A crunch *and a* pop... *Twang of tendons under his skin. Shock...bright, frightening pain...*

O'Kai stared down at his hyper-extended elbow, unaware he was screaming. MedTechs hustled over, laid him down on the sparring mat, and immediately set to work.

"Look here!" the instructor shouted to the class, pointing at the young trainee. "This is just the beginning!"

O'Kai felt two hot lines cut into his arm then forceps under his skin, fishing for detached tendons that had retracted up into his arm. Tools probing and weaving between muscles...burning sinews being refastened along with something else drilled directly into the bone...

He looked down as MedTechs removed their tools and zipped a bead of flesh weld down the incisions. Job done, they sterilized their tools, repacked their MedKits, and limped away to the edge of the room.

O'Kai rose from the mat and stared at his throbbing, aching arm. Tentatively, he closed his hand and flexed his biceps. His arm was strong again.

The instructor stepped up and took the young man's repaired arm in both hands. "We admire the diamond's hardness, yet even diamonds conform to the shape we impose." He inspected the closure of the incision, then braced the arm under the elbow and hoisted O'Kai off the ground.

O'Kai gasped, certain the joint would fly apart again. It held, and the young man dangled at his shoulder, awkwardly staring at his plank like arm.

"Soon, you'll understand," the instructor said to the class. "Once tempered, FLESH is the hardest substance in the universe."

OF
MORTAL CREATURES

OF
M O R T A L
CREATURES

F. ALLEN FARNHAM

CADRE ONE PUBLISHING
MILFORD, NH
2015

CADRE ONE PUBLISHING, LLC.
(WWW.CADREONEPUBLISHING.COM)

LIBRARY OF CONGRESS CONTROL NUMBER: 2015920327

SOFTCOVER ISBN: 978-0-9827116-5-1

Author Bio Photo by Kenny Thomas, 2010
Europa Ship Logo by Sara Richard (www.SaraRichard.com)
Book/Cover design and layout by Cadre One Publishing, LLC

CONTENTS

PART EIGHT

APPENDICES:

To Dr. HiFi and MC Myers for keeping the faith all these years.

To everyone else for your patience...

'Of Mortal Creatures, all that breathe and move,
Earth bears none frailer than mankind. What man
believes in woe to come when valor
and tough knees are supplied him by the gods?
But when the gods in bliss bring miseries on,
then willy-nilly, blindly, he endures.
Our minds are as the days are, dark or bright,
blown over by the father of gods and men.'

--*The Odyssey* by Homer, Book XVIII, Blows and a Queen's Beauty, lines 164-171
Translation by Robert Fitzgerald, 1961

CADRE ONE

PART SIX

TO THE SCRAPYARD, HENCE

Thompson sits at the edge of his bunk, stonefaced. Black and gray hair, more salt than pepper, juts from his head in untamed cowlicks. An elastic undershirt wraps him like a second skin, showing every rib and scar of his thinned frame. Dark gray uniform slacks fit loosely around his waist, and the fabric bunches where it tucks into his tight-laced boots.

Directly opposite, a faded gray uniform jacket and matching trousers hang on his wardrobe. He stares at his old Dress Grays, recalling the long years he wore them and how hard every decoration on the breast and collar was earned. Once, they were a source of pride. Now, they are relics from a former life. The longer he looks, the more certain he is that it all belongs to someone else, to another time.

The Gun who wore that uniform is dead, he thinks. *All that remains is this ghost, gazing at its own memorial.*

A long rifle leans on its butt against the wardrobe, barrel pointed straight up to the cabin ceiling. There is nothing unusual about its shape, no hidden feature he has not already seen a thousand times before. In fact, from having carried it throughout an unusually long term of service, he practically knows it by smell—the barely perceptible scent of ozone and vaporized metal, a hint of lithium grease, and the inevitable patina from regular handling that make this weapon as uniquely familiar as his undersuit. But as much as he needs the comfort of those perfectly molded grips in his hands, the rifle's deadly indifference is repellent.

With that rifle, I took lives. Not the enemy's, but Men, women... Colonists... I killed them. With that thing right there. Seventeen names. Doesn't matter if Maiella and Argo were involved. I had the lead.

He studies the rifle's lines, the attachments and fittings.

OF MORTAL CREATURES

I was a Gun. It's all I've ever been. Disgraced, exiled from the Corps...what am I?

His mind reaches far back, before the mission to a planet where humanity once thrived, before all of the Collection Rotations against the ancient enemy...

Standing at attention in the center of an oval arena, dressed only in a pair of loose nylon shorts, Thompson is two hundred thirteen centimeters of densely packed muscle. Wide, square shoulders narrow in a sharp V past plate-like pectorals and rigid abdominals to a trim waist. Legs bulge with enormous quadriceps and calves.

From shaved head to bare feet, the man is drenched in sweat and smeared with blood. Contusions swell in domes of red and purple on his legs, back, chest and cheeks. Lips and brows are split. Darkened orbits surround both eyes. Radius and Ulna protrude in a compound fracture above his left wrist like white daggers. Blood runs from the wound and drips from curved white fingers, pattering onto the floor mat.

Behind him stands a similarly battered but undaunted Brick. As muscular as Thompson is, the Brick is bigger, wider and bull-like, though not as tall. Knuckles of his huge fists are black as an anvil, and his great shoulders rise and fall with each deep breath. Blood rolls from hammered flat nostrils, crosses swollen lips, and drips from a square chin between huge pectorals. The Brick glances down at the floor beside him where MedTechs work to revive another Brick and Gun. As cudgeled as the standing men are, the two laid out on their backs are even more so.

At the arena's edge a mix of Guns, Geeks, and Bricks observe in dress gray uniforms. Most are shaved bald, baring myriad scars of intense combat. One steps from the group and marches to a halt centimeters from Thompson. He scrutinizes, drills a hard stare into the candidate's blackened eyes, then, loud enough to fill the small arena, announces, "Corporal Thompson, I think today we met the real you. You have my attention. Is there something you wish to ask?"

Thompson arches his back and shouts, "Major Zaius, I request entrance to the Operator Corps, sir!"

Zaius tilts his head, juts his lip. "In what capacity?"

"As Gun, sir!"

Zaius peers around Thompson at the two Operators being tended on the arena floor then he looks at the Brick standing behind Thompson. Zaius flicks his head toward the other Operators watching and orders,

"Go on, Argo. Get yourself cleaned up."

"Aye, sir!" Argo answers. With a last glance at his unconscious comrades and a wary glance at Thompson, Argo strides away to join his comrades at the arena's edge.

Zaius returns his gaze to Thompson.

"You've got the aggressive instincts," the major says, "but are you smart enough?"

"Sir?"

"I've seen candidates with this kind of talent before. They think they can handle anything. But they get so focused on what they're doing they can't fight and give orders at the same time. That gets Operators killed. So why don't you start by proving you understand what you're asking?"

Thompsom nods once. "Sir, just as it is for a Geek and a Brick, a Gun is a total sum of Operator and his kit. One is useless without the other. Only in concert do they comprise a Gun, and once united, only death may separate them."

Zaius grunts. "Overstated. But even a drone knows this. What else?"

Thompson blinks. "Likewise, an Operator team must be seamless, a unit, each part completing the others. The way I guard and use my body in combat I will guard and use my team, because they are my ears, my eyes, my speed and reflex. I am their breath, their thoughts, their cunning and killing instinct. To return from rotation without my team is to return an amputee. I can imagine no greater disgrace or failure."

"Interesting..." Zaius says, squinting. "I doubt you truly comprehend the weight of those words. Some day you will." He sniffs, lowers his arms, and straightens his stance. "Well, then, first thing's first." The major turns to the silent audience behind him and addresses a tall woman with gray hair pulled back into a bun.

"Colonel Enyo, with your permission?"

*The gray-haired woman crosses her powerful arms
and nods.*

*Zaius looks to the Operators as a group and shouts,
"Has Corporal Thompson demonstrated his quality?"*

As one, the Corps thunders, "SIR, YES, SIR!"

Thompson soaks in his recollections like bath water, but the water
has gone dingy and cold from bitter experience.

So brash. No greater disgrace or failure? He shakes his head. *I had
no idea...a naive fool.* The Gun's head droops toward his lap.

Gear gets broken, he thinks. *Worn out. It has to be replaced from
time to time. Like my first rifle... Was only my second rotation, and it misfired
so badly it was a smoking wreck in my hands.*

*Three Operators carried and maintained that weapon before it came
to me. I never abused it, but there's me—a fresh sergeant in the Corps—
with a blown out rifle. The others, they must've thought I couldn't properly
maintain the most crucial part of my kit. Unbearable...*

*HOURS I spent hammering, honing, and restoring that old weapon
to prove I was worthy of carrying it...*

*Got it to fire a couple times, but never got it dialed in. Thing
was cooked at the molecular level. Nothing short of a total melt and re-
manufacture could make it true again.*

With a twinge, he recalls Zaius finding him seated at a bench
sweating over it, trying desperately to pound life back into it. The discussion
was brief:

"Got it working?"

"Almost, Major. I've just about—"

"Stop. Give it to me."

*With a grimace, Thompson passes over the rifle body
to the major. Zaius scowls at it then passes it back.*

*"I'm going to ask you directly, Sergeant: would
you trust your life or the lives of your comrades to this
weapon?"*

*Thompson looks down at the thing he has been
working so hard to mend, but the answer is obvious.*

"No, sir."

*"These are the tools of our survival, Thompson.
If you can't rely on a thing anymore, you* scrap *it. Because
keeping something unreliable in service is dangerous. Not to*

mention stupid. *Now quit wasting time and turn that in to the Quartermaster. I'll requisition a replacement."*

"Sir, with a bit more—"

"A bit more what? Anyone with eyes can see that thing's all metal fatigue, so stop thinking you did something wrong. If anyone's to blame it's me for letting an Operator go on rotation with stressed gear like that. Now get off your ass and do as I say. And don't ever again *make me tell you twice."*

You were right, Zaius, Thompson thinks. *Sometimes a thing can't be fixed. But it isn't the rifle that's broken this time.*

He leans back on his bunk, propping himself against the metal wall. His mind carries him back to Earth, to the suicide mission that would have finalized his exile from Cadre One and served as death sentence for his crimes.

Sneaking past enemy ships in orbit, cutting through the ruins of Washington, DC, deadly games of hide an seek with a surprised enemy, fighting through hundreds—possibly thousands—of screaming Blueskins...

Zeal to recover a shred of dignity, to earn back even a tacit nod of approval from General O'Kai, driving him beyond exhaustion and injury until he could fight no more...

In retrospect, there is no pride in the job done, no satisfaction or accomplishment. While O'Kai was immensely pleased with the information discovered about *Cadre Two*, the general was more displeased at Beckert's condition upon return. What makes the disapproval so sharp is that it mirrors his own.

Beckert...immensely capable...but inexperienced... He relied on me, and I'm as bent as my first rifle. How could I have led him into combat? Should have given command to Argo. Kid might have had a chance, then.

Thompson sits upright on his bunk, eyes wide, staring through the close walls of his cabin at the awful memory.

Standing on a short flight of stairs in a richly appointed Blueskin transport, looking into the cockpit... Argo at the controls...Beckert slumps against the center console. The young Geek only has one of his four limbs;

the rest are ragged stumps capped with wire mesh and expanding medical foam. The bones of his face smashed beneath the skin, blind red eyes seeking about the cabin...

In the lounge behind Thompson, a tall Blueskin hunches on a plush sofa too terrified to move, diaphanous gown drawn tight against its aqua colored skin, whip tail wound around its legs. Its saffron eyes flick anxiously from Thompson to the gutted reptilian bodies at his feet.

Facing front, Thompson looks through the cockpit windscreen. Large bay doors are open to space, closing quickly. In the black of space beyond, hundreds of bright specks maneuver to intercept.

Mission's end, *he thinks.*

"Get 'im home, Argo," he says.

A draining, wasting sensation...the little strength left flows out through the violent perforations in his hide. Awareness of falling backward off the short stairs but not feeling the landing...

Awakening, floating amid gently churning currents... Opening his eyes and seeing Cadre One's MedLab through the lenses of a strapped on mask and the curved walls of a translucent tank... To his right, a tank like his own, empty... To his left, a fluid-filled tank containing a shunted and wired blob of flesh with a single curved limb and swollen red eyes...

Fresh scars on his legs, arms, and torso. Unfamiliar patches of skin, not his own... A lopsided feeling of breath inside his chest...

A tiny colonist woman on the opposite side of the plexisteel tank. Through the intercom she tells him her name is Sahara Taggart, that Argo refused to let go of him and that she won't either...

Then, decantation. Standing on two frail and wobbling legs, sunken gut heaving with waves of nausea and burning... Intravenous feedings until his irradiated insides could take nutrition again... Two months of physical therapy, listlessly pushing weights around to rebuild a body that no longer mattered to him. And afterward, graduating from physical therapy to psychiatric therapy, three tedious sessions a week with the Counselor to discuss pointless 'thoughts' and 'feelings.'

A gleam in the Counselor's eye at mention of a curved blade Beckert found in the D.C. ruins... The Counselor opening an archive, eager to share about warriors who carried such weapons on Earth long ago...

Why did they bother to keep me alive? Thompson wonders. *I'm just marking time now...getting older, slower, weaker. There's nothing for me to do anymore. Anyone with eyes can see: I've lived too long.*

The words come automatically to his lips, "If you can't rely on a thing anymore, you *scrap* it."

He nods at the truth of Zaius's words as he says them then looks to his right. On the bunk beside him lies his bayonet. A white cloth wraps the middle of the serrated black blade.

I really do understand what you were trying to show me, Counselor. There were others like me in the past—others every bit as devout in their sense of honor and service...

Thompson strips off his undershirt.

How they lived not just for their Bushido code but also for grace and simple perfections. How they cherished 'Life in every breath.'

He takes the blade by the white cloth and gazes at its edge.

You wanted me to understand how they lived. But what I understand best is how they died: they could not outlive their shame.

Thompson's other hand grips the hilt.

And neither can I.

He points the blade at himself.

First, a deep slice across the stomach, below the rib cage, into the liver...

He traces the blade across his bare abdomen in preparation of the act. The razor's mere touch leaves a faint red line in the skin behind it.

Another cut, vertically, to assure success.

He rotates the blade in his grip and traces a line from his waist up over his navel.

And if that doesn't suffice? Then into the neck, and rip out.

He lifts the blade in front of his throat and makes a stabbing motion from one side to the other, then jerks the blade forward in pantomime of the coup de grâce.

Retirement, at last.

Thompson slides down from the bunk onto his knees. He aims the bayonet at his mid-section and tightens his grip. Serrated points prick his hand through the cloth. The tip bites into his skin. Abdominal muscles tense up for the cut as a single crimson drop forms above the blade and rolls over the side. He watches the drop spill down, over, and around his rough pink scars, into the trough between abdominal muscles, until it disappears into the waistline of his uniform pants. That one meandering trail of red on his skin captivates him, and it reminds him what is just below the surface: the organs, the sinews, the biological machine that does not belong to him. Raised under meticulous attention of Cadre MedTechs, this body was weeded of genetic flaws then tuned for speed, strength, and aggression. Of each crop, fewer than five in a hundred ever reach Operator quality. The rest suffer incurable defects, lacking bilateral symmetry, or suffering impairments of speech, comprehension, vision, and hearing. He is one of the lucky five percent.

Moreover, this issued flesh carries precious replacement parts. One of the lungs in his chest. Half of the liver he is about to slash. Liters of transfused blood. Bone, muscle, and skin grafts, all from Cadre donors whom could scarcely afford to part with them.

This body could be used to save others...and I'm about to waste it?

He hurls the blade from himself, and the tip sinks into the base of his hygiene station.

What's WRONG with me?

Thompson rises to his feet and paces across his narrow cabin.

How could I have done that? Am I SO broken that I could throw this all away? His hands clap to the sides of his face as though catching it, and he halts his manic pacing.

Can't think straight. Can't make good decisions anymore... This brain is defective.

He looks up at his reflection above the hygiene station. What he sees is a patchwork of a man with hollow cheeks and confused, glassy eyes—a complete stranger, lost and anxious, leaking from a shallow cut across his belly.

"Reconstitution. It's the only thing that makes sense. Yes. I have to go right now, before I do damage to myself. Before I hurt someone else..."

Thompson strides for the door, and it swishes aside at his approach. He turns left, then right, not knowing which way is correct, in an urgent rush to be anywhere else.

GASP OF AIR

Thompson hastens through the *Europa's* dingy corridors, past crumpled paper boxes, torn clothing, broken tools, and empty canisters. He notices none of it.

Did Argo and Maiella struggle like this? If they did, how did they cope? How did they survive it?

He stops cold in his march.

Counselor said they both departed for Cadre Two over a year ago. Are they even alive?

No, no, no, I'm not going to think about that. And once reconstitution is done, I'll never have to think about anything again.

Resolved, his arms swing as he strides onward. But as he considers how to accomplish his new mission, his steps become less certain.

I've been exiled from Cadre One... Won't matter if they agree I should be reconstituted, they won't let me in for the procedure.

And Sahara has sworn she'll never perform a reconstitution. No one in Europa's *MedLab would dare go against her orders. So...where am I going?*

Just as before, Thompson stops dead in his tracks. He searches for a suggestion of where to go, finding instead more trash-strewn corridors and crude graffiti. For weeks, he has shuffled past it all, so distraught that the shoddy conditions scarcely registered. Now, he stares at words that have grown like mold throughout the *Europa's* halls:

"SABOTAGE"

"CADRE PIGS FUCK OFF"

His mouth forms the syllables as he reads them, but the words are hateful and he cannot utter them. Instead, he looks down and sees the rubbish, the grime, the stains and spilled paint left to dry. Countless footprints track through the stains, blotting the floors as far as he can see.

His hands clench into fists.

This ship is their life! The colony apparatus, the embryos, the means to carry them to a planet they could settle so they can begin again... Sabotage? Could any of them really DO that?

He reaches out to the defaced wall with both hands and spreads his fingers. The words themselves are more than mere slashes of fluorescent red and orange. To Thompson they are marks on the face of an abused friend—a friend that has endured far beyond her expected lifetime to preserve the people inside. Vehemently, he drags his hands back and forth until the words are dimmed behind a fog of their own color. Despite his scouring, however, the words will not erase.

A tinny tumbling sound comes from a corridor ahead, and Thompson turns toward it, watching an empty spray canister roll into the intersection. Soon after, he hears the rumple of paper trampled underfoot, a man's voice, and the subtle thud of hurried footsteps. He searches the floor around himself, picks up a dingy rag that was once someone's undershirt, and grinds his orange hands into it.

The footfalls grow louder, with the attendant shuffling of trash, until Gregor jogs to a halt in the intersection. Two Cadre Guns arrive behind him, one male, one female, fully armored with faceplates raised, rifles slung across their shoulders. Gregor stoops, picks up the empty spray canister and shakes it before tossing it back to the trash-strewn floor.

"*Shit,*" the Russian curses. "Almost had 'em."

He looks left, spotting Thompson.

"Hey, Thom, you see anyone run through here?"

Thompson shakes his head.

Gregor gives the bare-chested man an up and down glance as he walks over. "Good to see you out of your cabin for a change." But his face scrunches when he takes in Thompson's wild hair, orange hands, and the faint T cut into his abdomen.

"You, ah...um... The *hell* are you up to?"

Instead of answering, Thompson turns to the wall. Gregor follows his glance and reads the hazy words there.

"Fucking malcontents," the Russian says. He hikes a thumb over his shoulder at the two Guns towering behind him. "They don't like these guys looking over their shoulders while they wreck the ship. But don't worry. Whoever's doing this, we'll get them."

Thompson turns his gray eyes to Gregor's escorts, taking in the fit of their armor, the width of their shoulders, the marks crossing their faces. Both carry an expression of seasoned detachment. They do not disdain, they simply do not seem to notice him at all.

From the Operators, Thompson turns to Gregor. Though tall for a colonist, he is a full head shorter than his escorts and half the mass. Still, the Russian bears the calm demeanor of someone comfortable with his rank and confident in his abilities.

"We labored for *months*, Gregor," Thompson says. "You and I worked these halls 'til they were gleaming."

"Yeah, I know. Pisses me off. These people, making a mess of it—"

"No, you're not getting me," Thompson interrupts. He turns square to the Colonist. "I don't see a mess. I see a Captain who has *totally* lost command."

Gregor smirks in reluctant agreement. "Yeah, the new Skipper hasn't meshed with the crew so well—"

"And his first officer is letting it happen."

Gregor's eyes widen. His cheeks and ears redden.

"Oh, you want to play the BLAME GAME? You're way ahead in that one, *droog*. SEVENTEEN to *ZERO*!"

Thompson slumps against the wall. Gregor looks away and brings a hand to his forehead, scuffed wedding band glinting in the corridor's artificial light.

"I can't believe I just said that. Didn't mean it, not at all." The Russian shakes his head and shifts his weight to one leg. "But you *know* I got a temper. Don't throw shit in my face like that." He lowers his hand and looks at the band of gold. His face twitches.

Behind him, the male Gun speaks into his helmet microphone, "Cadre One, Gun Maddock reporting patrol delay, corridor seven, C-Deck."

Gregor turns on them, annoyed. "Well *go on*, then, if you're in such a damned hurry!"

Maddock shakes his head. "Orders are to escort and defend against any assault or attempt to abduct."

"No one's gonna try that on me. Just go. I'll catch up."

"Negative. Remaining on task."

Gregor sighs. "Fine. Then just stand there and keep it to yourselves." The Russian faces Thompson, about to speak, but Thompson beats him to it.

"No one would try to attack you, would they?"

"Nah, it's just shit-talk. But folks are pissed about Herzfeld. Gonna take a while for that to simmer down."

"Herzfeld?"

"Yeah. You missed a lot while you were floating in your tank. So *Europa's* been docked here at Cadre One a few years, right? And all that time we're giving free power, free food to the Cadre. Not even a 'thank you.'"

Thompson tilts his head.

"Yeah, yeah, I know, we can't stick up for ourselves," Gregor adds, "and the Cadre's watching out for us. I know, it's a good deal. Just seems like more and more, that arrangement's getting lopsided. We keep busting our asses to keep the Cadre all stocked up, but they aren't doing shit. Even stopped the collection rotations. They're happy taking everything from us."

"*That's* how you see it?"

"Pretty much. But then we find out our old Cap'n Keller...that he's one of the guys that turned it all to *gavno*... Slaughtered Lizards at New Dresden and provoked them to come and wipe us all out. Earth and the Colonies? Everything...gone." Gregor's hands rise in front of him like he is clutching something and crushing it. "Had him in my hands, too." His eyes become wild, insanely focused on the narrowing gap between his palms.

Thompson frowns and squints. "No way. Not Keller. I don't believe it."

Gregor drops his hands, and the crazed expression fades. "It's true. You didn't know? Beckert and Argo did. It was on that video you guys brought back from Earth. The one with the skinny Latina news lady."

"Never got a chance to see it."

"Well you should. Keller, *that gav-no-yed*, was testing viral weapons at New Dresden. Thought the Lizards were primitives who couldn't fight back. Cleared out whole villages."

Thompson smirks with skepticism, and Gregor turns square, pointing at himself.

"He admitted it *right to my face*, Thompson, so don't look at me like I'm making this up. Said he was given a job to do and he just did it. Like that was some kind of excuse... And then the bag of assholes makes a deal with O'Kai for protection down at Cadre One, where we can't get to him."

Thompson's head rocks back as he tries to accept what he is hearing.

"There are a few, like me, who were born in flight," Gregor says. "I don't know what it was like to live on Earth. But others? They *do*. They've been in and out of cryo since the beginning, so they remember what it was like. They told me stories about cities, sky, houses...*families*. And there's Keller, one of the guys that made it all go away, and he's *right in front of us*. What happens? O'Kai takes him in. Shields him. Keeps him from us, lets him get away to *Cadre Two*. Another thing the Cadre took! It was just too much. That was it. We'd had it."

"Keller knew things, important things," Thompson counters. "The way I hear it, we never would've found *Cadre Two* otherwise."

"So what? Fat lot of good it's done. *Cadre Two*... We don't even know if..." Gregor censors himself as if saying the words could cause them to come true. "They'd *better* come back. You don't know how bad we need to roast Keller. He's *SO* guilty, Thom, he's *got* to pay."

"Won't change anything."

"No, it won't." Gregor leans in with a cold leer. "But we'll feel a whole lot better."

Thompson crosses his arms, put off by the Russian's eager hostility. "So, you were saying about Herzfeld?"

"Right. Herzfeld's just one of those guys... Not that different from people like you and me, he just really knows how to say what we're thinking. Wasn't afraid to say it, either. Got folks pretty stirred up."

"You went along with him?"

"Hell, no! I mean, I get what he was saying. But ordering sabotage of the power relay down to Cadre One? That was fuckin' *nuts*. So one of Ortega's first act as new Captain was stuffing Herzfeld back into stasis. If anything, I think that was too soft. But a lot of the crew just *lost it* after that. A few took swings at Ortega for it. Bashed him good before some Operators broke it up. Sides have been drawn ever since."

"And what side are *you* on, Gregor?"

"*Fuck you*, what side I'm on! I back my CO, and I'll crack a head when someone tries it again! Don't fucking lecture me about letting all this happen! Tell me my ship's a mess? *You're* a fucking mess. And what's this?" He points at Thompson's midsection. "You're *cutting* on yourself now? Emo, schoolboy crap. Like you don't have scars enough, you need a touch up?"

Thompson looks past Gregor, past the disinterested Operators who scan the hallways around them.

"Oh, right," Gregor says, "you think I don't get it. There's no way I could know what you're going through, right? Well, I watched Argo and Maiella both go through this in their own ways. Maybe I don't know what it's like to kill someone, but what I *do* know is if they could see you now..."

Thompson thunks his head against the wall, defeated.

"For Chrissake, Thom, you used to scare the piss out of me. Now? I want to slap the fuck outta you. Get a *grip*, man. Get yourself together."

"This isn't about me, Gregor. The *Europa's* all that matters. She's the only thing left of Earth, the only thing standing between you and extinction. Letting her go like this, it's..."

"It's giving up," Gregor finishes.

Thompson returns from his infinite gaze and lifts his head from the wall, orange paint tinting the hair of his temple in a blotch. The Russian nudges an empty spray can with his toe, his arms crossed.

"It's been hard to like you, Thom." Gregor looks at the walls, floor and ceiling. "Especially when you lay all this mess on me. But it's a direct hit. You're right. I have let her go to hell. We all did. That has to change." His eyes turn fiery and he points a finger at Thompson's chest. "And YOU'RE a goddamned HYPOCRITE. I *hate* seeing you like this. Whether you know it or not folks look up to you, and the way you feel looking at this ship, all run down and dirty, well...that's how they feel looking at you."

Thompson squints in disbelief, crooking a finger toward himself.

"Yeah, they do," the Russian adds. "Open your eyes and pay attention once in a while."

Thompson stands upright, spine and face straighter. He nods.

"Look," Gregor says, "I gotta go or *Koshchei* and *Baba Yaga* here are gonna get testy. You need to chat or anything, let me know. Or the Counselor. He likes hearing your bullshit, too."

Thompson puts his hands together and rubs at the paint between his fingers. "Thanks, Gregor. Appreciate it."

"Yeah, yeah. Now go put a shirt on. You Operators look like you enjoy swimming through heaps of scrap metal. And for fuck's sake, *eat something*, will you, you twiggy bastard?" The Russian turns to his escorts. "You ready?"

The senior Operator speaks into his helmet mic, "Cadre One, Maddock and Dagmar resuming patrol, corridor seven, C-Deck. ETA eight minutes, barring further delay."

Gregor grimaces and heads off on his original path. The Guns turn as one and march behind him. Thompson looks into their backs until they turn left at the intersection and stride out of sight.

Alone, he thinks about Maiella and Argo.

If they were standing in front of me right now, what would *they think?*

He winces.

"No," he says to himself. "They're not going to see me like this." His eyes lift from the littered floor to the walls and ceiling around him, to the dusty light sconces and vent grills. "And you," he says to the ship, "you deserve better."

Thompson takes a deep breath and lifts his head. As ever, Gregor's words have a cutting edge. This time, they have sliced through his indecision, doubt, and self-loathing. Too much time alone, and they grow like weeds in his conscious mind, feeding on the tatters of his will and confidence, choking him inside and out. He exhales and shakes his head.

All this has been happening and I didn't even notice? Was I really that far out of it? His jaw flexes. *Some guy named Herzfeld that Ortega had locked up and frozen... And that about Keller bringing the war...? Is it true?*

A rumbling growl comes from his mid-section. He covers it with a hand and looks down in surprise at the first hunger pangs he has felt in days. When he sees the thin tracing of his blade and the flaking trail of blood, he drives himself through the last of his suicidal stupor.

"First thing's first," he tells himself as he marches back to his cabin. In automation, he strides to his hygiene station. Snatching up a razor, his hair is sheared to regulation length. Facial stubble is shaved away. Residue of paint and blood is wiped clean with a treated towel. When finished, he looks into the mirror, finally recognizing the man looking back.

He turns and grabs his undershirt from the bunk. It slips easily over his head and arms. Last, he yanks his bayonet free of the hygiene station. Turning it over, he understands the naked blade is not a fantasized path to oblivion, not a means to regain some dignity or honor. It is simply a sharp tool in his hand, nothing more.

Thompson cleans the blooded tip with the towel and retracts the blade. In a practiced motion, the soldier snaps the bayonet to the end of his rifle and locks it in place before leaning the weapon back against his wardrobe. He is about to walk out when he looks back at the rifle. Like the bayonet, it no longer seems imbued with cruel indifference. It is only a tool to be used or not used as required.

Thompson takes the weapon from its place and holds it. It feels heavier than usual in his weakened arms, but the grips are warm and solid.

At once, he realizes that, in the same way he was caught in the spiders' threads back on Earth, his mind was caught in a web of his own making. Every action became a labor, an agonizing fight with futility, such that just rising out of his bunk was a battle. Diagnosis of depression and post traumatic stress (however the Counselor chose to explain it) is irrelevant. In Thompson's mind self-destructive thoughts were whispers of rational truth, leading him to act upon the only logical choice: removing himself from existence.

With rifle in hand and Gregor's harsh words in mind, the idea of self-murder feels banal. Petty. Indulgence of weakness, cowardice, and selfishness. Regardless of the humiliation at being seen in such a state, there is a greater feeling of relief—a mental gasp of air after nearly drowning.

With an embarrassed smile, he replaces his rifle against the wardrobe. Head lifted, shoulders and back straight, he strides out of his gloomy cabin, turns left, and heads straight for the Dining Hall.

SUDDEN GRAVITY

Thompson's teeth grind. He closes his eyes, growling through the pain in his rebuilt shoulder, and pushes away from the gym floor in a handstand position.

"Forty-*eight*!"

The Gun flexes his elbows, nearly kissing the mat beneath him. Again, he strains, legs straight above like planks, back arched. His arms wobble then lock at full extension.

"Forty-*nine*!" he grunts, breathing hard, heart pounding. His legs tilt, and he staggers on his palms, nearly toppling. Anger flares in him for being weak, for getting soft, for falling below the Operator standard. He shifts weight from one hand to the other and flaps the free hand to work blood back into it.

Once calm, he evens his handstand, looks into the floor mat, and lowers himself. With a long, agonizing groan, he presses himself up, triceps and shoulders burning, back spasming, legs teetering until he fully extends his arms.

"Fifty!"

Thompson tucks and rolls like a diver then rises to his feet, clutching his left shoulder, jabbing a thumb into stiff sinews until the knotted muscles unclench.

At least I did THAT many, he thinks, swinging his arms in big limbering circles. With a long, lunging step forward he lowers himself into a stretch. A sharp twinge in his groin halts him.

"Ow, *OW*!" he shouts in surprise. The Gun keeps his posture, works through it, then switches legs into another deep stretch. A similar twinge on his opposite side makes him grimace, but he holds the pose the proper count.

When he rises, his right knee and hip pop.

"*Damn it*, am I falling apart?" he shouts at the vacant gymnasium. For a moment, there is a denial of ownership as if this body could not possibly be his. Memory and expectation of ability clash with a stiff, atrophied physique that is confining, disobedient, disappointing.

This is my fault. Weakness of mind became weakness of body. I WILL recover.

Shaking his head, he kneads his fist into his hip joint, using the knuckles to grind out the complaints. When finished, he straightens the waistband on his loose-fitting nylon shorts and takes a southpaw fighting stance. Hands rise to the sides of his face, fingers curled. Shoulders lift but are not hunched. Head dips forward, chin tucked. He stares through his eyebrows at the distant wall ahead and draws a deep breath.

The movement starts from his back leg, calf muscle flexing, heel lifting, rocking his whole body forward. His waist rotates, driving his right shoulder forward; and his shoulder rises beside his cheek as his arm extends, fist sliding out in a slow-motion jab. At full extension, he draws it back, rotates his hips, swings his shoulders, and extends his left arm for the cross punch. Satisfied his form is correct, he breathes again and repeats the sequence. His body coordinates in a thousand perfect flexions and extensions, moving faster with each repetition. Breath hisses through clenched teeth, driven by the force of his diaphragm.

Jab, cross. Jab, cross. Jab, cross, cross.

Like a piston engine revving up, Thompson's fists fly, balanced, poised, swift, and powerful. His drawn back right arm crooks and swings horizontally across his body, alternating from left to right with each set.

Jab, cross, hook. Jab, cross, hook. Jab, cross, hook.

He ignores the twinges in his shoulders, ignores the quivering leg muscles that threaten to cramp. The Gun pulls his left fist back, leans slightly to his right and powers his right fist upward in front of himself.

Jab, cross, uppercut. Jab, cross, uppercut. Jab, cross, uppercut.

Like a runaway machine breaking free of its mounts, Thompson jerks away from his fixed stance. His feet slide, never far apart, and he side steps, bobs, weaves, jabs, crosses, and lunges with elbow smashes. Gauging some unseen opponent, he weaves and ducks imagined strikes, then steps in, hooks hands behind an invisible neck and hauls down onto a rising knee with a resounding slap. In the same movement, he hops with his opposite leg and swings it in a devastating roundhouse kick, lands, and steps through into spinning side-kick.

"GAAAH!"

Thompson crumples to the mat and grips the inside of his left thigh. Beneath the skin, torn muscles ignite. Teeth bared, he pushes himself up into a kneeling position and thumps his fist into the mat.

"Get up," he growls at himself. "*Get up!*"

The Gun brings his right leg beneath himself and he stands. Breathing through his nose, he forces himself to put weight on the injured leg.

Once more, the Gun takes fighting stance. His hands rise beside his face and curl to unclenched fists.

"*Ah, please pardon the interruption, Mr. Thompson,*" the overly loud intercom blares, "*the Counselor is asking if you will be arriving for your scheduled appointment.*"

Thompson lifts his head and lowers his hands, annoyed, then raises his fists beside his head again.

"I'm not going today. Too much to do."

"*Uh, well,*" the intercom says, "*he says it's very important. An urgent matter.*"

"I'm sure it can wait."

There is a pause, then the voice says in a hushed tone, "*Can it wait?*"

"*No,*" the Counselor's voice says in the background. "*Tell him it's important.*"

"*Well I did that already, and—*"

"*Just give me the mic.*"

"*I would, but Captain Ortega doesn't want anyone else using the intercom, so—*"

The intercom thumps twice from the microphone's rough handling.

"*Thompson? This is the Counselor.*"

"I'm busy."

"*Yes, I see that. And I'm glad for it. One of the things we need to talk about, so we can end your sessions.*"

Thompson's head lifts. His eyebrows lift. "End the sessions?"

"*Yes.*"

The Gun looks around the empty gymnasium, thinking his diminished physique is far more in need of attention than whatever nonsense the Counselor could throw at him. Even so, the idea of being freed from discussions of guilt mechanisms and subconscious wish fulfillment is a compelling offer.

"We'll end the sessions?"

"*That's what I said. So will you just come to my office? It's important.*"

"All right, Counselor. I'll be there."

"*Thank you. I'll see you soon.*" The intercom falls silent.

Thompson limps to a row of exercise machines, snatches a towel draped over one of them, and dries himself. Next, he pulls on a T-shirt, slips socks over his feet, and dons his boots without lacing them. The rest of the free weights, gloves, and lifting belts he leaves out, knowing he will be coming right back for them.

Outside the gym, trash that once littered the halls has been collected. Defacements and stains still mar the once bright corridors, however, and, to his infinite aggravation, many of the scrubbed patches are overwritten with a fresh layer of graffiti.

"SIC SEMPER TYRANNIS"

"DISOBEY"

"MUTINY"

The Gun grits his teeth and looks away, focusing on his path. Down the next corridor, he spots a gray-haired man leaning against the wall ahead intent on something around the corner. The man wears orange coveralls, and his waist is wider than his broad shoulders, but tightness of the sleeves suggest he is no weakling. As Thompson gets closer, he recognizes the man is Dave DeLauro, department head of Plumbing and Conduits aboard the *Europa.*

Thompson's unlaced boots clomp with each step, announcing his approach. Dave turns, pats the air with a flat hand, and lays a finger over his mouth.

Thompson nods, rolling his feet to quiet his approach. From around the corner, hissing noises come in short, smooth bursts. Dave smirks and whispers, "Watch this."

The old pipe fitter stands upright and strides around the corner, shouting, "HEY, *DICKHEADS!*"

Thompson peers around the corner. Several meters down, two colonists in blue jumpsuits and hoods startle then run in the opposite direction. A Brick steps into their path, and the hooded pair slams face first into him, heads jolting back in unison. They both fall to the floor, shiny spray cans rolling from their hands. The Brick looks down at them, folds his massive arms, and scowls.

"I *got* you!" Dave barks, marching to the two laid out on the deck. They try to sit up, get to their elbows, and cower from the huge Operator barring their escape.

Dave leans over and hauls one of the two up from the floor. He knocks the hood back, uncovering a shock of bleached blonde hair. Beneath the wild yellow strands hunches a timid looking man.

"Chulito," Dave says, shaking his head in disappointment. "Should have known you were involved. Let's see who your friend is." Dave stoops and rips the accomplice up from the floor. He knocks the hood back and pulls down the scarf tied over nose and mouth. A pouty woman glares back at him through bangs of dyed black hair.

"Mika! How sweet. You two confessing your secret love on the walls here? Let's have a look."

Dave steps back to where the two were spraying and reads.

"STARVE THEM OUT," he reads aloud. "THE GUILTY MUST..."

The old pipe fitter looks at his arrested crewmates.

"The guilty must *what*?"

Chulito lifts his gaze from the floor, eyes tinged with red. "You *know*, Dave. Don't be a prick about it."

Dave nods patronizingly. "Right, right. *I'm* the prick."

"You gonna beat us up?" Mika rails. "Or, you gonna sic your Cadre gorilla on us? Is *that* who you are now?"

"I can't believe you two passed the SoVar entrance exam," Dave says, looking at his boots. He squats down to pick up one of the loose cans of paint, hefting it to see how much is left. "I'm on watch," he says rising to his feet. "That means I'm looking out for *you*, and for *this ship*. I don't have an axe to grind. But if you think for a *second* that I'm gonna let you get away with this..." He shakes the can vigorously, clacking the internal mixing ball.

"Vandalizing things," he says, knocking his free hand against the wall, "is *not* how you get heard. I have to admit, though, it does look like fun. Let's find out..."

Chulito ducks, and Dave sprays a long blast of red paint into his bleached hair.

"You like this? It's just your color, I think. And here..." Dave spins him around and paints a big A onto his back. "There's your Scarlet Letter. A, for *asshole*."

He turns on Mika.

"You, too." He sprays her hair down and rubs it in to the scalp. Next he spins her about and paints a big A on her back as well. When done he drops the can to the floor and turns her forward.

"Now you two *listen up*. You got something to say, you bring it to the meeting hall and you say it *there*. You don't put this garbage up in the shadows, you stand up and speak your minds like members of this crew. *Get me*?"

The two look up from beneath hair limp with paint, eyes sideways in suspicion.

"I said, *do you get me?*"

Chulito sneaks a glance at Mika then looks up at Dave. "You aren't turning us in?"

"Turn you in? To *whom?*"

"To Ortega! He's chucking everyone that disagrees with him into the freezers!"

Dave's eyes roll. He brings a hand up to his forehead, and says to the air around him, "There must be rubbing alcohol in the water..."

He drills a hard glare into Chulito.

"Herzfeld is the only one that got the freeze, and he *damn well deserved it*. Sabotage? That's *mutiny*. Out here in the black, that's a heavy crime. Herzfeld got off light."

Chulito and Mika look at one another but do not speak.

"Bottom line," Dave says, "we're getting this over and done. No more of this 'revolution' crap. We assemble tomorrow in the meeting hall at eighteen hundred. Anyone who wants to speak will be heard. Until then stay out of my sight."

"You're letting us go?" Mika asks.

Dave nods while keeping his eyes riveted on her. "Yes, I am. But if I catch you two taking your gripes out on the *Europa* again, I will kick the ever-loving crap out of you. Read me?"

"Yeah," Chulito says.

"How's that?" Dave asks, head turned slightly.

"I mean, *yes, sir!*"

Dave straightens, loses the aggressive posture. He gestures down the corridor, and the Brick stands aside.

Chulito and Mika look at one another, then scurry away like mice.

Dave watches them go and shakes his head. Turning, he says with a grin, "Enjoyed that." But Thompson is no longer there.

*****

The Gun moves with purpose through the *Europa's* corridors, eager to start the meeting with the Counselor so he can get to its end. Outside the Counselor's office, however, he pauses at the door and looks himself over.

Bootlaces dangle, untied. Tongues of his boots loll to one side. The Gun stoops to make himself more presentable, but halfway down his leg feels like it is being welded with high current. Exhaling through his mouth, Thompson sinks the rest of the way to the floor.

As the Gun laces his boots the door slides aside, and he sees the Counselor seated at a desk, off-center of the room to the right.

Without looking up from his desk, the therapist says, "You're fine the way you are, Thompson. Come on in."

Thompson pulls his laces tight, rises awkwardly, and heads toward the plush couch. The Gun stares at the crushed cushions, knowing how much it will hurt lowering himself into them.

"You should see Sahara first," the Counselor says, still focused on his desktop terminal. "I can see your leg is bothering you."

"It's nothing," Thompson counters. His face a stoic mask, he turns and drops himself into the flattened cushions.

The Counselor looks up from his terminal. He shakes his head.

"Doesn't make any sense to tear yourself down faster than you can build yourself up. But you'll do what you please..."

He closes the holowindow above his desk and rolls back in his chair, swiveling to face his guest.

"So. How've you been?"

"Let's cut to it, doc. You said we can end these sessions."

The Counselor looks down into his lap, eyebrows raised. He juts his lower lip and nods. "Okay, then." He fishes a tablet out of his lab coat pocket and tosses it onto his desk then rolls himself toward his patient. "This isn't an official therapy session and this isn't on-the-record."

Thompson eyeballs the Counselor, impatience visible in the tilt of his head and the slight down turn of his mouth.

"When Keller took you aboard, you became part of our crew," the Counselor says. "Whether or not you enjoy our meetings, it doesn't matter to me. What does interest me is the health and well-being of everyone in my care. Everyone. That includes you."

"Meaning?"

"Meaning we'll continue to meet until I'm satisfied you're no longer a danger to yourself."

Thompson grabs the bridge of his nose and looks at the floor beside him, expecting a lecture to follow. When it does not come he drops his hand and looks up at his host. The Counselor sits patiently, one leg crossed over the other, arms resting on the sides of his chair. Thompson rounds his shoulders and slumps back into the couch.

"Okay," the Gun says, hands raised, palms up, "I'm here. You said it was important."

"It is." The Counselor uncrosses his legs and leans forward onto his knees. "You know our usual routine. I try to draw you out, and I listen to what you choose to tell me. You'll fence with me at times, others you're direct. And I listen. This time, I want you to hear what I have to say."

"Fine."

"I saw you in your cabin."

Thompson's eyes narrow. "Saw what?"

"I saw you take your own knife, prepare it for seppuku. And I cursed myself for showing you that archive on Samurai culture. I should have known there was a risk in that. But when it comes right down to it, if you were determined to kill yourself, you would have found any number of ways. At least in such a suggestion, I believed I knew the place you'd choose, and that I might be able to watch for it. Might be able to stop you."

Thompson stares off in silence.

"I also should have known you would have come to that decision quickly," the Counselor continues. "You're used to making life and death decisions in an instant. I was a fool to think that, because others come to it gradually, I had time to watch for it in you."

Thompson turns his gaze directly on his host. "Others?"

"I won't discuss other clients, Thompson. You know that. I simply want you to know that you're not struggling alone."

The Gun looks away. His face scrunches, and he turns back. "You *saw* me?"

The Counselor nods. "I have two cameras in your cabin. One hidden, one in plain sight. Interesting that you found neither."

Thompson shakes his head. "I'd have found them."

"You didn't." The Counselor swivels to his desk and activates the holowindow. With a tap, he pulls up the camera feed from Thompson's cabin. The view is a wide angle from a ceiling corner, looking down at the bunk. Most of the room is imaged in a single fish eye image. "This is your cabin as you left it this morning. And I'm glad to see it this way, let me tell you."

"You just put that camera in now."

"No, it's been there for quite a while." The Counselor swipes a finger across the desktop and taps twice. The holoscreen switches to another file and plays back a recording from the same view. In it, Thompson steps in, shoulders slouched, head lowered. The Gun steps to his bunk and sits, staring at the floor.

The Counselor hits fast forward on the playback and, in the span of seconds, rolls through hours of video. The despondent man on screen does not move, maintaining his gaze into the floor.

"Seems you don't look up much," the Counselor says.

Thompson watches the holoscreen, unable to believe he is the catatonic figure seated there. "How long... How long was I like that?"

"Pretty much since you left Sahara's tank," the Counselor answers, scrolling through a list of recordings before closing the application. "I wondered if you were working through something or if you were stuck. You said less and less in our sessions, which made it hard to tell. Seemed like you were disappearing. I thought by showing you the Samurai you might find some connection to another warrior culture, something you could identify with and hold onto. When you mentioned the sword that Beckert found on Earth, it seemed like the right opportunity. You were interested, sure enough, just...not in the parts I'd hoped."

"Beckert..." Thompson says. Gloomy thoughts sweep into his mind like the onset of rain. "He was a fine Geek. And he's ruined because of me."

"That's not how he sees it."

"You spoke to him? He's out of the tank?"

The Counselor nods demurely. "Yes, with elevated duties, I hear. Now you, Argo, and Beckert were on the Earth rotation. Beckert knows he would have died if not for you and Argo. Argo told me the same. Frankly, I don't know how any of you made it back, but here you are."

He shuts down the holoscreen videos of Thompson's cabin and swivels to face his guest again.

"Before I get side tracked, I want to go ahead and tell you why I asked you here. Are you ready?"

Thompson leans forward in the sunken cushions, hands clasped, and nods.

"It's hard to know how to help someone until you try," the Counselor explains. "Sometimes, I see a patient stumble, and I want to catch them before they fall, or at least soften the landing. But that didn't work for you. You were determined to fall. I don't understand why. Some people are just like that. I do what I can, but my efforts only strengthen that person's will to crash.

"So I took hands off. Let go. I don't think you have any idea how hard that is for me to do. But I had to let you hit bottom, knowing you'd either bounce or break."

"Did you know?"

"That you'd bounce? No, I didn't. Your experiences are heavy burdens, and I know there can be a physical pain from carrying them. Can make a person fall into such a deep depression that death starts to look appealing. An end to weariness. A cure-all for troubles real and imagined. I've seen it happen."

Thompson fades back into the soft couch, ill at ease as the Counselor continues.

"But there's an ethos of the Cadre that's engraved into your being: the idea that the self is meaningless and only the group matters. I was counting on that core ethic to be stronger in you than any self-destructive impulse. The idea that, while you live, there's an opportunity to serve in some way."

"I was going to volunteer for reconstitution," Thompson says.

"That's one direction I saw you headed. Isn't any better than suicide, though. There are people on this ship who have strong feelings about you."

"Gregor said something like that recently."

The Counselor nods. "For the people aboard this ship to see you, someone they know, lobotomized...walking around lifeless inside, numb...a kind of living death... It's disturbing. Some of us can accept, with difficulty, that there are already drones at Cadre One. But to see someone we know become one? Chills right to the bone. You have to know we could never accept that. That fate is so terrifying that it could drive a permanent wedge between Colonist and Cadre, Thompson. That's why I begged Gregor to go find you, quickly."

"Huh. Wasn't a chance meeting, then?"

"You should know by now, I don't believe in chance. Besides, Gregor had some words of his own for you. Wanted him to finally say them instead of bottling them up inside."

"He didn't pull his punches."

"Good. Because your type is immune to subtlety."

"My type? You mean like Argo and Maiella?"

The Counselor smiles and shakes his head. "I'm not going to discuss other clients with you. Just know that your struggle is not unique. And I'm very glad to see you coming through it."

"So that's it? I'm cured?"

The Counselor chortles and repositions himself in his chair. "Ease down, there. We've barely touched on the reasons I asked you here. But we'll get to them, and don't worry, this isn't going to keep you very long."

Thompson takes a long, deep breath through his nose.

"I know you've been distracted lately," the Counselor says. "But you must have noticed by now...things are not going well aboard our ship."

"That's obvious. Maintenance has lapsed, refuse everywhere... The *Europa's* own crew are defacing the walls...advocating sabotage... If I were an Operator on patrol..."

"Yes?" the Counselor says when Thompson trails off.

"If I were still an Operator, I'd recommend General O'Kai assume command to preserve the ship and her assets."

The Counselor nods shrewdly. "I understand. When it comes to the security of the *Europa*, you and I both know your concerns are valid. Yet half of the crew is with Ortega, the rest against. Seems that whatever one side does, the other undoes. The result is stalemate. And the *Europa* has fallen into disrepair."

"But why work in opposition? How could there be any division? We're so few, the enemy so numerous... I can't see any reason to it."

"Ah. The ability to do as one chooses... There are varying degrees of commitment, but there are enough who'll risk anything to preserve it. Moreover, they'll prove that commitment to anyone who tests them."

"What *test*? There's a flow of authority here, just as there is at Cadre One, from ship's Captain down. If half of the crew simply *decides* that authority no longer applies to them, then their Captain needs to *prove* that it does."

"Okay. I see your point. Now consider this: The Colonists, every one of them, come from societies that vote in matters that affect their future. In every way that you were molded to hold the values you have today, they were raised to have a say in how their lives are led, to be free to choose for themselves the things that matter most. They put that on hold to join this crew and complete their mission. But it was always understood that this mission would *end*. Not a single person of this crew imagined when they signed up they'd have to live this way forever."

"They seemed content enough when Keller was in command."

"Keller was...well, before we found out what he'd done...Keller was our protector. He was constant, a kind of father. He was good at his job, and the crew trusted him. Provided normalcy in very strange times. Now that he's out, no one really knows what to do, but everybody's sure about one thing: they're *sick* of living this way. They're tired and they're scared. Bottom line, they don't want to die having travelled from one system to another, in some pointless, meaningless journey. If there is no future where they can lay down their burdens, many are willing to lay them down right here and start having some kind of life worth living."

"Ridiculous. They *can't* live normally again. I saw what they had on Earth, Counselor. I saw the ruins of cities, how the Blueskins blasted them into plains of black glass. There's nothing left of their lives outside of this ship. Holding on to such ideals? It's a *waste*."

"Are you *so* unsympathetic?"

"Of course! There's colonist delusion, and there's reality. Better we all lived in reality."

"I see. Then let me ask you: are you content in your current life?"
Thompson glares.

"Let me answer that for you," the Counselor says. "You're *not*.
When you were an Operator, you knew your role. You were good at it. You
were honored and respected. Those things matter to you. But they're beyond
your reach now, aren't they? And what you're left with is the memory of
when life was better. The difference between then and now...isn't that the
whole reason you wrestle with existence?"

"You *know* it is. But I can't change it," Thompson says, nearly
shouting. He points a finger toward the door and adds, "*They* should know
they can't change it, either."

"What if you're wrong? What if it can be changed?"

"It can't."

"Sure about that?"

A chilly silence ensues.

"What are you getting at?" Thompson asks. "It's like you're...
trying to *corner* me with words! I *know* what happened, and I *know* I can't
change what I've done. The Colonists should know just as well that this is
what they've got. Insubordination and petty acts of destruction get them
nowhere!"

"Well then, surely you know more about psychology than I do. So
what do you prescribe, Dr. Thompson? Do you think everyone who struggles
with life should behave as you have? Should they all look death in the eye
and see who blinks?"

Thompson looks up at his therapist. The Counselor's expression is as
cold as his words.

"It would be understatement for me to say I dislike it when you draw
lines between yourself and others," the lab-coated man says. "Do you have
any idea how many times you made yourself seem more reasonable than
those who think differently? Just in the last five minutes?"

He points at his desk.

"Do you want to see again how *reasonable* you look in your cabin?"

Thompson drops his head into his hands.

"Look at me," the Counselor insists.

Thompson's head lifts, face glum and penitent.

"I really wanted to get to this point another way," the therapist says,
"but you had to discover for yourself the root of our problems. This crew
is splitting apart, Thompson. Lines have been drawn, and every day, the
divide gets wider. We've lost sight of the fact that we have to stick together
because we keep focusing on our *differences*. Differences how we work, how

we think, how we organize, how we eat, even. We've lost sight that we all need one another to stay alive. We've gone off the rails, here, and we could lose everything. So when I hear someone underscoring how different others are and saying it's wrong... Well *that's* the problem. Talk like that becomes action. And it's *tearing us apart*. We *must* do better, Thompson. Do you understand?"

Genuinely, Thompson says, "I do."

"Good." The Counselor reclines in his chair. "Now that we're past all that, I can tell you what I need from you. You see the gaps between us, between Cadre and Colonist. I need bridges, not wedges. To start, we have to draw this crew back together. I can't do that alone."

"I'd help, but...how?"

"You may think you're neither Cadre nor Colonist, that you're an exile, off on your own. Truth is, you're the best hope we have toward building understanding."

"You taking your own pills, Counselor?"

"No, I'm not. So let me ask you: who has lived in both Cadre One and the *Europa*?"

"Maiella, Argo, myself..."

"And we all hope to see Maiella and Argo home safe. So who does that leave?"

Thompson sighs. "Just me."

"Right."

"But what good am I?"

The Counselor folds his hands in his lap. "Think back, when we were on our way here, to Cadre One. The *Europa* had already doubled her expected lifespan, and it showed. Skeleton crews meant lax maintenance schedules. And there was an indifference that made it easy to overlook how rundown she had become. But you, Argo, and Maiella came aboard with fresh eyes and saw what needed to be done. Didn't wait to be told, you just got to work. And the improvements you were making inspired us. Made us want to get involved, to be a part of it. Together, we made the *Europa* well again. We need that from you, Thompson. We need leadership through positive action."

"I know. And I'm not saying this to start a fight: I truly don't understand how anyone could consciously allow their lifeboat to fall apart. And I cannot comprehend *at all* the urge to take it apart."

"Well it's more complicated than that, unfortunately."

Thompson mutters under his breath, "Always is."

The Counselor grimaces, then waits until he has Thompson's

attention again. "Not everyone has forgotten it, and worse, they know it better than most."

"Wait, *what*?"

"Some are threatening the *Europa* to get what they want."

"That's *insane...*"

"Careful, Thompson. Judgment's going around aplenty, and more than enough for you."

The Gun shows his palms in surrender.

"It's called 'extortion,' the Counselor explains. "Some use it to get what they want. Like it or not, we have to deal with it."

"What could anyone want more than life?"

"Well, it's a calculated risk, because the person believes others will capitulate. Then, they can have their lives *and* something more."

"Which is?"

"Self-determination and freedom."

"*Freedom*? Of what? Freedom of *movement*? Who's keeping them? The only person I know who's been restricted is Herzfeld and he's—"

"No, no, nothing that simple. And I know I'm going to lose you on this, but I'm going to tell you anyway: being free from domination is vital to every Colonist on this ship. Many would die for it. A few would kill for it."

Thompson blanches. The memory of pulling the trigger in smoke and haze, of cutting down glowing blobs in his infrared vision, believing they were the enemy and finding the bodies of human colonists instead...

"That anyone could kill their brothers and sisters willingly," Thompson says, "that anyone could consciously kill another, knowing what he or she was doing...no accident, eyes open and aware... A corruption right to the core! It *can't* be natural, it *can't* be normal. Please, you can't expect me to believe that anyone would willingly kill another just because they want to make their own choices. There simply *can't* be that kind of freedom, not anywhere!" He smacks the back of his hand into the other for emphasis, adding, "Someone must *always* be in charge. Someone *has* to give orders and those orders *must* be followed. If everyone made up their own mind about what they would do, what could get done? Nothing! And what makes them qualified to decide everything? Are they rated in all the knowledge sets required to make these decisions?"

The Gun rises to his feet with an involuntary groan.

"How can anyone justify murder in *any* circumstance? I bear the judgment of seventeen lives, and *it has destroyed me*, Counselor. EVERY DAY I see their faces, the agony of what I did frozen in their final expressions... You're telling me there are people aboard this ship who could take life *willingly*? Without guilt, without responsibility? These people who think this way are allowed to move freely, inflicting this harm? *How can they be allowed to roam*? What makes them different from the enemy? No society could ever survive this way! It would *eat itself from the inside* and *collapse* under the weight of its own *selfish impulse*, and...and... *Why are you smiling*?"

The Counselor looks up from his chair, hands still folded in his lap, contended grin on his face.

"Thompson, societies like this have endured for centuries. And history has proven that they're far more stable than any dictatorship."

The Gun's mouth gapes. "This is humor. It must be."

"It's a fact. And I understand your confusion. If one were to think of it in terms of numbers, to give everyone a decision over everything in their lives, suddenly the range of choices, multiplied by frequency, becomes astronomical, even in a society as small as ours. Imagining it on the scale of entire nations stretches belief. Mathematically, it seems like it couldn't possibly work, yet it does.

"Now don't worry. I'm not here to convince you this is how you should think. I know better than to try and sell you on the idea that freedom could be worth such risks. My point is only to prove to you that you're descended from the very people you think are so irrational and impossible to understand. This is what it means to be human, Thompson. To have different ideas and different perspectives. To maintain a healthy diversity so that a group doesn't stagnate or calcify and become inflexible. I know this will sound counterintuitive, but history has proven that when a society becomes too alike, it becomes rigid and can't adapt to new situations. Given time, something always comes along that challenges those long held values, and if the society can't cope, it dies."

"Wrong. The Cadre has met every challenge and bested it because the entire group is aligned on the same path."

"Oh? Like now, for example?"

Thompson squints. "Hmm?"

"We're in the middle of this mess right now because both of our societies are so inflexible! We've had it our own way so long we're struggling to live with each other, even though we both want peace and harmony."

Thompson's arms droop at his sides and he sinks back down to the couch.

"I don't know much about genetics," the Counselor admits, "but I do know this: the Cadre is nearly identical. Same blood type, same features, same dietary requirements. There are some minor tweaks that make one a Geek, Gun, Brick, or MedTech, but you all come from the same basic DNA blueprint. That virus you brought back from Earth? If Cadre One didn't have all the precautionary measures in place, it could have killed you all in one swoop."

Thompson looks sideways at the Counselor, uncomfortable with the truth of his statement.

"Diversity is absolutely essential for survival," the Counselor continues, "and I don't just mean biological diversity. A wide range of perspectives, thoughts, and ideas is vital. The Cadre needs us, Thompson, every bit as much as we need them. We have to build these bridges and we have to find a way to live as one. Because who knows what the next shock will be, the next crisis, the next...?"

Thompson leans back into the couch and looks up at the ceiling.

"Have I lost you?" the Counselor asks.

"No," Thompson answers, still gazing at the ceiling. "Just saturated. So please, stop talking."

The Counselor laughs. "The sponge is full. All right, then. We're done for the day."

Thompson looks at the Counselor and arches an eyebrow. "For the day? Thought you said we were done for good."

"The therapy sessions, yes. I think we're done with those. There's a lot more we should discuss, though. Wouldn't mind if you dropped in from time to time."

Thompson stands, this time making no effort to hide his injury.

"Going to have that looked at?" the Counselor asks.

Thompson slaps his thigh with a flat hand. "Just stiff, is all. I'll work through it."

The Counselor peers through his eyebrows at the Gun. "Do I have to *order* you to MedLab?"

"Order me? You can do that?"

"While you're under my care, I certainly can."

"Thought this was our last session."

"Isn't over yet."

The two squint at each other.

"*Fine,*" Thompson says. "I'll go see Dr. Taggart. Like she hasn't seen enough of me." He starts toward the door and pauses.

The Counselor swivels in his seat. "Something else on your mind?"

"I've been caught up," Thompson says, inarticulately. "Kind of trapped, I'd say. Made it hard for me to see the bigger picture. Now that I do..."

"Yes?"

Thompson turns slowly. "It's all starting to sink in. I'm certain that if anyone does damage the *Europa*, O'Kai *will* take over."

"I think you're right. He would. So let me ask: do you think he'd be right in doing so?"

"Absolutely."

"Well, you may not have thought it through. Right now, half the crew is bordering on mutiny. One reason is because they think Captain Ortega is too much like O'Kai. Another reason is they think Ortega assumed the rank out of privilege, not because he's the best candidate."

"It's chain of command. He's totally within his right."

The Counselor nods in agreement. "That's true. But there are plenty who want a say in who replaces Keller. Moreover, Ortega was Keller's Executive Officer. By sliding into the big chair without any kind of review or approval process, he's automatically inheriting Keller's guilt by association."

Thompson smirks. "That's absurd."

"I agree. But again, that's what people think. And any time Ortega punishes a crewman, he seems more like a dictator than a ship's captain."

"A ship's captain *is* a dictator. Has to be."

"Well, it's a semantic difference, but at the moment, it matters. On the one hand we have part of the crew with sense of duty and loyalty enough to fall in line. On the other we have those who are desperate for change, people who are stressed to the point of breaking. What we need is less pressure, not more. But if O'Kai comes in, we *will* see sabotage, Thompson. We *will* see deaths. Believe that."

"Once O'Kai weighs the situation, it's mathematical. He'll judge the consequences and act."

"Yes, he will."

Thompson peers at the Counselor, waiting for an answer to his unvoiced question. "Seriously? Do I have to ask?"

The Counselor nods.

"Is O'Kai going to take over?"

The Counselor leans back in his chair. "For the moment, no. We've discussed this at length, in as many angles as we can. For all his formality, he wants us to find a way forward for the betterment of all. I don't think this crew gives him nearly enough credit, actually."

"But if something does happen, there's no way he'll stand by."

"Patrols have doubled in the last three weeks. You must have seen them. He's watching *very* carefully."

"And that has the Colonists spooked..."

"Which makes them more nervous..."

"...and more likely to do something stupid."

The Counselor nods with grim candor. "So you see why I need everyone, especially you, involved in this?"

Thompson sighs deeply. "Okay. I'll go find an engineering team and get started."

"*After* you've seen Dr. Taggart, of course."

Thompson snorts. "Yeah, yeah. After." When he turns to leave, awareness of events occurring just beyond the Counselor's office land with a sudden gravity. The Gun looks at the door the way someone might look down at a chair they have been lounging in only to find it packed with old, sweating dynamite.

"*Damn*," the Gun says.

The door slides aside as he limps toward it and seals after he passes.

MEAGER ACCOMMODATIONS

Deep within Cadre One, below Sub-Level Three, a basic floor plan is complete. Each room is coarsely hewn from the asteroid's native stone. Slim, wide channels have been chiseled out for ventilation ducts. Conduits for power and plumbing have been drilled. The main halls are lit and the entire space is pressurized, air regulators keeping the section breathable. All is staged and ready for completion once the future generation incubating above is ready to take residence.

One room is different from the others, a model for the rest, though not *quite* ready for human habitation. The light panel flushed into the ceiling never dims. There is a combination toilet/washbasin made from stainless steel. A simple hole in the wall above it streams water in an arc, which lands without splashing along the steep sides of the basin, and is vacuumed down the drain at the bottom. Air flows into the room from a slot near the ceiling and exits through a matching slot in the floor, thermally managed to maintain a constant temperature. The only furniture is an unpadded bench fused to the wall. Upon it, a lone creature turns uncomfortably.

She draws her long legs up against her body trying to stay warm in a room never quite warm enough. What little remains of her gown—once an elegant masterpiece of translucent, breathable fabric—drapes against her form in ragged clumps. She hugs it tightly, tucking her long reptilian chin against her chest to trap as much body heat as she can.

From time to time, the entry door parts enough that a doughy bar and a tube of cloudy gel can be tossed in. Whether it is supposed to be food she cannot tell for it has almost no aroma and even less taste. All she knows is that when she eats them, the gnawing hunger in her belly turns into slightly less painful cramps of indigestion.

For days at a time (who can say how many, with no clock and constant illumination) she weeps into her hands, isolated and lonely, missing friends, missing daily contact with her family and the intimate touch of her 'other self.' Dreams of gunfire, screams, explosions, the ragged bodies that shielded her from the blasts, are horrors that shake her from sleep. So many killed in a senseless attack that accomplished...*what*?

At times, she paces the sparse cabin, pressing against the walls for the resistive exercise, stretching out as much as she can, practicing meditative forms. Too often, she thinks about her obligations, about how much work there is to be done, if her responsibilities are being handled adequately, if those who survived the violence are receiving care, if the military is sufficiently vigilant to protect her subjects from another assault. One thing she no longer thinks of is rescue. Even if she could get a message out, she has no clue to her location, no idea where to guide her people. And at this point, if they have not been able to track her stolen limousine they likely never will.

She lies sideways on the hard bench, staring glumly at the opposite wall with saffron yellow eyes. She taps a scuffed talon against the bench's metal surface, making a dull clunk. As bored and glum as she is, the sensations are, at first, better than the endless silence until the mindless tapping becomes irritating. She sits up on the bench, letting her whip tail fall beside her legs, and she sighs deeply.

Must be calm. Must be patient. Must endure.

As an afterthought, she looks down at her fingertips and sees how long her claws have grown.

That's one way to tell how long this one has remained here, she thinks with a cynical smirk, and she rubs each talon against the rough stone wall until they are a more presentable length. Next, she rounds each tip, blunting and shaping it as though she were preparing for a gala event. She hums to herself as she works, pleased at her progress, happy to have a project until her last talon is done and anymore shaping threatens to open the soft quick under the surface. Boredom descends, once more.

She sucks her teeth. She clears her throat. She plays games with herself to see how long she can hold her breath, how long she can go without blinking, how long she can ignore the itch on her back, how high she can count. At six million, she quits.

A soft flow of air begins overhead, only audible due to the chamber's otherwise perfect silence. Ringing in her ears stopped quite a long time ago, and she welcomes a sound other than her own sighs. Absently, she drums her fingers against her leg and pats a rhythm. The rhythm brings a small bit of happiness to her elongated face, and she hums a melodic accompaniment. Dread seizes her in an instant and she stops, attention locked on the cell door.

When she was first dragged in, her protests were met with a stick so painful it left her writhing on the gritty floor. Fear of that stick kept her mute, and she would not have believed anything could make her willingly risk such a sensation again. Yet the boredom is so overwhelming that she longs for any change to the gray scenery. Quietly at first, with anxious glances at the door, she opens her mouth and shapes her throat to produce gentle tones.

No one comes.

Emboldened, she opens her jaw wider. Her vocal box elongates and constricts for greater volume. Words come to her lips, words that speak in her tongue about captivity and how sweet it is to be released, through escape, liberation, or death.

No prison forever detains, the words say, *No walls can endless confine. The captive will inevitably be free. Separation is but a moment in time, and one only need be patient and content, because captors cannot keep a spirit.*

Her chest fills with deep breaths, her voice resounds passionate and strong in the small stone cell.

Let the body fade, give them nothing to hold. The insolent deserve nothing and nothing is what they shall have.

Conviction puts bass in her voice. Her throat tightens in long held sustains. The words roll from her diaphragm, powerful and honest.

Indelible and everlasting is the soul, she sings, *and once you accept this simple truth, you are already free.*

The cell door reverberates with a pounding fist on the far side.

"Don't try to silence!" she shouts back in her language. "Take this one away from her people and keep her caged for no reason? This one will MAKE you hear, do you understand? You can't ignore anym—"

The cell door slides aside. The monster steps through in head to toe black armor that steals light like an eclipse. Black eyepieces convey soulless menace without a trace of anything alive inside. But she has seen what lies beneath that malevolent exterior, having glimpsed the fragile creatures within:

> *Aboard her capital ship... Announcements of violent intruders? Impossible!*
>
> *Bodyguards rushing into her chambers, demanding her evacuation... Staff packing essentials and ushering her to the limousine...*

Hallways gone dark... Tremors in the floor plates of far away explosions... Sooty burns on the walls and the smell of vaporized metal...

The limousine ramp only a few paces ahead...an entourage of bodyguards and aides, begging her to hurry...

A flash from behind and a gust that slams her onto her face... Vision blurred, head lolling, thick white smoke everywhere... Strobes of violet light in the haze...

Heavy weight on top of her, hard to breathe, can barely move...rolling part way over and looking into gawking dead eyes of her bodyguards...

Security forces running over to her, crouching nearby, shooting back into the haze then toppling backward one by one, pieces of their heads bursting in a mist of brain and bone...

Lost in barbaric noise, straining against the baggage and bodies pinning her...unable to get free...

A towering shadow in the haze, sprinting at her... mottled gray and black, glistening with dark blood... The Ravenous Ghost she refused to believe was real...

Clutching her wounded shoulder, looking up into the demon's face as it stoops over her... Red-rimmed gray eyes behind the wreckage of armor plating... A face of new and old scars... A savage beast tortured to the epitome of violence and desperation...

Her saffron eyes drop from the monster's faceplate to the truncheon in its enormous fist. Her back and legs twinge at the sight of it, how she stumbled in her forced march to the cell and how that baton electrified her until she was back on her feet. But even such a hulking, armored brute with a painful stick is less intimidating than the diminutive, hunchbacked figure lurking beside it, for even though one of its hands is clenched into an arthritically locked claw, the other holds an auto-syringe. Its reservoir is filled with bilious yellow fluid.

Immediately, the prisoner calms herself and places her palms on the bench where she sits, but she does not avert her eyes.

"This one is glad she was finally heard," she says in a conversational tone. "She misses talking to someone, even if it must be you."

The huge soldier maintains a steady gaze with its impenetrable dark lenses. But the hunched human caps the needle of the auto-syringe and places it into the deep pocket of her white coat. She says something in her own tongue, touching the enormous soldier lightly at the elbow, and the two back out of the cell.

"Wait!" the prisoner cries, rising from the bench. "Please don't go! We can talk to each other, we can learn to speak to one another. Will you try? Please, let us *try* to communicate, let us *try* to understand. *This one does not want to be alone anymore!*"

The door seals and she is left standing in the cold gray stone cell. Tears well and she wraps her arms around herself as she sinks to the floor.

Must remain, she reminds herself, pushing back the anguish of solitude. *Must be patient. Because this one will be free.*

*****

Lying on the hard bench, staring at the light panel in the ceiling, she meditates so the nervous cramps in her gut will relax. Rather than let up, they intensify, and she hurries to the sparse and uncomfortable toilet. Clearly, the designers made no account for tails, and she has to contort herself sideways across the narrow opening, one leg raised against the wall, teetering on the other in precarious balance. She gathers up the rags of her garments and groans as her body drives out disagreeable Cadre sustenance.

The things one takes for granted, like proper meals and simple eliminations...

Still perched in her awkward stance, she reaches blindly behind her to find the lever for the water stream. Her talon slips off of it twice before she realizes why it is so slick. An urge to cry wells inside, then is immediately overruled by a laugh, and yields to tears again.

*****

The door opens a crack and something is lobbed in. The door seals.

The prisoner lifts her head from the bench and sees another plasticine wrapped protein bar on the floor. Her belly rumbles with hunger, and she scowls at it.

My stomach is a traitor.

Rather than acknowledge the protein bar as any kind of food, she lies back and thinks about singing again. But the thought of the needle and its yellow cargo ends that plan. She interlaces her fingers, working out her next move, when there is a knock at the door almost polite in its brevity.

"Yes, enter," she says, and the door slides open.

Outside stands a human male dressed in black shoes, gray slacks, wrinkled white shirt and lab coat. His clothes hang limp against his frame, as though the fabric has worn so thin there is no longer any stiffness to it at all. Chaotic locks of black hair overlap each other, making her think of ocean waves during a nighttime storm. He notices her attention on his hair and he smiles, dragging a hand through it, then he straightens and to her extreme surprise says in her tongue,

"Channel open, ready to receive."

That's an odd thing to say, she thinks. *His words are correct, and pronunciation is good, but...is that the way they speak to one another?*

Like a lightning bolt, she recognizes the precise language.

That's how our ships hail one another in space... He must think that's our greeting!

The captive bows modestly and replies, "Among the people, this one is known as Aeolia Shondrekar Bakkar, and she is pleased to meet you. My place among the people is—"

The man holds his hands up, and says, "Not to..." His head tilts and his expression contorts as if unsure how to proceed.

He wants to talk, she realizes with joy, *but he doesn't know how. Let's start with basics.*

She directs her fingers toward her chest and says, "Shondre."

"Shon-dra?" the man echoes.

Shondre smiles politely, lips together, then extends her hand toward him.

The man mimics her gesture, pointing with all fingers at his chest, and says something in his tongue, a word gruff and sibilant unlike anything in her vocabulary.

"Kon-Zil-Urr?" she struggles to repeat.

The man smiles and nods quickly.

Shondre moves away from the bench and offers it to him with an inviting gesture, but he refuses. He says something in his tongue, bows, and then backs out of the room.

"Be well, Kon-Zil-Urr," she says in parting. The huge soldier steps in front of the door and looks in before sealing the cell.

Her blood races, making her giddy with excitement.

Have I made contact?

Just as swiftly, she thinks about the massive soldier and the small woman with her needle.

Or did I just remind them to toss me out an air lock?

STOP YOUR GOB

Thompson strides unevenly through the *Europa's* hallways. MedLab is only a short distance ahead, yet when he reaches the transparent outer doors he sighs inwardly with relief.

You took far worse than this on Earth, he chides himself. *Colonist lifestyle has made you weak in mind as well as body. Succumbing to sickness...allowing yourself to become mentally ill...and, now, hobbled by a minor injury...* He grimaces. *How did you ever reach Major in the Corps?*

The MedLab doors slide apart then slow with high-pitched squeals before nesting in their recesses. As he limps through, the wounded man squints at the doorframe.

I'm not the only thing that's run down around here, he thinks, making a mental note to come back and lubricate the tracks.

Inside, MedLab is quiet. A heavy set, dark-skinned man in light blue scrubs concentrates on a tray of covered circular dishes and the irregular pink dots inside them. His counterpart, a round pale woman with short gray hair, is identically dressed and studies a three-dimensional diagram of internal organs. Both look up at him briefly then resume their work.

Thompson moves past the receiving desk, stealing a glance at the woman's anatomical diagram. Between spongy cavities in an anonymous rib cage, where a heart would be, three muscular tubes curve in an arch and throb in regular cadence.

That's the Blueskin Bull's-eye, right there. Probably the captive down at Cadre One. But why are they studying its anatomy?

The Gun continues past research stations and medical test benches, past staged gurneys and examination tables to a screened-off area in the back. He takes hold of a thick drape and pulls it aside, revealing the *Europa's* main surgical facility. Three movable steel tables stand in a triangular formation near the center. Bright articulating lamps hang from the ceiling, aimed at each table. Carts stand ready at the room's center with immaculate steel and plastic surgical tools arrayed atop light blue cloths under a layer of clear film.

Along the back wall tall transparent cylinders stand vacant, air and fluid hoses hanging ready inside. Clear plastic covers the mouthpieces with attached labels that read, STERILE.

The new layout is nearly identical to the MedLab at Cadre One, and for a moment Thompson wonders if this was the room of his, Beckert's, and Argo's recovery. But a quick glance is enough to prove the narrow cylinders are far too slim for even a modestly built Brick.

As he takes in the seamless blend of Cadre and Colonist technologies arranged before him, part of what the Counselor was trying to tell him in an earlier session starts making sense:

> *Where the Cadre focuses on treating wounds,*
> *Colonists focus on treating the patient.*

At the time the difference seemed irrelevant, philosophical, and was easy to dismiss. Now, he sees the two perspectives encouraged development of very different medical tools, techniques, and processes. Because of that, Cadre and Colonist had much they could share with one another, and in blending those technologies they have both enhanced their healing capabilities.

Maybe differences CAN be strength... he thinks to himself.

"Hello, Thompson," Sahara says from her workstation on the room's far left. "Come on in."

Her back is to him, and her long, dark ponytail hangs down to the waist of her white lab coat. When she turns about, she shows him a warm smile and pushes her spectacles up from the end of her nose.

"Won't you have a seat on that table there? Be right with you."

Thompson limps to the indicated table while Sahara tucks her tablet under an arm and draws the curtain dividing the Operating Room from rest of MedLab.

"Jules," Sahara calls to the male nurse on the far side of the curtain, "would you join us, please? And bring in '*The Cart.*'" She pulls the drape the rest of the way and steps over to Thompson.

"Let's have your boots, then. We'll need your pants, as well."

Thompson complies, kicking off the boot on his good leg. Then he closes his eyes and grits his teeth as he works the boot off his injured leg.

Sahara observes while Thompson strips down, tapping notes into her tablet. Once he gets his uniform trousers off, the trouble is immediately obvious. Beneath the thin stretch fabric of his undersuit, a purple and red mound rises on the middle of his inner thigh.

"I think I found the problem," Sahara says, shaking her head. "So you were going to just work through this, were you?"

Thompson nods as if the answer is obvious.

Sahara grunts. "Trying to undo all my good work? Wasn't easy fixing you, you know. You'd *better* start taking care of yourself."

"Yes, ma'am."

Sahara looks up at him a moment then resumes her visual diagnosis. "Thought you were going to argue with me like yeh usually do. Did Counselor finally get through that hard head?"

Thompson snorts, smirks, and looks straight ahead. "You could say that."

Sahara shoots him a sly glance. "Good to know 'tain't all rocks in your noggin. Here, now. Up ye go. On the table."

Thompson sets himself onto the table as ordered.

There is a clatter of metal rings and a rustle of thick fabric from the dividing drape. Sahara and her patient both turn to see Jules pull the curtain shut, then he turns about and pushes a cart toward them. Arranged on top of a white cloth is a hideous assortment: blunt hammer, toothed extractors, hooked spreaders, drill bits, handsaw, and blades of varying shapes. Thompson does not give them a second glance.

"Lie back" Sahara orders. "Jules, give 'im a hand with his leg, will you?"

Jules nods and hurries to take Thompson's injured leg by the back of the knee and ankle. "Whoa," he says upon seeing the swelling and discoloration, "looks like a bad strain."

"That's my guess," she confirms. "Let's see how bad." Sahara takes the white tablet from under her arm, and while Jules is positioning Thompson's leg, she slides the tablet under the injury. Next she reaches up toward the cluster of ceiling mounted lamps and pulls down one that is elongated and cylindrical, parking it a half-meter above Thompson's thigh.

"All right, Thompson, lie still. Don't move. We'll be right back." Sahara and Jules move to the room's corner and pull out a slim barrier from the wall. Standing behind it, she calls out, "In three...two...one..."

The elongated lamp issues a series of bangs like a hard plastic mallet striking metal and rapidly curves through a forty-five degree arc. It then returns to starting position and curves through another forty-five degree arc on the opposite side.

By the time Sahara and Jules walk back to the table, a hologram projects above it. In the three-dimensional rendering, the muscles of Thompson's inner thigh are highlighted.

"Mm, hmm," Sahara grumbles, "will you look at that?"

Thompson picks his head up off the table and peers at the skinless projection of his own leg. "Look at what?"

"You don't see it? Here, let me show you." Sahara reaches into the projection and drags it closer to Thompson's face. Keeping grip on the projection, she rotates it and spreads her fingers, enlarging the injured area.

"These," she says, pointing with her free hand, "are your Gracilis and Adductor Longus muscles. And these notches here? That's where you nearly ripped them off the tendons."

"Yeah, I didn't feel it separate," Thompson says, laying his head back on the table. "Knew it was minor."

Sahara turns to her surgical nurse. "They said diamonds were the hardest things around... Had no idea about this one's skull, did they?" She looks down at her patient. "I don't need to operate on this. If you take your time, ice it and stretch carefully, you'll be fine in a few weeks."

"A few *weeks*?" Thompson sits up in alarm. "I've been down for months, already! You've got all the tools out. Patch me up."

Sahara puts a hand on his chest and urges him back onto the table. "I had no intention of using anything on this cart. I bring it out with all these pointy sharp bits to scare hypochondriacs into taking better care of themselves. Effort was wasted on you, clearly. But I tell you what: do as I say and you'll be fine."

"In a few weeks? C'mon, stitch me up."

"Good Lord, it's not that long! Be over before you know it!"

"You don't understand... I *can't* be laid up." Thompson's eyes widen; his eyebrows draw together. "I *have* to be ready."

Taken back by his urgent tone, she asks, "Ready for what?"

"*Anything.*"

Sahara squints at her patient. "What have you heard? Is something coming?"

"No, but... If something does happen, I can't be idle, I HAVE to be ready the inst—"

"All right, *all right*! Stop your gob!" She looks at the floor, then turns to the cart. "Jules, mix me up some local anesthetic and some flesh binder, Cadre formula. That one'll work best on this knucklehead."

"Thank you," Thompson begins.

"See, now," Sahara says, angrily, "I don't like doing surgeries I don't have to. My MedLab's been nice and quiet lately, and that's how I like it. Getting yourself hurt like this is just careless. Uses up my supplies, and that pisses me off, boyo. If I do this for you, you're going to follow my instructions on recovery. *Understand?*"

Thompson swallows. "Yes, ma'am."

"You'd better. 'Cause if you don't, I'm gonna brand the word *Imbecile* into your forehead." Sahara strides off to a deep basin near her workstation and washes up.

Jules returns from a wall sconce with a small tray. On it is a loaded syringe, a small scalpel, and a tube of binding agent with a pen-like tip. His hands are covered in thin blue gloves, his mouth and nose are covered by a white medical mask. Carefully, he sets the tray beside the other implements on the cart.

"Thompson, we'll need you to remove your undersuit," Jules says.

After the Gun does so, Jules shaves the area, paints it with brown fluid, and lays a patch of transparent plastic wrap over the injury. Next, he places sterile blue linens under Thompson's leg and drapes smaller cloths around the area.

Thompson looks around in boredom as the two prepare, and his eyes pause on the empty cylindrical tanks at the back of the room.

"I heard Beckert is out of the tank," the Gun says.

Jules nods. "That's right. He's taken Colonel Anders' quarters, in fact."

"Colonel Anders was promoted to Council?"

Jules grimaces and shakes his head before answering, "They called it, 'retirement.'"

Thompson lowers his eyes. "Oh. That's a loss..."

"Yeah." Jules looks through the wall of the MedLab momentarily. "Doc Taggart told me what his life was like, how hard it was. Can't blame him for being worn out and wanting an end to it all, but... I think he was more involved in things than we realized."

Sahara strides back to the table, hands raised in front of her. "How're we looking, Jules?"

"Prepped and ready, Doctor." The nurse stretches a pair of blue gloves over Sahara's raised hands.

"This won't take long," she tells her patient. Then turning to her nurse, she says, "Give him the local."

"I don't need it," Thompson says.

"*Me* Doctor. *You* patient. I don't want you twitching or squirming, so shut yer yap. Jules, *stick him*."

"Yes, Doctor." Jules consults the holoprojection above, then gently inserts the needle, hitting the points intended with a steady hand.

"Anesthetic delivered," he announces.

"We'll give it a few seconds," Sahara says.

Thompson peeks over his chest at his surgeon. "Have you talked to Beckert since he was released?"

"Oh, sure. I visit him to check on his progress."

"How is he?"

Sahara glances at Thompson to gauge how sincere her answer should be. "He's still in a lot of pain, but we manage it for him. Gradually, he's healing, and as he heals, the pain is less." Her eyes glaze in recollection. "Still can't believe he pulled through. Tough buggers, you lot."

"Can he talk? Is he... Is he all there?"

"Mentally? Oh, aye. Sharp as a laser, that one. That HDI is some of the best head protection I've ever seen." Her face contorts. "Not sure I like how you go about cramming all that tech in a boy's head, but it's amazing what he can do once it's in there. Clear as a bell why you protect it so well." Sahara lifts her gaze to the wall across from her, eyes tracking across the devices and equipment. "Had some mates who specialized in neurology. Head and spine traumas, mostly. Their days were full of SAC-V and skimbike wrecks. If those kids had headgear like Beckert's, my mates wouldda had a lot more days off playing golf."

"Golf?"

Sahara nods. "It's a game people used to play on Earth. Don't know the rules, but most of them seem to revolve around spending stupid amounts of money clubbing a wee ball around unproductive land. That, and driving yourself mad with frustration while dressed like a complete arse." She returns her attention to the swollen leg.

"And how is he physically?" Thompson digs.

"We're working on prosthetics for him," the doctor says, " but there was so much gangrene we cannae get 'em to interface. MedTechs have a motorized chair for him when he needs to get around. Don't have anything better at the moment. Anders had the same mobility issues Beckert does now, so the colonel's old spot was a good fit, all things considered."

She lightly taps a finger against Thompson's wounded leg. "Feel that?"

"Feel what?"

She grins. "He's ready." Turning to Jules, she says, "Dress and mask."

Jules pulls a folded white smock from a drawer of the cart and holds it up. Sahara slides her hands through the sleeves and waits for him to fasten it in the back.

"Beckert's getting some augments to his HDI," she continues. "O'Kai and Munro said he'd need 'em to handle additional processing requests. I objected at first. Wanted to be sure he'd healed enough from your last rotation. But every test, he passed. And where he can't move about, it allows him a fuller kind of service. That's really important to him, so I couldn't deny him that. He'll be getting upgrades through this week and next."

Jules covers her mouth with a surgical mask and ties it behind her head, adding, "When Chusan transferred him from the Operator Corps to Ralla, she promoted him to First Lieutenant. You never saw a kid so proud in your life."

The thought of Beckert's face upon receiving promotion warms Thompson's heart. It chills quickly when he considers how broken the young Geek is.

"He deserved better than to serve under me," Thompson says.

Sahara clucks her tongue. "*There's* a load of shite! Argo swears he never would have made it back without you, and so does Beckert. They're not exactly prone to exaggeration, you know. You *didn't* fail Beckert or Argo, Thompson. You saved *their* lives, and they saved *yours*. You should know that." She looks up from Thompson's leg and peers at Jules. "I think I'm gonna brand his forehead, anyway. Now, look," she says to Thompson, "I'm getting to work. No more talking 'til I'm done, do yeh understand?"

"Yes, ma'am."

"Good. Jules, gimme the cutter, and have sponges ready." She holds a hand out and Jules places a scalpel into it. Sahara leans close to Thompson's thick leg, peering through her spectacles. With the utmost precision, control, and skill, the surgeon mends her patient.

VOICE OF DISSENT

Ortega strides through the *Europa's* hallways, flanked by the Counselor on his left and Gregor on his right. Ahead of them march two Cadre Guns, and behind them two Cadre Bricks keep step. The Operators' heels strike in unison with muted thuds.

The corridors no longer bear angry slogans of revolt, and where graffiti once marred the surfaces, the wall coatings have been stripped down to bare metal. But there is still a palpable tension festering beneath, as if the disease has been driven from the surface into the very bones of the ship.

"You got your speech worked out?" Gregor asks him.

Ortega snorts. "No. Been preparing in my cabin for weeks, but... I can't see which way this'll go. Why? You have a suggestion?"

Gregor's mouth opens, then he glances over his shoulder at the Bricks and censors himself. "Not my place, sir."

Ortega frowns and tilts his head. "Never mind them. Out with it."

Gregor barely hesitates before saying, "Letting Herzfeld go? That was a risk. He's gonna have them foaming at the mouth before we even get there. And walking in with the goon squad, here? That plays right into his hands."

Ortega points to the dark ring under his left eye. "You think I should let them beat on me again? *That's* projecting strength?"

"Not my call," Gregor replies, attempting humility.

Ortega exhales in frustration. "Speak your mind, Lieutenant."

"Sir, I think walking in with these guys says you *are* afraid, that they *can* intimidate you. Send 'em off and let's just go, the three of us."

Ortega frets and turns to the Counselor. "Do you agree?"

"For different reasons, but yes," the Counselor says. "I think walking in escorted like this plays to fear and suspicion. Could make it harder to pull the crew together."

"So you think I'm a coward, then?"

"Not at all! It plays on their fears that you're aligned with what are, in essence...fascists."

"*Fascists*? Are you joking?"

"No, I'm not."

Ortega looks into the backs of the Operators ahead, his eyebrows crushed together in exasperation.

"The Cadre doesn't have time for such a game as politics," Ortega says with a sneer. "Call them fascists? That's an *insult*. They fight to the death for survival, ours and theirs! And you say they make politics out of that?"

The Counselor frets. "Captain, when you boil it right down, politics is about power, about getting others to do what you want. It can be through persuasion, authority, or force, but it's still about power. The Cadre may not have any use for influence, favors, or rhetoric, but they *certainly* have authority and force."

"In abundance," Gregor adds.

Ortega maintains his forward gaze, the corners of his mouth turned down in disgust.

"I know they're here for us," Gregor continues. "I know they'll give their lives to protect us without the slightest hesitation. They'd never toy with us in some kind of manipulative power play... But just look at them and tell me you don't see the Brownshirts of the nineteen thirties."

Ortega walks in silence, contemplating his counsel. He watches the square shoulders of the Guns ahead of him, how they swing together as if invisible bars connected them.

"They've proved themselves again and again," Ortega says. "They're brave. They don't drift along, helpless...like we do. They MAKE their future, and they are carrying us along! That's strength we should learn from."

Gregor peeks at the Counselor behind Ortega's head and the Counselor looks back in concern.

"Captain," the Counselor says, "I agree, but... I think saying that would turn the crew against you."

Ortega scowls, keeping a fixed gaze forward.

Knowing he missed the target, the Counselor looks at Gregor again, urging with his eyebrows to say something.

"Skipper, we're with you, however this goes," Gregor says.

"Are you?"

"Of course we are!" Gregor blurts.

"We're not saying you've done anything wrong," the Counselor adds. "We're saying there may be a better message than preaching *tough love*."

Ortega looks at the Counselor directly, eyebrows arched with impatience.

"Well?"

"You saw it as often as I did back on Earth: some major new law would come before the General Assembly—something that would truly benefit a vast majority of people—only to get voted down by popular referendum time and time again. It was always fear of change...the fear that no matter what the people were told, change would bring something worse than the status quo."

Ortega nods and he faces forward. "I'm listening."

"Allay their fears, Captain. Stand before them and let them see you. Show them that they don't need to fear you or the Cadre. Tell them plainly and directly, and then let *them* speak. Look them in the eye, talk to them. Listen to them. *That* will prove your strength better than a hundred Cadre Operators at your back."

Ortega mulls the advice before turning to his acting first officer. "You think this, as well?"

Gregor answers immediately, "Yes, sir, I do."

Ortega holds his head up high and takes a deep breath. His lips bunch and his cheeks draw in as if sucking on something.

"Halt," he orders.

The Operators halt their march and stamp once.

"Dismissed," Ortega says.

"Negative," the lead Gun replies. "Orders are to ensure safety of VIPs en route to Colonist meeting hall. Will comply."

"This is not the Cadre, and you are not at home, Sergeant. As captain, my directive supersedes any order from General O'Kai. Now I said, *dismissed*!"

The lead Gun speaks into his helmet mic, "Major Chusan, Captain Ortega has given me a direct order to part his company. Please advise correct action, over."

Ortega cannot hear Chusan's radioed response, but the Sergeant turns on his heel, salutes, and states plainly, "We are dismissed. Will patrol within one hundred meters and remain on-call for assistance."

The Gun points at his three comrades, and flicks his head. The Operators stride past and form into a two by two formation, arms swinging with each stride like pendulums of synchronized clocks.

Ortega watches them march away: how their right hands clutch the shoulder strap of their weapons in exactly the same spot, how despite their size, their combined footfalls are so quiet. Soon, there is no sound in his ears but his own breath and the gentle whoosh of ventilation.

"Now that it's just us," Gregor says, "can we be less candid in front of O'Kai's lackeys? Don't like the general eavesdropping on our every word."

"On the contrary," Ortega says, scowling, "I *want* O'Kai knowing what's going on. If he doesn't, he's more likely to intervene, I think."

"Captain," the Counselor says cautiously, "remember we pushed hard to maintain our sovereignty aboard the *Europa*. We used that as a condition of remaining at Cadre One, in fact. If nothing else, O'Kai is a man of his word, and you should feel complete confidence he'll honor that arrangement."

"Confidence..." Ortega mutters, staring far down the corridor. His hands search his trousers for pockets to hide in, but find none. He looks at his hands, annoyed, then drops them down by his side. "Let's go," he says, head raised, chest out, and the three resume their path.

Before they near the emptied storage-bay-turned-meeting-hall, all three notice a susurration from afar. Ortega turns his favored ear forward. The sound grows louder as they approach, a steady roar in the distance.

"We're not even in the storage *section*!" the Spaniard gripes. "Already we hear their anger? I can see that cabrón now, on the platform, fists in the air, telling his lies about me!"

Ortega stops in the middle of the hallway and rubs his hands. Gregor and the Counselor stop beside him, waiting.

"I am...concerned," the Spaniard says.

"I understand," the Counselor replies, looking far ahead.

"Why can't I do this from the bridge? It's easy enough to conference in by video."

"You could," the Counselor begins, "and maybe that will do for future meetings, but... This is a critical time. They need to see you in person, not just a face on a screen."

"Want to do this for me, Gregor?" Ortega offers.

"*Sir?*" The Russian asks in disbelief. He shakes his head. "No way, not my place. Just gonna keep my mouth shut and back you up."

Ortega looks to his left, one eyebrow raised expectantly.

"You know I can't," the Counselor says heavily. "I can say a few words at the beginning, but the real speech...it has to be you."

"I was *joking*, you fools," Ortega lies. He stares into the distance and forces himself onward like a condemned man on his way to the gallows. "This... This will be difficult."

The three walk quietly together, each alone in their thoughts. When Ortega realizes he is wringing his hands, he clasps them together. His head bows, and he silently prays.

Lord, I cannot say it outright, but I am afraid. I pray for wisdom and guidance. Let me see past the pettiness and bitterness inside me. May I find a path that is true through this time of confusion. May I conquer fear, and come not to death at the hands of those I would serve. But if I do, I beg your forgiveness for my many sins and may you, in infinite mercy, grant me eternal life at your side.

Glory be to the Father, and to the Son, and to the Holy Spirit, as it was in the beginning, is now, and ever shall be, world without...end. Amen.

Ortega lifts his head, grimly amused by the ending of his prayer. They are words he has used at the end of every important prayer. But the world did end. And waves of discontent from the meeting hall ahead erode his confidence faster than he can build it.

Keller would face them, he thinks. *He would face them all, no matter what. He would look them all in the eye. That's what he would do. That's what I must do, or be unworthy of this post. I have to face them all and look them in the eye. If I can't do that, I can't be their captain...and their hatred... it will be justified.*

Ortega covers his belly to calm its queasy rumbling. His jaw clenches and his stride becomes rigid.

"How are you doing?" the Counselor asks.

"I-I'm fine," Ortega says, eyes locked on the nearing door to the meeting hall. He shakes the tremors from his hands and breathes deeply. "We'll...we'll be fine."

Gregor's ears slide back. "Not to worry, skipper. Anybody takes a swing, I'll knock 'em flat. Can't show them—"

"I'M *NOT* A COWARD!" Ortega roars.

Gregor stiffens, blanks his expression, and faces front. The Counselor does likewise before Ortega can turn on him. The rest of the way the men walk in silence.

Individual words emerge from the shouted noise ahead—ragged fragments of speech like flotsam hurled back and forth in a storm. Keller's name rings clearly as does a demand for his blood. The *Europa's* old captain is vilified, demonized, then torn apart in verbal effigy, a violent

52

dismemberment of his memory, of his every accomplishment. But far from satisfied, the storm rages fiercer, its appetite whetted and ready for another victim.

"I will fear no evil," Oretga whispers, "for Thou art with me... I will fear no evil... I will fear no evil..."

Two Cadre Guns stand sentry at the entrance to the meeting hall dressed in full kit, rifles slung over one shoulder. At Ortega's approach, the Gun on the left salutes.

"We will escort you inside," the Gun states.

"No, Maddock, thank you," the Spaniard answers, staring straight at the closed door before him. Maddock looks to Gregor and the Russian confirms with a subtle shake of his head.

"Very well. We'll take position inside and guarantee your safety."

"No. You won't. You'll stay right here. This is an internal matter, and the Cadre has no part of it."

Maddock is undaunted, his gray eyes narrowed. "Say what you like, Captain. This crowd is agitated. We will keep our post and observe. If there is a threat to life, we must intervene."

Any other time the Gun's cool determination might have been taken as a challenge, but at this moment it is exactly what Ortega needs. Unlike Gregor's offer, which made him feel weak and unable to defend himself, Maddock's statement is an assurance, an independent certainty, that security will be maintained, that his life will be preserved.

"As ever, we're grateful to you," Ortega says, looking the two Guns in the eye. To the Counselor and Gregor, he adds, "Let's get this done."

Maddock punches the button and the wide doors slide aside. A raging din pours through the gap then lulls as hundreds of colonists notice the open doorway. Ortega stands mute, his breath frozen in his throat. He glances from one face to the next, forcing himself not to buckle under the weight of their total attention. Faces contort at the sight of him; eyes lock on to him like cannons of loathing.

He looks past the crush of angry faces to an elevated platform outfitted with two microphone stands and sturdy metal railings. A path to it is held open by uniformed crew loyal to their captain, their locked arms just able to hold back the tide of anger pressing against them.

I may not survive this... Ortega thinks.

Maddock gestures the way inside.

...but I have to face them. And I will show them I am unafraid.

Ortega breathes deeply and steps forward with the two Guns.

"Captain, wait..." the Counselor begins, but Ortega ignores him.

The Guns step through and take position on the opposite side as Ortega strides shoulder to shoulder between them, head raised, chest out. Immediately, the shouts resume their furor.

"Damn it, he walked right in with them!" Gregor curses. "Did he hear a *thing* we said?"

"C'mon!" the Counselor says, and the two hurry to catch up with their captain.

While Ortega focuses on the platform, Gregor watches the colonists' eyes shift from the Cadre Operators to Ortega and back, seeing in their faces the assumptions of collusion. The Russian's brow lowers and his shoulders lift in anticipation of attack.

The Counselor takes a softer body posture, shoulders rounded, palms up and fingers spread. He nods deferentially, engaging as many as he can with pleading eyes, silently begging them to be calm.

As the three move to the platform, red faces poke between the uniformed men and women standing akimbo. The faces are yelling at Ortega, threatening, spitting words like bullets.

"You sold us out!" one man shouts.

"Made us Cadre slaves!" another roars.

"He let Keller get away!" a red-faced woman shrills, stabbing an accusing finger past the row of people holding her back. "He's just as guilty!" She lurches against the row of uniformed men, clawing at Ortega's shoulder. Gregor bats her arm away and shoves her back. A scuffle breaks out behind the human barriers, and the people holding them back press with chests and shoulders, shouting at the crowd to *get back*, to *calm down* and *cool it*. The Counselor looks into the fury, placating with gentle gestures wherever he can. Ortega, however, keeps his gaze on the platform, ignoring the epithets and threats hurled at him.

I will show them I am unafraid.

At the base of the short stairs leading up to the platform, a Cadre Brick stands like an obsidian boulder. His massive arms are crossed, and he looks over the crowd without anxiety. Unlike the rest of the path that seems on the verge of collapse, no one pushes near the massive soldier.

Upon sight of the huge Brick, Ortega's spirit lifts. "Halgrim, glad you're here," the captain says as he climbs the stairs. Halgrim acknowledges with a head nod and keeps his vigil. Gregor and the Counselor ascend after Ortega, careful to avoid eye contact—and any visible affiliation—with the massive soldier.

Atop the platform, the two stand beside their captain and gaze out over an enraged mob. Fists are thrust repeatedly on outstretched arms. Teeth show between parted lips.

Leaning in to the closer of the two microphones, Ortega says, "Your attention."

His amplified voice drowns among the shouts and hisses.

"Your attention, *please*," he says louder than before, and then again. Every time the Spaniard raises his voice, the shouts get louder until the entire hall reverberates. In frustration, he turns up his hands and looks out across what was once an orderly crew, people he has known and lived with for decades, people who were once sane.

Until Herzfeld's lawyering, Ortega thinks. *And where is he? Skulking in the shadows, no doubt. Burrowed in like a rat in an attic, spreading his fleas and plagues!*

There is a tug at his arm, and Ortega turns to see the Counselor looking at him.

"May I?" the Counselor asks.

Ortega steps back from the microphone and gestures toward it with both hands.

The Counselor looks down a moment, then lifts his gaze to the shouting crowd around him. He turns all the way to his left, and sweeps his gaze all the way to the right. He folds his hands before himself and waits. Before long, the shouts lose their intensity and fade to a rumble. Some voices far in the back still clamor to be heard, but the noise falls to a constant simmer.

The Counselor angles the microphone lower toward himself and he leans into it, speaking very softly. Even with the reduced volume in the hall, his words are lost. Rather than raise his voice to be heard, he continues speaking softly into the microphone. Shouts become murmurs and calls for,

"Quiet!"

"SHHH!"

"Let him speak!"

"Can't hear you, Counselor!"

"Louder!"

"Speak up!"

The Counselor looks up from the microphone to the crowd. Random comments pass back and forth among some, but compared to the tumult just moments earlier it is remarkably still. He smiles modestly.

"Thank you," the Counselor says into the microphone. He thinks a moment. Then, with head slightly tilted, he asks rhetorically, "How did we come to this?"

The question hangs in the humid air like a rain cloud.

"I've sat with every single one of you," the Counselor says. "We've talked at length, we've shared stories. We've come to know each other." He cranes his head from side to side looking into as many faces as he can.

"We've all worked hard together. We've struggled, felt each other's losses. We've propped each other up and limped our way back from the brink because we didn't give up on one another. From shipmates we became friends, and then, through the bonds of our shared lives, we became family."

He pauses.

"Do families disagree?" He grunts and nods vigorously. "Yes, they do. And it gets heated sometimes. But there's no reason we should ever allow it to divide us."

The Counselor looks at the platform beneath him.

"I'm worried that we've let this anger cut too deep, that we've allowed ourselves not to care. That we're so exhausted there isn't enough left in us to try anymore."

The Counselor takes a moment to look at individuals in the crowd, connecting with his audience one face at a time.

"I'm worried that we're drawing borders that may never be erased. I'm scared...yes, *scared*...that those divisions leave us weaker and vulnerable." The Counselor lifts his hands, palms up.

"The biggest problem is that we stopped talking. We severed ties to one another and where we've cut, we've left awful scars." The Counselor shakes his head. "We're losing ourselves to bitterness and hate."

He lowers his hands and pauses for reflection. The assembly is silent.

"This man," the Counselor says, gesturing at Ortega, "is here to listen. Not to judge. Not to punish. He wants to hear you and understand. Because I've sat with him just as I've sat with all of you. I know him, like I know you. And I can tell you without any hesitation that he cares deeply about everyone in this crew. He has words he'd like to share, if you'll let him. I think it sounds better coming from him than second hand through me or someone else. So tell me, please: will you listen?"

A sullen quiet is his only response.

"Please, I need you all to tell me: Will you listen?"

Gradually, reluctantly, mutters of acquiescence circulate among the crowd.

The Counselor steps back and allows Ortega to retake the microphone.

"Uh, thank you, Counselor," he says, repositioning the microphone. It slips in his nervous hands, sending a jarring *thump* through the amplified speaker system. "Whoops, sorry about that."

Ortega clears his throat, having readied himself for a battle; and now, standing before an audience willingly giving its attention, he is unsure how to start. He closes his eyes and breathes until he is calm.

"I'm not going to tell you a long story. I'm not here to make you see things my way. I'm simply going to say this: I'm not proud of my performance as your Captain."

"You're not MY Captain!" shouts a voice from the back.

Ortega looks toward the voice, cheeks and ears flushing at the insubordination. He brings a fist up to his mouth, clears his throat again, and forces himself to let it pass.

"The whole point of leadership is to keep the crew together, as one," Ortega says. "To lead us where we need to go, sometimes willingly, sometimes unwillingly. It's not an easy thing to do."

Mutters and grumbles pass back and forth through the audience.

"When there was a vacuum, I rushed to fill it, because I believed we needed someone to be in charge, someone who could make the tough decisions, someone who could deal with the Cadre—"

Overlapping voices in the crowd hurl words like ballista shots, "We see how you're dealing with the Cadre!"

"...cozied right up to 'em..."

"...buncha head bashers!"

"No, no!" Ortega counters, trying hard not to react the way his instincts are pulling him. "The Cadre has always been our protector... I'm glad to have them watching over us, aren't you?"

"Filchers! Like sucker fish now..."

"...more like sharks..."

"...swallow us whole!"

"Look at 'em, trying to intimidate us...aching to take over!"

"Please!" Ortega says, voice straining. "I know you have concerns, and I *will* listen. First, I need you to hear what I have to say. Hmm?"

Boos and obscene gestures answer him.

With an exasperated sigh, Ortega continues, "These soldiers protect us from the enemy. Do you want them to leave?"

"HELL, YES! Get 'em outta here..."

"...we don't need police..."

"...or a police STATE!"

"Get them out!" a voice in the back calls out in deliberate syllables. Others pick up the chant in quick succession, clapping hands and stamping feet until the platform shakes. "Get them out! Get them out! GET THEM OUT!"

"All right, all right! *Enough!*" Ortega shouts, eyes wide. He gazes, dumbfounded, at people he simply cannot fathom. The Spaniard steps away from the microphone to the front railing, holding his hands up and waving them in a desperate attempt to disrupt the chant before it grows too strong. Gregor and the Counselor mimic Ortega's gestures as a show of unity and, with their assistance, the chant rolls off.

The Spaniard steps back to the microphone and says, "Maddock, we need you and your Operators to step outside."

All eyes turn as one to the Gun standing watch by the entrance. Maddock's head swivels side to side warily. He speaks into his helmet microphone while the crowd shouts at him.

"Leave us be!"

"...don't need big brother watching us..."

"...this ain't your home!"

"...Cap'n said, *piss off!*"

"...get the FUCK out!"

Shouts devolve to hoots and vicious jeers, all of them directed at the few Operators standing guard. The soldiers hold their ground without alarm. Finally, Maddock's head bobs, and he thrusts a hand up into the air. His lips move in inaudible speech and with a hand gesture, he orders his Operators out of the meeting hall. Wild cheers and whistles follow them out, and when the doors close behind them applause fills the hall.

Ortega looks out at a sea of faces that have vacillated from primal anger to exultation in the span of mere minutes.

Who ARE these people? I don't recognize any of them. So quick to judge...ruled by impulse and shortsightedness... How did Keller do it?

He lets the cheering go on, hoping it will eventually burn itself out and leave the crowd less energetic. It continues longer than he believed it could.

Do they think they won something? Alienating the ones who defend us...and they cheer in victory? I try to save them from their idiotic choices... and they HATE me for it!

At last, the cheering fades. Ortega opens his mouth to speak again when singing breaks out in the back left corner of the hall. The song catches on, more and more colonists joining into one voice.

They've gone insane. No reason left at all. Like lemmings, they'll run to their deaths. And they'll take the Europa *with them. They'll take ALL of us with them!*

Ortega switches off the microphone and bows his head, disillusioned so badly his heart aches. He props himself against the cold metal railing. His eyes water.

Again, there is a tug at his sleeve.

"What is it?" he growls.

The Counselor leans close to his ear and says, "They're singing."

"Yes, yes! I can see them, the *fools!*"

"No, they're singing *together.* Everyone. Look!"

Ortega brushes the dampness from his eyes and looks out. At first he misses it, and then he sees: those who once stood akimbo against an angry mob are now swaying with them. Arms that were once locked together as barriers are now thrown over shoulders, hugging necks. Hands once clenched as fists are patting neighbors. And everyone's head is back, mouths wide in song.

Dios mío...he's right... They stand together... This ONE thing I did, sending the Cadre away, was enough to unite them?

He turns to Gregor and finds the Russian with hand over heart, singing along. As he watches the crowd, realization bursts into his mind like sunlight through parting clouds.

The Cadre still scares them, but I let the soldiers in. I let them in to protect and watch over everything we do. To keep us safe. But it was too soon. They aren't ready...

When Ortega looks back at the Counselor, he finds him singing, as well. The Counselor dips his head and moves his hand in front of himself like he is turning a crank, urging the captain to join in.

The heaviness drops from Ortega's chest, and he chuckles to himself.

Sending the soldiers away... That's all I had to do to win them back? I'M the fool...

He shakes his head in disbelief, pushes himself off the railing; and, feeling the song in his chest, he allows himself to join in.

"...All this time, so many days,
stumbling blind along the way,
to find a home that we could share.
When I'm with you, we're already there.

Then duty called me, 'Commodore,'
and parting pain we humbly bore.
Bedecked in bars and uniform,
a long, cold ride to distant shore.

But now, at last, I'm at your door,

home again from bitter war.
We swiftly healed what grief had torn,
our love restored with each new morn'.

...our love restored with each new morn'!"

When the song ends Ortega lifts his head and finds the colonists are all looking at him, waiting. He switches his mic back on.

"I needed that," Ortega confesses.

Heads bob, and murmurs of agreement ripple through the assembly.

Ortega looks out over his crew. "Whoever started our song, you can be our new music director, hmm?"

"*You betcher ass!*" a lone voice shouts from the corner.

Laughs filter through the crowd.

Ortega takes the microphone from the stand carefully. He moves to the railing and props himself against it with his free hand.

"When we all joined up, we signed the same contract: for the duration of the mission, we would submit to command authority. But who among us could have imagined that this mission would last forever? We all believed our journey would end, yes? We'd build the Colony of New Vancouver, and once our contracts were up we could do as we liked. Not one of us believed that we'd be stuck here, on this ship, for the rest of our lives."

Ortega pauses, thinking about the last twelve months of his command and how swift was the descent into bickering and defiance.

"I can't remember what it was like to not be living in fear," Ortega explains. "Fear of the enemy. Fear of never finding a home, fear of wandering the stars until the *Europa* finally gives out. Fear of our people dying out, completely. No security, no resting place. Worst of all, no meaning...

"It was better for me, I think, because I could make decisions. I could influence what we did, where we went. I had some control over my life. That was a freedom I enjoyed, and it seemed natural that we simply continue that way, since it had always worked for us. So why not stick with what works, I thought?"

The crowd's hard earned attention sours quickly. Sneers and sideways glances abound.

"I'm not saying that was correct," Ortega recovers. "The point is, I see that it was wrong and we're going to make changes."

Voices rise with their own suggestions, overlapping. As each voice stacks in greater volume, individuals shout to be heard above their neighbors.

Again, Ortega has to wave his arms and wait for the clamor to die down.

"Yes, we all have ideas on that! And we're going to hear them in orderly fashion. But do you see what happens when we have no structure? No authority? When we all yell we can't hear one another."

The crowd settles, except for one voice that carries in the sudden hush.

"Arrogant bastard! You want to keep yourself in charge!"

Ortega grits his teeth in recognition. *So THERE you are, Herzfeld.*

"You think this is easy?" the Spaniard calls out. "You think it's comfortable? You have no idea how hard this is!"

"That's right, and we never will so long as you keep your claws on the big chair!"

The insult of this man! Ortega thinks. *How he dares to speak of things as if he knew ANYTHING about them!*

"I wondered when we would hear from you, Herzfeld. So glad you came out of your hole so you could—"

A gentle hand on Ortega's arm distracts him. When he turns to see, he finds the Counselor's wary eyes cautioning against saying more. He is tempted to brush the Counselor off until he looks back at the crowd of faces. When he sees nearly everyone in his sight regarding him with narrowed, suspicious eyes, the Spaniard clears his head.

Herzfeld is trying to provoke me. He wants to draw me into a trap. I will be more clever, by far.

"The greater the authority, the greater the burden of service, Mr. Herzfeld. To be Captain of the *Europa* is a heavy burden, indeed. If there is a better person, I am happy to relinquish command."

"Then do it! Right now!"

"To *whom*, Mr. Herzfeld? To you? I think you would find it beyond your abilities."

"You hear that?" Herzfeld asks the crowd around him. "You see how he holds on? How he belittles anyone for suggesting there could be someone better?"

Voices chime in around Herzfeld, in agitated agreement.

"I DO NOT WANT TO BE CAPTAIN!" Ortega thunders. The crowd goes silent at the sudden conviction in his voice, and the last word bounces off the hall's symmetrical walls in fading echoes.

"It is a burden I struggle to bear, but I will...so long as I *must*. Now I ask you again, Mr. Herzfeld, to whom shall I give command? Who can we all trust, without question, RIGHT NOW? Who is qualified to oversee the *Europa's* systems? To make the decisions where resources are allocated? To provide as normal a life as possible every day? Hmm?"

"There could be dozens!" Herzfeld shouts back. "But as long as they're all under your thumb, they'll never get the chance!"

Ortega drops his gaze to the floor, muting himself until he can reply without anger. He turns to look at Gregor. The Russian nods his head then flicks it toward the crowd, urging his captain to keep going.

Ortega raises his head and meets eyes with Herzfeld. "If this crew comes together and decides, by election, caucus, or review that there is a better Captain, I will relinquish my post that instant. Until that time, I CANNOT ABANDON MY POST. I cannot simply wave aside my responsibilities, and I cannot ignore the safety of this crew! It would be so much easier to be like you, Mr. Herzfeld, being the voice of dissent, casually stirring up revolts that tear us apart from the inside. But that is not who I am. I cannot simply step aside without knowing for certain that this crew will be provided for, that this crew will be protected. We are the last few who still breathe, and that thought haunts me EVERY SINGLE DAY. As much as I dislike you, Herzfeld, I would GIVE MY LIFE TO SAVE YOU AND EVERYONE ELSE IN THIS CREW. DO YOU UNDERSTAND WHAT THAT MEANS?"

People stand gaping, stunned by Ortega's sudden fire, surprised to find a man who was always so aloof aroused to a passion. Interested in the change, they see him anew through lenses of uncertainty and guarded optimism.

Ortega stands straight and brings a hand to his forehead.

"I'm sorry for that. I did not want to lose my temper. Keller made it seem so easy, but it's—"

The crowd breaks wild at Keller's name, yelling, clamoring, surging in fury. Ortega looks out in shock, seeing his blunder reflected in hundreds of reddened faces.

Every time I calm the flames, the slightest spark sets them alight! Are they made of Benzine?

"Yes! Yes, I see your anger! I feel it, too! But I did not speak his name to upset you!"

A voice shouts in rage, "What have you done with Keller?"

The crowd animates again, voices echoing the question like an indictment. Ortega raises his arms and dips his head until he can be heard.

"You may believe me or not. I do not know where he is."

"Bull-SHIT!"

"LIAR!"

A wrench hurtles up from the crowd at Ortega and barely misses his head, whizzing as it flies by.

"HEY!" Gregor bellows, stepping in front of Ortega, leaning against the rail, and pointing a finger in the direction it came from. "You want to fuck around, YOU TRY IT WITH ME!"

Ortega places a hand on Gregor's shoulder, and pats it until his first officer stands aside. He frowns at an undulating press of angry faces around the platform then draws a deep breath.

"You think I DON'T want him to pay?" he bellows. "You think I don't dream of seeing him put to death for his crime? I found myself in my cabin praying for this! And then, I was ashamed. To ask God for vengeance...I knew was a sin! When we find Keller, there WILL be justice I SWEAR to you. But it will be done according to the rules we have set down so it will be *clean*." Ortega pauses, letting his words sink in. "We must not dirty ourselves and soil what is righteous. It must be done *right*, so we can come through this agony renewed in spirit, still able to trust one another. Yes, *so we may still trust one another...*"

Ortega stares out across the crowd daring anyone to argue before continuing.

"Vigilantes always believe they are righteous. But justice carried out in the shadows is *evil*. None of us must live with the possibility that someday, we could be ambushed and murdered because a handful of people believe we deserve it. Justice belongs to us ALL. We must not be robbed of it by a few who cannot wait...by those who would act so quickly, so impatiently. Because in such haste, THEY COULD BE *WRONG*."

The Spaniard steals a glance at Gregor. The Russian's head dips, a modest show of contrition for his own attempt on Keller's life.

"None of us will live in fear of this," Ortega says with conviction, "because we deserve better."

"THEN WHERE *IS* HE?" a voice in the crowd roars.

Ortega looks down and clasps his hands before answering. "I cannot say exactly, only that he left with the others for Cadre Two."

"Why didn't you tell us?"

"...holding out on us?"

Ortega shows his palms. "That's a fair question. I didn't know how you would take it. If you would think I let him get away, if you would think I was helping him somehow... That you would see me as the reason he escaped and hate me more for it. Possibly kill me." He points to his black eye. "I had reason to believe that could happen. I allowed this to cloud my judgment." The captain looks down at his feet.

Fear. It has been our demon for as long as I can remember. We will always feel small and out of control if we cannot see past it.

Ortega looks to his left, and says, "The Counselor has given me good advice." He turns to his right. "So has Lieutenant Petrova. I'm lucky to have them." He looks out at the crowd. "But I need more than just their counsel. I need *yours* as well. This must never again be a place where fear rules our decisions. This must never be a place where we do things out of intimidation. We must speak our minds to one another without fear of incarceration, or punishments. We must be allowed our ideas and opinions. But first I want you all to ask yourselves, how can we have the things we want and still ensure that we are doing what we must to survive? How can we have both meaningful lives and security? Don't answer now, just think about it. We'll meet again in two weeks to discuss your ideas."

Ortega scans the murmuring crowd for one man in particular. When he spots him, their eyes lock.

"Until then I have something to ask you, Herzfeld. And it's good that everyone can hear and see us at the same time. Tell me, do you deny inciting sabotage aboard the *Europa*?"

Herzfeld glares. His arms cross.

"Detonating the power relay could have ruptured the hull, possibly led to cascade of depressurized compartments. On a ship this old, there's no way of knowing for sure all the safety measures would activate. It might have killed us all.

"I placed you into stasis, because I didn't know what else to do with you," Ortega says. "I acted as I thought a captain should, to protect the ship and her crew. I see my mistake, however. I carried out your sentence with no trial, no consultation, allowed no defense. I denied this crew their chance to weigh you and your actions. The Counselor helped me see that by imposing an immediate sentence you all had reason to fear me. If I could stuff one man into cryo, I might stuff anyone into cryo. To mute opposition. To consolidate power. Of course, I would never do these things, yet my actions had spoken louder than my words. That was a *grave* mistake on my part.

"I have no interest in punishing you further, Herzfeld. I have to face the mistakes I've made. I have to accept that things must change and that we will do things differently than we used to. It's wrong of me to expect that I should be your captain simply because the chain of command falls to me. That's not a system we agreed to live under forever. The harder I held on to the old ways, the more I divided this crew. For that, I am truly sorry.

"What I will *not* apologize for is acting to save our ship and to save lives. I see the way I acted was wrong, but to not act would have been far worse. I can accept your anger at me, so long as you are alive to be angry with me. That's part of taking the Big Chair. But whoever leads this crew, they cannot tolerate acts that threaten our survival."

The Spaniard takes a breath, and he presses onward.

"While I'm on the subject, I will step into a purely administrative role until we, as one crew...one family...can decide who is best among us to lead. We can decide for ourselves who should hold authority. We don't even have to have a 'Captain.' We can call it President, or Prime Minister, or whatever else you like. We can *do* as we like, so long as we can agree on it as a unified crew. We can bring positive change when we come together and discuss our thoughts openly, when we feel free to speak without reprisal. What do you say?"

Grunts of assent at first, then open words of agreement rise from the assembly. Heads nod soberly.

"I'm going to turn over the mic to your questions, but before I do, I have one last question for you: What should we do if the *Europa* is sabotaged again?"

Silence. Blank stares as far as Ortega can see.

"Should we let it go? Just allow it? I'm asking you. You tell me the answer. Should we let that happen?"

"*Hell*, No!"

"...no way!"

Ortega nods in satisfaction. "What happens to the person who sabotages the ship? I'm asking you. Tell me now."

"Hang the sum bitch!"

"...air lock 'im!"

"Whoa, whoa! Hold on!" Ortega says, raising his hands in a warding gesture. "I don't want you to start thinking like that. I'm relieved to hear that you care for this ship and you care for your crewmates. But we can't let ourselves think that way. Now this is not meant to give anyone a black eye. As you can see, I have plenty already." Ortega points at himself, hoping for a laugh, but an anemic chuckle is all he gets. "I'm relieved that we came to this point. I feel like we nearly lost something important...something crucial. I saw this crew fracturing. I did what I could to keep it together. What matters now is that we get through, remain together, and recognize that everyone— including you, Herzfeld—has a valid point to contribute. Can we hold on to that? I'm asking you now. Tell me your answer."

"DAMN RIGHT!"

"YEAH, WE CAN!"

"...YOU BET!"

"Okay. Good. Please form an orderly line for the microphones and you will be heard."

Ortega looks at Gregor and points at the second microphone still in its stand.

Gregor takes the microphone from the stand and walks down the short steps into the crowd. Dozens of hands fly up around him as people beg for his attention. The Russian raises both arms over head and brings them down like slowly falling trees, indicating where he wants the line to form. Colonists jostle their way in and queue up as directed.

"When is Keller coming back?" the first woman in line asks. "And what happens when he does?"

"I don't know the answer to that first part," Ortega admits. "They've been gone for a year and a half now. Could be tomorrow, could be never. But when they do, we will insist that Keller be remanded to us for trial. And he *will* get a fair trial, I assure you. Next, please."

"What's with the Cadre patrols?" asks a gray-haired man in a faded blue jumpsuit. "Why are they watchdogging us?"

"We struggle sometimes in ways they can't understand, so when it looks like we might hurt one another, or when the *Europa* is damaged, they want to be close by where they can assist. I can see what it might look like to many of you, but they were only here to protect us."

"Is O'Kai going to take over?" asks an older, yet still rugged man in a sleeveless orange jumpsuit. "Will he try?"

Ortega wrestles with the question before answering, as it is one he has silently wondered, himself. "O'Kai has given his word not to interfere, but you have to remember: the Cadre will act to preserve all human lives. Gun Maddock told me on the way in, if anyone is threatened, they will intervene. If they do intervene, it will only be to separate those who are fighting and restore order. Like a parent separating two children fighting."

"What, are we friggin' *kids* to them?" the man asks in irritation.

"It's a bad analogy. Don't read into it. Next, please."

"Any word from Cadre Two?" a slender woman in faded green jumpsuit asks. "From Sharon?"

"No, unfortunately. The moment we hear something, we'll announce immediately. You have my word on that. Next?"

"How do we choose a new captain? What process? Do we need a constitution, or...?" The man at the mic shrugs with palms up, and looks around at his crewmates.

"Those are big questions and I don't have an answer," Ortega replies. "I ask that we come together again like this in two weeks so we can figure it out. Until then, I'd like all of us to think hard and bring ideas to that meeting for discussion. Next?"

"The Cadre has been doing combat maneuvers for over a year now, with no collection rotations," says a man in a heavily-mended brown coat. "Are they planning something? Or are they just gonna leech off us forever?"

The crowd animates, cheering the question and echoing it with shouts. Ortega nods in acceptance and holds his hands up until he can be heard. "For the time being, we have enough that we can spare for them. Personally, I'd rather have them here, in force, to defend us than out on rotation. And remember: as long as they're here, they aren't stirring things up out there. Makes it less likely the enemy could follow them home. That said, O'Kai and Chusan tell me that in the event of shortfall, they will resume collection rotations. In the meantime, they are conducting war games based on the data Argo, Thompson, and Beckert brought back from Earth. Testing against enemy tactics to see if there's a successful counter. This is a good thing, so they'll be better prepared if they have to face the enemy in a larger force. Next?"

A woman steps tentatively to the microphone, gathering the top of her faded red jumpsuit and holding it closed at her neck. "Are they still making...drones?"

Ortega slumps slightly. "Yes. They need everyone they incubate to serve in whatever capacity they can. I don't like it, either, but it's how they survive."

"Will Thompson become one?"

"*No*," Ortega answers, "definitely *not*. And let me be clear, that will *never* happen to anyone in this crew. We'd be better off on our own if that were the case." Ortega pauses, letting that message sink in before asking, "Next?"

"What about the embryos at Cadre One?" asks a woman wearing layered long-and short-sleeved gray shirts. "They said they needed our DNA to breed out defects, but did it work? Will we...will we have children again?"

The question draws follow up questions from the crowd like a magnet. People reach for the microphone, tugging it close enough to ask,

"Are they mutated?"

"What do they look like?"

"Will we recognize them?"

"Will they belong to us or to the Cadre?"

"How do we raise them? Can't be a shared parenting..."

"Will they all be Operators? I don't want them forced into that life."

"What if they can't be Operators? MedTechs, then?"

"Or drones? Good God, no! Not that!"

Gregor pushes into the crowd, gets a grip of the microphone and takes it away, raising his arm to queue up again. The crowd shouts at him, demanding the microphone back.

"Please!" Ortega shouts. "Please, one at a time! I'll have to get you better answers, but for now, I will tell you." He pauses again, waiting for the crowd to turn their attention toward the platform. "The first generation of embryos at Cadre One has gone in to incubation, and... We don't have any kind of legal basis for this, but... Strictly speaking, we donated our DNA to them—"

"HOLD ON, NOW!"

"He CAN'T be serious!"

"Whoa, easy!" Ortega soothes. "We worked this out loooong ago when we first got here. We are going to provide input how they are raised, what kind of skills they will learn, what kind of lives they lead...balanced by the Cadre's most basic needs.

"As for mutations," he continues, "Colonel Munro tells me it's the most perfect class he's ever decanted. Sixty-eight percent Operator quality, he said. So be prepared: if any of you plan to babysit, you'll need to sew up some *really* big diapers."

Laughs go around the crowd along with sighs of relief. A line reforms where Gregor indicated and the first woman in line takes the microphone gingerly.

"What about the Lizard down at Cadre One? Are you talking to it, Counselor?"

Leaning over to Ortega's microphone, the Counselor answers, "Yes. Or, at least I'm trying to. We're figuring out how. Language is quite different."

"Has it told us anything? What has it said?"

"Very little, aside from her name, and what she does," the Counselor replies.

The woman turns to her friends nearby, asking, "Why are we even keeping it?"

Many muttered comments pass back and forth. Derisive words are spit through frowning lips.

"Anything we learn about this creature will be useful," Ortega states, "which is why I've asked the Counselor to keep trying. Thank you for these questions. I know there's a lot on your minds, and getting answers helps take the load off. Any additional questions, get them to the Counselor. I'll get you answers as soon as I can. Now, then, there's one last thing we have to talk about, and it's the *Europa's* maintenance. There's a long backlog of needed service. We can assign teams, but would anyone like to volunteer?"

Dozens of arms rise with willing shouts. Those who did not immediately volunteer look around at their comrades and lift their arms. Herzfeld keeps his arms crossed.

Ortega exhales in relief and flexes his free hand, feeling the layer of anxious sweat in his palms evaporate. "That's what I hoped." He smiles. "I don't know about you, but I could use a drink. Anyone else?"

Even Gregor's eyes go wide at the shouts and cheers, whistling and applause.

Ortega parks his microphone in its stand and walks down the stairs into the crowd. Unafraid, without judgment, he extends his hand to everyone he can, shaking vigorously as if reuniting with long lost friends. The crowd gathers around Ortega and moves with him toward the exit.

Gregor folds in with the rest, letting himself be moved along with the flow, getting punched in the arm by mates and punching them back.

While the rest of the Colonists laugh and joke with each other on their way out of the hall, the Counselor watches from the platform. He leans down to the railing, propping himself, and smiles in silent pride.

THE RIGHT THING

Sahara sits at her workstation in the *Europa's* MedLab, gazing into a tablet propped up in front of her. On the tablet's screen is a magnification of bluish-pink cellular tissue, alike in color and densely packed in a honeycomb of irregular hexagons. The indigo-stained nucleus of each cell stands out prominently; the smaller bodies inside are barely perceptible fibers.

Beside the tablet is a black and steel device, about a meter tall, fashioned from tubes, knobs, and precision optics. One of its barrel-shaped tubes stares down at a glass slide that is backlit by a disc of brilliant, diffuse white light; and when Sahara drags her finger across the tablet screen, the slide shifts with a sigh of electric motors.

"For the most part, the tissue is consistent," she narrates into the tablet's recorder. "Unremarkable groupings of apparently homogenous cells." She spreads two fingers across the tablet surface and zooms in to a random cell. The grainy features resolve with remarkable clarity.

"Porous nucleonic membrane, of comparable structure to human cell... Genetic material likely inside. Analogous structures include free Ribosomes, possible Golgi Apparatus, and Endoplasmic Reticulii. Mitochondria notably absent, however."

She squints at the image, scanning over cyst-like bubbles within the cell itself.

"Unrecognized spherical structures in cytoplasm."

She spreads her fingers on the tablet again, and the black microscope sighs as it dials up the magnification. Her eyebrows lift in surprise when she finds the spherical bubble has a thin tail that undulates.

"Spherical structure possesses a flagellum. What are we looking at, here? Is this a foreign body? An infection? Or..."

Sahara pinches the screen surface again and again to zoom out, then she swipes across her sample to another random spot. As before, she zooms in on a cell and magnifies the spherical structures inside. Every cell she investigates has the same cyst-like structures, and each of them has a tiny undulating tail.

"Seems to be a universal structure in this sample. Wouldn't surprise me if it had its own genetic material."

The doctor widens her field of view, until she is looking at thousands of densely packed cells.

"All appear healthy," she notes, and then her head tilts. "Hello, what's this?"

She double taps on a region with a thin blue line through it then drags a finger across the tablet, following the blue line like a road to an intersection of more fibrous blue lines.

"What we're assuming is the subject's liver, or at least an *equivalent* of a liver," she narrates into the tablet's recorder, "bears minor scarring. What one would expect in a human subject with rich, fatty food or daily alcohol intake. Maybe residual damage from 'College Days?'" she says with a wry smile. "Otherwise, the organ appears to be in good health..."

Sahara swipes the screen repeatedly and the slide tracks smoothly to a new area. The farther she goes, the more the fibrous blue lines converge until she reaches a circular spot with lines radiating out from it.

"Wait a tick..."

She centers the anomaly and zooms in until the spot fills most of her screen.

"Intersecting fascicles of atypical cells... No, no, this is more recent. Indications of fibrosis?"

"Doctor Taggart?" Jules calls from the front room.

"Yes?" she answers, still gazing into her screen.

"There's a call from Cadre One, a Specialist Obet. He's asking for you."

"I'll take it."

Sahara taps a button on her tablet. "Transcribe and save," she says to it. The device confirms file was successfully transcribed to text and saved. Sahara taps another button and a window opens in the display screen. Obet's face fills it.

"Top o' the morning, Obet. What's up?"

Obet lifts his head to look at the ceiling. He frowns, his eyes narrow, and he tilts his head. "Alloyed metal plating. Ventilation grilles. And illumination panels. I don't understand why that is important."

Sahara rests an elbow on her work surface and props her head on her hand, donning her most patronizing smile. "I was saying, 'Hello,' and, 'What do you want?'"

"Ah. Colonel Munro is interested to know what you've discovered from the biopsy samples."

"Not a whole lot, yet. Just getting started, really. Different physiology. Going to take a while to study."

"That's unfortunate."

"Why, is there something I'm supposed to find?"

"Well, the captive refuses to rise from its bunk."

She snorts. "Having a bad day, huh?"

"It no longer responds to stimuli."

Sahara sits upright, mouth straight. "Did it fall down, or something?"

"No, the subject was showing increasingly erratic behavior and then it became less active each day. Today it shows no sign of awareness."

"I'm coming down. Tell Munro I need clearance and transport."

"That won't be necess—"

Sahara switches off before Obet can finish. "Jules?" she calls through the half-drawn curtain. "Are you at a place you can stop?"

"Yes," he calls back.

"Can you get my bag and make sure it's complete? I'm making a house call to Cadre One."

"Sure thing," he says.

Sahara rises from her chair and snatches her white coat from the back of it. She zips one arm through a sleeve, then the other, and buttons it in front.

"Take over for me here. There's a sequence of slides already prepped, arranged anatomically. Depending what I find down there, I may need you to pull a few and have a look for me."

Jules hurries in, carrying a hard red case with a white cross on both sides. He holds it by its shoulder straps.

"Here you go," he offers.

Sahara slides into it and cinches the straps tight, stooping to compensate for the weight.

"After I've left, can you tell Javier where I'm going?" she asks.

"After?"

"Yes, after. He'll say, 'no,' if I ask."

"You sure you oughtta be going, then?"

"Yeah," she says, "I don't think you got to see this thing when it came in. It's *delicate*. And these Cadre lads have all the tenderness of a tax audit."

"I don't even know why we're keeping it alive," Jules says as he steps to Sahara's workstation. He looks over a selection of slides and picks one up. Holding it up to the light, he peers through it and adds, "Not like they'd bother to keep us breathing."

The comment gives Sahara a chill. "I'm going anyway. Might learn something from it. One way or other." The doctor slips her thumbs under the shoulder straps and readjusts. "Right. I'm off. You've got MedLab while I'm gone. Rouse your mate and bring him 'round for coverage 'til I get back."

"You got it." Jules sits down into Sahara's chair and he swivels toward the workstation. Still holding the slide he picked, he exchanges it for the one in the microscope and activates the tablet display.

On the way out, Sahara snatches a comm device and parks it on her ear. The MedLab doors slide aside as she trots toward them.

"Call Munro," she says, and the small comm device tones gently until it connects.

"*This is Munro,*" answers a deep basso voice, "*go ahead.*"

"Colonel, this is Sahara. I'm headed to air lock on *Europa's* starboard side, B-Deck, forward. Respond."

"*Understood. Routing shuttle for pickup. Europa B-Deck, starboard, forward. ETA, thirty seconds.*"

That was quick, she thinks, and the doctor breaks into a fast jog to make the rendezvous. "Can you brief me on the way? Obet said subject was unresponsive..."

"*Correct, unresponsive to verbal or physical stimuli.*"

"Define 'physical stimuli,'" she says anxiously.

"*Flat hand to face and electric shock.*"

Good Lord, they'll kill it before I get there! "Please, no more of that, then, all right?" she asks. "Were there any indications before collapse?"

Sahara reaches the air lock to find the Cadre shuttle already waiting. At the controls a Geek sits patiently, his goggles streaming occasional lines of code. She runs through the open air lock, belts herself on the bench seat, and listens as Munro gives her the full account.

"*Subject showed decreased appetite and chronic fatigue, which we at first assumed was due to inactivity. But then the subject had difficulty moving about its cell. It became increasingly hostile whenever we entered its cabin, until it was too weak to resist.*"

Sahara shakes her head and looks out of the transport's porthole. *Cabin, eh? Like it's on some kind of cruise...*

The Geek turns front in his seat, seals the air lock behind them and detaches the shuttle from its docking clamps. There is the briefest moment of weightlessness before the pilot thrusts into a graceful corkscrew toward the crater-nested facility below.

"How long has this been going on?" Sahara demands.

"*Seventeen days, sixteen hours, since initial onset of symptoms*," Munro replies.

"More than a fortnight! Why wait so long to start treatment?"

"*We needed to rule out possibility of contagion.*"

Sahara scowls at the patient neglect when a more troubling thought occurs to her. *Counselor was in sessions with the thing... Why wouldn't he have told me it was sick? He's never held anything like that back before...*

"Munro, can you explain why the Counselor wouldn't have told me about this?"

"*The subject is a Cadre Asset. The Counselor's access was secured by his assurance of secrecy.*"

Sahara tilts her head. "I have a hard time believing the Counselor would stand by in silence on this! Besides, everyone knows your boys dragged that thing back from Earth. Hardly a secret!"

"*The Counselor did not stand by in silence. He petitioned General O'Kai to involve you with irritating persistence. He has never insisted so forcefully on any previous matter.*"

"Glad you unclogged your ears, finally! So let's cut to it, Colonel: how can I help?"

"*We've reached the limit of our understanding. We'd value your insights.*"

"Here's an insight for you: stop *abusing* the thing maybe it won't die on you!"

"*None of the tests were life-threatening.*"

"Oh, aye, clearly." Sahara leans forward on her bench seat, easing the weight of the MedKit straps on her shoulders. "Better pray it isn't too late. *Damn it*, Munro, you *know* I'll help you no matter what! Make me sign O'Kai's secrecy oath if you have to."

"*That won't be necessary.*"

The Geek pilot swings the craft through Cadre One's open bay door and backs into a custom-fit port. Dual clamps reach out for the shuttle, grab it, and draw it into the port where it locks in with a series of clanks. When she undoes her belt and stands, it occurs to her that she has just crossed through the weightlessness of open space, yet the pilot's maneuvers kept her planted in her seat. Moreover, the transition to the artificial gravity enhancement at Cadre One was completely seamless. She glances at the back of the Geek's head, recalling the gentle turns of the trip, aware of the skill and finesse required to maintain such an even sensation of gravity.

"Smooth flying, there, Geek, uh...What's your name?"

"Geek Kibwe," the pilot replies, swiveling about.

"In the Ambulance Service, our MedEvac drops were downright brutal. I could have brought my tea on this one and not lost a drop."

"You were a MedTech?"

Sahara thinks about it. "Of a sort, yeah, but not nearly as skilled as your lot. I was just starting out. Knew a bit about patching holes, not much else."

Kibwe nods then swings back toward his controls. "Many Colonists are sensitive to micro-G, so we make transports as comfortable as possible."

Sahara smiles. "Much appreciated."

When the shuttle door and air lock open, Obet is there to greet her. Despite the curve of his spine, he stands as straight as he can, shoulders nearly level. With his good hand, he gestures her inside.

"Right this way, Doctor."

Sahara follows, pleased that he is trying hard to make a good impression. Even so, she cannot help recalling the last time she saw him: how rude he was to Argo when the wounded Brick emerged from his healing tank, how Obet offered condescension to a man who had just been through the most grueling ordeal she could imagine. It got under her skin, and she sent the young MedTech out of her sight with the threat of a poor competency report. The irony, however, was that Argo did not seem to care a bit.

Maybe it wasn't even meant as an insult, she thinks. *Maybe that's just how they talk to one another.*

As they walk, she glances casually at Obet, noting his height, in particular.

You'd have been a Gun, I bet...if they could have straightened you out.

After a few steps, Sahara notices Obet's arms are not swinging. Rather, they extend stiffly down to each side. On his face is a look of concentration, tiny dimples in his chin, lips held together firmly.

"Obet," she says, "be at ease. You don't have to make appearances for me."

The MedTech looks down at her quickly, eyebrows raised slightly. "I am ashamed of my previous performance. I...I want you to be pleased with my service, Doctor. This time, I will perform without error. Y-you can rely on me."

Obet looks straight ahead, keeping his shoulders as level as he can, rigidly maintaining a posture his body does not naturally take.

Sahara looks again at the tall MedTech, suddenly self-conscious. *He's like a whipped puppy... What did I say to him?*

"Obet, it's all right. It wasn't that bad."

"I think you're trying to be, what is it you say...'kind?' But there can be no tolerance of poor performance. We have to be at our best, always." He lowers his eyes. "Being relieved of duty is a measure of last resort. It's a sign of incompetence or negligence so severe that the individual has to be removed from a project to ensure its success. What was worse is that I could not see how I had failed. So I requested demotion and re-education to restore my skill sets. Failing that, I would have requested reconstitution."

Sahara stops in her tracks, hand over her mouth. "Obet... That was over a year ago!"

He nods grimly. "I must try harder in all things. I must never fail again."

Sahara stands dumbfounded at the staggering scale of Obet's overreaction, yet feelings of guilt give her an uneasy twinge. She looks inward, searching her memories of that day in MedLab, trying to recall context, words used, tone. While Sahara cannot recall exactly what Obet said that made her so angry, she remembers how righteous it felt to rip his name tag from his chest and say,

> *"Specialist Obet, what a shame you had to be transferred for incompetence and insubordination. Colonel Munro will be so disappointed."*

And to her infinite chagrin, she remembers flinging his name tag at the MedLab doors with the parting shot,

> *"Get ye gone, lad."*

Her eyes close. *Oh, no...I really did send him away. I really did relieve him of duty...*

When Obet sees that she has stopped walking, he turns, and with eyes wide in terror, he asks, "Have I disappointed you again?"

"Oh, GOD, no! I am SO sorry, Obet. I hadn't the *slightest* clue what I was saying to you!"

"Again, I think you are making light of a very serious—"

"Look," she interrupts, "I want you to listen to me. I never should have said what I did, and I certainly shouldn't have dismissed you that way. I had the notion you're all tough as nails and I'd never have believed some stupid-arsed words from me could do any damage."

Obet frowns in thought, and Sahara puts a hand on his arm. He flinches.

"We'll talk more about this, but for now I want you to relax, and be yourself, lad. No pretense, okay? Can you do that?"

Obet blinks at her then looks down into his hands, comparing his good hand to the one with arthritically locked joints. With a mild sigh, he lets his shoulders tilt to their regular angle, right arm drooping from the lowered shoulder, left arm hanging across his body from the elevated shoulder. The look of intense concentration departs, leaving his face and chin without dimple or stress lines.

"*Much* better," Sahara says. "Now let's go see our patient, aye?"

Obet nods and the two stride through Cadre One's polished metal corridors.

Typically, Sahara's visits lead to a single place: Cadre MedLab. But at the first intersection, where she usually heads straight, Obet points toward the right corridor and leads her in that direction. Soon, she finds herself in an unexplored part of Cadre One, filled with distant rumbles and mechanical rhythms telegraphed through the solid floor plates. Occasionally, a high-pitched shriek pierces the sounds of heavy industry, making her wonder why anyone would keep a captive in such a disagreeable place.

"Umm, where are we going?" she asks, voice raised above the din.

"To C-Lift. It's the only one that goes all the way down to Sub-Level Four."

"Four? I thought there were only three Sub-Levels."

"Four is unfinished. Easy to contain the captive there. And nothing it could damage if it got out of its cabin." The tall MedTech ushers Sahara with his good hand to a bank of sliding doors embedded in the curved outer wall. "Here's the lift." He hurries ahead with his lop-sided gait to call the elevator. While they wait, Sahara listens to the squeals, clanks, and bangs.

I'd go mental here, she thinks with an annoyed smirk. But the smirk straightens immediately. *Is that what they're doing? Are they trying to break it?*

The elevator dings on arrival and the heavy door slides aside.

"This way, Doctor," Obet says, and they both step into the spacious lift. Once inside, Obet aims his finger at a holographic panel. The three-dimensional image challenges him with a pass code, presenting a choice of alphanumeric options. He punches in the correct sequence, and the panel shifts to green. When the door slides shut there is an initial jolt, and then a low hum is the only indication that the car is in motion.

The two stand, hands clasped in front, awkwardly silent.

"May I ask you a question?" Obet says.

"You just did," Sahara quips.

Obet squints, shakes his head, then says, "May I ask you a direct question?"

"Sure."

"How is it that all of you are so physically perfect?"

Sahara half-snorts, half-chokes. "We're far from perfect, Obet."

Obet juts his lip and restates with sincerity, "Not even our finest Operators are decanted without flaws. But every Colonist has a proper spine, legs and arms of equal length, dexterity of both hands, symmetry of hearing and vision... Every one of you could be Operator-trained. So why aren't you?"

"Because we're not soldiers, that's why."

"You could be."

Sahara runs a gauntlet of responses through her mind, but none seem remotely adequate. When Obet sees her stymied for reply, he looks down in embarrassment.

"I'm sorry, I was curious. Did not intend to make you uncomfortable."

"No, no, it's quite all right," Sahara says. "It's not a bad question, really. Something I hadn't thought about. And it's perfectly fine to ask. No harm done."

Obet nods, visibly fighting the urge to level his shoulders and stand straight.

"When we get done down here, I'm going to have a look at you," Sahara volunteers. "See if we can't do something about that curvature."

"You're welcome to look, but Colonel Munro, himself, has tried. The thoracic section of my spine, from T4 through T12, is rotated almost ninety degrees to the rest of the spinal column. Error in my genetic code, not just a physical deformation. They talked about surgeries, but trying to rotate the vertebrae would almost certainly leave me paralyzed from the waist down. They decided to leave it alone. Isn't that bad, really."

"Well, I'm still going to have a look."

The lift jolts to a halt, the holographic panel dings, and the wide door slides aside. At this depth, strident noise of industry above is dimmed to deep thumps that telegraph through the unfinished stone.

In the hallway opposite the open lift, a Gun on guard duty salutes crisply. Sahara is amazed to see the Gun's skin tone many shades darker than the typical light olive.

"Hmm," she says, "thought you all looked the same..." Both hands slap to her forehead. *What is WRONG with me today?*

"Never mind me," Sahara says through her hands. "Just took my crazy pill. It'll wear off soon."

Obet and the Gun tilt their heads in exactly the same manner. Sahara slides her thumbs under the straps of her medical case and readjusts it on her shoulders.

"Where's the subject? This case is getting heavy."

"This way," the Gun says with a husky female voice.

Sahara puckers her mouth and her eyes widen. *Would not have guessed that was a woman.* She drums her fingers against the shoulder straps and follows along.

The Gun leads them through dim, roughly cut stone corridors to a single plain door, like every other cabin door at Cadre One. Beside the door, however, is a complicated communication panel showing vital statistics of the occupant, camera feeds, thermostat, activity schedule, occurrences of feeding and waste removal. Evenly spaced cables run vertically up the wall from the panel to the ceiling then dive into conduits that run along the ceiling back toward the elevator shaft.

Sahara peeks around her two escorts for a look at the panel screen. In the video feed window she sees the back of a very large man leaning over a bunk in an undecorated cell. The only sign of the creature inside is the tip of a tail hanging over one end of the bunk.

"Colonel Munro is already inside," the Gun announces to Sahara. "He's expecting you. You may enter."

"Thank you, um... Your name is?"

"Branka."

"Branka, yes, thank you."

The Gun casts a suspicious glance at Sahara then enters a code sequence into the pad. The door slides aside, and Obet announces himself.

"Colonel Munro, Specialist Obet reporting with Doctor Taggart." He swings his good hand up to his brow.

Munro turns his great head to look over his shoulder. "Good, you're both here." He places the cap on a very long and thick needle, then returns it to his MedKit beneath the bunk. "Doctor Taggart, we've conferenced a few hundred times over comms, but I'm glad to finally meet you in person."

"Likewise," she replies politely. "You'd think we would have run into each other at some point."

"Our duties pull us in many directions, as you know too well." Munro takes a cloth from his belt with his left hand. It is not until Sahara sees him rubbing both hands with the cloth that she realizes how much smaller his left arm is than his right. On any other man, the smaller of his arms would seem muscular and well-built, but on Munro's massive frame it looks downright puny.

So that's why Gregor calls him, 'the Fiddler Crab'...

Munro extends his great hand in greeting, and when he clasps Sahara's hand it disappears half way to her elbow. She grits her teeth, nervous that her arm will be pulverized; but the Colonel's grip is measured with gentility, and the petite woman is relieved to get all of her bones back unbroken.

Such a light touch for such a huge man—like the concern for comfort Kibwe showed earlier—it's bizarrely at odds with their warrior ethos...

Munro tucks the cloth back into his tool belt and looks down at a gaunt, emaciated creature, lying on its side. Stained rags of a diaphanous gown cling in blotched patches. Withered limbs droop over the bunk's edge like bent saplings. Everywhere, its skin is chalky, cracked, and peeling. And in contrast to the rest of its thinned body, the creature's belly is badly distended.

A bag of transparent fluid hangs from a tiny cart at the head of the bunk. It drips into a small plastic chamber that feeds into the creature's armpit via a transparent tube.

Sahara purses her lips, taking in the state of her newest patient. "Fer Chrissake, Munro, are yeh feedin' the bloody thing?"

"Standard ration, every day. Caloric requirements are right on target."

"Takes more than just calories, you know."

"Its diet is fully supplemented, same as our Operators get. Best we can offer."

Sahara shakes her head, recalling a time in the distant past when physicians were not required to understand basic nutrition before practicing medicine—how many chronic illnesses were 'miraculously' cured once wholesome, nourishing food replaced pills in a doctor's prescription.

Damned ignorance is what this is, she curses as she kneels beside the bunk. *But everything they eat comes out of a machine. Not like they can reprogram the whole line just to feed this poor bugger. Probably really is the best they can offer.*

"What's good for your Operators clearly isn't working for this one, here," Sahara says, surveying her patient head to tail. "Let's get the basics out of the way." The doctor starts her examination by lifting the creature's arm. She turns over its hand, inspects the nail beds at the fingertips, notes how rough and brittle the claws are, how the nail beds have retreated. Her eyes trace the chalky peeling skin of its arm to the creature's face. Shallow breaths issue past cracked and bleeding lips.

Sahara lifts its barely parted eyelids. Dull yellow eyes stare at the opposite wall. Sahara snaps her fingers in front of them, but the creature remains oblivious.

"Catatonic?" she asks.

"Or stupor," Munro answers. "Withdrawal, possibly."

The petite doctor grips the creature's long, delicate jaw and she peels back the lips. Large white teeth, perfectly even except for the pointed canines, stand in pale green, receded gums. A stale, rank odor issues with every exhale.

Sahara removes her MedKit from her shoulders and opens the latches. "Where, uh, where do you take its pulse?"

"The vessels in the neck are too deep, so we use the armpit or inner thigh. You can also place your scope just off center of the breastplate, here," Munro says pointing to the creature's chest. "The aortic cluster is there. You'll know when you hear it. It's a beat of three."

Sahara pulls a shiny metal disk from her kit with two finger-sized loops on the back. She slides the loops over her index and middle finger, then taps a button on her earpiece. It switches modes and beeps twice to confirm connection with the disc.

Leaning in, she notices two darker areas of skin on the side of the torso. Not only is the skin cracked and peeling, it is blistered. She shakes her head in disgust.

Electrocution to rouse an ailing patient? Note to self: never get sick here...

She feels around with the disc, listening for a regular three-count rhythm. She finds it, thready and faint, like someone gently drumming their fingers on a tabletop: *Ba-Da-Dub, Ba-Da-Dub, Ba-Da-Dub.*

From the creature's chest, Sahara moves the disc around to the creature's back, listening for air moving through what she assumes are lungs. Even with such shallow breaths, she hears ticks and pops of fluid rattling inside.

From the creature's back, she moves to the distended belly. It bulges as if pregnant, wildly out of proportion with the rest of the creature's frail extremities. Inside, the gut gurgles with infrequent pops and pings.

81

Sahara points at the clear bag hanging at the head of the bunk and asks, "What's in your I.V.?"

"Standard isotonic hydration, with electrolytes," Obet answers. "Sodium, Potassium, Calcium and Chloride."

"All were present in the blood before administration?"

"Yes, and levels have been falling off recently. We're trying to reverse that."

Sahara frets. "I'd like to draw some blood, but weak as it is, I don't know that I should. And without a better understanding of this thing's physiology, any treatment I recommend could make it worse."

"Do you have a diagnosis?" Munro asks.

Sahara looks at him then returns her gaze to her patient. "Looks like advanced malnutrition and severe dehydration. Poor thing. I really wish you'd called me sooner." The slim woman turns from her patient to the walls of the cell, taking in the cold, bare stone walls, the minimal fixtures, the unending artificial light. The more she looks, the more she feels like a bug trapped in a child's jar, one where the kid has forgotten to punch holes in the lid.

"Have you checked this room for contaminants?" she asks.

Munro pulls his labset from his MedKit. He thumbs the controls then holds it low to the floor and reads the display. Next, he lifts it to the ceiling and reads the display again. He shakes his head.

"We're getting waste gasses and some metal particulates from manufacturing above. Probably coming down the elevator shaft in trace amounts."

"You think it could be poisoning the subject?" Obet asks.

"It's on the edge of detectable," Munro says, "I wouldn't think it could do harm, but who knows? Could be really toxic to them."

"Then we need to move it out of here," Sahara states.

Munro scowls, shaking his head. "It's easy enough to set up a scrubber on the ventilation system."

"Well, in my medical opinion, that isn't the only problem your patient is suffering from. Toxic compounds or not, it's horribly malnourished."

Hand on chin, Munro says, "No argument there. Could we use one of the food processors aboard the *Europa* to craft something edible?"

"We could, but anything we make would be a guess. I mean, who knows what these things eat? Could be filet mignon, could be cardboard. No idea."

Obet shifts his stance. "Colonel, may I make a suggestion?"

"Of course."

"Why not pull a processor from one of our collected ships?"

Munro and Sahara turn as one to look at Obet.

"They all came with at least one," the MedTech continues. "That old passenger liner had a lot more."

"That's a fine idea," Munro says, "but those've been retrofitted for human consumption. A restoration to original condition would take time and resources."

"Then you have to ask yourself," Sahara begins, "how much is your prisoner worth to you?"

Munro looks down at the ailing alien. "General O'Kai does not wish to expend additional resources maintaining this creature's life."

"And what about you, Colonel? Do you agree with that?"

Munro gives Sahara a warning glance.

Branka peeks in from the corridor. "Sir, what about this Blueskin's vessel, the one Team Forestall collected from Earth? My team was aboard last week, testing it as an assault platform. It hasn't been fitted for human support yet."

Munro lifts an eyebrow. "That's right... It's been hollowed out, but the interior components are still staged for retrofit." He nods to himself. "I'll pull the food processor and have it installed here."

Sahara folds her arms and looks at the cell's interior. "Not a lot of space here. Will it fit?"

"We won't install it inside. We'll put it in an adjacent room, and the guard can serve meals at intervals."

She sighs in exasperation then says bluntly, "Colonel, never mind the contaminants, this *cell* is toxic to life."

Munro and Obet look at one another, not comprehending.

"I'll tell you this," she continues, "you Cadre lads are brilliant at surgery and genetics. You can do things in the field with a portable kit that I'd need a full O.R. to match. I'm not just saying this, I truly admire your skills. But when it comes to how you treat your patients..."

Munro waits for Sahara to finish, and when she does not, he prods her, "You were saying?"

Her eyes flash with anger. "I'm saying that even if you gave me a machine that spat out chocolate truffles and black cherry ice cream, I'd *still* die in here."

Obet's face scrunches. "Chock-luht truff-fulls and—?"

"Why?" Munro says, ignoring the confused MedTech. "If we can meet all your basic needs, then—"

"This doesn't even come *close* to meeting basic needs!" Sahara volleys back. "Maybe for you, living in a hollowed out rock is natural. But not for me. And apparently not for it, either. This place is depressing and cold. Let me take it up to MedLab on the *Europa*."

"Out of the question."

"Why?"

"Risk of escape. Risk of sabotage. Risk of it sending communication to its kind."

Sahara eyes the creature slumped on the bunk. She snorts in mock amusement. "Oh, aye. A fearsome risk, this one. Gonna muscle right out of here, I can tell yeh!"

Munro frowns at her.

"Look, I get why you never brought these things home with you before," Sahara says. "But it's here now, and it's a chance to learn about them. It's a chance to communicate and understand something of what happened, why it all went to shite. If we let it die, then I say we're just plain too stupid to live."

Munro spreads his large and small arms. "I don't disagree with you on any particular point."

"Then let me take it to the *Europa*. Post guards if you have to. Keep a camera on it. Do whatever you need to satisfy O'Kai. But this patient needs a more livable environment than this dungeon. If you want it to survive, let me treat it as my patient, the way I treat everyone in my care: with dignity and respect. And some basic decency, for fook's sake."

As Sahara imagines herself trapped inside such a place a smothering desolation takes hold. Arms crossed, her mouth a tight line, she looks down at the ailing creature and shakes her head.

Nothing should have to live this way.

"I'd let you take it, but..." Munro scratches his head. "I can't think of a way to convince the General."

"Call it a medical emergency. Call it a medical necessity. Call it whatever you like. But this thing's only hope is to be out of here, out of this place. If it recovers, then we can discuss where it sleeps, but right now...I just hope we aren't too late."

Munro crosses his arms, as well, and stares down at his dying patient. "I've never heard you make a claim you couldn't substantiate."

"Then give me Obet as an assistant and let me try."

Obet's head rocks back and his eyes widen. "Me?"

"Obet?" Munro asks in equal surprise. "Are you sure you want him as an assistant?"

"Absolutely. I don't want anyone else." Sahara nods. "And I've been meaning to tell you, Munro, I was completely wrong to dismiss him before. It was a misunderstanding on my part."

"A *misunderstanding*?" Munro says, amazed. "Are you saying Obet *did not* impair the vital functions of your MedLab?"

"No, not as such."

"Then Obet was a threat to Argo's life?"

"My goodness, no!"

"And you *relieved him of duty*?"

Sahara sniffs self-consciously, flexes her jaw, and answers, "When someone is out of line, we sometimes send them away. It's not unusual. But like I said, it was a misunderstanding."

Munro grips his chin again, staring into a corner of the cell in deep thought. "And they say *our* methods are severe..." He turns to Obet suddenly and says, "Specialist, you've been requested to assist the Chief Medical Officer of the *Europa*. Will you serve her as you've served me?"

Eyes still wide in disbelief, Obet replies, "Without fail, Colonel."

To Sahara, Munro says, "I'll authorize twenty-four hour access to this room. You may come and go as often as needed to—"

"Colonel, that's just not going to cut it. It's *dying* here. If we don't get it to a healthier environment, we're going to lose it. That's my medical opinion, and I'll stake my reputation on it."

Munro grips his chin and peers down at the reptilian. "That's unnecessary. Your reputation has never been in doubt."

"Then think of all the things this creature knows," Sahara persists, "*who* it knows, *where* it's been, what it's seen.... O'Kai has *got* to be interested in that, at least, as a source of intelligence. Seems to me that would be a lot to lose. And I don't relish the thought of disappointing him."

Munro continues his stare.

"Munro, there's a reason you're the first MedTech ever to sit at the general's side in Council: you've proven your worth. He trusts you. If you committed to a decision, would he question it?"

"No," he says plainly.

Sahara moves beside him and matches his gaze down at the softly wheezing creature. "Then what's the hold up?"

"General O'Kai will not approve of this transfer," Munro admits. "He will be displeased."

"I know what you mean. Ortega's gonna be fuming I left without getting permission first."

"You didn't obtain clearance?" Munro asks, incredulous.

"Nope. He might have ordered me not to come, and I couldn't risk that. Some things are too important to be left to protocol."

"We..." Munro searches for words. "We cannot allow that kind of... *flexibility*...in interpreting a superior's intentions."

Sahara nods in understanding. "Even so, we must be free to act; we have to have latitude in our decisions, regardless how others view them. Now, I'd never tell Ortega how to run his ship. But medical matters are entirely my call, and I'll never apologize for making a call I know is right. If that 'displeases' him, well, I can live with that." She places a hand on the colonel's arm. "We can't let our patient slip away, Munro, not while there's more we can do. Please, help me save this life. Let me take it back to the *Europa*."

Munro drops his arms to his sides, closes his eyes, and sighs. "Obet?"

"Sir?"

"Prepare the subject for transport to *Europa* MedLab."

"Aye, sir!" Obet says with a salute. He steps out to the wall-mounted comm panel, and taps commands into it with his good hand.

"Doctor Taggart," Munro asks, "will you proceed ahead and ensure your facility is ready to receive?"

"My facility is always ready." She stoops and packs her MedKit before hoisting it onto her shoulders. "I'll tell Ortega and Jules to expect a food processor coming up from Cadre One." She looks at Munro. "You'll have someone to help us install it?"

The big colonel nods. "If I need to do it myself."

Sahara smiles in gratitude, moves toward the door then stops herself. She turns about, walks up to Munro, and takes his big hand.

"Thank you, Colonel."

"Please keep me informed," he says, "and anything you require, ask."

"Will do."

"Doctor Taggart?" Branka calls from the doorway. "This way, please."

Sahara looks the Gun up and down, slipping her thumbs under her shoulder straps. "Lead on," she says.

After only a few steps into the corridor, Sahara freezes in her tracks.

I just made the survival of this thing ENTIRELY my own responsibility.

Her ears slide back and her mouth forms a straight line across her face.

If it dies, it'll be all my fault...

But just as quickly, the heaviness dissipates.

It wouldn't have a chance, otherwise. I'm doing the right thing. That's what matters.

Head lifted, she catches up with her escort, rides transport back to the *Europa*, and strolls happily into her MedLab, where Ortega waits, seething.

WE HAVE NO FUTURE

Ortega stands on the raised platform in the *Europa's* improvised meeting hall. Nights of restless sleep, skipped meals, and dependence on low-grade stims have left him thin with dark rings under his eyes. The wireless headset he wears is warm from long hours of use, and he hunches with exhaustion against the platform's railing. Even with the ambitious agenda he has slogged through already, there are still dozens more crew members queued up at the microphones.

The drudgery of it all gathers in the muscles of his neck, shoulders, and back, manifesting in the most severe headache he has ever known. Time after time, he wants to rip the headset from his ear, hurl it into the crowd, and tell them to figure it all out on their own, because a man can only take so much pettiness from whining children. Usually, he can hide his disdain behind a practiced mask of stoicism. But today their insolent, entitled mewling has eroded the last of his patience, and he scowls bitterly.

"That's it! No more! This meeting is closed. I cannot listen to any more of your complaints. You have your assignments. Now *go*, and *do them*."

Curses and insults fly at him like rotten tomatoes from the assembly.

"What do you mean *that's it*?" says the woman at the microphone. "We've been waiting for two weeks! You can't shut the door on us like that! Where do you get off—?"

Even with the powerful speakers amplifying, the woman's voice drowns in a tide of shouts, boos, and hisses hurled at the *Europa's* captain.

Ortega pushes off the railing. "Since when do you think you deserve these things, eh? Your magical fairy godmothers coming to grant all your wishes? Maybe you hang a hammock in your rooms and make pretend you're on Caribbean holiday, huh? Maybe you think you relax and somebody brings you piña colada! I'm *disgusted* by this selfishness! All I hear are the shrieks of *spoiled children!*"

Confused, angry, and sullen eyes stare up at him from the floor. The crowd is stunned to silence, except for one.

"Ortega!" Herzfeld shouts, pushing his way forward until he reaches a microphone. "How *dare* you?"

"And there he is," Ortega announces with a sweep of his arm. "What day could be complete without my dose of poison ivy?"

"Poison ivy? What the hell are you talking about?"

"Every time you speak, Herzfeld, you *give me a rash.*"

Herzfeld's eyes widen, but his head bobs lightly before he speaks. "Ah. That's your guilty conscience fighting its way out."

"Save your insults! We are adjourned. We meet again in two weeks. I cannot wait to hear more of your complaining then."

"Hey! This isn't about me! YOU PROMISED *THEM.*" The hall echoes with Herzfeld's amplified syllables.

Ortega halts his retreat from the platform.

Maybe I should take O'Kai's suggestion. Maybe I SHOULD start adding inhibitors to the food processors...

In slow motion, he turns back toward the railing, looking his antagonist in the eye.

"There is only so much time in a day. You squander it with squabbling and I have no more patience to give. Blame yourselves that you do not get what you want."

"You think I'm just an instigator, don't you?" Herzfeld fires back. "You think I'm just trying to get in your way and make things harder? Well the fact is, I'm trying to get your attention 'cause you aren't listening anymore! You're not dealing with the real issue!"

"Ah, yes. This is the part where you astound everyone with your powers of persuasion, and then some part of the ship explodes. Do I have it right?"

Herzfeld looks at the floor, exasperated, yet restrains his indignation. When he looks up his eyes are glassy.

"I know you think you're having a hell of a time. That this crew can't be bothered to take care of their ship. And it's so *obvious* it has to be done that you can't believe you have to whip people into doing it. You're frustrated and irritated, and you clearly haven't been sleeping. So you can't see what's *right in front of your face.*"

Ortega's haughty demeanor cracks. Herzfeld's summary feels spot on, a direct hit onto what has made his job such a burden. His guard does not drop entirely, however.

"Tell me then, Mr. Herzfeld. What is it you think I cannot see?"

Herzfeld looks around at his fellows. They look back at him as carefully as Ortega does.

"You think this crew has forgotten that the *Europa* is our lifeboat. That this is it. All we have left. And you can't understand how she's fallen to such a state. You think the burden's all on you to keep it together, to smack us around if you have to, to make sure the ship endures, so that we all have a future."

"I'll admit, Mr. Herzfeld, your summary so far is a fair one."

Herzfeld bows his head, his face as solemn as a judge passing sentence. "Ortega, the condition of the *Europa* no longer matters because *we have no future*."

Ortega's eyes narrow, his mouth curls into a hateful frown. "That's what I expect from you. Keep tearing us apart, keep tearing us down."

"Will you shut up for *one second*, you old windbag? Because this is exactly what you're missing: you, me, and almost everyone else here...we're too old to have children. Maybe we thought there was more time. Maybe we were too scared to think about it in the last few years. But even the kids we had in flight, they're right on the edge of safe childbearing years. Think about that for a second."

Herzfeld clasps his hands in front of himself and watches Ortega. The Spaniard steps forward to the railing. He wants to shoot back with something devastating that will embarrass or humiliate this man at the microphone, anything that would shut his mouth for good. But the awful fact is that his words shine light on a path he has not seen. There is a glimmer in the distant recess of his mind that warns him about something he has missed, something that a captain should have foreseen but did not. Instead of speaking, Ortega lifts his chin and waves his hand in a rolling gesture, urging his antagonist to get on with it.

"Thank you," Herzfeld says. He turns to the crowd around him, holding the microphone close to his mouth and speaking calmly. "Some of you have come to me and asked, what will happen if we stay here? Well I don't need a crystal ball. The only children being raised are the ones decanted down at Cadre One. From their first day, they'll be indoctrinated, raised to march and fight and soldier and take orders. They won't be like us at all. They won't be a part of our lives. How much longer until we grow old and die out, with nothing left of us but the DNA we gave to Cadre One? How long until the Cadre consumes the last trace of us and they *own* the *Europa* completely? Twenty years? Thirty? There are no guarantees for the future because *Keller left us none.* He let everyone down, and Ortega hasn't got the answers, either. So why don't we take our children back from Cadre One and *go?* We don't want to get 'appropriated' into the Cadre system. Besides, we have the Lizard in our own MedLab, under Doctor Taggart's expert care. If we treat it right, that could be our way to reconcile with the enemy. If we learn what we can from it and give it a decent life, we *can* communicate with it, possibly convince its kind to leave us in peace. We have no weapons and, really, we don't need any! We're no threat! So how does it make any sense to hunt after us?" Herzfeld pauses, looking among faces that gaze at him attentively. "No matter how you look at it, staying with the Cadre means our death. Either a slow gradual death as we die out with no one to take after us, or a violent death when the Lizards finally track down their stolen ships. And they *will.* We all know it's just a matter of time. The *only* choice is to leave. And that is the plan I will enact if granted the authority to lead you."

Ortega's head falls back, his jaw drops, and he stares at the ceiling.

A campaign speech. I gave him an open microphone for a campaign speech against me. And I played right into it!

He takes the headset from his ear, shaking his head, ignoring the people shouting at him for his response. Even the ones who disagree with Herzfeld, the loyal ones, he can no longer hear.

I'm done with this. I no longer have the stomach for it.

Ortega bows his head.

Lord, I have done what I can. Please take pity on these, the last of your children. Protect them from themselves and may they find a true guardian. One who can shepherd them to salvation. In Jesus' name, I pray. Amen.

Ortega shuffles from the platform, down the short flight of stairs. His name is shouted all around him, voices ranging from desperate pleas to aggressive threats.

"Where are you going?"

"Captain! Don't leave us! *Hey!*"

"Are you *insane?*"

"Ah, let him leave!"

"He doesn't have a clue!"

"He's still the captain! Show some respect!"

"Shut your *fat fucking face!*"

"Come shut me up, *cocksucker.*"

"I'll bend this wrench on your skull!"

"*Try* it, motherFUCKER!"

The crowd roils. Hands clutch at collars and shoulders. A fist swings across a man's jaw and a cluster of orange, blue, and green coveralls falls into a struggling heap. Screams and shouts of rage volley like cannon shots, intense and overwhelming.

The hall doors open and Operators, dressed in full kit, surge through. They dive into the thickest tangles, parting them with swift chops. A wrench clangs against ceramic armor. A mailed fist answers it, bashing a man's nose with a splat of red. Grown men and women are hauled up by their clothing, tossed aside with hisses of tearing fabric. Curses, groans, cries of pain, clack of sticks and tools. A loud *snap* and a howl of agony.

"Aaaaaaaa, *my arm*! You *broke* my *fucking arm*!"

Ortega shuffles away from it all, through the open doorway, down the corridor, past more Operators racing by toward the meeting hall. He takes the lift up, plods into his cabin, and collapses face first into his bunk.

CADRE TWO

PART SEVEN

A COLONEL'S RESPONSIBILITY

Maiella dozes in the pilot's chair of a sow-like transport, feet up on the console, arms crossed, chin resting on her armored chest. Tiny lights shine on breaker panels, blinking with the normal operation of ship systems. A single lanyard connects her HDI to the ship's controls, and performance metrics cycle by in her goggles, each showing green bars.

For all the peaceful calm inside the ship, a maelstrom of channeled energy rages just beyond the hull. Positive and negative fields, fed by regular discharges from the ship's engines, contort space-time into opposing lobes that both push and pull the ship to superluminal speeds. At present output, the ship crosses billions of kilometers in an hour. Were it not for the prismatic smears of passing stars in the viewscreen, it would be impossible to tell that the ship was moving at all.

When she first took the helm, there was excitement of new technology and unimagined performance, not to mention eagerness to put the madness of Cadre Two behind her. As fast as the ship is, however, the return trip to Cadre One has been long. Having explored every feature, compartment, and panel, Maiella finds boredom to be the one enemy in her life she cannot defeat.

Colonel Shao-Lo is as tight-lipped as ever, which means both Argo and Keiko are, as well. Sharon is consumed in long, brooding silences, unwilling or unable to speak about the heavy thoughts that make her perpetually slouch in her cabin. The only other passenger is Keller's frozen body, the rest of the expedition lost to the mad artificial intelligences running amok at Cadre Two. Without meaningful interaction to bide the time, Maiella lets the hypnotic lensing of stars lull her into a meditative torpor; and the light years flow by in fitful starts of awareness.

A gentle tone sounds in her ear, rousing her from half-sleep. After a couple of deliberate blinks, she focuses on new words displayed in her goggles:

APPROACHING DESTINATION

The words are no surprise, as she has known the time and distance remaining since departure. Nonetheless, they are a welcome signpost in the journey home and a fresh reminder that she will see Thompson soon.

The Geek interlaces her fingers and flexes them backwards until the knuckles crack. Then, following a drawn out stretch and exaggerated yawn, she takes her boots down from the console and grips the controls. Data streams into her goggles as she requests it from the ship: all the last minute security and function checks required before entering Cadre One's regional space. Again, she sees all green bars.

With a thought through her HDI, Maiella activates cameras in each of the occupied cabins, and she opens four separate windows in the viewscreen. In the cabin farthest aft Sharon sits on her bunk, thumbing Argo's borrowed Labset. Organic molecules and human anatomy display on the Labset's screen, while a male voice with Hindi inflection narrates relevant details about his discoveries. Sharon cringes at some images, then leans in with fascination at others.

In the adjacent cabin, Argo guides Keiko through a set of calisthenics. Keiko is bare-chested, revealing a torso so covered in new scar tissue it looks as if she has been splashed with hot pink wax. As she moves, Argo observes the closure of her most recent wounds and tests her range of motion, giving encouragement when her amputated right arm complicates an otherwise simple exercise.

Shao-Lo sits cross-legged on the floor of her cabin, dressed in a heavily-mended undersuit. Delicate tools spread in a neat fan in front of the muscular woman, and a rifle lies in parts to her right atop a folded bunk sheet. She handles the rifle's body, turning it over and over, scrutinizing blemishes, checking her repairs. Satisfied, she flips the release latch and peers inside with intense concentration, obsessing over the main coil and lasing optics. In the corner behind her, two more rifles stand on their butts and Argo's cannon squats like a malevolent anvil. All three have benefitted from the colonel's meticulous attention, finished with fresh doping of light-absorbing carbon.

The only occupants of Argo's cabin are three suits of armor, joints locked, standing shoulder to shoulder in the narrow space. Whole sections of plating are missing, exposing the skeletal frame and patched fiber mesh beneath. Despite Argo's work, the suits still look like husks of hammer-smashed crustaceans.

The last cabin is dark, occupied by the shrouded body of Braemar Keller, ex-captain of SoVar Colony Vessel *Europa*. Maiella leaves the light off in respect for his eternal rest.

Thumbing the "Comm" button on her control wheel, she announces to all cabins, "ETA Cadre One, fifteen minutes. Colonel Shao-Lo to the flight deck, please."

The occupants of each cabin look up at their own camera. Argo and Keiko smile broadly to one another and clap each other on the shoulder. Shao-Lo nods. Sharon merely stares.

"Be there in three," Shao-Lo says, slapping rifle parts together in rapid succession. "Keiko, Argo," she shouts across the hall, "dress and cover."

"Aye, sir!" they shout as one.

Sharon stands from her bunk, clutching Argo's Labset to her chest like a four-year-old with an encyclopedia. She smiles at first, and then the smile straightens. A line forms across her forehead and she remains still, staring at the door of her cabin.

Maiella studies Sharon's expression, guesses at her thoughts, then switches off the camera feeds.

"Cutting C-Plus drives," Maiella announces. "Transition in three... two...one..."

The Geek thinks a string of commands from her HDI and the drives power down with a series of rapid pulses, sending a slight shimmy down the length of the transport. Smeared stars in the viewscreen collapse to brilliant pinpoints.

"Updating positional references, calibrating NAV points," she announces. With an easy turn of the controls, she swings the craft toward a brilliant blue-white star. Her goggles and the transport's viewscreen automatically dim to compensate.

Muffled conversation carries forward from the rear cabins, along with clanking of gear and snapping of latches. Maiella marks none of it, however, for all she thinks about is Thompson: the thousands of orders he gave, the calm confidence, his precision in every rotation...the lines of his jaw, his sharp gray eyes, the scent of his exertion...and how badly she wants his hands on her bare skin.

Memories play through her mind, beginning with her assignment to

Team Spectre, to moments of intense enemy action, to the bright memory of wrestling in slippery oil.

And then the *Europa* encounter—approaching the colossal ship, certain she had found the fattest enemy prize yet. Boring through the hull and blasting their way to the bridge, only to discover the *Europa* was a colony ship launched from Earth orbit mere months before the Blueskin genocide.

Violently torn bodies of human men and women... An unimaginable crime, the unending shame of it reflected in the eyes of every Colonist aboard who survived the assault...

Disgrace and exile from the Cadre Operator Corps... Deemed so irreparably flawed, she was not even fit to join Argo and Thompson on a suicidal recon mission to Earth...

Standing at Cadre One, huddled against Thompson and Argo moments prior to their departure, not knowing if she would ever see them again. And the last thing Thompson said to her:

"Be strong."

Those two words were an imperative, an order that buoyed her in the darkest moments, a reminder that her life was not hers to take...

At her lowest, standing at the *Europa's* inner reactor access door, beyond which was merciful incineration. The Counselor may have found the right words to reel her back from that door, but it was Thompson's mandate that made her hesitate in the first place.

He knew, she thinks. *Thompson always knew what I'd do before I did.*

Thoughts of Argo and Thompson leaving for Earth on a one-way transport, replacement Geek at their side, is an old wound that will never heal. And no matter that Argo is just a few meters away, he has never felt so distant. The Brick turned his back on her to prove he was worthy of rejoining the Operator Corps. His success in restoring himself to honorable service underscores her own failures and inadequacies. Her combat prowess has never been sharper, yet the Cadre has written her off as irredeemable, so mentally diseased that mere association could infect other Operators and corrupt the Corps from within. Argo, the anchor of her team, the man she adored like an older brother, is lost to her forever.

Has Thompson gone back to the Corps, as well? Will he knock me back like Argo did?

Her heart flutters in her chest, threatening to climb up her throat and out of her mouth. In the few years she has been free from Cadre inhibitors, she has learned to cope with the intense emotional surges, but the thought of losing Thompson is overwhelming. Breaths come too quickly, amplifying a swing to the verge of panic.

No, no, no, you showed your worth at Cadre Two! Keep it together, Geek. You WILL NOT fall apart now.

Maiella draws a deep breath and holds it, eyes closed, hands firmly gripping the controls. Her heart slows its manic pounding, heat recedes from her cheeks, ears, and neck. As panic ebbs there is still unexpended tension in her veins, and the Counselor's calming advice comes to her from what feels like a thousand years ago:

> *"You'll continue to have these wild swings. When you feel them coming on, I want you to take a breath and intercept them, just until you can give them creative expression."*

Maiella exhales and looks over her shoulder, knowing it is far too late in the voyage to start another physically intensive "Art Project" like the one she completed aboard the *Europa*. But thoughts of the Counselor bring their own unpleasantness. The humble, plain-faced man in the lab coat who exists only to serve others, a man whose face she came to trust with difficulty, only to learn it belonged to someone else first.

When I look at the Counselor I'm going to see his maker, Mikato.
Her shoulders bunch.

Counselor's never done me wrong. Far as I know, he's never done anyone wrong... But what I saw at Cadre Two, he IS Mikato, or at least a part of him. Could he ever do the things Mikato has done?

She draws another deep breath.

All these people, I thought I knew. Every one has a secret they hold back, some other side they don't show. Is it possible to really know anyone?

Muted footfalls behind her announce Shao-Lo's approach. Maiella blanks her expression.

The colonel ducks into the dim cockpit, clad in the remains of her armor, faceplate of her helmet raised. She squints at the brilliant blue-white star in the distance.

"Rotation's end is supposed to be the best part," the tall colonel says with a fond half-smile. The smile straightens, and she stares straight out. "Except when there are casualties to report... Figured those days were behind me."

Maiella sneaks a glance then looks away quickly, wondering, *Did*

I see what I think I did? A Cadre Officer showing emotion? The idea is so bizarre that Maiella desperately wants to look again. She does not get the opportunity.

"Standard approach," Shao-Lo says. "Close to three hundred thousand and squawk flash."

"Aye, Colonel."

Maiella guides the transport to the distance ordered and flashes the transponder. Keying her radio, she announces, "Cadre One, this is Transport Shao-Lo returning from rotation, acknowledge."

Seconds later, her reply comes, *"Transport Shao-Lo, do not approach. Hold position and transmit ID codes, over."*

"Wilco, Cadre One. Stand by." She releases the radio button and looks over at the colonel. "Was never given IFF keys for this rotation. Can you talk to them?"

Shao-Lo's head rocks back slightly and she grimaces. "Ah, that's right. You stowed away. Patch me through."

"Channel open."

"Cadre One, voice and visual ident, Shao-Lo, Colonel, Victor-Echo-Uniform-Kilo. Acknowledge."

Seconds later, the radio replies, *"Remove headgear and present for visual confirmation."*

"Received, Cadre One. Geek, open a window."

Maiella's goggles flash once and a two-way communication window appears in the viewscreen. Shao-Lo takes a knee so she can look directly into it. After removing her helmet she turns her head from left to right and back.

"Cadre One, confirm authentication, voice and visual ident," the kneeling colonel orders.

"Transport Shao-Lo, hold position. Acknowledge, then maintain radio silence until further instruction."

"Acknowledged, Cadre One, going radio silent," Maiella answers.

A thought occurs to Maiella as they wait for Cadre One's next transmission. There is a moment of inner debate, whether or not she should voice it, and then she speaks.

"Now that Honniker's seen us, it'd be easy for him to beat a voice and visual ident."

"I was thinking the same," Shao-Lo says, staring into the empty comm window. "Next step will be a DNA match, but..."

"We left plenty of that behind at Cadre Two," Maiella adds.

They both stare patiently into the viewscreen, when the slightest ripple in the star field catches Maiella's eye. "Contact, Colonel."

The Geek's goggles flash, and Maiella frames the distortion on-screen with an aqua box. The ripple grows larger as it approaches.

"Is everything all right?" asks an uneasy voice from behind them.

Shao-Lo glances over her shoulder and nods. "Standard procedures, Sharon. We'll be debarking shortly. Is your gear ready?"

"Yeah," Sharon answers, looking down at her roughly-patched and stapled brown pressure suit. "I'm wearing it, in fact."

"Good. Please wait in your cabin. We'll let you know when it's time."

"Oh. Okay, then," Sharon says, stalling, tracing her gloved fingers over the doorframe. "Nothing I can do in the meantime?"

"No, Sharon. Thank you."

"Well, I'll just go back to my cabin, then," she announces, hiking a thumb over her shoulder, "where I've been for the last four and a half *months*." She turns and shuffles away, letting her boots clomp on the corridor floor plates. "Maybe I'll have another go at Jin-Sung's journal. It's only a photo-documented account of *moral horrors*. It's no problem at all, really. Because I've grown immune to nightmares. It'll be fun this time, no doubt..."

Shao-Lo shakes her head as Sharon's sarcastic tirade trails off down the short hallway. "I'll never understand why Colonists feel the need to say so much more than is necessary."

Maiella smirks lopsidedly.

"*Transport Shao-Lo,*" the radio says, "*steer three-two-zero, mark, zero-zero-five. Hands-on approach. Maneuvering thrusters, only. Respond.*"

"Understood, Cadre One. Three-two-zero, mark zero-zero-five. Hands on, thrusters only. Over."

Maiella turns the transport to the given heading, and the nose of the vessel points directly at the aqua-framed anomaly on screen.

"Uh, Colonel? We going to hit something?"

"Steady as she goes, Geek."

Maiella reaches out with the ship's detection and ranging systems, feeling for some hint of her destination, and the radio immediately barks at her.

"*DISABLE ACTIVE SENSING.*"

With a flourish of code in her goggles she replies, "Acknowledged, active sensing disabled!"

"*Remain on course, maintain present speed,*" the radio states.

Rippling distortion of the star field swells as the transport thrusts toward it. The aqua frame enlarges past the border of the viewscreen and the universe ahead undulates with twinkling dots of prismatic color. There

103

is momentary resistance to the craft's progress as if flying into an invisible curtain, and the transport passes through into stark white light. Maiella's goggles compensate against the glare, and the Geek finds she has piloted the transport inside an immense container ship, many times larger than suggested by the ripple in her viewscreen. Vast rack and rail systems, all of which are collapsed and retracted in stored position, line the walls of a vaguely spheroid interior. Powerful lamps shine from all directions, and the transport's passive sensors tell the Geek the hull is being painted by hundreds of different scanning wavelengths at once.

"*Transfer flight control, acknowledge,*" the radio demands.

"Sending Prefix C2 codes. Confirm receipt, over."

"*Codes received.*"

The control stick jumps out of Maiella's hands and locks against the console. System feeds in her goggles disappear and every diode in the dim cockpit switches to amber.

"*Transport Shao-Lo, prepare for boarding. All passengers submit to DNA verification. Cadre One, out.*"

Shao-Lo rises from her knee and strides aft.

A droning whine telegraphs through the bones of the ship as the transport's belly doors swing open. Maiella is about to get out of the pilot's chair, but she pauses and looks through the viewscreen at the enormous container ship she finds herself inside.

Must be one of the old high-mass freighters, she thinks. *Thought they were too big for stealth generators... Solved that problem, I guess...*

A black speck leaps from one of the catwalks high on the left and glides directly toward the transport. She watches through the viewscreen as it nears, resolving two thick arms, spread wide at the shoulders, a great round head, and two thick legs, bent at the knees. Light absorbing armor covers it head to foot, making it hard to tell just how far away it is. Every time she thinks it is about to make contact with the transport, it keeps getting larger.

Can't believe the size of the new Bricks... Another generation or two, and they'll have to crawl *through Cadre One.*

The entire transport jolts with the Brick's landing. His magnetic boots *klank* against the hull as the big soldier tromps down the ship's port side to the open cargo doors.

"Geek," Shao-Lo calls from the corridor.

"Yeah. Coming."

Maiella rises from her chair and retracts her HDI lanyard, taking a last look around the flight deck, silently admiring the ship's smooth, swift capability.

Some solid engineering in this crate. But no way this thing is Mikato's best. He wouldn't have given away his top gear, not to us. What did he call us? Children with fire?

The Geek opens a locker on her left and takes her pistols out of it. She gives each a flip around her trigger fingers and clips them to her back. Last, she grabs her helmet and, stooping, slides it over her head.

Crazy old man... Wish he would've come back with us.

She turns and ducks through the low cockpit doorway to the main corridor along the spine of the transport. Argo, Keiko, and Shao-Lo are in their own cabins, policing up their gear.

Sharon peeks out from a darkened cabin on the right. Her face is glum and her breath condenses from the cold air within.

"Maiella...would you give us a hand, please?"

"Sure."

The Geek flips the light switch for the cabin, and the overhead panel illuminates gradually. The room is bare white and minimally appointed. Beside the light switch is a hacked thermostat panel, re-programmed to cool the room to minus five centigrade. A vanity with mirror stands in the back corner, its glass and shiny metal fixtures fogged by a thin layer of frost. A bunk with bare mattress juts from the left wall and atop it is a long figure, shrouded from head to toe in white sheets.

Maiella looks at Keller's frozen body, understanding exactly what Sharon is asking.

"Well carry him properly," Maiella says. Turning around, she calls, "Colonel?"

"Yes?" Shao-Lo says from her cabin.

"With your permission, we'd like to bear Keller in honor."

Shao-Lo appears at her cabin doorway, two rifles slung over her shoulders. Her mouth is already open to deny the request, but upon sight of Sharon, the tall colonel closes her mouth. She peers into the chilled room.

"Keiko! Argo!" Shao-Lo calls.

Keiko and Argo hurry from their cabins, dressed in their pocked and cracked armor, weapons hanging from frayed straps over their shoulders, battered helmets in hand.

"Sir?" Keiko states.

"Assist Commander Jones in funeral honors."

"For Keller?" Keiko asks, eyebrow raised.

Shao-Lo nods, her mouth a serious, straight line.

Argo and Keiko slip an arm through the neck and open face of their helmets, parking the headgear on their elbow, then slide past Sharon into the frosted cabin. Maiella steps in behind them. Together, the three soldiers hoist Keller's tightly-wrapped remains up to their shoulders. The body is stiff as a plank and nearly as thin, requiring little effort to lift.

Sharon steps in, looking for a place to grip. The Operators' high shoulders make it an awkward reach, but she takes hold of the shroud and walks along in somber procession toward the pressure door near the back of the transport's short hallway.

Before they arrive, there is a series of knocks at the pressure door. Shao-Lo steps ahead and hauls it open. On the opposite side stands an enormous Brick in light absorbing armor, dark brown eyes just visible through the lenses of his helmet. He swings a flat hand to his brow. Shao-Lo returns the salute crisply.

"Permission to come aboard, sir?" the Brick asks.

"Granted, Halgrim," Shao-Lo says, stepping backward to allow him in.

Halgrim moves inside, then hauls the pressure door shut behind him.

"I need to verify your DNA, please," he says while pulling his Labset from his waist.

"Of course. How do you want it? Skin? Hair?"

"Blood." Halgrim thumbs the control pad on his labset and detaches a small phial. "Look up for me, sir?"

Shao-Lo lifts her chin, exposing the injection port in her neck armor. Halgrim plugs the phial into it, and it hisses as it fills. With a deft motion, he transfers the phial to his Labset, and the device ingests its contents. He studies the results, his closed faceplate making it impossible to tell if he is pleased or not.

"Gun Keiko," he states.

Keiko shifts her one-armed grip of Keller and presents the injection port at her neck. Halgrim repeats the process with a separate phial, for her, Argo, and Maiella, then he pauses at Sharon.

"Do you really need *that much* for a DNA test?" Sharon asks, eyeing the phial in Halgrim's armored hand.

"We are testing for more than DNA. A larger sample is required."

"What else are you looking for?" Sharon asks.

Halgrim takes an impatient breath behind his faceplate. "Standard practice now includes full screening for pathogens and parasites prior to admission to Cadre One. A necessary precaution after Team Forestall's return from Earth. We also test blood chemistry to identify imbalances, which indicate latent or emerging mental illness."

"You can't tell that from a blood test!"

"We can. Nutritional deficiency or blood toxicity have proven to be excellent markers for neurotransmitter imbalances."

"What, was there an outbreak of crazy recently?" Maiella asks.

Halgrim turns his dark eyes on Maiella, dowsing her amusement. "Yes. There was."

The Brick takes a pistol-like hypodermic from his belt and loads a clean phial into it. "Please, Commander Jones, this will only take seconds."

Sharon looks away and raises her chin.

"Hold still," Halgrim states.

"Barbarians," Sharon gripes. "You doctors still love all your evil little pointy bits, don't you? In thousands of years, you haven't learned a th—" She draws a sharp inhale through her teeth as the needle pierces her skin and draws her blood. "Oh, God. Oh, God. Oh, God. OH, *GOD!*"

Halgrim releases the trigger, retracting the needle. He shakes his head at Sharon then transfers the phial to his Labset. Sharon claps her free hand to her neck, glaring at the Brick as he works.

"Findings?" Shao-Lo asks.

"DNA matches on file records. No unusual pathogens or antibodies. Your hormone levels are all off, however. Have you experienced any unusual symptoms?"

"Emotional responses to inactivity," Shao-Lo replies. "Sensation of confinement. Getting soft, losing our edge. Frustration. Quick tempers."

"Explanation?"

"Food machine aboard won't produce Cadre formula," Argo answers. "Missing inhibitors and supplements. Been living like Colonists for the last four months."

Halgrim's spine straightens. "We'll get you a proper interval straight away."

"Well, then, Brick, do we pass?" Shao-Lo demands.

"Yes, sir," Halgrim replies modestly. "Please forgive the necessary delay, but I must ask: Is Deepak, Carter, Zuri, or Asha aboard?"

Shao-Lo's jaw flexes, and her lips turn down with fiercely restrained feeling. "K-I-A. Unrecoverable."

Halgrim's head bows. "I will inform General O'Kai—"

"*No,*" Shao-Lo counters. "That's *my* responsibility."

The Brick nods in deference, then turns his attention to the sheet wrapped figure riding on Argo's, Keiko's, and Maiella's shoulders. "Is that Keller?"

Shao-Lo blinks slowly and nods.

"I'll need to verify," Halgrim states.

"Of course."

As Sharon is about to protest, Argo's free hand lands gently on her shoulder. She turns to him, eyes glassy, a question forming on her arched tongue.

"It's all right, Sharon," Argo says. "He'll be respectful."

As Argo predicted, Halgrim is delicate in loosening the wrapped sheet around Keller's face. Before he pulls it back, he pauses and waits for Sharon's approval.

Sharon's gaze flicks back and forth from Halgrim's hands to his eyes, unsure if she is ready to see Keller's face again. She nods rapidly and turns away, listening to the soft rustle of sheets, the tap of armored fingers on a Labset, a brief discussion of where to draw a sample, and finally the re-wrapping of Keller's shroud.

"You're all cleared," Halgrim states. Cadre One is prepared to receive. Colonel Shao-Lo, shall I arrange alternate transport for Commander Jones and the exile?"

Maiella looks away and her eyes close.

"No," Shao-Lo says without hesitation. "We owe Keller our lives. He deserves all of us to carry him home. That includes Maiella."

Halgrim turns a perplexed expression toward the exiled Geek then looks back at Shao-Lo.

"Very well, sir. Follow me to transport." The huge Brick turns about, strides toward the pressure door, hauls it open, and stands aside.

Shao-Lo glances at Keiko, and with a flick of her head, the five survivors bear Keller through the open door, down the slow lift in the cargo bay, and onto a shuttle hovering just inside the open cargo bay doors.

Taps

Sharon sits on the shuttle's bench, swallowing wet burps. Arrival at Cadre One has blunted the edge of her anxiety, ending a journey of horrors with a bit of safety and security. But keeping food down has been a challenge ever since she left Cadre Two and the shuttle's lack of gravity enhancement is not helping.

Maiella is strapped in to Sharon's right, Keiko strapped in to her left. Keller's shrouded body hangs weightlessly over their laps, held in place by Keiko's and Maiella's arms draping over him.

Opposite, Argo and Halgrim share a bench, nearly filling it between the two of them. Halgrim holds Argo's labset, thumbing through several files. Argo points at it occasionally, guiding with one or two-word directions.

Shao-Lo stands just behind the pilot, bracing herself against the ceiling with one hand, the other gripping the back of the pilot's chair. She watches over the Geek's shoulder as the craft exits the bright white cargo hold and emerges into an infinite expanse of star-filled space. Ahead, a nearly spherical asteroid looms. Enormous parabolic dishes, perched on the limb of the asteroid, aim directly at a blue-white sun out of view to the left.

Sharon looks down at the plank-like body across her knees. For the entire journey back to Cadre One her mind has been deadlocked between verdicts of guilt and exoneration, and a eulogy is no closer than it was four months ago. No matter how she tries to recall the positive about Keller, hateful memories insist on clouding her recollections.

She turns as far around as her harness allows for a glance out of the shuttle's bubble-shaped viewport. Nearby, on parallel course, is a late-capture warship. The skin of the ship is muted black but running lights and flood lamps trace its sharp angles in profile. Weapon batteries extend from recesses straight at the shuttle, ringed and flanged barrels glowing violet with capacitance.

She turns the opposite way, looking back the way they came for a glimpse of the gigantic freighter. All she sees is a faint shimmer in an infinite field of stars.

"Colonel," Sharon asks, "what was the point of flying inside that big ship?"

Shao-Lo looks over her shoulder then faces front again without answering.

"Wasn't exactly a standard welcome," Maiella adds. "Did they think we grew tails or something?"

Halgrim looks up from Argo's labset. "Thoroughness and caution are to be commended," he states coarsely.

Maiella pops her eyebrows and grunts at the dissatisfying reply. She looks through the porthole beside Sharon, and asks, "How'd you adapt the stealth generators to something that big?"

Halgrim does not bother to look up this time. "Need to know, only."

Maiella turns from the porthole, frowning at the rebuff. "Need to know? *Seriously?*"

Sharon shifts her gaze from Maiella to Halgrim to Shao-Lo, wanting to stick up for her friend, wanting to take Shao-Lo by the arm and ask, *After everything Maiella did for you at Cadre Two, just what* exactly *would it take for her to get some respect?* Most infuriating is the colonel's indifference to Halgrim's slight, as if belittling Maiella is appropriate and acceptable.

Maiella notices Sharon's hostile glare into the back of Shao-Lo's head, and the Geek leans forward to break it. With a shake of the head and a taut smirk, Maiella tells Sharon silently, *Thanks, but don't.*

Sharon folds her arms and slumps back in her seat.

Cadre One looms large in the shuttle's viewscreen, and the pilot rolls the craft into a smooth arc toward the crater-nestled facility below. Sharon feels the push of her body against the bench beneath her and Keller's body falls against her thighs. As usual, the pilot steers the shuttle into a corkscrew approach, creating a sensation of weight that transitions seamlessly to the gravity enhancement of Cadre One. At the last moment, the shuttle swings about and backs into its docking cradle. Clamps attach at the stern and draw the craft firmly against the air lock with strident klanks. Air hisses as pressure equalizes.

"Arrived, Cadre One," the pilot states.

The shuttle hatch and air lock slide aside with a wisp of condensation. Cadre MedTechs stand in orderly rows against the wide corridor walls, all of them craning their necks to catch a glimpse of returning heroes. Operators stand among them like stoic pillars.

Shao-Lo adjusts the two rifles hanging from her shoulder, strides to the rear hatch, and halts. "Honor guard, fall in."

Argo, Halgrim, Keiko, Maiella, and Sharon unbuckle their lap belts. Gripping Keller's body by the tightly wrapped shroud, Maiella and Keiko stand. Argo and Keiko take position at Keller's head. Maiella moves to Keller's legs, parking the feet on her shoulder and holding them with one hand. Again, Sharon has to reach for the sheet wrapping her former captain.

"Hey," Maiella whispers, "can we bring him down a bit?"

Keiko and Argo both look back to see Sharon awkwardly hanging on to a fold of Keller's cloth. They readjust their grip, lowering the rigid body to waist level so Sharon can more easily hold the shroud.

"Thank you," Sharon says, lower lip trembling.

"Forward, *march*," Shao-Lo orders, and the colonel leads the way. Argo, Keiko, and Maiella stride forward in step, much faster than Sharon anticipates. She hustles to catch up, having to take two steps for every stride of the tall Operators. Halgrim follows at a respectful distance.

MedTechs, excited at first to witness a successful return from Cadre Two, stand mute with bowed heads as the funeral procession strides by. Operators remain at attention with open helmets. Sharon steals glances at them as she passes, finding even they are not immune to the heavy mood.

General O'Kai stands at the end of the entry corridor in dress gray uniform, flanked by Colonel Munro, Major Ralla, and Major Chusan. Shao Lo marches up to O'Kai, stamps to attention, and snaps a crisp salute. O'Kai matches posture and returns the salute.

"Welcome home, Colonel. *At ease.*"

Shao-Lo drops her salute and takes Deepak's rifle from her shoulder. With the humility and precision of a freshly trained cadet, she proves the weapon is not loaded and is powered down before presenting it to her superior.

O'Kai takes Deepak's rifle, the corners of his mouth turned down. "Thank you, Colonel," he says, spinning the weapon deftly around one hand and throwing the strap over his head. "This weapon will not remain an orphan."

Shao-Lo nods and takes a step back.

"You will report to Council chamber for mission debrief," he tells her. "Before then, is there anything you'd like to say?"

"Yes, General, there is."

O'Kai gestures toward the assembly. Shao-Lo turns about stiffly.

"This rotation was the hardest I've ever known," she begins. "To survive required everything we had. For others, it required more."

Her head dips before continuing.

"Asha. Zuri. Deepak. Carter. They fought with the skill and courage that define Operators of the finest kind. Their lives were not *lost*. Their lives were *spent* so that we could return with our discoveries...so that the Cadre can endure, stronger and more vital than before."

She looks at the sheet-wrapped body. "Keller's sacrifice was no less. He fought with all the cunning and determination of any seasoned Geek, Gun, or Brick. There was no dead weight on this rotation." Shao-Lo's gaze falls directly on Maiella. "Without *everyone*...this mission would have failed."

The colonel looks out across the silent and still assembly.

"As we learn the applications of technologies recovered, our Cadre will be more resilient to future threats, will enjoy enhanced capabilities, will be less burdened by limitations. For this, we decorate Gun Keiko and Brick Argo in recognition of their accomplishments. We give thanks to Sharon and Maiella for bringing fresh perspectives, for illuminating possibilities we would not have otherwise seen. And we bestow highest honor upon Geek Asha, Geek Zuri, Brick Carter, Gun Deepak, and Braemar Keller, that we should remember their sacrifices and keep them alive in our memories for all time.

"Show your respect as we bear them to eternal fame."

She salutes.

Chusan bellows, "PRESENT *ARMS*!"

Operators and MedTechs alike snap a salute as one unified organism. No one speaks. No one shuffles or slouches. No one coughs or clears their throat.

Suppressed emotions rise in Sharon all at once: horrors of the mission, violent deaths of companions (and, she reluctantly admits to herself, loved ones). Shao-Lo's straight-to-the-point delivery leaves no cloudy gray contemplation, only awareness of loss and affirmation that the lost did not die in vain.

Sharon's breath catches in her throat. She swallows it hard, not wanting to disturb the reverent silence, not wanting to be a blubbering girl among those keeping a stiff upper lip. The longer she stands, however, the easier it becomes. Complexity falls away. Reasons, hidden and lied about, words spoken in anger or haste, misunderstandings and disagreements, all are irrelevant now. As she clings to Keller's shroud, she finally understands why Shao-Lo changed her obvious first impulse and afforded Keller military honors: because Keller proved beyond any trace of doubt that his priorities were correct, that he loved others more than he loved himself.

Sharon wipes the water from her eyes before it can fall and she raises her head high. Where the words refused to come in the four and a half month flight home, she finally knows what she will tell her crew about him.

"Honor guard," Shao-Lo announces, "to the left, *MARCH*!"

Sharon strides in step, not about to be left behind again.

GOOD HUNTING

Shao-Lo strides through the corridors of Cadre One, intent on Council chambers. Her heels strike hard, given extra force by the frustration in her veins.

So little gained for the cost of four seasoned Operators and a warship, she thinks. *What did we bring back? A small, unarmored transport...medical information, mostly redundant to Cadre One's own archive...genetic research detailing the hybrid of human and blueskin...*

The tall woman looks down at the brass shell cradled in her left arm.

And this? We don't know if it will affect the enemy at all. Could be another one of Honniker's elaborate deceptions.

Things of real value I left behind: ample living quarters, food synthesis, abundant energy, radical new weapons, excellent defenses, a standing army that could repel almost any assault...

A scowl settles onto her face, drawing her thin cheeks in.

Another sent in my place would have returned with the keys to Cadre Two in hand. Would have pacified and erased Honniker/Mikato and could have prevented Maiella's upload. Would have snatched the best of Mikato's armada and brought it home with her full team aboard. Could have brought Voss and Keller back, alive...

At a junction ahead Munro waits, lightly smacking a pair of plasticine-wrapped protein bars against the palm of his larger hand. He turns into the corridor beside Shao-Lo and matches pace with her.

"Here," he says, offering the protein bars, "heard you haven't had a proper interval in months."

Shao-Lo glances at the bars and frowns. "Got something faster? I can't stand these swings anymore."

"I could give you an injection."

Shao-Lo halts, turns toward Munro, and lifts her chin. "Please," she says between gritted teeth.

"Won't be instantaneous. You'll have to build it up in your system over a couple of days."

"*Do* it."

Munro nods, takes a hypo-gun from his waist belt, and slides back the top rail. "When I was still raw," he says, "my instructor asked one of the class to skip inhibitors for a week. I volunteered."

Shao-Lo maintains her rigid stare at the ceiling.

"It wasn't good," Munro continues, taking a phial from a pouch at his waist and loading it into the open injector. "*Powerfully* destructive impulses. Desires, both selfish and indulgent. That was just a week."

He closes the rail and presses the hypo to Shao-Lo's jugular.

"Hold still."

Shao-Lo waits with strangled patience as the medicine shoots into her blood stream.

"I'm told Maiella's been off inhibitors for more than two years now," Munro says as he takes the gun from Shao-Lo's neck. "Don't know how she even *functions*."

"I don't think anyone ever will," Shao-Lo says, rubbing her throat. Her face blanks and her eyes focus to a distant point. "And that's unfortunate."

Munro regards his colleague with some skepticism. "Why is that?"

Shao-Lo returns from her mental journey, and she looks at Munro squarely. "Because we need fighters like her." The tall woman flicks her head and the two of them resume their path.

"So Maiella's back in the Corps?" he asks.

"NO." Shao-Lo's jaw clenches.

Munro waits for an elaboration. When it does not come, he faces forward and falls in with Shao-Lo's long strides.

Two Guns flank the entry to Council Chambers ahead. They salute crisply as the colonels approach, and the door they guard slides aside. Shao-Lo and Munro return the respectful salutes, Shao-Lo taking the lead as they pass through single-file. Inside, Ralla and Chusan stand in conference with O'Kai, who sits on the table's edge, arms folded. The general rises to his feet.

"Take your seats," O'Kai says as he makes his way to the rounded center of the semi-circular table. "Let's begin."

Ralla and Chusan take their places at the table's corners. Munro takes his chair between O'Kai and Ralla. Shao-Lo takes her chair between

O'Kai and Chusan, setting the brass shell onto the table in front of her. It draws stares.

"We have questions about Cadre Two," O'Kai states, taking his eyes off the shiny shell. "Rather than wait for your full report, we're going to need answers, right now."

"Something happen?" Shao-Lo asks, scanning the faces of her comrades. Chusan, Ralla, and Munro look at the table.

"We'll discuss that," O'Kai states. "But let's get to it. Your team took a beating, Colonel. We assume there's a potent and hostile presence at Cadre Two. Is this correct?"

"Yes, it is."

"If *all* of our assets are deployed, can we pacify Cadre Two for occupation?"

Shao-Lo's spine stiffens. "No," she says reluctantly. "The facility has overwhelming superiority."

"How'd you get in?" Chusan asks.

"Keller invented a story about the *Enyo's* offensive potential, claiming it could cripple Cadre Two's power plant if we weren't allowed in. Don't know if the story worked, or if Honniker had other plans for us. Regardless, neither lies nor force will get us inside again."

"Honniker?" Munro asks.

Shao-Lo takes a deep breath as memory pulls her to a distant place:

> *Huddled back to back with Argo and Keiko in a pitch-dark room... Massive tanks of electrolyte, towering beside them and glowing with warmth in her visor...*
>
> *Innumerable beasts surrounding them, genetically torqued-up killers rumbling with menace and creeping closer one razor-clawed paw at a time... In every maw, metal-capped teeth bared for show... Hot panting breaths, merging into a whirling fog in infrared...*
>
> *Argo, swinging his cannon toward the massive tank of electrolyte...*
>
> *Snarls rising to rabid howls and barks...*
>
> *And Honniker's disembodied voice,*
>
> *"Such fuss is unnecessary, Colonel. If you would merely give yourself to my project, I would need no other. What remains of your team could return home, perhaps with some small trifle to please your General... But if you do not, I will have you all on my tables. It would be simpler for you*

to spare them a pointless and agonizing death, do you not agree? Or rather, not...quite...death. Because long after their minds collapse, they will continue to do my bidding..."

Shao-Lo's teeth grind. She looks at Munro, then at Ralla, O'Kai, and Chusan. Their eyes are fixed on her, waiting.

"There's an artificial entity in control of Cadre Two that calls itself, 'Honniker'," she says. "Loosely based on one of the original researchers at Cadre Two. Insisted on a reproductively viable female to replace its stem cell inventories. Showed a preference for Commander Jones, but would've accepted another in her place."

Munro tilts his head and asks, "Does that mean *none* of the original inhabitants of Cadre Two survive?"

Slouching, drooling automatons with lifeless eyes, stitched together with artificial implants and scraps from the Graveyard...

Shao-Lo grunts. "None."

"Providing tissue for stem-cell cultivation doesn't sound like a big ask," Munro says, his smaller hand clasped inside the larger one. "A subject can remain in a productive capacity for years and still be capable of robust work, provided they aren't carrying a fetus to term."

Shao-Lo frowns at the thought. "That's true, Munro, but I've seen first-hand what Honniker intends. Confinement to an open recliner, frontal lobotomy, and intubation. Hormone therapy to keep the subject in a perpetual cycle of fertility and pregnancy. The uterus and ovaries are harvested for the rest of an artificially extended life."

Ralla glances at the others around the table. "That isn't so different from how we obtain our own—"

"We use *drones* for that," Shao-Lo interrupts, "not fully-realized individuals with a lifetime of experience and skill..."

Tentacles of anger reach through Shao-Lo's mind, grasping at memories of *The Vault...*

A nude woman in a stainless medical recliner with purple-striped, distended abdomen. Long reddish-gray hair, sparse and slick with unwashed body oils. Contorted hands drawn hard against a bony chest. Tall black numerals tattooed over double mastectomy scars. Untrimmed nails

hanging in vine-like ribbons. Eyes and lips sewn shut as if
to deprive the senses and make the mind a prisoner in the
body...

"It was *sickness*," Shao-Lo burrs, "satisfaction from the infliction of pain. Her mind was wrecked, her body spent. All we could do was grant her retirement."

O'Kai's eyes narrow. "If the subject was properly lobotomized, there would be no pain."

Shao-Lo's fist slams the table.

"ROSENTHAL WAS *NOT* A DRONE."

In the sudden silence, Shao-Lo looks at her fist on the table. There it sits, proof of her actions, a visible crack in the dam of her emotional conditioning. Her mouth slides back into a horrified grimace. She pulls her fist into her lap and laces her fingers together. Beneath armored gloves, her hands crush each other white.

"I apologize for my outburst, General."

When Shao-Lo builds the nerve to look up, she sees Munro leaning away from O'Kai's ear. O'Kai nods soberly, and asks, "Shao-Lo, are you able to continue, or do you require a recess?"

Shao-Lo clears her lungs. "I am composed, General. And I repeat my apology to all. There is no excuse."

"Never mind that. Munro explained you've been off inhibitors for months. Can you continue?"

"Aye, sir," Shao-Lo states. "I'm in control."

"Very well," O'Kai says with a nod. "So this Honniker is in possession of Cadre Two?"

"Affirmative. With another entity called, 'Mikato.'"

"They're both hostile?"

Shao-Lo's eyebrows knit. "Not a clear line between them. Separate personalities, but facets of the same entity."

Munro leans forward onto his large arm. "An artificial intelligence... with multiple identities?"

"As described to me, more like conjoined fraternal twins."

"Bizarre..." Munro says and turns to Ralla. "Could that happen in a machine environment?"

Ralla's eyes narrow as she considers it, then she shrugs.

"The two were once distinct," Shao-Lo adds, "until the residents of Cadre Two tried to shut them down. Hardware was damaged, some of their software was successfully deleted. To survive, Honniker and Mikato merged code. Some attributes are shared while others are distinct. But it's safe to say, what one knows, the other does, as well. Whatever their morphology, neither seemed interested in having us there unless we moved into their cells and submitted to Honniker's 'experiments.'"

"I'd rather take our chances against the Blueskins," Ralla says to O'Kai.

Shao-Lo looks down the table at the cool-eyed Major with the polished silver contact terminals. "You're planning an Op?"

Ralla looks to O'Kai, deferring the question.

"We are," the General answers. "The *Europa* will resume her mission, taking our MedTechs along. The rest of us are headed elsewhere. The information you provide will determine our destination."

"We're *evacuating*?" Shao-Lo's heart races. "Was Cadre One discovered?"

O'Kai nods. "An object appeared in our vicinity three weeks ago, no reply to our challenges. From its vantage, it would have had a clear view of the solar collectors and many of the moored vessels before we shot it down."

"Do the Colonists know?"

"No. The crew of the *Europa* has rejected their new Captain and is nearly in revolt. Informing them will only aggravate their irrational tendencies."

"That may be so," Shao-Lo says, "but to delay is unwise. Why isn't the *Europa* on her way?"

O'Kai looks down the table at Chusan.

"We made pre-flight checks during patrols," the burn-scarred major replies. "Her crew has been so preoccupied with arguing that maintenance has lapsed. Found evidence of sabotage. In sum, *Europa* is not space worthy."

Shao-Lo stares at Chusan as if he were deliberately trying to misinform. "Sabotage? Are they *insane*?" She turns to Munro. "Or suicidal?"

Munro shakes his head. "We asked ourselves the same. For now, our Operators have restored order and we're supervising crucial overhauls. Once Colonist command authority is rebuilt and the ship restored to minimal function, *Europa* will resume her mission. While underway, our MedTechs can work through the back maintenance...keep her going, even if her own crew won't."

Irritation tightens Shao-Lo's shoulders and neck. She nearly dismisses the Colonists as incurable evolutionary mistakes and declares their separation a blessing, after all, but that thought is squelched by Mikato's poignant lecture back at Cadre Two:

*"...if all of your kind were so aggressive, Honniker
would have no choice but to exterminate you to ensure
his survival. If all of you were like Ms. Jones, there would
be no cost to him gathering all of your kind and twisting
them in his experiments. But together, some of you show an
inclination toward peace while others show an inclination
toward aggression. So long as the two of you remain blended
in the same group, there is peaceful restraint keeping you
from conquering all you see, yet there is also a powerful
deterrent to attacking you. There is balance there, which
suggests a lasting stability... So long as you remain unified,
that is..."*

Shao-Lo hangs her head, sensing truth in Mikato's words, that
somehow they truly are stronger when joined, even if she cannot see how,
even if the Cadre has to do everything to maintain that unity.

"We're *sure* it was an imaging device?" Shao-Lo asks, lifting her
head.

"Positive," Munro answers. "Twin transmitters around the sides,
permitting three-hundred sixty degree broadcast. Two-meter disc at its
leading edge. Imaging optic, no doubt in my mind."

"And we're certain it was the Blueskins? Honniker knows where we
are. He might have sent a fast moving probe to watch us."

"Not unless he builds to Blueskin spec," Munro counters. "We netted
the debris and went over it thoroughly. Circuit design overlaps with Blueskin
tech too closely to be anything else. Unless..."

Ralla picks up on Munro's thread. "Could this Honniker thing have
captured any of the enemy's vessels, like we have? Mimicked the design?"

Shao-Lo thinks back to vaults and corridors stacked with Blueskin
corpses, to the mobs of drone-like, shuffling reptilians. Cadre Two had a
large inventory of Blueskin corpses, she recalls, but not a trace of their tech,
nothing at all to indicate they had access to it.

And Sharon's story on the flight back—what Keller told her, how he
thought the Blueskins were primitives until he found proof otherwise...

"No," Shao-Lo counters. "Everything we found at Cadre Two told
the same story: once the colonies and Earth fell, Cadre Two went radio silent
and stayed dark ever after. It was self-sufficient, at least for the artificial life
forms that survived. No reason for them to go out and risk discovery. And the
Enyo... That's a piece of Blueskin hardware that Honniker didn't recognize.

He was obsessed with taking it."

Asha was aboard the Enyo *when Honniker blasted it... Killed for nothing...*

Shao-Lo squirms in her seat with the bitter memory, but forces herself to remain composed, adding, "There'd be no reason for Honniker to work so hard to capture the *Enyo* if he was already sitting on Blueskin tech."

"The *Enyo* was *captured?*" O'Kai asks. Both he and Ralla raise an eyebrow at one another and look back toward Shao-Lo.

"Aye," the tall Colonel says, "in a show of force to deter us from returning."

"Lost to enemy capture..." O'Kai repeats to himself.

In the general's distant stare Shao-Lo reads the same dismay that she felt as she looked out upon the *Enyo's* wreckage, surrounded by an armada of vessels poised to blow her out of the sky.

Not once in Cadre history, not ever, has a mission commander lost an asset to enemy capture, Shao-Lo thinks. *An asset wrested from the enemy through blood and toil, then stripped, rebuilt, and equipped with the best of Cadre tech. Most likely torn down on Mikato's production floor now, being analyzed, rated, and improved. Who knows if we'll we see the* Enyo *again? Or if she'll be one of the last things our Operators ever see...*

"Honniker blasted the whole front third away," Shao-Lo says. "Unlikely that Asha saw it coming, or she could have detonated the whole vessel."

"If Honniker can sneak up on one of our best Geeks and zero her out," Ralla adds, "we have a problem."

"Possibly... But if Cadre Two has been sealed up since the genocide," Chusan posits, "then I'm uncertain Honniker has the operational expertise to utilize his fleet effectively."

"The quantity and variety of weapon systems were remarkable," Shao-Lo counters. "If Honniker's forces were close to ours in speed and firepower, there could be discussion of an assault. But they're significantly advanced and outnumber us *at least* ten to one. The real number may be much higher."

"Why do you say that?" Munro asks.

"Because in all the time since the genocide, the experiments of Cadre Two have continued. Directed energy, power storage, propulsion, advanced armor, self-repairing machinery, autonomous droids... Mikato's production has gone on without interruption."

Shao-Lo pauses and she stares into the table, the corners of her mouth drawing back into the beginnings of a smile. "Almost..."

"You have something?" O'Kai asks.

Shao-Lo looks up from the table. "Organic polymers."

O'Kai glances at Munro. Munro shrugs and shows his palms.

"Care to expand, Colonel?" O'Kai insists.

"Cadre Two is nestled inside a planetary core remnant," Shao-Lo explains. "Uranium, minerals, and metals are abundant. But Mikato said the facility was missing organic polymers. Needed resins, adhesives, and solvents, mostly plastics. Mikato said he stripped as much from the station as he dared. There wasn't nearly enough. And he didn't want to render the bodies in the Graveyard. Those were reserved for Honniker's *other* projects..."

"*Plastic?*" O'Kai echoes.

"That's right," Shao-Lo says.

"Blueskin ships are *crammed* with it," Munro notes with a look of ironic amusement. "Every exposed surface is sealed, like they're afraid of touching or even seeing metal. And every locker, cabinet, or pocket is full of plastic junk. Takes weeks to strip it all out before we can start our retrofits."

"That's good leverage," Ralla states.

"Depends what this Mikato needs it for," Chusan says. "If it's the finishing piece for a NovaTrigger, we'd best not hand it over."

"True," O'Kai states. "But that makes two things we know these entities want. And we have them both." He faces Ralla. "*Very* good leverage."

"It's a risk to return," Shao-Lo says, leaning back in her seat. "Our last visit was costly."

"We're all or nothing at this point," O'Kai counters. "If Cadre Two is fortified as you say, has refuge enough for all of us, and a fleet of heavily armed ships... If we can offer something in trade that could secure all that, we're taking that risk." The general pauses, looking his council in the eye for any sign of debate. Munro, Ralla, and Chusan take the edict as a matter of course. Shao-Lo's every nerve jangles at the idea of taking residence in a place where the very circuits and machines have gone mad, but she buries any trace of dissent and nods approvingly.

"Now then," O'Kai says, leaning forward onto his elbows and pointing at the brass shell, "tell us about *that.*"

Shao-Lo grips the shell and hands it to O'Kai. "By Keller's description, it carries a viral load. A hardy strain that endures in an environment, carried by indigenous fauna, dormant, until the correct host appears. This one, he said, was coded to the Blueskin genotype."

Munro's eyes widen. "Has it been tested?"

"We didn't tamper with it in-flight. Wanted to have a controlled environment before cracking it in case Honniker packed in a surprise. But if it really is as effective as Keller said... We'll want to manufacture in bulk."

O'Kai's eyes shine as he turns the shell over and over, studying it. "Munro, verify the viral load." He sets the shell onto its flat end and slides it to Munro. "If it checks out, manufacture as much as you can until we evacuate."

"Sir?" Munro asks. "There's no room in Incub—"

"They won't mature in time," O'Kai interrupts, "and they won't survive transport. We'd have to flush them one way or other."

Munro's jaw hangs open. His head droops, and his shoulders slump. "I'll get started right away." He takes the brass shell from the table and rolls it over in his large and small hands. "But, uh, there's only one sure way I know of to test this."

"The captive?" O'Kai asks.

"Aye."

O'Kai thinks hard before replying. "I don't expect Doctor Taggart will release her patient willingly."

"I can make do with tissue samples," Munro says.

"Approved. But first, you'll flight prep the transport for return to Cadre Two. Pack four embryo production Drones, and fill the cargo hold with as much plastic as will fit."

"That'll only be a fraction of what I have on hand," Munro says. "Got *mounds* of the stuff."

"Even better. We can send a peace offering and tempt Honniker with future shipments to keep him interested. And, as Chusan wisely cautioned, we don't want to give away everything a potential enemy could need."

"It will be done," Munro states. "Where do we store the extra inventory? If we're evacuating, then..."

"The passenger liner will become your barge, Colonel. Park it somewhere distant, yet accessible."

"Aye, sir."

O'Kai turns to the major on his right. "Chusan, getting the *Europa* back in shape is a tall order. On the issue of labor allocation alone, you're going to need Colonist compliance and participation. Focus purely on the ship and stay out of their internal conflicts, unless lives are threatened. Now, having said that, you must temper your directives with patience. If Cadre Two cannot be pacified, we need our MedTechs to be welcome guests with the colonists for as long as necessary. It's a fine line you walk, Major."

Chusan nods in acceptance.

O'Kai looks down the table to his left. "Ralla, outfit a two ship escort for the *Europa*. We can't spare Geeks to pilot them, so be thorough in your programming. After, you and I will coordinate evacuation of Cadre One, final defense, and Earth assault."

Ralla's head dips modestly and she replies, "Aye, sir."

"*Earth assault?*" Shao-Lo echoes.

O'Kai nods. "You've convinced me a direct assault on Cadre Two will fail, and sending our fleet off with the *Europa* increases the chance she'll be spotted. Therefore, we send the fleet to Earth. We're losing our home ground, and we'll never be as strong as we are at this moment. An attack now has the greatest chance of success. If we win, we restore humanity to our rightful place and we guard against the enemy's return. If defeated, we will have covered the *Europa's* escape and rendered Earth a ruin, devoid of life, unfit for habitation. Better the planet is destroyed than remain in enemy hands.

"Shao-Lo, you'll return to Cadre Two aboard the transport and deliver the cargo with our terms. In return, we expect access to Cadre Two's research and a serious negotiation for our residence. You know these entities first-hand. You'll be better able to detect any attempts at deception."

"Honniker will demand more than we're offering," Shao-Lo says. "He doesn't want Drones. He wants fully aware subjects for his experiments."

O'Kai looks directly at her. "Can you deliver on those demands?"

Shao-Lo's ears slide back.

> *Cold steel table and constrictive restraints, mechanical arms tipped with blades, saws, drills, and chisels... Head and spine in a jar, just like Summers...but alive and conscious of it all...*

There is tightness in her throat that is difficult to swallow, yet she speaks without hesitation, "Yes, General. I can. And I will."

"Good." O'Kai rises and his officers all rise with him. "This operation dwarfs any we've ever attempted. You four are the only ones who can accomplish it. Urgency presses us to cut sleep, so triple shifts with stims are authorized. Watch for signs of fatigue in your teams and in each other. You have your orders. Dismissed."

Chusan, Ralla, Munro, and Shao-Lo swing a flat hand up to their brows. They slide their chairs under the table and stride for the exit.

"Shao-Lo," O'Kai calls, "a moment."

Shao-Lo watches the rest of the Council leave then faces O'Kai. "Sir?"

"Close the door and come here."

The tall woman punches the button on the door panel and returns to the table.

"I've lost Operators before, Shao-Lo. Don't think I haven't. And we both know it never gets easier."

Shao-Lo's mouth opens to reply, but O'Kai shuts her off.

"I can see it in your face. You think you failed at Cadre Two. I don't have to know what happened on this rotation. I know *you*. And that means this is the best outcome we could have expected."

Shao-Lo looks down, unable to agree with her general's assessment.

"This is no time for your confidence to slip, Colonel," O'Kai scolds, "because this is our last stand. *Everything* hangs on our performance. Cadre Two will either become an ally or an enemy to us. There is no in-between. You are to do everything in your power to rally those assets to our side, *anything* at all. But if this Honniker thing refuses to cooperate...then you make it PAY for Carter, Asha, Zuri, and Deepak. And if your life is required, then you make it pay DOUBLE. *Do you read me?*"

Shao-Lo looks eye to eye with O'Kai. Her spine is straight, her shoulders square.

"Clarion, sir."

The hard lines around O'Kai's eyes soften, his eyebrows rise. "Go see the quartermaster and update your kit. Be ready to depart the moment Munro completes the transport lading. And one last thing, Colonel."

"Sir?"

O'Kai extends his hand. Shao-Lo looks at his outstretched hand then grips it firmly.

"Your service has been *exemplary*."

O'Kai's free hand lands on Shao-Lo's shoulder. Shao-Lo grips O'Kai's shoulder in return. The two wordlessly contemplate the hard fought rotations together as younger Operators, the competition between them and the teamwork that made them so lethal in combat, the crush of responsibility that increased exponentially with every promotion, and most of all the respect for lives spent in absolute devotion to the Cadre.

"Good hunting, Colonel."

"You, too, sir."

O'Kai releases Shao-Lo and flicks his head at the door. She turns on her heel and strides from the room.

HARD TO LET GO

Sahara stands at the rear of the transport, waiting for the docking clamps to finish reeling it in to Cadre One. In deference to her hosts, she wears her hair back in a tight bun and her white lab coat is buttoned up to the collar in Cadre fashion. A bulky white plastic medical case hangs by a strap over her shoulder.

There is a harsh *klank*, a hiss of air, and the transport door moves aside.

The hallway ahead of her is a blur of activity. Carts piled high with equipment speed by, driven by metal-capped Drones. MedTechs weave between them, shouting directions, keeping lanes of traffic flowing smoothly.

Sahara steps off the transport, her head swiveling to find a spot where she will not get flattened in the shuffle. No sooner has she cleared the transport doorway than a burly Drone shoves through a clattering line of carts. The door seals, the clamps release, and the transport thrusts away with its cargo.

Good Lord, Sahara thinks, *it's chaos on the* Europa, *but it's positively frantic here... What the hell are they up to?*

A Gun in full kit approaches, faceplate raised, cheeks rough with black stubble. He eyes her badge before standing to one side.

"Thank you for coming, Doctor Taggart. Are those the samples from the captive?"

"Yes," Sahara replies, lifting the strap over her head and passing the case over.

The Gun takes it and hands it off to a MedTech. "Take this to Colonel Munro immediately."

The MedTech throws the case strap over his head, salutes with a hand missing all four fingers, and rushes away.

The Gun gestures away from the transport air lock. "Please, doctor, this way."

Sahara follows the Gun's lead down the center of the corridor, having to jog to keep up with his long strides. Drones and MedTechs hustle by on each side, hauling large wheeled carriers, carts, and pallet jacks. Most carts are heaped with pelletized plastic, others are crammed with frosted metal canisters that trail gently curling vapors. Still more are stacked with uninstalled photonics, their cords and cables dangling in tightly coiled bunches.

Drones share the same stoic expression and move with robotic ease. But MedTechs sweat from red faces, pushing carts as fast as their crippled bodies will let them. When they speak, their words are pressurized by effort, more like barks than speech.

"Keep the pace!"

"To your right. TO YOUR RIGHT!"

"Ho! You're Slipping! CATCH IT! CATCH IT!"

"Clear a path for VIP!" the Gun shouts into the fray. "Hug the walls!"

Feeling like a deer trapped between opposing lanes of honking trucks, the petite woman tucks in behind her escort.

"What's going on here?" Sahara yells above the din.

"Reorganization," the Gun answers over his shoulder.

All this for a re-org? Sahara thinks to herself with a grimace. *Cadre doesn't do anything leisurely, do they?*

"So...is Sharon injured?" she asks. "Or sick, or...?"

"We find nothing wrong with Commander Jones," the Gun says, "but she refuses to leave Reclamation. Insists on remaining with Keller's body and will not allow us to process the remains. Colonel Munro thinks if you speak with her, you may persuade her to return to the *Europa*."

Sahara's mouth bunches up on one side of her face and her eyebrows dip.

Keller gave us all reason to hate him. For Sharon, it was worse... more personal. I'd think she'd hate him more than anyone... Why would she want to be anywhere near him, living or dead?

The two make their way through the main corridors of the ring-shaped facility, ride down two levels by elevator, and approach the wide entryway of Cadre One's Reclamation and Recycling facility. Deep carts, piled high with scrap, ore, rags, and junk stand queued before a heavily reinforced door on the left. Enormous Drones in grungy coveralls stand motionless behind the carts, gripping the handlebars and waiting for their turn to advance. When the reinforced door opens, a hellish noise of squeals and metallic groans rolls out, punctuated by a series of sharp snaps and cracks. Hydraulic motors whine as the smasher reaches full extension then abruptly change pitch when the compactor pistons reverse. A faint reddish glow from inside silhouettes a Drone and his empty cart as he strides out. The next Drone in line pushes his cart inside, the door seals, and the corridor is quiet again.

On the right, stainless steel gurneys are staged before an ordinary metal door. Each is draped by a white sheet, humanoid shapes concealed beneath, and the queue runs out of sight to the right. Slender Reconstitutes in white medical dress stand like mannequins behind each gurney, their lens-covered eyes staring straight into the back of the metal-capped Reconstitute ahead.

While the deep carts on the left advance in orderly fashion, the gurneys on the right are stalled.

"I'm sorry," Sahara says to her escort, "your name is?"

"Gun Maddock."

"Maddock..." she begins, eyeing the long line of gurneys and craning her neck to see how far down the hall it goes. "Was there an accident I wasn't told about?"

"These Drones were nearing the end of useful function. They've been granted early retirement."

Sahara's jaw drops. *Jesus... I'll never understand these people.*

Maddock strides ahead and opens the sliding door on the right. Cooler air from inside raises hair on Sahara's arms, bringing with it a subtle scent of chlorine bleach. She peers inside.

Diffuse white light gleams from the ceiling panel overhead and reflects off institutional-gray walls. To the right and left, bright steel cutting tools hang from magnetic racks in even rows. Tubes and hoses of varying thickness hang from taps in the walls, and a half-meter wide chute occupies the rear wall, dead center. Shiny white tile covers the floor in a slight grade toward the central drain.

Two Reconstitutes stand at the back of the room, wearing heavy rubberized aprons with detachable sleeves, clipped at the shoulders, and tall white numerals printed across the front. Overhead lighting glints off their metal craniums. They are as motionless as furniture, staring straight out with dark lens-covered eyes.

At the room's center, Keller's body lies on a stainless steel table with raised edges. A plain white sheet covers him from feet to chest. His pale arms lie atop the sheet, hands over his sternum. Sharon sits on a padded stool beside him, hands in her lap, looking down at him.

Sahara takes in the room's ghastly ambience—the scalpels, serrated blades, cleavers, saws, and chisels, the chilly temperature, the antiseptic sting in her sinuses, the chute in back too narrow for a whole person to slide through, and the statuesque approximations of life watching from the back wall.

Can't imagine deliberately spending a second in this place, much less a full day...

She eases her way over to Sharon with a wary glare at the Reconstitutes.

"Heya, Jonesie."

Sharon looks up, sees Sahara, and smiles. She rises from her stool without enthusiasm, and gives her friend a hug.

"Good to see you, China. Missed you."

"Missed you, as well." The women pull apart and Sahara looks Sharon up and down for signs of injury. "You okay? Maiella said it was pretty hairy out there."

"That's one way to say it," Sharon answers. "*Fooking nightmare* is another. But yeah, I'm all right."

The two turn and look at Keller in silence. Muted creaks and hisses from the smasher next door intrude through the adjacent wall.

"You coming back any time soon?" Sahara asks.

Sharon sighs, sitting back onto her stool and resuming her gaze at Keller. She lifts a hand to her ear and tugs absently at the lobe. "Thought I had this one all figured out, you know? Keller was the bastard who turned it all to shite. All of it. His fault. I was happier when I actually believed it."

"What, that isn't how it goes?"

"Not even close."

Sahara's head slides back on her shoulders, her eyes narrow, and she frowns. "Well, now, do tell."

"Still trying to put it all together," Sharon says. "It's a huge jumble, whirling around in my head. But some really big pieces have fallen into place."

"Like?"

"Keller used to be a soldier. Like the Operators here. Did you know that?"

"Keller?" Sahara crosses her arms. "That's a laugh!"

Sharon shakes her head. "He was. And he was bloody damn good at his job, apparently." She looks off through the adjacent wall, listening to the muffled groan and crack of compacting metal.

"He'd been to Cadre Two before. That's how he knew where it was. Actually, we've all been to Cadre Two. We just didn't know it."

"Sorry, I don't follow."

Sharon looks at Sahara with an expression like she is about to deliver bad news, but instead she turns back to the lifeless man on the table.

"Keller was tied in deep to the experiments at Cadre Two. Not pulling the strings, more of an errand boy I think... This was before he took command of the *Europa*. Before any of us knew him. The more I think about it, the more I realize he was used. Willingly, but he was used all the same."

"So he was a hired stooge. I'm missing the part how that doesn't make him a total bastard."

"He hated that it was him and not someone else...that he might be remembered with the likes of Stalin as one of history's all-time killers rattled him to the core. Never seen him cry before."

Sahara leans in, questions rising in a flood from Sharon's disjointed story. Not wanting to interrupt quite yet, she listens.

"All this time, he knew he brought the Eleto on us," Sharon continues, "provoked them to come and murder every one of us they could find. He lived with that every single day, and he said he thought about killing himself. But he couldn't, because he had to find a place for us first. It was something he had to do to buy back at least a part of his soul. Sounded selfish at first, but it really was true. He wouldn't give up."

"Um, sorry, you've lost me."

Sharon turns on the stool to look at her friend. "He wouldn't give up on us, Sahara. He was barely in his thirties, remember, when we shipped out to build New Vancouver. But the planet was too radioactive to settle." Sharon lifts her eyes toward the ceiling. "Hunh. Makes sense now why they shipped us off without sending a full analysis team first... SoVar must've known the Eleto were coming...rushed us out of there."

Sahara's mouth opens to ask a question, but she cannot fathom how to frame it. So she drops her arms to her sides and keeps listening in hope that answers will come.

"When we couldn't land at New Vancouver," Sharon continues, "he started taking double shifts to the rest of us, looking for another planet. He spent the rest of his life searching. Never found a world we could settle. Told me he knew he was getting old and he was desperate to find somewhere safe for us before he died. Knew we'd hang him once we found out he was connected to all of it, but at least we'd be safe. So he brought us here."

"Wait...you're saying he knew about Cadre One, as well? And he brought us here *on purpose?*"

Sharon nods and her eyes glaze over. "Bringing us here was last resort. So it wasn't chance we met with Maiella, Argo, and Thompson. He was checking back on his old stomping grounds to see if anyone was still home."

Sahara reels. "Are you sure? I mean..."

"We found shipping manifests at Cadre Two, bound for Cadre One. Keller's name right at the bottom. There are artificial intelligences there, Sahara, and they knew him...recognized him. So did Mikato, that nutty old codger..."

"Who the hell is Mikato? Darling, you're not making a whole lot of sense."

"Yeah, I think if I had a hundred years I could just about tell you everything." The heavy look comes back across Sharon's face. Sahara tunes in, waiting for the news.

"Damn him for what he did, but...if not him, SoVar would've found someone else to do it. I believe that now."

"You've been through a lot," Sahara says, laying a hand on her friend's arm. "You don't have to sort everything right now. What you're saying is coming out jumbled, anyway. Why not come home? Give yourself some time, and we can work all this through together."

Sharon looks down at her hands and spreads the fingers, then sighs and drops her hands to her lap.

"There won't, actually. The moment I leave this room, he'll be gone. If I don't work this out now, I don't think I ever will."

"Why it should matter if Keller's body is here or not is a mystery to me, but okay, fine." Sahara finds herself a stool against the far wall, picks it up, and plunks it down next to Sharon. Climbing onto it, she pats Sharon's thigh and says, "All right, mate. Tell me what's eating at you."

Sharon smiles at her friend, but when she looks down at Keller the smile turns to a frown.

"Keller held us together through really hard times. We all know he's guilty. Every one of us screamed for his blood. And here's the thing: I don't think anyone else could have gotten us this far. We needed him, Sahara. More than any of us want to admit."

Sahara looks at the emaciated figure lying on the table, wrestling with the idea this man could be anything other than entirely despicable.

"That may be so. How do we see past all the rest?" Sahara asks.

Sharon shrugs. "Been asking myself that. He tried to explain himself to me. I wouldn't listen, naturally. If I had, I might have answered my own question."

"Yeah, you got a hard head sometimes," Sahara says with a grin.

Sharon pops her eyebrows. "Anyway he called me out for being a hypocrite. Pissed me off. Got me listening, though. He was telling me about how everything had happened, and I started thinking about what I would have done in his place. In all honesty I'm not sure I'd have done things that much differently. Except for the bit about leaving Soares and the others behind."

"Soares... He was part of some ice mining expedition that went wrong...an explosion, was that it?"

Sharon looks at her friend. "That was Keller's story, but there was no ice mining expedition. Keller sent them in to Cadre Two, to look around and see if anyone had survived, see if the place was livable. They got trapped, and Keller... He left them behind..." Sharon's eyes close, her shoulders droop as she unloads the burden. "Soares and Michaela burned up in the transport. But Summers and Aaronson... Voss... Rosenthal... *Oh God*!" Sharon dives into her hands.

Sahara wraps an arm around her friend and asking, "What? What was it, girl?"

When Sharon looks up, her eyes are rimmed red, glistening. "Torture," she says, her voice as flat and lifeless as her expression. "Sadistic, evil torture. He murdered them, one cut at a time. And Rosie...strapped to a recliner, harvested for *decades*..."

Sahara shivers. She claps her hands against her upper arms trying to warm herself against a chill much colder than the room's air.

"Well you're the bleeding Navigator, aren't you?" the doctor asks, her unease giving the question more of an edge than intended. "How is it you didn't know what was going on?"

"Different flight crew. I was in Cryo. Soares had my post at the time."

"Well, there must have been a log entry, or way point or *something* that would tell you where the *Europa* had been, right?"

"Keller was the only one on the bridge. He covered his tracks well. I never knew any better."

"Stop," Sahara says, hand raised. "How are we still sitting here pining for this man? If Keller left his own crew to die and then lied about it to the rest of us, the bloke is right evil. Cast 'im off!"

Sharon rubs her damp face, sniffs, and wipes her hands on her pants.

"Sounds simple, yeah? But I saw what was in that place, Sahara. Every hellish thing there tried to rip us open, and I understood what he did was right. If Keller hadn't left as fast as he did, Honniker might have caught the *Europa* and we'd all be getting stretched on his tables." Sharon shakes her head, haunted. "I don't know if I could make that call. Or if I could live with myself afterward."

Sahara looks down at her old captain on the table, the weight of ambivalence making her grimace. "Jaysus... That's a feckin' dose, all right. I think I just caught a cold thinking about it." Her face scrunches up. "After all that, can you imagine pushing on for Cadre One?"

Sharon nods in agreement. "He didn't see any other choice. Then that whole mess with Maiella, Thompson, and Argo? He blamed himself for that, as well. I remember he was hiding behind the consoles with the rest of us, and that wasn't like him at all. He must've been just *gutted*, thinking he'd finally done us all in. I've never had to face a moment like that. I've never had to risk that much. And when I look at him now, I can't believe he held us together through it all."

Sahara nods. "We like our issues wrapped up in pretty little packages, don't we? Good, bad. Right, wrong. It's never like that, is it?"

"Nope. Never is." Sharon falls quiet, staring through walls. "Keller insisted I go with the team out to Cadre Two. Did you know that? Said it was to toughen me up for command. I wanted to smash him with a spanner right then and there because I thought for *certain* that place was going to kill me. But then, we were getting out...we really were getting out of there... And I thought we'd have the whole ride back to come to grips with it all. He gave me some story about an off-switch inside him, something Honniker had done that would kill him if he ever left Cadre Two. I figured he was just afraid to come back and face a trial."

"Off-switch? Don't think I'd believe it, either."

"Yeah, well, he wasn't lying. I'll show you." Sharon moves Keller's hands and pulls back the sheet, revealing a thin pink seam on his chest. "Honniker replaced his heart with a mechanical one, a heart that could be controlled remotely."

Sahara adjusts her specs, squinting to see the fine bead of pink skin and flesh binder. "This is good work," the doctor says. "Who did it?"

"The machines at Cadre Two are alive. One calls itself 'Honniker.' He... *It* did this."

Sahara looks up from Keller's chest. "*Living* machines did this?"

Sharon nods. "Just as we were getting away, he collapsed. We tried to...we *tried*, but...but we *couldn't*..."

Sharon bows her head, tears coming fast. Sahara embraces her friend, trying to cope with all the bizarre things she has heard, wondering how much more there might be to hear.

"I hated him *so fucking much*," Sharon sobs into her friend's shoulder, "I didn't want to hear his reasons. I didn't *want* there to be reasons, I just wanted to hate him for what he'd done! I don't know why it was so easy to hate him. Now that he's gone, I... I can't believe how much I want to say. It's too late, now. *It's too late!*"

"You can tell me," Sahara offers.

Sharon sniffs hard and looks up through red, puffed eyes. Embarrassed, she peels herself away and sets herself back on her stool.

"I want to confess something. Will you swear you won't repeat it?"

Sahara holds up her pinky. "On pain of death."

Sharon gazes into Keller's face. "He was so handsome. So confident. I loved him, once."

Sahara smirks. "Ah, that's no secret, girl."

Sharon looks over in shock.

"Caught you staring more'n once," Sahara continues. "Big doe eyes when you thought no one was lookin'." Sahara's smirk straightens and she looks at the floor. "Hurts more when someone close lets you down. I figured you'd hate this prick more'n anyone. More the fool, I am."

"I turned on him. Just like everyone else." Sharon's raps her fists against her thighs. "I had four months in the transport. I can't believe this is all coming out now!"

"I'm thinking a ride full of Operators would make a lousy support group."

Sharon snorts. "Maiella tried, at least." Her expression blanks and she stares through the wall again. "Gor, that girl... You wouldn't believe what she can do, Sahara. I didn't think anything in the universe could be so deadly. Still trying to wrap my head around it, and I was there."

Sahara draws her arms in again.

"What, like on the *Europa*, when—?"

"God no!" Sharon counters. With less certainty she adds, "Eh. Sort of. What happened on the *Europa* was mistaken identity, no question. What I mean is at Cadre Two we were up against it, and she fought to the gristle. I had no idea what it really takes to survive." She looks directly at Keller. "What you have to do, what you have to face... So many times, I was ready to lie down...so much easier. But to keep fighting, to never give up... I had no idea how strong you really have to be." Sharon looks down into her own hands, sees the slick moisture. "A fine officer I turned out to be. Can you believe the old man actually suggested I should take command? Punch drunk old sod..."

"Not such a bad call, really. Maybe you need to ease into the idea."

Sharon snorts. "Hah! There was a time, but I'm not ambitious anymore."

"You say Keller preferred you? Did he say why?"

"He said Javier was an aristocrat, that he knew how to look down on people, not lead them."

Sahara arches her eyebrows and sighs.

"What, was he right?" Sharon digs.

"Yeah, unfortunately. Ortega expected the chain of command would remain, that he would step in for Keller and everyone would fall in line. Herzfeld challenged him, and it got ugly before Ortega folded. Threw up his hands and walked off like a pissy teenager. I tell you, Sharon, things are not good. We really need you back, if you can."

Sharon looks at her friend, sees the urgency in deepened lines of her face. "You mean, I can't sit here like a mopey little schoolgirl anymore?"

Sahara shakes her head. "Not what I'm saying at all."

Sharon stands from her stool, takes Keller's cold limp hand in hers and replaces it on his chest. "So much I need to say to you, Braemar, but I missed my chance. Makes it hard to let you go, you know?" She swallows the lump in her throat and glances at Sahara. "But I have to get on with it, yeah? Yeah, I do."

Sharon caresses his bristly cheek, leans over and kisses his forehead. "Good-bye, old man. I miss you."

Sahara places a hand on Sharon's shoulder, seeing Keller differently than when she first walked in.

Maybe not a monster, after all, the doctor thinks.

"I'm ready," Sharon says.

"Sure?"

"Yeah."

As the two women walk out together, Reconstitutes at the back wall animate. One takes a hooked blade and a bone saw from the magnetic rack. The other attaches a long brass needle to the end of a thick red hose. The door slides shut and reclamation begins.

SOONER THE BETTER

Thompson roams the *Europa's* halls in faded coveralls. The upper half fits too snugly in the shoulders, pulling the top open into a wide V at his chest. The sleeves, split under the arms to accommodate his biceps, are rolled to the elbow. High-water pant legs end several centimeters above his boots. The waist, however, is ample, bunched into pleats by a wide belt.

Armed with a pistol-gripped scan tool in one hand and a data tablet in the other, he stops at printed tags marking recent repairs. New pipe fittings, electrical junctions, welds, distribution hubs, and motors receive careful inspection and sweeps of the scan tool's beam. If all is satisfactory, he marks the repair 'complete' and strikes it from his list in the tablet. If not, he updates the tag with the reason for failure and schedules a follow-up repair.

Simple work passes time in what feels like a productive manner, every completed task a step closer toward restoring the *Europa* to her proper condition. Yet the list in Thompson's tablet contains thousands of identified problems. With an unhappy glance at the walls, he wonders how many more have not been found, how many that will become apparent at the most inopportune time.

Keep going, he thinks. *Ship can't fix herself.*

His list takes him by one of the two dining halls, and activity inside makes him pause by the entrance. At the far wall, several MedTechs cluster around a partially disassembled food machine. They pore over the inner workings, studying and probing, pointing out differences and punching notes into a tablet of their own.

Reverse engineering the solution for Cadre One? It's about time they got around to that.

He leaves them to their study.

His next stop is a bare metal panel, swirled with abrasion marks. It swings easily on its hinges, and behind the panel Thompson finds a rebuilt electrical node. The inside of the box is still black with soot, but all of the burnt cables have been trimmed back and spliced with new terminals. Each repaired cable is plugged into a remanufactured junction. Tiny diodes pulse above each socket.

A coiled cable hangs from the inside of the panel door, which he takes. One end he plugs into a diagnostic port on the junction, the other he plugs into the base of his scanner. In seconds, the tool analyses the junction's health and displays a series of green bars.

"Good, good," he says to himself, marking the job complete in his tablet. "They finally fixed this one right."

The Gun disconnects his scanner, hangs the cable back on the panel door and closes it. Consulting his tablet, he sees the next repair is a third of the ship's length away, so in the monotonous walk toward it he lets his mind wander.

What did they find at Cadre Two? Losing two Geeks, a Gun, a Brick, and the Enyo... He shakes his head. *Can't imagine* anything *being worth all that.*

Thompson passes a weld point in the hull like many others he has already inspected. This one is a complete circle, however, roughly a meter across. He stops and his arms go slack when he recognizes the cut.

This is where it all went wrong...

He lifts a hand and feels the raised metal scar.

...where Argo, Maiella, and I came through, weapons free.

Self-loathing stirs in his gut, but he crushes it.

It's done. There's nothing you can do about it. Get back to work.

The weld is tagged with satisfactory repair, but he sweeps his scan tool around the full circumference, anyway.

Green bars. Good.

He strides off to the next on his list, waving or nodding at Colonists he passes on the way.

Now that Argo's back in the Corps, I'll probably never see him to ask about Cadre Two. But where is Maiella? Thought I'd have seen her by now. Maybe she's as busy as everyone else. Plenty of work to go around, that's for sure.

And what about Beckert? Has he really taken Anders' old post? Makes sense, physically, but is he equal to Anders' intellect? If he's that smart, I should have asked for more of his input on our rotation. So why didn't I?

He scowls.

Because he isn't Maiella, that's why.

The thought stings his conscience, rankling his Operator discipline.

Got too attached to my team. Should have been rotating in other Operators for balance. But the three of us together...we were good*... Every rotation, we came through. What we had worked. Argo and Maiella were the best of the Corps. I knew what they could do, and they knew what I'd ask before I asked it. You don't get that high-level calibration when you swap teammates every other mission, and... Hold up...*

Thompson halts, taking a careful look at his surroundings. The turns of the corridors, the distance between each intersection along the way, the patched up plating are all uncomfortably familiar. Random small holes, filled with epoxy, dot the walls. Several wall plates are wrinkled with hammered-out dents. Some of the doorways have no doors.

Every filled hole, a shot from my rifle. Every hammered-out dent, a ricochet from Maiella's pistols... And every doorframe without its door, a blast from Argo's cannon...

I'm walking our path to the bridge. I've avoided these corridors for years.

Thompson lowers his head, intent on getting away and taking another route to his next job; but when he spots a tight cluster of perforations, right at chest height, he stops and stares. The old wish for disintegration seeps in, perching like a crow on his shoulder and pecking words into his ear.

Murder. The worst of all crimes.

The old Gun forces himself to not look away, forces himself to stand and confront the proof of his actions.

Always remember what you've done. You owe them that. And more. Much more.

Thompson lifts his head and moves on, taking a more thoughtful tour, pausing where a colonist fell to his team, reliving the moments when they were mere blobs of heat in his infrared vision, how they screamed and lurched as they were cut down. And after the attack was over, identifying the bodies, the reading of names...

In time, Thompson comes to the warped circular entryway of the *Europa's* Bridge. The blast doors are cut down to their roots and he visually traces the framing.

The way Argo peeled 'em, no amount of hammering would ever get 'em flat again. Not like they slowed him much, anyway...

On the far side of the portal is his next task: a printed tag, dangling from a panel of buttons. Thompson heads straight for it, casting a casual glance into the bridge as he crosses the entryway.

In the navigator's chair sits a Geek Thompson does not recognize. The young Operator is armored up to his neck, HDI riding on the silver contact terminals of his shaved head. The Geek's helmet is parked on the console looking back at him. Its visor reflects leisurely pulses of his goggles.

Major Chusan stands dead center of the bridge where Keller's chair used to be, wearing his charcoal grays and a slim headset. Halgrim, Maddock, and Dagmar attend the burn-scarred major in full kit, faceplates raised, weapons slung over their shoulders. They nod as Chusan gives them orders.

"Dismissed," Chusan states, and the three Operators salute before departing.

Thompson arrives at the tagged panel, reads the notes on the printed tag, and props the panel open. As the Operators stride by, Thompson looks over at them. Dagmar and Maddock pay him no attention, but Halgrim casts a glance that is difficult to decipher. The Brick looks with narrowed eyes, eyebrows gathered slightly together, mouth a straight line.

Thompson watches the Brick march away and turn out of sight, marveling at Halgrim's size.

He almost fills the corridor... Great strength, sure, but a large target. A Brick that size...is it practical?

"Progress?" Chusan demands.

Thompson turns and finds the major only a meter away, staring directly at him.

"The tagging system was a good idea, sir," Thompson answers. "We're able to track Colonist techs and hold them to account for poor repairs. Finally getting some good work out of them."

"We were getting *no* work from them before we took over here. But they resent my Operators' supervision. I think they value this notion of 'liberty' more than their own survival."

"They can't be free if they're dead, sir."

"My thought *precisely*." Chusan leans forward to glance at the tablet in Thompson's hand. "How far down your list are you?"

"This is the last of my current assignment. I'll be ready for another once I finish here."

Chusan leans back on to his heels. He lifts his head slightly, looks down his flattened nose. "You're on the Colonist schedule. You've finished a twelve-hour shift, that means you're due for rest."

"With respect, Major, that's a short shift. And I've been idle too long. There's much to be done."

"That's a fact. And little time to do it."

Thompson tilts his head. "Has something come up?"

Chusan's eyes narrow shrewdly. "We must always be ready, at a moment's notice. Have you forgotten?"

"Not ever, sir." Thompson turns to the panel and triggers his scan tool at the repaired circuit board inside. The display on the tool shows green bars, so he updates the tag and marks the task 'complete' in his tablet.

"Tell me something," Chusan says, crossing his thick arms and widening his stance. "You've lived among the Colonists. Can you tell me why they are unable to take care of themselves? What makes them so weak and dysfunctional?"

Thompson closes the panel slowly, thinking of an appropriate reply. "The Colonists value strength and efficiency almost as much as the Cadre. But the difference is that they want it to come from one of their own, not an outsider."

"Go on."

"Keller was their strength. He held this crew together, and they were accustomed to his leadership. Now that he's gone, there's a vacuum they struggle to fill, because not one of the Colonists is like Keller. They want strong leadership. The problem is they don't know how to be strong."

"Perhaps you can teach them."

"Me? I'm not one of them, sir. Their ways are not mine."

Chusan looks Thompson up and down, his eyes stopping at the high-water cuffs above his Cadre-issued boots.

"I can see that. Colonist life suits you as well as those coveralls. You look ridiculous. Did they have nothing else for you to wear?"

"They had some that were thicker in the middle. Nothing that was longer."

"And your uniform? What have you done with that?"

Thompson stiffens. "Sir, I'm no longer worthy of Cadre Grays."

"That's not for you to decide."

Thompson looks directly at Chusan, sees the major's hard, steel-gray eyes peering at him between layers of skin grafts.

"Is the major suggesting something?"

"The major is *suggesting* nothing. I'm *telling* you that Argo found his way back to the Corps. As long as he stays away from Maiella, he'll remain."

Chusan squints at Thompson's thinned arms, narrowed shoulders and chest.

"But you're unfit, underweight. A new uniform would hang on you like a bunk sheet. What are you doing about that?"

"I'm on a regimen of weight-training and aerobic exercise—"

"On Colonist rations?" Chusan interrupts.

"Aye, sir."

"You'll never get there, and we don't have time to wait. I'll see to it you get proper intervals."

"Sir, you've mentioned a shortness of time twice now. Are we prepping for action?"

"If we were, would that motivate the Colonists?"

"Would more likely alarm them, make them more scared than usual."

"And we see how much they get done when they're alarmed and scared. So what do you recommend?"

Again, he didn't answer the question, Thompson thinks, but he replies, "The work is good for them. Gives them something better to do than gripe. To *keep* them working, however, we need to give them incentives, not orders."

"*In-senn-tivs*? I don't know this term."

"When they do something you want, give them something they want in return."

"What could I give them that they'd want?"

"You should talk to the Counselor. He can guide you."

"I'm asking you."

Thompson looks down at his scan tool in thought. "Recognition would be a good start. I was thinking of these repairs, in fact."

"Yes?"

"A Colonist likes to hear what they're doing well. Makes them feel valued and respected. Like when we'd bring in a good haul from Rotation. That feeling we were doing good for others, that we were providing... Was all I needed."

Chusan nods with interest. "What shall we recognize?"

"If I tally the number of these jobs that were done right the first time, and mark the tech assigned to the job, I'll find the most efficient Colonist workers. We share that with everyone. Give them pride in good work. More motivating than calling them 'weak' and 'dysfunctional.'"

"You have a completed list there. Tell me who rates highest."

Thompson thumbs in the data query. Five names appear on screen, and he hands the tablet to Chusan.

The major glances at the list and scoffs. "The highest rating on this list is only ninety-two percent." He looks up from the tablet, incredulous. "Eight percent of all repair efforts fail? And that's their *best*? That's not something to be proud of."

"It's a start, Major."

Chusan looks down at the tablet again and frowns. "I don't want to know what the worst rating could be."

"We need to focus on the positive, and build on it."

"The positive, you say?" Chusan shakes his head. "All right. When task lists are distributed, the top five Colonist Techs in efficiency will be at the heading where all can see them. I'm told that competition might work, as well. Should we break them up into teams?"

"That's a good idea, so long as we rotate the members often. Don't want to breed an 'us versus them' mentality. Too much of that in the crew already." Thompson thinks a moment. "The winning team will expect a prize, however."

"*Pry-ze?*"

"Elite status over their fellows, a special award or privilege. Doesn't have to be much. Just something they find enjoyable."

Chusan hands the tablet back. "It strains belief we have to reinforce behaviors that *don't* lead to extinction. Thompson, your plan is approved. I'll leave it to you to figure out what the award or privilege will be. Work with the Counselor if you must. Now then, if you're ready for more assignments, here they come." Over his shoulder, Chusan barks out, "*Kibwe!*"

"Sir!" answers the Geek seated in the pilot's chair.

"Send Thompson a new work assignment. And surrender your nutrition interval."

The Geek's goggles strobe momentarily then he reaches down to the floor beside him. "Incoming!" the Geek shouts, and he lobs a plasticine wrapped bar to the major. Chusan catches it without looking and offers it to Thompson.

Thompson looks at the bar in Chusan's hand.

Is this the right way to go?

Thompson takes the bar and drops it into a deep pocket of his coveralls, then checks his tablet. A fresh list of installations populates his schedule, and his eyes widen when he skims the hardware list.

"Stealth Generators for the *Europa*?"

"That's correct," Chusan states. "Can you handle that?"

"Aye, sir."

"Your insights were valuable. Now get back to work." Chusan turns and strides back toward his post.

"Major," Thompson calls.

Chusan halts and turns about, the hairless skin of his brow raised expectantly.

"You never answered my question," Thompson says.

"That's right. I didn't." Chusan stares at Thompson without interest or irritation.

"Sir, if I may be bold, what did Shao-Lo find at Cadre Two?"

"That information is shared with Leadership Council and the Operator Corps. No one else."

Thompson feels a flush of frustration at Chusan's obstinacy, but he restrains himself from expressing it. Instead, he asks, "Then tell me this: was it worth it?"

Chusan turns squarely toward Thompson, his face rigid and serious. "Yes, it was."

The major returns to the center of the bridge, gazing into an array of holowindows, hands clasped behind his back. Various areas of the colony ship cycle through the windows like a rotating security feed.

"That's all you're going to get, Thompson, no matter how long you stand there. You said, yourself, there's much work to be done. Sooner, the better."

By the time Chusan looks over his shoulder again, Thompson is gone.

*****

The old Gun winds his way back toward his cabin, mind spinning with the hints Chusan dropped. He pulls at the collar of his ill-fitting coveralls, embarrassed by them, and he thinks about his faded, threadbare uniform. Like his rifle, his uniform is second nature, something familiar from a better time. Having heard Chusan say he could once again be suited for Cadre Grays makes him long for the comfortable fit.

At each junction, he looks about, hoping to catch a glimpse of Maiella. Oddly, he sees no one at all in the quiet hallways.

Maybe they're at one of their big meetings again, he thinks. *They're* always *at meetings.*

He looks down at himself once more.

You do *look ridiculous. Time you were dressed properly.*

Thompson turns from his work detail for a brief trip to his cabin.

Don't want Maiella seeing me like this, he thinks, and it surprises him how important it feels to be back in his uniform, how correct Chusan was when he said that Colonist life fits as well as his coveralls. It is absurdity for him to try being anything other than what he is: a Cadre Operator, bred to serve through and through.

Argo and I, brothers again in honorable service...

The idea brings a smile to his face, until he considers the flip side.

Would they ever let Maiella back? Likely not.

The tall soldier stands at the door of his cabin, hesitating before entering.

I don't want to be separated from either of them again. Will I have to choose one or the other?

He enters the lock code on the door panel, and his cabin opens. At the back of it stands a tall, slender woman with square shoulders, curved hips, back toward him. Form-fitting olive drab trousers are tucked into tall black boots. Her stretch black t-shirt is tucked in at the waist. Polished gold contact terminals gleam above her close-cropped hair. When she turns, he sees a familiar face of old and new scars. Her brown eyes are cautious.

"MAIELLA!"

At the sound of her name, and the excitement in his voice, she smiles. Thompson crosses to her in an instant and hauls her in close. The sight of her, the feel of her, the smell of her banishes every other concern in his mind.

"Missed you," she says at last. She pushes back to look up at him then leans in and presses her lips firmly against his.

Confused by the contact, but enjoying the sensation, he is sure he feels her tongue swipe between his parted lips. His eyes close, concentrating on her movements, how one of her hands has reached behind the small of his back and pulls him against her, how her other hand holds the back of his neck, how she rubs the soft flesh of her chest ever so slightly against him, and how the tips are so much firmer than the rest.

She pulls her head back, letting his lower lip slide between hers, and draws a stuttering breath.

"You have *no idea* how much," Maiella says. Her face is flushed; her body radiates warmth. An inviting undertone in her voice makes the hairs of his body stand at attention.

"I missed you, too," is all he can think of to say.

She nods hurriedly, kisses him again, then pushes him, shuffling her feet, guiding him back toward his bunk. He slides along, letting her steer him until he feels the edge of the frame behind his legs.

Maiella puts a hand at the center of his chest and shoves him down onto the bunk. Straddling his leg, she works the tight-fitting coveralls from his shoulders.

He has no idea what is happening, not a single clue, but he wants it to continue. The movement of her thighs against his, her focused attention, her warm breath, the sensitivity of his skin at her touch is exhilarating in a way never felt before. He leans toward her, pulling out her tucked in t-shirt. There is humidity of perspiration, the faintest scent, alluring and exciting.

Maiella falls down on top of him, knocking him flat. She lays herself astride him, hugging his neck, rocking her hips, kissing him hard.

He allows his hands to explore the firmness of her strength, the smoothness of her shape, the way her clothing clings to her and accentuates her new curves. Punching through the layers of his operator conditioning is an inexplicable urge to combine with this woman, to fall into her in some way that he does not comprehend. The sensations are so odd they seem wrong, as though he has gotten a taste of something dangerous, something the Cadre fears enough to utterly suppress with hard drugs and dogmatic code. He wants to indulge it, to keep it going, to finally experience what the Colonists talk about constantly...but there is work to do.

"Maiella..." he mumbles with her mouth on his.

She pulls back, looking him in the eye. With the slightest pout, she says, "You're on duty."

"Yeah."

Maiella's eyes roll. As she slides off, she groans for emphasis, "*Fine.*"

With reluctance, she rises from the bunk, and, with reluctance, he lets her go. But his eyes follow her movements with an appetite all their own.

The Gun sits up at the edge of his bunk and loosens the laces of his boots. "Just came in to get changed. This colonist clothing doesn't work for me."

Maiella smirks. "Got that right. Happy to help you out of it." She looks at him through the mirror above the hygiene station and arches her eyebrow.

"Won't be a moment," he says, missing her innuendo entirely. Thompson kicks his boots off by the heels and rips the coveralls down to his feet before stepping out of them.

Maiella turns and reclines against the basin, hands behind her, watching him strip to his thin white undersuit. Her face scrunches.

"Don't they feed you here?"

Thompson grimaces. "Yeah, just got an earful from Chusan about that." He pulls a plasticine wrapped bar from the pocket of the coveralls and tosses it onto the table. Maiella glances at the bar as if it was some kind of silver vermin.

"You don't need *that*," she says as he heads to his wardrobe and opens it. With a sly smile, she adds, "I think we just need to find you a better workout."

Thompson pulls out a hanger with his faded gray uniform. Maiella winces when she sees it and turns away to look at her reflection.

"Chusan wouldn't say a thing about Cadre Two," Thompson says, stepping into his uniform trousers. "Said it was for Leadership Council and Operators only." He pauses in thought. "The way he said it, seemed like he was saying I should work my way back to the Corps, like Argo did."

Maiella's ears slide back, and she squelches a grimace. "Is that so?" Her eyes drop to the basin.

"Yeah. I mean, what could be valuable enough to trade so many Operators and the *Enyo*?" He takes his uniform coat off the hanger and pauses. "Keller, too." He shakes his head and punches his arms through the sturdy garment. "All Chusan said was it was worth it, but that's hard to believe."

The Gun retrieves his boots and slides his feet into them.

"You're quiet all of a sudden," he says.

"Hmm? Yeah, well." Maiella turns to face him and crosses her arms. "You want a hand on your shift? Can tell you what you want to know along the way."

"Definitely." He tucks his trouser legs into his boots and draws his laces tight. "Plenty to do around here. Would be good to have someone who knows their way around a welder's torch."

Thompson stands and fastens the front of his uniform coat. All the decoration has been stripped of it, making it little more than clothing, but wearing it, he feels taller.

"So, should I ask how you got in?" he says. "After the sabotage, we've been ordered to keep our cabins locked."

"I'm all fixed up," Maiella answers, pointing to her head. "Not like I needed to be. Security here is pathetic." The mirth in her eyes is gone as she looks Thompson up and down in his Cadre Grays.

"Doctor Taggart figured out how to fix you?" the Gun asks.

"No. It was at Cadre Two. They knew how to fix me."

"They?"

"I'll tell you about it on the shift. But yeah. I'm all fixed. Better maybe."

She could get back to the Corps, as well... he thinks. *All three of us, together again...*

Thompson smooths down his uniform. "How do I look?"

"Great," Maiella says with tight jaw. "Got your gear?"

While Thompson collects his tablet and scan tool, Maiella collects her HDI, stealthily pocketing a media card with a hand-drawn heart that she had left on the basin. On her way out, she claps Thompson on the back and says,

"You won't believe what I have to tell you about the Counselor."

MASTER CLASS

Sharon strides deliberately toward the *Europa's* meeting hall. Her uniform coveralls are faded and worn, yet clean. Her brown hair is tied neatly back in a short ponytail, and she wrings her hands, trying to organize all the thoughts in her head into a coherent speech. But every few paces, a half-completed repair or a patch of hazy graffiti steals her concentration.

Can't believe the state the ship's in, she thinks. *Taking everyone off refit for another meeting is a risk, but...even in our worst days, I've never seen the crew like this.*

Chusan wouldn't lie, I know... It just strains belief... Javier attacked? Sabotage? Here? It's all too much, really.

We've got to get past this fighting and bickering! And they've got to know about Keller. They deserve to hear it, whether they like it or not.

Intersections pass quickly by, the alphanumeric markers at the corners telling her exactly how close she is to the meeting hall. Then she hears them, the full assembly's merged voices telegraphing through the bones of the ship, and the colony vessel feels much smaller than before. Adrenaline electrifies her fingertips and dampens her palms.

What would Keller do? Probably grab someone by the lower lip and tell them how it's gonna be. Just get right to it. Like chopping wood. Don't dally, don't try to soften it. Just bring the axe down and make the cut.

When Sharon rounds the last bend, she finds the Counselor is outside the entrance to the meeting hall. Two Cadre Guns attend him in full kit, faceplates sealed. The Counselor welcomes her with friendly smile. But his appearance is identical to the eccentric genius she met at Cadre Two—a man who realized too late he had given his people the power to completely destroy themselves. Regardless how long she has lived with the Counselor aboard the *Europa*, she finds it difficult to look at him now.

"I met your maker, Counselor," she says.

"Really?" he asks, hopeful.

"You look exactly like him," Sharon says, finally making eye contact. "Did you know that?"

The Counselor nods. "I did."

"You're not going to tell me you knew about Cadre Two, as well, are you?"

"No, no. Doctor Mikato worked from his labs on Earth when he shaped me. But that was a long time ago. I assumed he died there with everyone else." The Counselor dips his head momentarily. "Was he lucid? Was he...sane?"

"He was an *icicle* when we arrived. Don't think the lengthy cryo suspension did his mood any favors, but I get the impression he's more or less as he was. At least he used to be."

"Is...Doctor Mikato no longer alive?"

"He took his own life as we left. Said he was paying a debt, or some such bollocks."

The corners of the Counselor's mouth turn down and he clasps his hands.

"You all right?" Sharon asks.

"The closest person I had to a father was just resurrected and then died again in the span of thirty seconds. The information is difficult to collate. But, please, come. The crew needs to hear from you." He gestures towards the closed doors.

Sharon hikes a thumb at the Operators and asks, "How long have they been here?"

"Months, I'm afraid. There were some acts of violence, even sabotage."

"Yeah, Chusan clued me in when I came aboard. Can't say that was an easy pill to swallow." Sharon looks up at rusty stains on the ceiling. "Proof of it's all around, though."

"People do strange and desperate things in times of crisis. Without strong leadership, it's worse."

Sharon levels her gaze at the Counselor. "Javier had command. How could this have happened?"

"Captain Ortega folded."

"Javier *folded*?"

The Counselor nods reluctantly. "He couldn't cut through the hatred and distrust, so he gave up. It got scary for a while, then O'Kai ordered

Chusan in to restore control. Plenty are nursing some big swelling lumps, but they're alive. Would have been deaths, otherwise, I'm sure of it. The problem now is the Cadre's like an occupying power. All that hatred and distrust has focused on them."

"Gor... It's a right bleeding mess, yeah?"

The Counselor nods again. "Yes, it is. C'mon, let's go on in."

The Guns step aside, and the Counselor punches the door panel. A dull roar pours through the widening gap with hundreds of Colonists all chatting, shouting, arguing, in dozens of simultaneous conversations. Those nearest the entrance turn to the open doorway, and ripples of quiet spread from them, fanning out across the crowd.

The Guns step through first and take guard positions on each side of the doorway, earning scowls and hisses. When Sharon and the Counselor step through, however, Colonist faces brighten with pleasant surprise.

As Sharon walks the path to the platform, sunny greetings from the colonists are followed by rapid-fire questions about Cadre Two.

"What was at Cadre Two?"

"Is anyone alive there?"

"Is it safe to go?"

Sharon nods, making eye contact, smiling fondly at friends she has not seen in nearly two years, and answers loudly, *"Hold on, we're going to cover it, I assure you!"*

Before she is half-way to the platform the questions take an ugly turn. Angry faces shove their way through the crush, hounding her for answers.

"Where's Keller hiding, Lieutenant?"

"The bastard still at Cadre Two? Why isn't he here?"

"He's got a trial comin'! We'll go get 'im if we have to!"

"Better tell us, Jones!"

Sharon looks away and focuses on the platform, ignoring the hostile shouts. She climbs the short stairway and takes the microphone from the stand. Hall speakers thump from the microphone's rough handling, and the navigator looks out into a sea of people with faces gnarled in loathing.

"KELLER IS DEAD," she says into the mic.

Expressions turn from anger to suspicion then turn sour with vengeance spoiled. There is a slight lull in the shouts, replaced by muttered curses. Sharon seizes the moment.

"I don't expect that satisfies any of you. Not that it could. Even if I told you *how* he died. That it was long and agonizing. That he was tortured before he died. Yes, he was *tortured*. And I don't expect that will satisfy anyone in the least. Because it didn't satisfy me."

She looks out across the crowd. A few grumbles pass back and forth near the back, but nearly every eye is on her.

"I wonder, do you think I'm going to make excuses for him? Do you think I'm going to tell you what a good man he was?"

Sharon lets the question hang, daring anyone to answer it.

"Well I can't do that. In fact, I could tell you all sorts of other things we didn't know about that would make you hate him more. But what's the point? You all know as well as I do what Keller did as a younger man. And even a long, painful death won't make that any easier to accept.

"I'll tell you this much, though: when he was our captain, this crew was united. Now that he's gone, we're on the verge of tearing ourselves and this ship apart. Do any of you think that's coincidence?"

Sharon looks into as many faces as she can, searching for any sign of argument. There are sullen glances, crossed arms, and frowns, but nothing that begs to differ.

"I'm not going to tell you what to believe," Sharon continues. "All I can do is tell you what I know. I've served as the *Europa's* navigator since we left Earth orbit, and that entire time Keller was our captain. I looked up to him, not just as a superior officer, but as a man. I admired him, never doubted him. We were alone out here. The last of our kind." She pauses, weighing the silence of the sullen audience. "I could take it, because I had a captain who knew where he was taking me. Just a matter of time, I thought. We'd make it, eventually.

"Then we find out our captain is one of the reasons we were alone out here in the first place! Maybe it wasn't his idea to slaughter Lizards, but he followed his orders well. How ironic that a man who brought humanity to the brink of extinction became responsible for its last survivors... Can you even *imagine*? Try it on for a moment."

Some in the crowd huff with dismissive smirks and mutter to crewmates. Others grimace or look away. The rest wait and listen with eyes narrowed in suspicion or interest.

"I didn't know why I was called for the Cadre Two trip," Sharon continues. "I was glad to be of assistance, of course. But once aboard the *Enyo*, I saw Keller. He pulled some strings to get me on the mission, and that got me boiling, let me tell you. I wanted nothing to do with him. Was hard to look at him, because the image I'd built was smashed. That man was *not* who I thought he was; he would never live up to what I'd made him out to be. And on top of all that, this man, who seemed so sure of where he was taking us, had NO BLOODY CLUE WHERE WE WERE GOING. All I wanted was to get away from him. But I couldn't. Had to keep chaffing against him, had to face that he was really just a man, after all. Not *Captain* Keller, not a kill-crazy demon, just Keller. Old, broken down Keller.

"Wasn't until we were on our way home...after he'd died...that I really started thinking about what it must've been like to be him. And I started to understand what a burden it really is being responsible for us all, that one person could *truly* make the survival of mankind their reason for being, that *anyone* could follow through on that responsibility day after day. *Knowing* there's no hope but manufacturing it in sufficient quantity for all of us to get a share. Could I do that? For a day? A week? A month?

"He tried to explain to me the level of devotion required, but I didn't want to understand. With his last breath, he *proved* what devotion truly means. Even I couldn't argue it anymore. And too late, I realized that this person who I hated so deeply...he loved us more than we could possibly know.

"I see some of you are struggling with that. I don't blame you. But again, I ask you to look inside yourselves and try to find a time when Keller acted selfishly, or abused us. Because I can't remember a time like that."

Sharon bows her head. The hall is still.

"I was with him at the end," she says softly, and when she looks up, her eyes are damp. "It surprised me how conflicted I was. Even after we'd howled for his blood, promised him red justice...he never gave up on us. None of us would have come back from Cadre Two if it weren't for Keller. He knew getting us out would cost him his life. And he gave it."

Emotion, suppressed for the sake of professionalism, surges. Tears stream down her cheeks. She groans, pressing the water from her eyes.

"*I can't hate him anymore,*" she says as forcefully as she can. "I *won't.*"

The Counselor pulls a white cloth from his pocket and offers it.

"Mm, *ta,*" Sharon says, and when she looks out across the crowd again, she sees less anger, less vehemence.

"There's something we have to decide," Sharon says to the assembly, "and this is more important than anything else. Like it or not, Keller is gone. And like it or not, we need someone to take his place. We have to find that strength among ourselves, because to be blunt, we can't have the Cadre baby sitting us anymore."

Coarse shouts of assent come from pockets among the crowd.

"Glad you agree! Because it's embarrassing, yeah? Doesn't matter who we choose, we need someone calling our shots *right now*. Whoever we choose, we have to *trust* them and stand behind them, *one hundred percent.*

So we're going to vote, *right now*. Herzfeld? Where are you? Get up here."

Herzfeld emerges from the crowd, his eyebrows bunched in suspicion. Sharon waves him up to the platform, and the man steps warily up the stairs.

"Counselor," Sharon calls, "you stand beside Herzfeld."

"I'm sorry, Commander, but I—"

"Shut it, Counselor. You'll get your chance in a minute. Gregor? Where the hell are you?"

Sharon scans the crowd and finds the Russian all the way at the back. He grimaces and waves a flat hand at his throat, shaking his head while he does so.

"Lieutenant Petrova, get your ass on this platform, *pronto*."

Gregor looks left and looks right, uncrosses his arms and makes his way through the crowd.

"Now, then. Commander Ortega, come forward, if you please."

"He's still down at Cadre One, the pompous *ass*," a nearby voice yells.

"Oh? Has he been there long?" Sharon asks, pretending she did not already know.

"Since he ran away, the baby!"

"Rather be in the Cadre, now..."

"Fuck that guy!"

"Ho, whoa, *whoa*! Back it up!" Sharon calls out. "Maybe he cracked under the pressure, but Javier's a good man. Besides, no one knows the colony apparatus as well as he does. Doesn't matter who gets picked for command, Ortega is going to come back to this crew, because *we don't throw people away*. Not him and not any of you."

Sharon takes a step forward and leans against the platform railing.

"All right, who else? C'mon, this is your chance. Throw your hat in now or hold your peace."

Many anxious faces turn to one another, enthusiasm wilting visibly.

"Hmm?" Sharon calls. "Let's go. Put your hand up where I can see it and I'll call you up. This is your chance to be in charge of everything. It's your chance to be responsible for the entire ship and everyone you know. C'mon, people, don't hold back."

The crowd shifts uncomfortably, and the ones most agitated at Sharon's entrance are the ones most muted now.

Gregor ascends the steps like a man at the gallows. He swallows hard and stands at attention, gazing out at the crowd.

Herzfeld rests a hand on Sharon's shoulder and speaks into her ear.

"You can't seriously expect this to stand, Commander. You don't just come in here and *call an election*, it's out of—"

Muting her microphone, Sharon spits back, "*Shut your fucking mouth*, Jonah, you're going to win by default. The Counselor's going to excuse himself, and no one else is thick enough to want the job."

"What, you'd just *hand* it over?"

"Yeah. You want it so fucking bad, you can have it. And if calling you, 'Sir', means we can pull ourselves together and get on with it, then *that's* what we're going to do."

Herzfeld's eyebrows lift, and he grunts. He steps back from Sharon and crosses his arms.

Switching the microphone back on, Sharon calls, "Last chance. Let me see some hands, yeah? No? No one else? Better be sure, because this is it."

Not a single person in the crowd raises a hand.

"*Done*. We have our candidates for election. The Counselor, Lieutenant Gregor Petrova, and Professor Jonah Herzfeld. All will have five minutes to make their case. We'll start with the Counselor."

Sharon thrusts the microphone into the Counselor's hands. He tries to give it back, but she refuses and points out to the audience. Glum, the lab-coated therapist takes the mic and faces the assembly.

"Friends," he says, "this is truly a high honor you offer me, but I'm sorry, I *must* decline candidacy. My role is to counsel, to advise. The moment I have authority over anyone, my motives become suspect. I can *advocate*, I can *serve*. I will continue to give my all in any way for you, except this. I *cannot* accept authority over others. Thank you for your consideration, but on this point I am resolute."

The Counselor passes the microphone back to Sharon.

"Thank you, Counselor," Sharon says. She turns to Gregor, and the Russian's eyes are large and round, his mouth a short straight line. Sharon plants the microphone in his unwilling grip, claps him on the shoulder and says, "Your turn."

Gregor stands at attention and says gravely, "I would accept this post only if every other candidate had refused. I believe in service, and I'm proud you've trusted me this far. But I do not crave this position and I cannot look you all in the eye and say I know everything I need to be captain. Until I've had greater experience, I humbly ask that you look elsewhere. I withdraw my candidacy. Thank you."

He passes the microphone back to Sharon, whispering, "Permission to be dismissed, ma'am?"

"Granted," Sharon replies. The Russian hustles down the steps and folds back into the crowd.

"Well," Sharon says, "that leaves you, Herzfeld. Unopposed. Let's get confirmation, shall we?"

Sharon turns to the crowd. "Let's hear it for Captain Herzfeld!"

Small pockets of enthusiastic applause erupt, but they quickly subside. Sharon thrusts the microphone at Herzfeld, and with deliberate scorn says,

"Welcome to your new command, sir. Would you take a moment to acquaint us with your agenda?"

Herzfeld eyes Sharon cautiously. With his ego justified by election, he steps to the front of the platform. Before he can get his first word out, someone shouts,

"*Hold up*! What about Jones?"

"Yeah! She should have a shot!"

"*Give the mic back to her*!"

"*C'mon*, Jonesie!"

A chant begins, "Sha-ron! Sha-*ron*! Sha-RON! SHA-*RON*! *SHA-RON*!" The hall thunders with coordinated hand claps and foot stomps. Herzfeld looks out across those he so nearly had mandate to lead, and his mouth hangs open. Sharon plucks the microphone from his hand and lifts an arm high for all to see. The chants and hand claps die down almost instantly.

"I'm not going to bullshit you," she says. "This is a huge undertaking. There's no way I can anticipate every angle, so if you choose me as your Captain I'm going to need your input and participation. Can you give me that?"

"*Hell* yeah!"

"You bet!"

"Sure will!"

"That said," Sharon continues, "once a decision is made, we have to end the discussion and act. No more divisions. No more sabotage. Can we agree to that?"

"*Yeah*, we can!"

"You got it, Jonesie!"

"If selected," Sharon states, "I pledge to continue the good examples of leadership I learned while serving as your Navigator. I swear to defend you all and the ship with my life, if required. You deserve nothing less."

Applause answers her, and she raises her arm again.

"One last thing." She turns to face Herzfeld.

Herzfeld looks back with controlled hostility and reluctant respect.

"You have good insights," she says to him. "You went about it the wrong way with Ortega, but you were right to call out his shortcomings. I'll expect that kind of vigilance from you. You have concerns, you come and tell me. In fact, I think whoever is elected today, the other should serve as spokesperson for the crew. Does that sound fair?"

The hostility vanishes, replaced by guarded surprise, and Herzfeld nods soberly.

"All right, then. Are we ready to decide, right here, right now, who will take command of the *Europa* and her crew?"

Cheers, whistles, and applause answer her.

"Okay. Counselor, will you call for votes, please?"

"*Hold*!" Herzfeld shouts, raising an arm. He steps close to Sharon, cups his hand over the microphone, and speaks softly into her ear, "You just gave a master class, Commander. I underestimated you, clearly. But your terms are acceptable. May I have the microphone?"

"Of course."

"*Ahem*. Ladies and gentlemen," Herzfeld says to the crowd, "I thank you for your consideration, but I would like to endorse Commander Jones and retract my candidacy. Perhaps we will revisit this process in three or four years' time."

Wholesome, dignified applause greets Herzfeld's words. He hands the microphone back to Sharon, and she takes it, trembling with realization of what she is about to inherit.

It's a hell of a legacy you left, Braemar. You'd better be right about me.

Sharon passes the microphone to the Counselor, who takes it with a smile.

Cupping the microphone in his hand, he says to her, "I'll be available for you any time of the day. You may confide in me with absolute discretion."

"I know. C'mon. Let's get this done before I change my bloody mind."

The Counselor pivots to the crowd, arm raised, microphone to his lips. "All in favor of Lieutenant Commander Sharon Jones assuming rank of Captain and taking command of the Colony Ship *Europa*, say, 'AYE.'"

The room rumbles with a singular reply, "*AYE*!"

"Opposed?"

The room is immediately quiet, echoes fading among the high ceiling supports.

"The 'Ayes' have it! Congratulations, *Captain Jones*!" The Counselor hands the microphone to Sharon and applauds her with a broad smile.

The crowd joins, clapping, hooting, whistling, and shouting. Sharon repeats her thanks into the microphone, unheard amid the roar of endorsement. She smiles, and raises her arms to be heard. The roar rolls away to distant claps and random shouts.

"We've been in a rut too long," Sharon says as the cheers fade. "We made a major change today, and it's good for us. But we've all been doing the exact same jobs for ages. Stagnation isn't healthy. If you want to stay in your roles, that's fine. We need expertise. But for anyone who yearns for something different, we'll begin a program of job cross-training. There's no reason we have to remain trapped in a life we find stale or meaningless."

Sharon looks over the crowd to the Operators guarding the set of doors she entered.

"Next, we can say, 'thank you, and good-bye,' to our Cadre sentries. We're grateful for your assistance, but it's time we stood on our own. We've got this, now. You are *dismissed*."

Gun Maddock tilts his head, radioing for orders. He nods once and stands straight. With two barked words from Maddock, the Operators move as a unified creature, departing from their posts and striding out through the exits. Before the doors seal behind them, Sharon shouts, "*Tell Chusan to put the chair back on the bridge, if you please!*"

"And finally," the *Europa's* new captain says with a sparkle in her eye, "let's have some cold ones and get reacquainted, yeah? Rec Rooms five, six, and seven! *Open bar!*"

If the cheers were loud before, this time they are positively seismic.

INSIDE OUT

Shao-Lo strides through the hallways of Cadre One, clad in the patched-up remains of her armor. She carries her helmet upside down in the crook of her arm with a roll of thick charcoal gray fabric stuffed inside it. In stark contrast to her piecemeal, lopsided armor, the rifle slung over her shoulder appears production line new, all parts meticulously repaired and doped with light-absorbing carbon.

Her chin is lowered as she strides toward the Cadre Armory, and her heels do not strike the floor with her usual zeal. Neither does she acknowledge the MedTechs and Operators saluting as she passes, for her mind is locked on her ultimate destination.

I'll be...dismantled. Taken apart then spliced with who knows what? There'll be pain beyond anything I've experienced, but worse than that... what will Honniker do with this body? Am I to be like Summers? A head in a jar? Or...a hybrid of Blueskin?

Her jaw flexes and her nostrils flare.

Or will I be used against my will like Voss? Turned it into some creature to kill those I'd protect?

She shudders. Her hands clench.

NEVER. I'll self-terminate first.

The entryway to the Armory is propped open. As she approaches, she watches MedTechs, drones, and Operators flow through it, running parts, batteries, and chemicals. When Shao-Lo steps inside, she finds what is ordinarily a tranquil storeroom humming with activity. Long racks against the left wall are stacked with caseless pistol ammunition and rifle cell packs in power chargers. MedTechs push trolleys up and down the rows, swapping charged cells for drained ones and collecting loaded pistol clips.

Racks and hangers line the right wall, most of them empty except for two armor suits, a machine pistol, four rifles, and a hand-held cannon. All dangle a red tag for repair, defective parts marked with a large 'X' in orange grease pencil.

Down the center of the Armory, long flat workbenches are occupied by seated MedTechs. Power tools dangle from the ceiling by retractable cords above each bench, and workers grasp them without needing to look. From what Shao-Lo can see, a few small arms are currently being serviced, a couple of Operator helmets and suits, as well. But the majority of MedTechs are packing grenades.

At front of it all is a man of huge shoulders, arms and torso, and a great round head with hair razed to the scalp. He rides in a rugged, circular cart and enters transfers into a waist high desk terminal. Dwarfed, shriveled legs hang beneath him, curled feet dangling centimeters above the floor.

"Colonel Shao-Lo," the man says, sweeping a flat hand to his brow and straightening his spine.

Shao-Lo salutes back. "Surrendering Operator kit to the Quartermaster," she says and she shrugs her rifle off her shoulder.

"The Quartermaster will receive," he says, taking Shao-Lo's rifle in both hands. He opens the catches and peers at the rifle, manipulating and rotating it, spinning it through his fingers, inspecting all angles as if he had three arms and photographic vision. Just as quickly, he spins the weapon back together, latching every catch with a flick of a thumb or fingertip.

"This is good. No need for service. Still want a replacement?"

"No."

The man lays the rifle on his desktop and pushes back from it, calling over his shoulder, "*Get me a cell stack and fresh suit for the colonel!*"

A Drone rolls a complete suit of armor over on a wheeled hanger. A MedTech limps to the desk and sets five rifle batteries on the surface. The Quartermaster logs the gear transfer into his terminal then rolls aside to inspect the replacement armor.

"Save it, Erik," Shao-Lo says. "It'd be wasted where I'm going."

The quartermaster rolls forward again. "Sir?"

Shao-Lo takes the rolled gray fabric from her helmet and sets the battered lid on Erik's counter. She unlatches the locking plates at her right shoulder and releases the mesh seam.

"Restore my kit and issue it to an initiate. The new Operator class is coming early and we're short on gear."

Erik rolls closer to the counter. "Colonel, I don't intend to send you off unprepared."

"No equipment can prepare me for this rotation, Erik." Shao-Lo opens the long seam down the side of her torso, rotates the waist-lock, and slides out of the upper half. She latches the shoulder lock and parks the upper suit on Erik's desk beside her helmet. Without its armor plating, the left arm droops by the limp inner webbing.

"I've done what I can with it," Shao-Lo says. "Needs a lot of work."

Erik looks at Shao-Lo's helmet and upper body armor. With a sigh and a sad glance, he takes both pieces and hangs them on ceiling hooks just behind him.

Shao-Lo works out of the rest of her armor until she stands in clean white undersuit and socked feet. Stretch fabric clings to her muscular frame like shrink wrap.

Erik takes the lower half of Shao-Lo's armor and hangs it beside the rest. "I can get you some boots at least." He puts two fingers in his mouth and blows a shrill whistle. *"Hey, Boris! Bring me a pair of twelve-eyes, size ten!"*

From the rear of the Armory, a MedTech pushes back from his workbench and shouts back, *"Aye, sir!"* Boris hops off his stool and hobbles to a set of lockers on the back wall.

The tall woman unrolls her charcoal uniform and steps into her trousers. The jacket, she slides into a sleeve at a time and closes the fasteners. By the time she finishes, a polished pair of boots is laced and waiting for her. She slips her calloused feet into them one at a time, props each up on the counter, and cinches the laces tight.

"Will we see you again, sir?" Erik asks.

"Unlikely. I'll arrange to have my quarters inventoried and cleared."

"No need, sir, I'll take care of it. Just mark your approval on my terminal."

Shao-Lo leans over to make her mark on the screen built in to Erik's desk, and she notices the Armory has gone strangely quiet. When she looks up, every MedTech is standing at attention and saluting. While Erik cannot stand on his own, he props himself with one hand on his cart, spine straight, shoulders back, chest out, flat hand at his brow.

"There are plenty of us who remember when you first joined the Corps, sir. Everything you've done for us, everything you're doing...we'll remember, *always.*"

Shao-Lo's mouth is a tight, thin line. She puts her heels together, stands tall, and snaps a salute.

"Thank you, Erik."

She drops her hand, about faces, and leaves.

Mind full, the colonel strides down the middle of the corridors, keeping out of the traffic running to and fro on each side. Every face she passes, she takes the time to acknowledge, nodding, addressing by name, or returning a hurried, yet respectful, salute.

On the way to Cadre One's main hangar bay, Shao-Lo suddenly realizes how naked she feels without her kit. Her uniform fits perfectly, every stitch custom made, yet it will offer no protection from the claws, spines, knives, and needles awaiting her at Cadre Two.

It's NOT a futile mission. In trade, my life could secure our residence there. I'm doing this for them. *And that's all that matters.*

In moments, she passes the wide gate to the hangar bay where the sow-like black transport is parked. A long line of Drones shuffles toward it, each pushing a cart piled high with plastic scrap. At the head of the line, she sees two lifters gripping the carts with forked limbs and heaving them up into the transport's spacious cargo hold. Bright light shines from inside the vessel, and the lifters lower emptied carts.

The transport itself appears exactly the same as she recalls, with the exception of white residue wrapping the ship's midsection like a belt.

What is that? Some kind of condensate from the main drive?

"Colonel!"

Shao-Lo lowers her gaze and sees Chusan stepping out from beneath the transport's open cargo hold. She falls in shoulder to shoulder beside him and they walk briskly beneath the transport.

"I have list of updates to this transport I'd like to review," he states.

"Very well, Maj—" Shao-Lo mutes herself when she spots the silver eagle on Chusan's collar. She looks forward. "Congratulations on your promotion, *Colonel*."

"Thank you," Chusan says. He gestures to the vessel's elevator and they both step onto the platform. As it rises, the safety catches *klank* with each half meter of travel.

Shao-Lo swallows hard and sucks her teeth. "Who'll be taking over the Corps?"

"The Corps will be split, Maddock taking half, Keiko taking the other. Would you like a rundown of the T.O.?"

"Not necessary. Let's continue."

"The food machines aboard have been programmed with Cadre formula. No more dietary deficiency in transit."

Shao-Lo nods and crosses her arms, looking around the transport's cargo hold as they ascend. The racks have been adapted to carry massive rectangular containers nearly as long as the hold, itself. At one corner of each container is a square funnel. The lifters heft carts up to the funnel and pour the contents in. With a brilliant flash of light, loose scrap is compacted and fused into a solid block. Drones inside each container catch the fused blocks and stack them, filling their container with cubes of solid plastic.

"What else?" she asks.

"Four of the cabins have been retrofitted to accommodate reproductively viable drone females. Munro inspected the modifications himself. Their nourishment and maintenance will be entirely automated during your flight."

The lift rises into a sealed box and jolts to a halt. The door ahead of them hisses and slides aside. Chusan steps out first, indicating two cabins on each side of the central hallway with open doors.

Shao-Lo looks into each of them, finding female drones strapped into medical recliners, eyes closed. Diagnostic and feeding machines are bolted onto the walls around them, readouts updating each second and showing green bars.

"What else?"

"You'll have no pilot, so your route is being plotted and loaded now. The vessel will take you there without need for input."

"And if I need to steer around something?"

"The ship will automatically course-correct for obstructions. Likewise, if an enemy vessel is detected, it will take evasive action. But if you want instruction how to pilot the ship, Maiella has uploaded a manual to the ship's computer."

"Maiella?"

Maiella emerges from the flight deck at the front of the vessel, HDI snapped onto her gold contact terminals.

"That's right," the Geek says, and she steps down the short stairway. "Chusan, would you give us a moment?"

Chusan nods and he leaves the way he came in.

"How'd you get into Cadre One?" Shao-Lo asks, somewhere between amused and irritated.

"Special Dispensation. O'Kai wanted a quick turn around on this beast, and I already had the full flight manual cataloged. So here I am." She looks over her shoulder toward the flight deck. "The hangar bay's as far as they'll let me in, though." She glances at the silver eagle insignia on Shao-Lo's collar then looks toward the lift at the rear of the corridor. "They could've waited to promote him until you left, at least."

"Doesn't matter." The tall colonel slides past Maiella, and she ducks into her cabin. Maiella follows, frowning. "Traveling light, aren't you?"

Shao-Lo turns a circle in the cabin, noting how the comfortable fixtures have been stripped down to the minimal.

"That's right," she answers. "No point in giving our gear away." Shao-Lo fixes a suspicious stare on Maiella. "Are you loitering for a reason?"

Maiella leans in the doorway. "We've had our differences, Colonel, but we both know where you're headed. No one should have to do this alone."

"Tell me, who can we spare?"

"Just *ask* me."

Shao-Lo's mouth twitches. "No," she says, finally.

"*Seriously*? Are you so fucking proud that you wouldn't have—"

"STOW IT, GEEK. There's *no one else* I'd rather have at my back in a fight, but *I'm not going there to fight*. I'm going there to trade what ever I can offer. To be blunt, adding you to the manifest is something Honniker does *not* deserve. I refuse to give him that satisfaction."

Maiella crosses her arms and leans against the wall, momentarily disarmed by what sounded like an honest complement. "Well... You know what Honniker's going to want."

Shao-Lo's eyes go cold. "Yes. I do."

"There's someone who can help you out."

"Oh?"

The Geek snorts. "He'd never go to a place like Cadre Two. Hasn't got the guts. But he knows about negotiation, power plays, trade, persuasion... Everything the Cadre is terrible at."

"Who?"

"His name's Herzfeld."

"I know that name. He's the one pulling the Colonists apart, isn't he? The one fomenting revolt and sabotage. The man is *cancerous*."

"I thought so, too. But you and I've already gone head to head against Honniker. If you're going to try and bargain with that thing, you should know what you're doing. From what I can tell, no one else is better than Herzfeld at that. So I asked him to put some reading material together."

"You're in *contact* with this man?"

"Yeah. Because dismissing what we don't understand isn't getting us anywhere."

Shao-Lo squints.

"I'm not trying to make your mind up for you," Maiella says, raising her hands. "Herzfeld pulled some titles from the *Europa's* archive on advanced negotiation tactics, political outcomes, psychology of choice and decision making. He even put together an interactive practice. It's all saved in the ship's computer. Have a look at it or don't, it's up to you. It's a long flight, so you'll have plenty of time to decide."

Maiella stands straight.

"Well. The ship knows where to go, and she's smart enough to get out of the way if something comes up. Don't need me holding you up anymore. Good hunting, Colonel."

Maiella turns sideways and slips past Shao-Lo on her way to the lift.

"Maiella."

Maiella pauses and looks back at Shao-Lo. "Hmm?"

"You'd have come if I asked?"

Maiella purses her lips and nods sincerely. "Yeah."

"What about Thompson? You were preoccupied with him the entire flight back."

"I, uh... I think he's gonna go back to the Corps. I've lost Argo, and that hurt goes straight through me. If I lose Thompson...I don't think I could take that."

"Scares you?"

"Inside out."

Shao-Lo thinks a moment. "This is my toughest rotation, because you're right: we both know what's waiting. But I'll never let fear drive me from what I must do. And neither will you."

Maiella looks down, face scrunched.

"Don't think for a second I approve of your attachment to Thompson. But if you want to serve this man the way you once served the Cadre, then remember: you will support what is best for him. Go, look him in the eye. Face that possibility and accept it's not your choice."

Maiella looks up at Shao-Lo in disbelief, but says clearly, "I will."

"And one last thing." Shao-Lo reaches to her collar and removes the silver eagles. "Will you see that these are returned to O'Kai?" She hands the insignias over.

The Geek turns the eagles over in the palm of her hand. "You don't think you're coming back, do you?"

Shao-Lo looks back with her usual austerity. "The Cadre has never required three full colonels."

"Colonel Shao-Lo," the transport's intercom blares, "lading is complete, vessel is fully fuelled. You are cleared for departure."

"Go on, Maiella. Get outta here."

"Is that an order?"

Shao-Lo smirks and shakes her head.

Maiella is about to leave when she turns back, looking down at the silver eagles in her hand. "I'm keeping these. To hell with O'Kai."

"On your way, Geek."

Maiella nods and heads toward the lift. Shao-Lo follows.

"You're walking me out?" Maiella asks.

"Making sure you don't stow away again."

"*Ha!* You know me too well." Once Maiella is on the lift, she stands straight, heels together, and snaps a respectful salute.

"You don't have to do that anymore, Maiella."

"It's not rank I'm saluting." The doors close and Maiella rides the lift down to the landing bay floor.

Shao-Lo breathes deeply then strides to the front of the vessel. She stoops into the low-ceilinged flight deck and pulls up an interior camera feed, watching Maiella leave.

She would have come along? Was brave of her to offer. But no, this mess is mine.

Shao-Lo straps herself into the pilot's seat, sorts out the controls, and keys her radio. "Cadre One, this is Cadre Two transport, green bars, ready for stars, over."

"*Received, Cadre Two transport. Landing bay evacuated and equalizing. Stand by.*"

Hydraulics whine as the transport's cargo doors swing shut. Shao-Lo looks through a reinforced plexisteel windscreen at amber lamps strobing on each side of Cadre One's Landing Bay doors. The doors part down the middle, sending a puff of gray dust out to the crater floor beyond. Blackness of space spreads above.

Even if I could come back, will there be anything to come back to?

"*Cadre Two transport,*" the radio squawks, "*manual control is disabled. Autopilot engaged. Maneuvering to departure window, acknowledge.*"

"Acknowledged, Cadre One," Shao-Lo states.

With a crackling hiss the transport rises from the deck and thrusts out from the brightly lit bay. Millions of pinpoints shine amid infinite sky overhead.

A low cycle hum begins from the rear of the transport then rises in pitch. Shao-Lo checks the monitors in the console in front of her and keys her radio,

"Cadre One, Deep Space Drive coming on-line, over."

"*Received, Cadre Two transport. Stand by.*"

While Shao-Lo waits she peers up at the *Europa* loitering overhead.

Its running lights are off and, typically, all she would see is a wide, triangular blot of the sky. Instead, the dingy hull is alive with tiny specks flitting about on long tethers, each with its own headlamp. The specks fuss over evenly spaced cubes, guiding them into position, welding them in place with a distant spray of sparks, stringing cables between them.

Good, we're installing stealth generators, she thinks. *Colonists just might get away from here undetected.*

Her transport rises out of the crater, smoothly banking around the massive colony ship, and both of the Cadre's high-mass freighters swing into view. One is long and rectangular, the other nearly spherical. Unlike the rest of the Cadre fleet that is covered in non-reflective black, the freighters still wear their original markings, including their scorches and cuts from collection. The freighters are centuries old, at least, having been two of the earliest vessels captured, and have remained parked for as long as Shao-Lo can recall. Now, they are a hive of activity with transports running to and fro. Newly constructed towers jut from the bows in massive tripods with reinforcements between the struts as rugged as the main towers themselves. Like the *Europa*, both ships are dotted with stealth generators.

Where is all this material coming from? Shao-Lo wonders until the transport soars past the freighters. Parked behind them is an even older vessel. Whole sections of hull are peeled from its circular ribs, leaving the entire structure open to space. Sparks of blue light shine from inside the hulk, reflecting off interior bulkheads as workers cut away more lengths of bracing.

Shao-Lo looks beyond all the activity, out into the depths of space, where she knows Cadre warships are patrolling.

Only our Operators can handle micro-G work... Means Ralla must be running patrols with just Geeks. She looks back at the heavy freighters. *Because a project of this scale would need every Gun and Brick we have.*

The monitor on her console flickers. O'Kai's head and shoulders fill the screen.

"Shao-Lo," O'Kai begins. "First, I regret keeping you in the dark regarding our on-going operations. Tactically and strategically, you're an asset I've come to depend on, and excluding you from planning is quite unnatural. However, if Honniker is able to crack your mind, we cannot allow him to have detailed knowledge of our intentions.

"Furthermore, you are authorized to employ *any* means at your disposal in gaining our long term access to Cadre Two. I cannot underscore how important those resources are to our survival. Cadre One will no longer shelter us, and if our assault at Earth fails then we have nowhere else to retreat. It won't matter if the enemy is unable to track all of us down. Starvation and asphyxiation will ultimately do the job for them.

"I'm aware that to accomplish your mission, you may be required to experience more physical pain than anyone ever has. If there were any other way I could assure success, if there was any other possibility, I would leap for it. But I must order you to endure at Cadre Two for as long as you are able. As mentioned earlier, there will be no other retreat for us. If you can wedge a door open for us, you'll have to be inside to do it.

"That said, if there is absolutely no chance to secure a collaborative arrangement, and if remaining at Cadre Two would only result in the waste of your life (or worse, having your life used against us), then you must escape or self-terminate. If escape is available to you, reunite with us and assist in our assault. This is an expiring option, as you can imagine, for once we make our initial strike, we will win or die. Arriving after the battle, you may find us in possession of the planet, or you may find an enemy task force. If the enemy wins, then your escape from Cadre Two will mean little.

"Even if you find us in possession of the planet, it is a fixed location. Should the enemy decide they have the will to retake the planet, it is unlikely we could defend it indefinitely. Thus, I reiterate: without a secure place of retreat, this is the end of our line.

"Good-Bye, Shao-Lo. It has been an honor."

The video ends and the monitor resumes its display of on-board diagnostics. The vessel steers itself robotically toward a bright yellow star that gleams intensely in the perfect blackness.

"*Cadre Two transport, prepare to engage deep space drive in three... two...one...mark.*"

The main drive engages, the field of stars lenses, and the transport plunges through space and time.

POWDER KEG

Sharon slumps in the re-installed Captain's chair aboard the *Europa*, head propped by one hand, elbow on the armrest. Multiple holowindows are open in front of her, showing areas of the ship where major repairs are proceeding. Other windows stream data on energy consumption, life support, reactor function, but the window she studies is an external view, wide angle, looking out across the asteroid's night side and the ships hovering above it. She stares into that serene scene of massive vessels and the tiny specks servicing them.

My God, I'm exhausted, she thinks.

Gregor sits at the first officer's console ahead and to the right of her. He looks over his shoulder and sees her eyes are slits.

"Need some rack time, Skipper? You've been at it almost thirty hours."

"No, thank you, Gregor. Well, maybe. Won't do if I nod off at my post, will it?" She sits up, her eyebrows scrunching together. "You've been here as long as I have... How's it you're still bright-eyed?"

"Scored a couple tabs of Cadre Stim they've been passing around. Some powerful shit." He drops his jaw, stretching his face and making exaggerated blinks. "I may never sleep again."

"Break me off a piece, yeah? Rather fancy the idea of never sleeping again."

"Still having the dreams?"

Sharon bunches her mouth on one side of her face, regretting the casual over-sharing with a junior officer.

He's always been a trusted friend, but I'm the captain now. Such things are no longer appropriate.

Instead of answering, she asks a question of her own. "What's got the Cadre so wound up? It's more than a damned re-org, I don't care what they say."

Gregor looks into the holowindow of space, studying the massive vessels. "Been wondering myself why they got everyone all hopped up."

"Well then, let's take a closer look." Sharon taps a control pad on her armrest and combines all windows into one magnified image of space. Two high-mass freighters occupy most of the view, and, now that they are enlarged, the colonists notice all of the tiny specks are moving away from them down toward Cadre One. Sharon and Gregor tilt their heads, trying to decipher what the sudden departures mean, when the freighters' long, thin engines surge with plasma; and the high tonnage vessels thrust toward deep space. Previously hidden, half the Cadre fleet is revealed as the enormous barges accelerate away. Long lines of transports, what Gregor and Sharon assumed were for the freighters, dock with the warships momentarily and rush back to Cadre One.

"Uh, they're probably testing things out," Gregor supposes unconvincingly. "Routine maneuvers. Turning over provisions. Proving the seals are good. That sort of thing."

Sharon rouses herself and sits upright in her chair. "Look how fast those freighters are pulling away... They've got to be empty."

"If they're empty," Gregor replies, "then where are they going?"

Before the mammoth ships are out of sight, both shimmer and disappear. Sharon stares into the holoscreen while Gregor checks his console.

"Freighters no longer appear on instruments," Gregor states. "That's stealth tech, sure as day."

"I'm getting to the bottom of it," Sharon says, but before she can dial a frequency on her comm panel, the holowindow displays an incoming call from Cadre One.

"Here's your chance," the Russian mutters.

Sharon opens the channel, and O'Kai's face peers at her from the cramped confines of a shuttle.

"Captain Jones," the stern-faced general says, "request permission to come aboard."

Sharon shifts in her seat. "That depends. Are you going to level with me what's going on?"

"That's the purpose of our visit."

"You can tell me *right now*. And don't give me any *cack* about re-organization. You're *mobilizing*!"

O'Kai's expression remains the same. "Not to be discussed over an open channel."

Sharon glares at the man in the screen, wrestling with how intimidated she is by him. She rises from her seat, and standing gives her more confidence, lessens her need to compensate.

"Permission granted," she says. "I'll ask the Counselor to receive you."

"Understood," O'Kai replies. "Arriving now. O'Kai out."

The screen blanks and restores the view of space.

"Here already?" Sharon says, shaking her head. She taps the comm button of her armrest. "Counselor...proceed to forward personnel hatch immediately to receive Cadre VIP. Acknowledge."

After a brief delay, the Counselor radios back, "*Understood, Captain. On my way.*"

Sharon closes the commlink and steps behind her chair, leaning over it to quell the butterflies in her stomach.

"It's never good news, is it?" she asks.

Gregor looks down at his console. "Nope."

Sharon paces while Gregor sits quietly at his terminal, trying to concentrate on his work. When the sound of unified foot steps come from the corridor behind them, Gregor rises from his terminal and Sharon turns to face the entryway. She runs fingers through her hair and smooths down the front of her uniform.

The Counselor steps through first, trotting to keep ahead of his guests. O'Kai and Munro stride in right behind him, followed by Chusan.

Jesus, I forget how tall they are... she thinks. Burying her anxiety, she blanks her expression and waits for them all to approach.

"Captain," the Counselor says, "General O'Kai, Colonel Munro, and Colonel Chusan."

"Welcome aboard, gentlemen," she says cordially.

"Thank you, Captain," O'Kai replies. "And congratulations on your promotion."

"Election," Sharon corrects.

All three Cadre officers tilt their heads.

"Let's just get to it, yeah?"

O'Kai looks down at the Counselor then back at Sharon. "The information we have to share is sensitive. Would you prefer a private discussion?"

Sharon crosses her arms, not about to be alone in a room with men who outweigh her three to one, each.

"Gregor and the Counselor have my full confidence. So quit stalling. What *exactly* are you up to, O'Kai?"

"First," O'Kai explains, "I did not want to withhold information this important. Lack of leadership and disunity in the *Europa's* crew made it necessary."

"Get on with it."

"Cadre One has been discovered. We are evacuating. The *Europa* must resume her mission."

Sharon's eyes flutter, and she involuntarily hunches with sickness. She draws her cheeks in and turns her back.

"*Fuck...*" Gregor says.

Out of all the questions that race into Sharon's mind, only one seems sensible to ask. "How do you know?"

"An imaging device appeared in local space. It had several seconds to image and transmit before we were able to destroy it."

"*And you're JUST NOW getting around to telling us?*"

"You saw for yourself how far the *Europa's* condition had decayed. She wasn't space worthy. Even if she was fit mechanically, her crew was not. Thus, we concluded that sharing this information would have created further chaos, leading to deteriorating conditions and loss of life. Now that you have drawn your crew together and the *Europa* is able to resume her mission, you must depart Cadre One immediately."

"What, *by ourselves*? You're coming with us, *yes*?"

"No," O'Kai counters. "Traveling with the fleet would create an energy signature detectable for parsecs. Stealth generators will minimize your profile and prevent detection by all but the most focused of sweeps."

"*And where shall we go*, General? The Lizards could be anywhere, waiting. At least Cadre One has defenses! Out in the black we're helpless! What could we possibly do if discovered aside from die?"

"It is highly unlikely the enemy will find you. Our plan is to lure the enemy to a location far away and engage them."

Sharon crosses her arms again, holding them close as if to restrain the thudding in her chest.

"What happened to sticking together, General? Not just you and me, I'm talking about the Cadre and the Colonists, *all of us*. You can't expect us to abandon you...honestly, *can you*? It's been a rough path, but we're finding our way together. For Christ's sake, our children...*our children* are growing in your MedLab!"

Munro's head dips suddenly, his lips turned in. Even O'Kai looks at the floor before replying.

"They were not mature enough to transport. We've preserved the DNA sequences and packed the incubators for flight. When you find a world you can settle, you may try again."

Sharon's ears slide back, her face blanches. "My God...you terminated them," she says into her hand as she crumbles into her seat.

"Gun Maddock witnessed your assumption of command. He described it as decisive and assertive," O'Kai states. "This led me to believe the *Europa* has found a strong replacement for Keller. Did I misjudge?"

O'Kai's icy tone stabs Sharon in the heart. Rather than let it defeat her, she turns cold, herself, and rises from her chair. "If you're telling me that you've terminated our next generation of children and you *don't* feel a crushing loss of hope from that...then maybe we *aren't* losing so much in this separation."

O'Kai absorbs the hit, the corners of his mouth drawing closer together. "Let's cut through it, Captain. This ship possesses the resources, the structures, the people required for the human race to begin again. There is nothing more valuable than that. I need not describe all of the sacrifices we've made to ensure you survive. But I do not intend for our people to be parted. Instead, I come to ask you personally if you'll take my MedTechs with you."

Sharon blinks in surprise. "There are so many... *Of course* they're welcome, but...can we handle the extra load?" Sharon looks at Gregor for backup.

"The draw on life support, the nutritional requirements, the strain on plumbing, sleeping arrangements..." Gregor lifts his hands in a helpless gesture. "I'm not sure we can accommodate them, General."

"We've already performed the assessment," Munro says. "Many can occupy the vacant cryo-cylinders, which won't tax existing systems. For the rest, we will build dormitories in the vacated storage bays. Only the barest essentials are required. Moreover, our MedTechs will assist in maintaining your vessel. They're excellent workers, Captain. I'm certain every one of them will prove themselves an asset."

"That's not in question!" Sharon fires back. "*Of course* I want them aboard, if we can have them!" She raises a hand to her forehead, massaging the deepening lines. "I'll have to review your plans and coordinate with our engineers. But how can we do this in time?"

"With respect," Munro states, "the majority of the work has already been done."

Gregor squints at Chusan then laughs cynically. "When you took over... You built your upgrades into our maintenance and retrofits, huh?"

Chusan confirms with a nod.

Gregor shakes his head like a man who has just been outplayed in a poker game. "You guys think pretty far ahead."

Sharon takes a deep breath and wrings out the tension in her hands. "Is there any other way?"

"The only advantage we've ever had is surprise," O'Kai says. "The enemy knows where we are. That means we cannot stay. No matter Cadre One's defenses, the enemy will overwhelm us. A fixed location is simply not defensible."

"How much time have we got?" Sharon asks.

"None to spare. The enemy could arrive this minute. Or months from now. We can't know until they appear. All we know for sure is if the *Europa* is still here, it's the end of our line, forever. Do you understand that, Captain?"

Sharon scowls at the patronizing tone, yet she contains her indignation. Turning to Gregor and the Counselor, she says, "This is a powder keg. We know what it'll do to the crew. But I'm not about to start lying now. I have to tell them."

"It'll be pretty obvious once all the MedTechs start moving in," Gregor says. "Should I round everyone up?"

"Gor, we don't have time for another fucking *assembly*!"

"You want to straight up announce it? Over intercom?" Gregor asks.

Sharon thinks about it, yet another crisis on top of crisis on top of crisis...

"Let me ask you this, General. What if the enemy never shows up?"

"That's unlikely."

"Well it's *possible*. Maybe you shot the thing down before it could get a message out. Maybe it didn't know what it was looking at, and you got to it in time."

"That's not a possibility we can afford to entertain."

"Are you going to throw your home away without knowing for sure? You might think about leaving the lights on in case they don't show up."

"We've planned for all conceivable contingencies," Chusan says with impatience.

"I must ask again," O'Kai says modestly. "Will you take my MedTechs?"

"Naturally, *YES*! Whether the *Europa* is ready for them or not, we'll find a way. When do you need them aboard?"

"They're waiting as we speak." O'Kai turns to Munro. "Supervise the transfer of personnel and equipment, then take the last shuttle up. You're going with them."

"*Sir?*" Munro says, his round face contorted with surprise. "I won't be... You want me *here?*"

"The *Europa* is where our people will be, Munro. We can't expect Doctor Taggart to tend all of them as well as her own crew. And this is where your expertise will count the most. Lend Captain Jones your skills and help her keep the *Europa* going. Obey her orders as if they were mine."

Squelching deep disappointment, Munro answers, "Aye, sir."

"Captain Jones," O'Kai says, "you may not realize how difficult it is to entrust the safety of my people to another. This choice is obvious, however. They *cannot* remain at Cadre One, and where we're going they must not follow. So they go with you. May you all prosper together. Someday, perhaps, we won't seem so strange to one another."

O'Kai looks to Chusan and flicks his head. The three Cadre officers turn as a unit and march toward the exit.

"And where *are* you going, General?" Sharon calls after them. O'Kai does not answer, and the sounds of their long strides fade down the corridor.

Sharon turns to look at her holoscreens. When she realizes she is chewing on her thumbnail, she looks down at it and grunts in annoyance.

"How can I help?" the Counselor asks.

Sharon turns to look at the Counselor, and she flinches at how much he reminds her of Mikato, how just the sight of him floods her with horrible memories.

Everyone's looking to me now, Sharon reminds herself. *If I think about it too long I might go mad. Action. That's what it takes. I have to act on this, quickly.*

"Gregor," she begins, "call Herzfeld and ask him to assemble the department heads. I'm going to tell them first. Then we send them out to inform their teams. When I make the announcement to the rest of the ship, they'll be there to handle questions, keep order."

The Russian replies, "Aye, Skipper."

"Counselor," Sharon says, "find Herzfeld and stay with him like a student loan. He was pushing for us to leave Cadre One, anyway. He could help us sell this idea. While I don't think he'd try to twist this for political points, I can't be sure. Need your eyes and level head through this."

"Of course," the Counselor says.

"Go now," she says.

Gregor salutes, the Counselor bows, and the two hustle off the bridge.

Sharon faces the large holowindow. *Keep it together*, she tells herself while chewing on a thumbnail.

O'Kai's got a plan. Everything'll be all right. It's only the infinite fucking reaches of space. Just keep it together, and everything'll be fine...

OUT OF TURN

Maiella marches through the halls of the *Europa*, irritated at being torn from a vital netware patch for yet another discussion.

Back and forth of pointless debates, she thinks. *Needy ego where decisiveness could be.*

As tedious as it is, listening to Colonists grind on, a single thought lightens her mood:

Maybe Thompson'll be there.

The route to the meeting hall is so familiar that muscle memory guides her through every step and turn. On personal autopilot, she reopens the patch program in her HDI and displays streaming lines of code on her goggles. Somewhere in the machine language is a bug keeping the *Europa's* stealth generators from meshing.

Traffic across the network increases exponentially after eight seconds, she thinks, *and latency drops the nodes out of synch... But a logic loop isn't something Beckert would miss. He's too sharp for that. Could it be hardware?*

Thompson spots her from an adjacent corridor and his dour face brightens.

"Maiella!"

"Heya," she replies, lifting her goggles for a better look at him. "You got called in, too?"

"Roger that," he says, turning into formation beside her. Their strides automatically fall into unison. "There are such things as *radio* and *intercom*. Don't need all these face to face groupthinks."

"Could be worse," Maiella counters. "At least we weren't ordered back to Cadre Two."

"So, it's true? O'Kai *really* sent Shao-Lo back to Cadre Two?"

"Yep. She's headed out solo, no backup." Maiella looks down the corridor at nothing in particular. "But how about you?" she asks, facing him again. "You're looking better. You, uh... You going back to the Corps?"

"If they'll have me. I think I should."

Maiella hides the hurt behind a stoic mask. "Yeah...yeah. You should go."

"You're coming, too. Couldn't trust any other Geek."

She nearly spits. "That was another life. Even if they'd take me I wouldn't go."

"Why not? The chance to serve again? You said your HDI's been restored, and there's nothing else that would keep you out. Argo paved the way for us. How could you not—"

"Will you fucking LEAVE it?"

Thompson blinks at the lashing and halts in the middle of the corridor. His eyes narrow.

"What's changed, Maiella?"

Maiella halts her march. "The *Cadre's* changed, Thompson. I can't put my finger on it, but O'Kai, Shao-Lo, Chusan, Ralla, right down the line... it isn't enough for them to survive anymore. They're after something bigger. Makes the hair on my neck stand on end."

"Like what?"

"I don't think they're interested in Collection Rotations anymore."

"Obviously. With the *Europa* here, they don't need to be."

"No, I'm not just talking about food and minerals. I sneaked a peek at a video O'Kai made for Shao-Lo before she went back to Cadre two."

"How'd you get access to that?"

"I prepped the transport for flight. And...that made it easy to skim all data in and out."

"You hacked a *private message* between officers of the *Leadership Council*?"

"Never mind all that! O'Kai mentioned an assault. I think they're heading for something *drastic*, Thompson. Something *final*—"

Two Colonist department heads round a corner behind the exiled Operators, chatting on their way to the meeting. One is a man with gray temples and bags under his eyes. A paunch fills the waist of his faded orange coveralls, and a threadbare patch over his chest labels him, *David*. His companion is a rugged looking woman of similar age in faded blue coveralls, labelled, *Sharma*. They both look ahead to see Thompson and Maiella facing each other in the corridor.

"Hey, Thom, Mai," greets the man as he nears. Sensing candor between the two, he becomes self-conscious. "Uh, sorry, didn't mean to interrupt."

"No, no, Dave, you didn't," Maiella assures him with a shake of her head. "We're on our way to the Mess Hall."

"Same here," Dave groans. "Skipper gives me a deadline for installing new water service to Storage Bay Nine, then keeps hauling me away from the job for another stinkin' meeting. That's some *pig logic* right there."

Thompson waits for Dave and Sharma to catch up then walks beside them. "How're things in Life Support?"

"Damn good, actually," David answers. "I know I bitched about the Cadre taking over here, and all, but they really beefed up our capacity. Scrubbers can handle about twice the volume as before. Hell of an upgrade."

"Same thing in Power Gen," Sharma says. "Ran whole new service into the emptied storage bays. We might be able to set up some workshops in there, do some light manufacturing, maybe. I mean, we were working the ship over, anyway. Might as well make the most of it, right?"

Thompson takes it all in as good news, but Maiella turns pensive, mulling why such major improvements to the *Europa's* infrastructure would be necessary.

"You got all the stealth generators installed?" Dave asks.

"With a *lot* of help from this one," Thompson says, aiming a thumb at Maiella. "Been too long since I did Micro-G work. She got me back up to speed."

"Soooo, we can just...disappear?" Sharma asks.

"Sort of," Thompson replies. "Working together, the generators emit a field that curves space-time above the hull and bends light around it. Up close, lensing of anything directly behind the ship is pretty obvious, but from a few thousand clicks, you gotta really know what you're looking for to notice. Beyond that, it's pretty much undetectable."

"Or it will be," Maiella adds, "once we figure out why they aren't all meshing."

"You'll figure it out," Dave says. "Say, Thom, when you finish up, would you mind swinging by Bay Nine? Got a section of pipe that's been a bear and we could use some muscle on it."

"Sure thing. What's the trouble?"

While Dave, Sharma, and Thompson delve into the subtle mysteries of plumbing, Maiella adds clues together.

Extra Life Support capacity...improved power service...stealth capabilities...we're being sent out, no question. But to where? Cadre Two? And if so, are we picking up? Or dropping off?

"Hey, Mai," Dave asks, "you all right? Look like you just swallowed a bug."

"Hmm?" Maiella shakes her head. "Nah, I'm fine. Thanks."

The doors to the cafeteria are wide open, and Maiella can see the other department heads have already arrived. Dave and Sharma stride ahead and fold into the group easily, reaching out in friendly contact, trading handshakes, hugs, and good-natured gripes. Laughs pass easily among them, giving the place a buzz of relaxed optimism.

Thompson and Maiella are met with hand waves, which they return. The two take their usual places at the rear of the hall.

Gregor and the Counselor stand at the opposite end with Herzfeld. Their body language is more serious with equal weight on both legs, shoulders square. When one of the three speaks, the other two listen with sober head nods.

Gregor turns from his tight circle, recognizes the tall ex-operators, and he shouts from the far end. "*Thompson! Can you get the doors?*"

Thompson juts his lower lip and pops his eyebrows at Maiella. "Closed meeting?" He punches the button and leans back against the wall. Maiella folds her arms and resumes debugging code in her goggles.

"Okay, people, settle in!" Gregor begins, allowing the relaxed murmuring to wind down. "I know the last thing you're looking for is another meeting, but you'll understand why we had to do it this way. What I'm about to tell you is absolute fact. The faster you accept it, the quicker we can deal with it. It's bad news, folks, so get ready for it. You ready?"

Maiella peers through the scrolling script in her goggles at a room gone silent. The light mood has been stamped flat and all eyes are on the Russian.

"Well, what the hell, Boss?" Dave shouts.

"Cadre One's been discovered. We have to leave immediately."

A pall fills the room, anxious, disbelieving.

"*Jesus*, Gregor," Sharma says, "*please* tell us you're joking!"

"I'm not. This is real, and we have to deal with it. Now look—you're leaders among the crew, and you're being told first. We're depending on you all to keep cool and handle this. When we announce to the rest of the crew, we need you right in front of them, maintaining calm and keeping order. First, I expect you to have some questions, so let's have 'em one at a time."

Hands lift, people stand, and before the shouts come Gregor raises both arms over his head.

"Keep it orderly, people! You're gonna be standing where I am soon, so think about how you want your people to behave. Now then, raise your hands and I'll get to you." Gregor points to a woman in a green jumpsuit, sleeves rolled up to her elbows. "Go ahead."

"Did one of their ships show up, or something?" the woman asks. "I mean, I work the scopes and I never saw so much as a blip the whole time we've been here."

"Was a probe of some kind," Gregor answers. "Wasn't one of O'Kai's and it wasn't one of ours, so that pretty much narrows it down. From its vantage, it would've had a view of the Cadre solar collectors along with part of the *Europa* before it was shot down. You, go ahead."

"Are we *sure* it was a probe? I mean, how do we know?"

"Munro scooped the wreckage and his MedTechs studied it. He's sure. Now let me say, I understand your curiosity, but the hows and whys aren't relevant at this point. Let's get some questions about how we're gonna handle this. *You.* What have you got?"

"Where will we go?"

"*That's* the real matter at hand. We're resuming our mission, exactly as if we hadn't stopped at Cadre One. Could be a very long journey, so we should get comfortable with the idea that this ship might be our forever home. Maiella, in the back, go ahead."

"All these upgrades," the Geek says while peering through her goggles, "they weren't just-in-case improvements, were they? The Cadre must have known about this for some time."

"That's correct. About four weeks now. They held it back, saying the ship wasn't in condition to leave, and we were too disorganized to handle it."

Angry grumbles and complaints roll toward the Russian, building into a wave of dissent.

"*Hey!*" Gregor shouts.

The colonists gaze at him with begrudging attention.

"We've been through some shit," the Russian says, "but to be blunt, I think they were right not to tell us straight off. All it would've done is cause panic. Anyway, we have to move on. You, what've you got?"

"Is the Cadre coming with us?"

"The MedTechs, yes. The Leadership Council and Operators, no. They're headed somewhere else. O'Kai won't say where."

While Colonists fire rapid questions at Gregor, Maiella saves then sweeps aside her de-bugging project. Code flares before her eyes as she enters the *Europa's* wireless network and works her way into communications. The first link she checks is the main commlink to Cadre

One. Though open on the *Europa's* side, the connection is closed on the Cadre end.

Next she tries radio traffic between vessels, tries alternate channels, tries emergency lines. Everything on the Cadre side has gone dark.

She dips into the *Europa's* sensing apparatus and pulls down live video feeds from regional space. The enormous freighters are gone, and stripped hulks loiter in their absence. Nearby, the old passenger liner parked above Cadre One receives transport after transport in a long line. Each transport tows a massive net of material behind it.

What are you up to, O'Kai?

While the others argue and fume, Maiella taps Thompson on the arm. "I gotta check something out."

Thompson nods and punches the door button for her. "I'll let you know if you miss anything."

"Thanks."

The Geek sprints back to her cabin, kicks off her shoes, strips down to her undersuit, and dives into her locker where her old armor hangs. The Geek steps into her boots, builds up the legs, clamps herself into the torso, and drops the helmet down over her HDI.

Machine pistols hang at the back of the locker with her last three clips of ammunition. She weighs them with her eyes.

Won't need 'em. She turns for the door then halts. *Or will I?*

The Geek returns to the locker and stares through her open faceplate at the rugged tools of her trade.

Better to have 'em, anyway.

She clicks the magazines to her thighs and clips her pistols to her back. With a deep breath, she looks into the mirror above her hygiene station. Her armored reflection is one she has seen hundreds of times, but now it seems ugly, unnatural. With an unhappy grunt, she turns and leaves her cabin.

Maiella dashes through the *Europa's* corridors, oblivious to the points and worried looks of those she passes.

I'll never get inside Cadre One by shuttle, she thinks. *They'll bounce me out of there as soon as I touch down. So how...?*

The umbilical! I'll slide down the umbilical in the shade, wait for a transport to come or go, then sneak through the open bay door. If I can get a hard network connection inside, even for a few seconds, might get some answers...

At the forward personnel hatch Maiella checks to make sure no one is watching then seals her faceplate. When her rebreather kicks on, she ducks into the air lock and hauls the door shut behind her. Air evacuates, the outer door slides aside, and she gazes out into blackest night.

The Geek stands at the open portal. Huge parabolic dishes near the asteroid's horizon cast long shadows across the crater-nested base below. She crawls out onto the hull with her magnetic boots, seals the air lock behind her, and crouches, watching the movements of transports in and out of the Landing Bay.

Regular and dependable, she thinks with a grin. But when she looks for the umbilical cable that transfers power from the *Europa* to Cadre One, she finds only empty space between the ship and the asteroid.

When did they cut the umbilical? Hell with it. I'm going.

She ponders the gap, calculating the physics with her HDI. A trajectory plots in her goggles, telling her exactly how much force is required to leap and how much thrust will be required at the end to not be smashed on impact. Keeping her boots strongly magnetized, the Geek repeatedly crouches then extends her legs, testing her jump speed and angle until her goggles confirm she is on target. Once sure she has it right, the Geek crouches and watches transports cycle in and out of the base.

Here I go...

Maiella aims herself at the asteroid, clicks off her boot magnets, and leaps. The distance crosses slowly at first, but she is calm and patient, contenting herself with the sound of her even breaths. The asteroid's weak gravity pulls her into a more vertical path and speeds her descent.

As she falls, she ponders the best way to get inside, how to engage the Cadre network without being noticed, how to get back to the *Europa* again. The crater swells beneath her, meters ticking away in her goggles toward zero. Unconcerned, she takes her pistols from her back and slaps the grips down over the clips on her thighs. She racks the actions, aims toward the surface in a narrow V, and triggers. Thudding pulses telescope up her rigid arms, silent flashes of light bloom at the tips of her pistols, and the ticking counter in her goggles slows. Clouds of dust billow beneath her then collapse just as quickly as the pistols fire dry. She slams hard onto her feet, rolls to one side, bashes against a boulder and flops onto her back, unbroken.

Blinking hard, Maiella looks up at the colony ship loitering above her. Most of the running lights are off, leaving only red and green pinpoints at the tips. She lies still, watching for any sign that she may have been noticed, any deviation in the movements of the transports and warships nearby. There is no change.

The Geek stalks toward the facility, vaulting over boulders, leaping fractures, occasionally stumbling in pockets of deep powder, until she arrives at the Landing Bay doors. A transport approaches, its forward facing lights painting the doors in a brilliant glare, and Maiella ducks behind a large stone. The craft hovers, waiting for the doors to part, then thrusts forward, lofting dust around it. Obscured by the cloud, Maiella races to the transport and runs beneath it as it enters the bay then flattens herself prone when the craft sets down onto its struts. Harsh lights shining down from the high ceiling keep her shadowed beneath the craft.

To reach a terminal I'll need to cross in the open. They'll spot me instantly... Should I hitch a ride on this thing to see where it goes?

One hard turn and I could be thrown off into space...

Where to go, where to go?

In answer, a dual-tracked loader lumbers up to the transport, hauling a massive cargo net of plastic debris. The Drone driving it stares with dark lenses, focused only on his task, and stops the loader centimeters away from the transport. Maiella scuttles into the gap between the loader's tracks, grips the undercarriage tightly, hooks her toes, and lifts herself off the deck.

In moments, the Drone secures his cargo net to the transport and drives the loader back into Cadre One. Maiella rides along, careful to keep herself hard against the undercarriage and avoid any telltale scrape of her armor.

The loader whizzes down corridors, electric motors whining at full speed. She bounces along until the loader pauses at an intersection for another loader to roar by. Maiella cranes her head left and right, making efforts not to tap the deck with the back of her helmet. There is no sign of Operators or MedTechs.

This spot is good as any.

She spreads the fingers of one hand and places the tips beneath her center of balance. Keeping her body planked, she lowers herself onto her padded fingertips then releases her grip on the loader. Once the Drone drives away, she uses both hands to press herself up so she can get the quiet treads of her boots beneath her, and the Geek races for the first room she can get inside. At the back wall is a terminal. She pulls a lanyard from her HDI and plugs in. Awareness transitions to digital and she merges her consciousness with the streams of code...

At first, she remains passive, sniffing packets of network traffic, but the only information available at this node is mundane, uninteresting.

Deeper...

Her goggles strobe as she assumes the terminal's identity and credentials. Then, pulse racing, she prepares for intrusion of the greater network.

OF MORTAL CREATURES

Unlike her all-out assault on Honniker at Cadre Two, the Geek opts for a covert entry. She filters her way in, masked as redundant packets routed across the network, sniffing and sampling. Network traffic is much lower than normal, however; and, as Maiella explores, the Geek finds entire nodes have gone dark. Manufacturing, Incubation, most of Life Support, and Reclamation are all dead silent. The farther she reaches across the network the more it seems she is virtually tiptoeing through some ancient place, long abandoned. Stranger still, the solar collectors and reactors are running at one hundred ten percent.

The chief power drains are off-line... Where's all that energy going?

Cadre Archives hold a fraction of the files they used to. Such emptiness mirrors the strange vacancy of the Cadre hallways, and the Geek wonders if she may have come too late. But then she finds one file set in the diminished Archive that is currently being accessed, labeled, "Europa *Star Charts.*"

Let's see what's going on...

The Geek merges with the stream and emerges inside a simulation of a solar system, running in fast-forward. Eight major planets, four small and four enormous, revolve around a dwarf yellow star at the model's center. A ninth dwarf planet revolves a few degrees off the orbital plane, slipping inside the orbit of the eighth for a fraction of its revolution then resumes its place at the edge of the system. Thousands of asteroids and comets are plotted, most of which have nearly circular orbits like the planets. Others are highly eccentric, swooping close to the central star then flinging themselves beyond the outer planets in narrow ellipses.

Maiella selects one of the eccentric asteroids and assumes its identity in the simulation. As she careens through the system she passes a gas giant with prominent rings, streaks by an even larger gas giant with alternating horizontal bands, and then passes through a belt of sparse, rocky debris. Two specks are plotted inside the belt, labeled with recognizable attributes of mass, thrust, angular momentum, and acceleration.

Are those the freighters?

The Geek zooms past a rusty, dry world on her way toward a planet of vast liquid oceans and living landmasses.

Did O'Kai find a habitable planet while we were at Cadre Two? No... That's EARTH!

Hundreds of locations are plotted on the planet's surface and in orbit above, but without labels none of them make sense. She stores the data and makes a mental note to ask Thompson later.

The closer she gets to the central star the faster she moves, streaking past a hellish world of sulfuric clouds and a smaller planet scorched to a metallic cinder. She loops around the blazing star and, on the far side, she spies an incoming comet, trailing a tail nearly an Astronomical Unit in length. The nucleus boils from the star's intensity, spouting huge jets of gas and dust. Behind the nucleus, where dust and ion tails overlap, are dozens of plotted points, each bearing its own legend of attributes.

What is that? Is that...the Cadre fleet?

Painful whiteness shoots into her mind, then blackness falls around her like a box of lead. The simulation is gone, and in its wake there is nothing at all, no space, no light as though space and time have collapsed and she is merely a sentient point. Maiella tries to explore her containment, but there is no exit, no direction she can move, no structure she can attack. All she can do is marvel at the totality of her entombment.

Ralla. It must be.

"Correct," Ralla says directly into her mind.

"Well?" Maiella yells back. "You gonna *do* something?"

There is another flash of white then *braps* of debilitating feedback. Brain buzzing, she hurtles back into her body and finds herself staring directly into metal floor plates. Every joint of her armor is locked. Her legs are bent at the knees, heels to her buttocks. Her hands grasp her elbows behind her back. She cannot move her head, but just within her range of sight are the tips of a Gun's boots. The end of a rifle barrel hangs beside them.

With grim conviction, the Gun says to her, "This was *not* your best idea."

"Maddock," Maiella grunts, squirming against her locked armor, "let me out of here, will you?"

Into his radio mic, Maddock says, "Major Ralla, intruder is apprehended, incapacitated. Shall I transfer to holding cell?"

A faint electronic buzz filters from the Gun's open faceplate, but not loud enough that Maiella can understand it.

"No, sir, her incendiaries have been disabled some time ago. No detonation risk."

His helmet buzzes again.

"Copy that, Major." Maddock steps back, keeping his rifle ready, and he says to someone standing out of view, "Take her to the Landing Bay. She goes with the next shuttle back to the *Europa*."

White canvas shoes of Cadre Drones step in front of her then take position on either side. The Drones heft her by the locked elbows like handles on a trunk. Together, they march her back the way she came, into the Landing Bay, up a ramp, and into a waiting shuttle. They drop her from waist height, letting her slam face first on the deck, and she growls.

Once the Drones leave the shuttle, there is a steady shuffling of feet up the ramp behind her. Maiella squirms in her locked armor for a peek, but her immobilization is total.

"*Damn it!*" she shouts. "Something's going on, just *tell* me! I can help!"

A cautious hand reaches down to her and flips her over. Maiella looks with wild red eyes up at Obet as he steps back, takes the pack from his crooked shoulder, and settles into a bench seat.

"What were you thinking?" the MedTech asks. "Going against Ralla in a net assault?" He shakes his head in awe. "You're as crazy as they say you are."

Maiella's eyes lift to her eyebrows. "I'm not going against *anyone*, Obet," the Geek says with exasperation. "I'm trying to find out *what's happening*."

"What's happening?" the MedTech says. He scoots over a bit to make room for another MedTech to sit beside him. "What's happening is we have to leave. We have to get out of here before the Blueskins come. What else is there to know?"

"Do you know where O'Kai is going?"

Obet juts his lip. "Why should we know that? We're not going. Besides, the fewer people who know, the less likely the enemy could be informed."

Maiella blinks at the insinuation. "You think I would do that, Obet? You think I *could*?"

Obet looks away, watches his comrades limp and hobble their way up the ramp with their personal bags of tools and clothing. "No one knows what you're capable of."

"I'm tired of having to prove my loyalty," Maiella grumbles through clenched teeth.

Obet's head swings toward her like an owl's and he looks at her directly. "*Loyalty*? You sneak in to Cadre One, armed and armored, hack into the network and attempt access to privileged information? How does *that* prove loyalty?"

Maiella slumps in her rigid armor, cornered by Obet's straight talk. In the corner of her eye, she sees Arjay climbing the shuttle ramp unsteadily, bag of belongings slung around her neck. Despite the MedTech's young face, her movement is elderly, toes pointing inward, a shaky hand reaching out ahead of her. At the top of the ramp, her toe catches on the lip of the hatch way and she topples forward. Other MedTechs reach out for her, but miss,

186

and Arjay crashes hard onto the deck.

Maiella watches, frustrated to the point of rage that if someone would have unlocked her she could have caught the poor woman. And then she wonders for a moment what it must be like for them, trapped in their crippled bodies. There is no way to turn a key and unlock their joints, their spines or coordination. No way to free them from nervous tics, no way to easily lengthen dwarfed limbs.

What do they think when they look at me, able-bodied but reduced to this?

With a frown on her face, Maiella says, "You're right, Obet. Sometimes I go too far. Doesn't matter if I'm doing the right thing. I give in to impulse. Makes it hard to trust me."

Obet wears a look of regret, himself. He reaches into his bag and pulls out Maiella's rugged pistols, setting them onto the bench beside him. The actions are locked open and a loop of welded metal runs up the empty grips, out through the ejection port, and connects back at the base of the grip. "I spoke out of turn. It isn't my place to say anything. I understand, it isn't entirely your fault. You're ill, and you just can't help yourself."

LASTING TERROR

O'Kai takes a solo tour through the halls of Cadre One, reacquainting himself with the fit and movements of his old armor. His kit is bulkier than modern Guns'—wider in the shoulders, more mass carried in the thigh plates, thicker helm. Fresh carbon doping masks the thousand indentations, slashes, pocks, fills, and welds.

The last time he wore his full kit he was a Major in the Operator Corps, a few kilograms heavier with muscle in the legs and shoulders. With satisfaction, he discovers that in the intervening ten years the dense internal padding is only a bit less snug than before.

Like his armor, the rifle over his shoulder is an older generation hand-me-down. Its long barrel houses hard optics, not the shorter plasma-focus issued to the latest Operators. If asked, Erik the Quartermaster would gladly have issued a modern replacement, but updates became unnecessary once O'Kai was promoted to the Leadership Council. There were to be no more rotations, and retrofits would only take resources from Operators still ranging the Black.

Now that he wears his cerametallic skin again, he recalls the things he did while wearing it, how intensely he explored the suit's strengths and limitations during his long service in the Corps. The precise assist of the liquid-smooth joints, the exact location of each icon in the visor, the correct postures to take hits so they slide and glance off of the hard angles are second nature. No matter if new suits are lighter, or if new rifles have better range with more penetrating power, he has never trained with them. A younger Operator would wear new gear to greater effect, and no one can wear this old suit better than he.

O'Kai's heels strike unusually loud in the otherwise silent corridors.

Such stillness was unimaginable before today. It would have been impossible to find a corridor without an Operator on patrol, a MedTech running gear, or a Drone hauling a load. Maintenance of the facility going back over a thousand years—improvements, updates, expansions, and upgrades to keep Cadre One habitable—required constant activity, constant oversight, endless care.

Now the facility is stripped to bones, guts ripped out and packed for flight. Its heart still beats inside the reactor well below, but Cadre One's soul—the MedTechs—have all crammed in with the colonists to be evacuated. And for O'Kai, that is the most savage blow. Being parted from them is unnatural, running counter to every impulse but the hard calculus of necessity.

The general approaches the double doors to MedLab and he halts outside them. No beam scans his identity, and the doors do not part. He clicks on his helmet lamps and shines them through the transparent doors into the darkened space beyond. All of the medical stations have been removed. The cabinets are open, displaying barren shelves. At the back of the lab, pipes and conduit jut a few centimeters from a wall where cylindrical healing tanks once stood. No cart or gurney remains, no chair, no smock nor medical mask, not even the disposal bins for bio-waste.

With a grunt, he moves on.

His solitary tour takes him past Incubation, Manufacturing, and the Forge. Like MedLab, they are hollowed out to the metal wall supports. The efficiency with which his orders were followed is small satisfaction when confronted by such intolerable emptiness.

Am I the cause of this? Was I overzealous sending Team Forestall to Earth? They weren't expected to return...but they did... Could the enemy have trucked them to Cadre One?

Or did I rile a drowsy enemy...rouse them from half-measures to greater action?

The captive's containment below was absolute...of that I'm certain. It could not have contacted its kin from Cadre One. After transfer to the Europa? No way to be sure. I should have ordered Munro to let it die, and not taken the chance.

He grips hands behind his back, spine straight, breathing the dry air deeply.

Perhaps it was just a matter of time. If the enemy got lucky with a random probe or if they've been systematically searching, it no longer matters. Our path is set.

Though his plan is resolved, a nagging uncertainty has plagued him for weeks, an idea that refused to clearly resolve. With the mobilization and evacuation of Cadre One to supervise, there was no time to indulge it. Now, in the uncanny silence, the thought stops him in his tracks.

Without people...without Cadre One...what purpose does a General serve?

The chilling thought cracks his authoritarian edifice, stirring something colder within.

If the enemy means to attack humanity's last refuge...scattering my people to the Black...then, yes, a General does serve a purpose: to pull justice from their cracked bones and weigh the sentence in their blood. I will teach the enemy a lasting terror of mankind.

O'Kai's jaw hardens and he resumes his tour along the facility's outer ring.

One emptied room after another passes without interruption until he reaches a convex section in the outer wall. In stark contrast to Cadre One's darkened rooms and hallways, the silo behind the bowed wall thrums with energy. O'Kai pauses at the wall, contemplates the potent sentry inside, and places his hand on the polished metal plating. Through the durable padding of his gauntlet, he can sense the Exciplex silo's eagerness to discharge. It mirrors his own.

Soon enough.

His tour of the first floor complete, O'Kai enters a lift and rides down one level. When the doors part, he looks into a corridor exactly like the one he left with the exception it is labeled, *Neonatal Selection, Vocational Aptitude, and Cognitive Potential*.

Sterile words hide the harsh regimentation and severity of tests, which evoked the most feral of aggression. As O'Kai looks upon these words, he recalls himself as a juvenile, nearly full grown by age thirteen, consumed by igneous rage and blood-red lust for violence.

Standing at attention. To his left and right, young men and women like him, dressed in skin-tight undersuits. Opposite, another line of young men and women. Some tall and muscular like he is, others shorter, more slight of build. The rest are hulks of muscle and bone. All of them shuddering, shoulders hunching in gathered tension, mouths involuntarily yawning and showing teeth, eyes tracking with white-rimmed insanity...

Looking into his own flexing, shivering hands, fuelled by adrenaline and the will to expend it on the nearest living object. Blinking hard, trying to converge hunting eyes, lips peeled away from gnashing white teeth.

Power in every sinew, so fit, so flexible, so skillful, his body yearning at the cellular level for savagery...

Lieutenant Munro striding between the lines, colossal and intimidating. The huge man stopped at a small cart, trading his injector for a short black rod.

"This is your first experience with combat stims," the huge man said. *"We must be sure you can control yourself under its influence. I will observe how you respond."*

Munro paced back down the lines, peering into adolescent faces that trembled in fragile restraint. *"YOU WILL MAINTAIN CONTROL,"* the lieutenant boomed. *"You will master what I have injected into you! That killing urge, the passion for violence, must always remain subordinate to your conscious restraint. In time you will use it. Right now, YOU WILL CONTAIN IT. If not..."* he added, raising the rod over his head, *"...you get this."*

O'Kai forced himself to lift his malevolent gaze from the floor, turning it on Munro...

Munro, meeting the gaze and striding at him, stopping centimeters away...

"Tell me, neonate, what would you like to do right now?"

Gouge your eyes. Smash your skull. Rip your throat with my teeth. WEAR. YOUR. BLOOD.

Munro tilted his head, staring through O'Kai's rage-watered eyes.

"You've something to say, neonate?"

O'Kai growled ape-like through his teeth, *"I AM... IN CONTROL."*

Crushing his eyes shut, no longer able to look at Munro for fear his hideous temptations might overwhelm him. Forcing his clenched fists open, drawing a long, cooling breath in through his sinuses, and lowering his shoulders...

Munro leveled his head, retracting the rod aimed at O'Kai's gut, and stood straight.

"Good," the lieutenant said without obvious

enthusiasm. His mouth opened to say more, then a scream from down the row...

Slap and thump of fists impacting, knees bashing, feet stomping...

Munro surged toward the fight like a bolt of electricity, jabbed the rod into the spine of a huge young man.

The young man convulsed away from his victim, head thrown back, spine arched, arms flung out, collapsing onto his side and lying so still he might be dead.

Munro, stepped back and shouted for all to hear, "NEONATE LEVY, REDESIGNATE: DRONE, EIGHT-FOUR-NINE." The big man looked from the collapsed figure to a muscular young woman on her back. She, propped on elbows, watching Munro with cautious, yet unafraid eyes...

"Are you going to lie there all day?" Munro asked.

The woman jumped to her feet, brushed herself off, and stood at a jittery attention.

Munro studied the swelling lumps on her face then peered directly into her eyes. He stooped over and hauled up the unconscious lad with his large arm. Holding him in front of the young woman like a sparring dummy, he asked her,

"Would you like to hit back, neonate?"

"Yes, sir, I would," the young woman said with surprising evenness. "But I won't."

"And why is that?"

"Because I don't want to be Drone Eight-Five-Zero."

Munro let a smile cut through his stony face. "Well done." Turning toward the doorway and pointing at a junior MedTech entering notes on a tablet, he added, "Arrange collection and have Drone eight-four-nine prepped for reconstitution."

"Understood, Lieutenant," the MedTech said, tapping in the transfer via tablet.

O'Kai looked at the floor in front of him, still at war with his own desires to throttle and crush.

How did she hold back? I couldn't've stopped...not until I'd kicked his head off his shoulders...

"To the rest of you," Munro said grandly, "the first

*few minutes are the hardest. Already, you may have noticed
the stim's effects are reaching a plateau. But this test is
FAR from the hardest you'll face. If you feel you struggled
today, practice your meditative technique, practice the forms
and movements, or YOU WILL NOT PASS WHAT LIES
AHEAD." With a nod to the young woman with bruised face,
he added, "You can all learn from Shao-Lo's example."*

O'Kai steps from the lift and turns left, pausing at an open set of
doors. As he stares into a wide room, roughly twenty meters square with
three-meter ceiling, it occurs to him he has not visited this place since he left
it as an Operator Candidate thirty years ago. Thick, heavily worn mats still
lie on the floor, and racks of battered free weights line the walls. The air is
stale with an acrid tang of old sweat and chlorine. He steps inside, and the
moment his boots sink into the mat, recollection comes barreling out of the
past:

A crunch *and a* pop... *Twang of tendons under his
skin. Shock...bright, frightening pain... O'Kai stared down at
his hyper-extended elbow, unaware he was screaming.*

*His sparring partner released the grip on O'Kai's
wrist, unwound his arms from around the unnaturally bent
limb, and stepped back.*

*MedTechs hustled over, laid O'Kai down on the
sparring mat, and immediately set to work.*

*"Look here!" the instructor shouted, pointing at the
young Operator candidate. "This is just the beginning!"*

*O'Kai felt two hot lines cut into his arm then
forceps under his skin, fishing for detached tendons that had
retracted up into his arm.*

*"To learn the proper technique," the instructor
continued, "you will break each others' bones, dislocate
joints, choke to unconsciousness, and strike at vital organs.
You will inflict immense pain upon one another, and you will
receive it in equal measure. Why?*

*"ONE, by experiencing the pain you inflict on
others, you understand the consequence of your actions. This
will determine whether or not you have the discipline to kill
and maim in combat.*

"TWO, every injury you sustain exposes a weakness.

*Our MedTechs will repair you and reinforce the injury so it
does not recur. Your bones will be cast in carbon mesh, your
joints cabled, your trachea armored, your skin toughened.
In time, you will come to appreciate how durable these
reinforcements make you.*

*"THREE, pain will be a regular part of your lives.
You will train your mesolimbic dopamine system to reward
this pain so that you will never again fear it. In the absence
of fear, all things are possible.*

*"FOUR, so you never have any doubt: this training
is for the sole purpose of DEFEATING OUR ENEMY.
Hesitation equals death. If you cannot be ruthless to your
enemy, YOU WILL NOT SERVE IN THE OPERATOR
CORPS.*

*"Now then, look at your partner. The person
across from you will cause you more pain than you've ever
experienced, and they will look you in the eye while doing it.
Soon, you'll thank them for it."*

*Tools probing and weaving between O'Kai's
muscles, the burning sinews being fastened to the bones on
each side of his elbow along with something else drilled
directly into the bone...*

*He looked down as MedTechs removed their tools
and zipped a bead of flesh weld down the incisions. Job
done, they sterilized their tools, repacked their MedKits, and
limped away to the edge of the room.*

*O'Kai rose to his feet and stared at his throbbing,
aching limb. Tentatively, he closed his hand and flexed his
biceps. His arm was strong again.*

*The instructor stepped up and took O'Kai's repaired
arm in both hands. "We admire the diamond's hardness,
yet even diamonds conform to the shape we impose." He
inspected the closure of the incision, then braced the arm
under the elbow and hoisted O'Kai off the ground.*

*O'Kai gasped, certain the joint would fly apart
again. It held, and the young man dangled at his shoulder,
awkwardly staring at his plank like arm.*

*"Soon, you'll understand," the instructor said to the
class, "that, once tempered, FLESH is the hardest substance
in the universe."*

O'Kai resumes his path. In the gloom, he activates his radio.

"Munro, respond."

After a brief delay, the Colonel replies, *"This is Munro, General. Go ahead."*

"Are all of our MedTechs aboard the *Europa*?"

"They are, sir. Finding accommodations now. Some of them look ready to fall over. I think they'll need more than four hours, standard."

"They've earned it. Grant whatever rest they need."

"Understood."

"Is the *Europa* ready to depart?"

"Captain Jones is announcing it as we speak."

"Can you get me audio?"

"Yes, sir."

Munro pipes the intercom through his radio, and Sharon's voice comes through O'Kai's helmet speakers.

"...have all heard that Cadre One has been discovered by our foe. It's true. But General O'Kai has a plan to keep us safe. That plan means leaving immediately and bringing the MedTechs with us while the Operators make their stand."

Random shouts break out in the background, only to be shouted down by others. O'Kai squints as he listens, trying to concentrate on Sharon's speech through the noise of the crowd.

"We're no good in a fight," Jones continues. *"We'd only be in the way. So we have to go and we have to look after our Cadre guests. Gonna be cramped, tempers may get short. But we've all come this far, because we're tough and we can take it. And because we* have *to take it. There isn't any other choice.*

"If Cadre One remains, we can return. But it isn't smart to stay when the enemy knows where you are. For now, we resume the search for a world we can colonize...a place we can finally set up our domes, raise our crops and our herds. In an infinite universe, it's only a matter of time. Possibly beyond our lifetimes, so we all must accept the Europa *may be our forever home. We have to love her and take care of her as she takes care of us. Just remember, there IS another world out there we can settle, one far away from our enemy. A world where we can begin normal life again. If we have to leave Cadre One, anyway, we might as well get looking for it.*

"Please help our Cadre friends adjust and make them feel welcome. It may be hard for us to understand one another sometimes, but we're all brothers and sisters. We've learned so much from them and they can learn as

much from us. We're lucky to have found each other. From here on, we do not rely on luck. We make our own.

"*Now, then, we'll let O'Kai and Chusan and Ralla do what they do best. And we know they are* bloody *good at it. So we can't be mucking about, spoiling their shots. We need to get out of their way, right now.*

"*With all of your efforts, the* Europa *is strong again. She's ready to take us where we need to go. Let's get cracking, yeah? To your posts!*"

There is a mixture of enthusiastic shouts from some while others strain to give orders over angry yells.

"*I think that's all,*" Munro says via radio.

"What do you see on your end? Are the Colonists handling it?"

"*Most that I can see, yes. Some not so much, but it looks like Jones is in control.*"

"Best we could've hoped for."

"*I agree.*" There is a silence, which Munro breaks. "*How is the reactor?*"

"Stable. Ralla's keeping close watch."

"*And the containment field?*"

"Holding."

"*Good, good... If I may, General...*"

"Yes?"

"*There's risk enough in breeding plasmas of Positrons and Antiprotons, but it's nothing compared to when we merge them into AntiHydrogen. I have as much confidence in Ralla as I do myself to manage the neutral trap multi-pole fields...but I must say again, before we move to the compression and injection phase, we should be sure everyone has moved to minimum safe distance.*"

"Understood, Munro. Any trouble with the incubators?"

"*No, sir. All of them properly boxed and stored.*"

"And they were decontaminated before transport?"

"*Thoroughly. Packed in like this, we're ripe for an outbreak, so we left no trace of residual virus in the breeding chambers.*"

"Good man. Anything else?"

"*There, uh... I'm useful as a field surgeon and engineer. I could save lives on the front line—*"

"Thank you, Colonel," O'Kai overrides. "You're where you'll do the most good."

Munro pauses, and lets out a deep breath. "*Aye, sir.*"

"One last thing, Munro."

"*Sir?*"

"Our Operators were never in better hands than yours, myself included. That's why you *must* go with the Colonists. I can't trust them to take care of themselves, much less our MedTechs. And to be blunt, their engineering solutions are shoddy, temporary, as if they're unconcerned with what future generations will inherit. I'd be a failure if I left our MedTechs with anyone less capable than you."

There is a pause on the line. "*Thank you, General.*"

"O'Kai out."

The general switches off his radio just as he arrives at his ultimate destination. The doors to the Cadre arena slide aside at his approach, and as he strides through, Chusan's voice thunders,

"ATTEN-*TION!*"

Dozens of Guns and Bricks turn toward the doorway, stamp to attention, and salute.

"As you were," O'Kai replies.

The group of Operators pulls apart at the middle, and in the gap between them, O'Kai sees the brightly lit Arena, occupied by thirty new Operator candidates. Ten are tall and muscular. Ten are massively built with wide shoulders and thick legs. Ten are slender, shaved heads planted with silver terminals. All of them are clothed in charcoal gray nylon shorts.

They remain at attention as Maddock and Keiko stride up and down their rows, scrutinizing, criticizing, chastising.

Chusan steps in beside O'Kai and walks with him to the arena's low wall. "They're not as tough as we need them to be," he says quietly. "With so many coming on-line at once, we had to supplement nutrition with colonist calories." Chusan scowls. "Better they were underweight than...*soft.*"

O'Kai frowns. "It's a long journey. You'll have to toughen them on the way. Can we outfit them all?"

"Just. Erik kept his MedTechs on stims for days, and they got it done. Full kit for each new candidate, whether they deserve it or not."

O'Kai watches Keiko and Maddock as they try to intimidate individual candidates in their rows. To the general's dismay, some of the new candidates visibly flinch.

"I see what you mean," O'Kai says. The general squints at Keiko, noticing the Gun appears to have two complete arms. "Keiko has a prosthetic?"

"Yes, sir. Munro and Sahara took some notes out of the Cadre Two medical archive Shao-Lo brought back. The prosthetic is delicate, but inside armor, it's almost as good as the real thing."

O'Kai nods while still frowning at the rows of candidates. "Are we ready to pull out?"

"Soon as we get this bunch sorted, we will be."

"And our fleet?"

"Geeks are at the helms now, keeping the ships heated in case the Blueskins jump in."

"And you're clear on your orders?"

"No question. Ralla and I split the fleet and head for Earth, leaving you two ships here at Cadre One." Chusan looks over his shoulder to make sure none of the Operators are listening in, then he asks, "General, why not come with us?"

"Have to give the impression we're still here, Chusan. We need the enemy to believe they caught us so we can lure them in close. Can't do that with Drones and machines. Speaking of, are the Drones reprogrammed?"

"Beckert's tweaking the algorithms now. Drones'll keep the machines running, do maintenance, make basic repairs, take care of their own needs. Won't be good for much else, though."

"It's enough."

The officers stare at the candidates in the Arena, silently marking the ones who are weathering Maddock's and Keiko's abuse.

"Too bad we can't get 'em out of here," Chusan states. "The Drones, I mean. May not be sentient, but still..."

"I know."

"Is the *Europa* on her way yet?"

"As we speak."

"Jones pulled it off? Never would have believed it."

O'Kai smirks, then he crosses his arms. "Are Munro's warheads loaded?"

"Affirmative. Every tenth shell carries a viral package. If all goes as planned, the Blueskins'll assume they're duds and wait until after the fight to dig 'em out."

"If we're lucky, whole crews will be exposed."

"And if we're *very* lucky, they'll get all the way home before realizing they're infected."

O'Kai squints at the candidates again. "Experience is going to be critical on this one, Chusan. We'll need every Operator, including this lot. Can Thompson be brought to the standard?"

"I thought so."

"But?"

"I asked Argo for a straight-up recommendation. He said, 'no.' Said Thompson was too involved with Maiella. Wouldn't integrate with another team."

O'Kai's brow bunches. "If anyone would have given a recommendation, it would've been Argo."

"Agreed."

The men stare into the Arena.

"You know what to do with this mess, Colonel."

"That I do, sir."

O'Kai turns on his heel and strides out through the Arena's automatic doors. Before they shut, Chusan's caustic shouts spill into the corridor as he berates every single operator candidate present.

CONFIRMED SIGHTING

Boredom. Inconceivable, intolerable boredom.

Dressed in his charcoal grays, O'Kai paces Council Chambers. His armor hangs in the corner on a moveable cart, each part staged and ready for rapid assembly. A slim, rectangular back rack rests at the bottom of the cart with a stout cable coiled beside it. His long rifle leans against the wall, tranquil and still in every way that he is not.

The *Europa* departed months ago, in a direction he prefers not to know. Ralla and Chusan left shortly after, leading their fleet of captured warships toward Earth at nearly three million kilometers per second. Cadre One's silos are charged to capacity, hard-wired to the Solar Collectors for continuous power feed. And the sub-level containment fields Munro engineered are nearly bursting with AntiHydrogen.

There is nothing to do but wait.

Could be minutes, O'Kai mulls. *Or years. Could be never. No way to know until the enemy arrives.*

For what feels like the thousandth time he mentally reviews the plan for Cadre One's defense, lack of other responsibilities allowing him to obsess over every meticulous detail.

I'm over thinking it. Good plans are ruined this way.

As he paces, the room suddenly seems confining, poorly optimized. He sets his eyes upon the heavy, semi-circular table at the room's center then shoves the flat side of it against the wall. It groans and squeals the entire way. The chairs he stacks on top, and it occurs to him this could be the first time in centuries the table has moved. Maybe the first time ever.

At the floor's center, etched into the deck plates where the table once stood, is a faint outline of the Cadre Hawk. Endless scuffing of boots under the table has scoured it away in five irregular patches, but the caption around the edge is still legible.

Covert Accelerated Defense Research (CADRe)
PROJECT ONE

O'Kai strips down to his undersuit and rests the dress grays on the table. Returning to the room's center, he tips himself forward and lands on the floor in push up position. His hands slide down to his waist and the general presses his entire body off the floor as a horizontal plank. His powerful arms do not quake.

O'Kai tilts his face toward the floor, elevates his legs, then presses himself up into a handstand. Like a giant lever, the man lowers himself horizontal again before sinking down to the floor and repeating the movement.

Regardless that the expenditure of calories is unnecessary, it feels correct to do something, to do anything but remain idle. And in mindless exertion, the general approaches the inner calm his unsettled pacing could not provide.

After his second set of twenty repetitions, O'Kai halts himself in handstand position. As he stares into the floor plates his mind wanders to a time just before the *Europa* departed and took all of his people away:

> *The Counselor, walking down the ramp of a transport in Cadre One's Landing Bay... a flat object in his hand...*
>
> *"General!" he shouted, over the racket of loaders and cargo movers. "I have something for you."*
>
> *Waiting for the android to approach, marking to himself how life-like a simulacrum of a Colonist, minus all of the vexing self-interests...*
>
> *"I want you to know how grateful we are," the Counselor began. "I can't imagine how hard it must be for you, being parted from those you live to serve."*
>
> *"Not necessary, Counselor. But I appreciate your concern."*
>
> *The Counselor extended his arm, offering a slim, flexible slate. "I'm sure you'll be able to keep yourself busy, but just in case you have some down time, I've prepped some*

reading material for you."

Taking the slate, and thumbing up a list of titles...

"What subjects?"

"There are some histories," the Counselor
explained, "some tactical and strategic guides, though I
doubt they'll be of much use to you. What I hope you'll find
interesting is the fiction."

"Fik-shun?"

"Yes. Fiction means these stories never actually
happened. Though most of them could have."

A scowl and a powerful urge to hand the gift back.
But asking instead, "What makes you think I would be
interested in false accounts?"

"False accounts? Uh... Well, you run simulations,
do you not?"

"Frequently."

"Those aren't actual battles, but you learn from
them, yes?"

"We do."

"Consider these stories simulations, then. The
situations the characters get in, the way they either succeed
or fail is illuminating. There's wisdom here, General, I
assure you."

Taking a second look... Dubious, but intrigued...

"You have a suggestion where I should begin?"
O'Kai asked.

"How about the one at the top?"

Scanning the list, and reading aloud, "One thousand
nine hundred eighty-four... This number is important?"

The Counselor, with his knowing smile, replied,
"You'll find out if you read it. And I really wish I could be
here once you've finished it."

"Reason?"

"Because for the life of me, I can't guess who you'll
think the hero is."

O'Kai lowers himself to the metal floor and sits cross-legged,
thinking back to when the boredom became too much to bear; and,
in desperation for some activity or stimulus, he finally gave in to the
Counselor's recommendation. Skeptically, he opened the book file and

read about a frail, prematurely decrepit man named, Winston—a man who consciously subverted the laws of his own society, a man who indulged in behaviors he knew would end his life, a man who kept company of another malcontent like himself (a person irritatingly similar to Maiella). Winston knew the rules that would permit him to live and contribute to society, yet he broke them anyway out of some latent suicidal instinct. The entire concept of such a man was absurd, an exaggeration of the Colonists' weakest attributes. Often, O'Kai put the slate down, but the absence of other responsibilities was maddening. His mind unoccupied, he picked the slate back up and continued to read simply because there was nothing better to do.

Large sections of the book were given to rambling treatises on ideology, which he gave a cursory glance. He was interested even less in the drawn out physical and psychological tortures the characters suffered toward the end. But there was one perfect moment in the middle that leapt off the page: as Winston gazed out through the window of a short-term living space, he watched an old woman hanging clothes to dry. Her wide body and rough red skin showed the hardness of a life spent bearing children then raising them. Winston was certain this woman was enslaved to these offspring, existing only to care for their needs, yet she sang as she worked. There was joy in her life from the good work she did in service to others. Hers was a fundamental inner beauty that transcended outward appearance. And in that precise moment, Winston understood that the future did not belong to people like himself, it belonged to those who could labor selflessly from birth to death and keep singing until the very end.

How forcefully that image struck, how clearly O'Kai recognized the same joy to serve, no matter the cost to oneself. The imperfections of his MedTechs, the scars of his Operators are no impediment to his esteem (quite the opposite, in fact); and, like the woman hanging laundry for her children, he sees the same inner beauty.

"Theirs is the future," O'Kai echoes. "And I am the dead."

"*GENERAL O'KAI, ENEMY CONTACT,*" blares Beckert's voice via intercom. "*Task force incoming, two-seven-one karem one-zero-five. Range eighteen million and closing. Mixed complement. Speed: point one C.*"

O'Kai leaps from the floor and sweeps the chairs from the top of the table, letting them crash and clatter to the floor. He punches his access code into the terminal nested inside the tabletop, and an array of holowindows projects in front of him. Around the periphery, dashboard gauges update with critical indications of Cadre One's systems. In the center, a three-dimensional image plots of a distant fleet spaced thousands of kilometers wide.

"Understood, Geek. Option Alpha is authorized."

"Received," Beckert replies. *"Stealthing. Going radio silent."*

O'Kai zooms in on the distant fleet, switching from one satellite view to another, analyzing deployment, ship class, attack strength. All around the incoming fleet, background stars shine brightly, but between the ships in vanguard a shimmering darkness forms. The general leans in, studying it. Before his eyes the incoming fleet disappears behind an undulating surface like infinitely black water.

From the corridor beyond Council Chambers comes a rapid thudding of heavy footfalls. In anticipation of his approaching visitor, O'Kai moves to the door, opens it, and hurries back to his screens. The thuds grow in intensity until Argo runs through the open doors, dressed in full kit, cannon slung across his back. He salutes.

"Sir! Confirmed sighting?" the Brick asks.

"Affirmative," O'Kai answers without looking away from the screens. He points into the heart of the holographic formation. "This field deployed between vessels... Have you seen it before?"

Argo peers over the general's shoulder at the enemy vanguard.

"Aye, sir. Blueskins tried to net us with it during escape from Earth. Energy bounces off it like a mirror."

"Does Beckert know that?"

"Aye, sir. He's wise to it."

O'Kai's jaw flexes as the range counter ticks below seventeen million kilometers. He is about to speak when he notices the shimmering field is altering its deployment, forming a concave dish. Shimmering intensifies with reflected starlight.

"An energy mirror..." he thinks aloud. The general types at his terminal, and the screen plots the parabolic shape, illustrating how any shot from Cadre One will be reflected directly back.

"So they're going to come straight at us?" the general says, striding to his armor. He plunges his legs through the lower half, steps into heavy boots, slides into his torso plating, punches his arms through the sleeves, and pulls on his gauntlets.

"Argo, get back to the virus ship and warm it up." He takes the heavy pack, lifts it over his head and guides it down the rails on his back. It latches with a solid click. "We're going to introduce ourselves."

"Aye, SIR!" Argo about-faces and dashes from the room.

O'Kai snatches his rifle and throws the strap over his head. Reaching behind himself, he finds the stout cable from the back rack and jams its plug into the rifle's battery port. The weapon hums immediately and settles at full charge.

Helmet in one hand, he strides back to the table and enters a string of commands with his free hand. The screen displays in large amber letters, AUTONOMOUS TARGETING, ENABLED. ENEMY IN RANGE, 10 SECONDS.

Into his radio, O'Kai orders, "Beckert and Kibwe, get me a hole in that parabolic field."

In the bright hologram two dots streak out of the distance, cross behind the shimmering wall, then streak away. Fiery detonations bloom around the periphery of the field, and a notch in the wall collapses. Through the gap, O'Kai spies a cluster of Blueskin warships huddled in tight formation. Already, the vanguard is redeploying to close the gap.

TARGETS SELECTED, IN RANGE, the screen proclaims.

Subsonic vibrations telegraph through the floor plates as Cadre One's Exciplex silos discharge. In the hologram, the lead vessel takes repeated hits on the bow, seeming to absorb them without effect until columns of vaporized metal spout into space around it. The vessel rolls and veers away, but Cadre lasers track with it, punching blast after blast through the side. Internal explosions bulge the hull, cracking it and puffing away entire sections like scales. Lasers target the new bulges and burn through weakened points, blistering more sections farther down its length. Tiny craft pour from the ship like bees from a smashed hive, chased by orange blooms of secondary explosions. All fight gored out of it, the ship's running lights darken and it no longer maneuvers.

Adjacent carriers jostle to evade the disintegrating, burning ship as it drifts through their formation, then they disgorge their own waves of fighter craft. Tiny dots swarm in O'Kai's holoscreens as enemy pilots try to negotiate the sudden traffic jam, spilling chaotically around the edge of the closing field.

Beckert and Kibwe race through the heart of the enemy formation again, and atomic detonations swell in their wake. O'Kai's holowindow whites-out. The sub-sonic vibrations subside.

SENSORS IN RECOVERY, the screen announces, and the general seeks impatiently for detail to emerge. At last, the glare in the holowindow fades and enemy positions plot in a rapidly expanding fog of debris. Less than a third of the small fighter craft remain. There is also a much larger gap in the reflective field.

"*Well done*, Geeks."

Subsonic vibrations resume, and Cadre One's weapons tear into the flash-blinded vessels. Invisible beams scorch and carve their way through enemy hulls, gutting them in brilliant flashes. Ships jockey for cover, crowding, colliding, disappearing in catastrophic sprays of plasma.

As satisfying a first round as it is, O'Kai frowns at debris filling the battlefield.

Beckert and Kibwe won't be able to make another high speed run through that... We get bloody from here.

O'Kai drops his helmet over his head, latches it securely, and swats down his faceplate. "Argo," O'Kai transmits via helmet radio, "I'm en route to Landing Bay. Be ready to depart on my arrival."

"*Received, Sir,*" Argo transmits.

The general casts a last glance at shifting formations in the Holowindow then sprints from Council Chambers into the central corridor, around the ring to the main entry hall, and into the Landing Bay. There, an idling virus ship squats low on spidery struts. At O'Kai's approach, idling engines rise in pitch.

O'Kai slides under the low craft and pops up through the open hatch. Argo is strapped into the pilot's recliner on the left. On the right, a barrel-shaped canister is strapped into a recliner, its only marking the stenciled letter H with a horizontal bar across the top. The general shoves his rifle into an overhead cradle, seals the hatch, and parks himself in the center recliner.

"Take us out, Brick."

"Aye, sir."

Not bothering to de-pressurize the bay, Argo remotely opens the doors, and a gust hits the virus ship from behind. The Brick kicks the thrusters and rides the gust between parting bay doors out over the crater floor, great billows of gray dust preceding them. With an easy pull of the stick, he arcs the craft upward into vast night.

O'Kai opens multiple holowindows above his console. One view is directly back at Cadre One. The station's quartet of battle optics angle toward the advancing enemy, tracking distant targets with minute corrections. Below each mirror the faintest violet glow emanates from silos as they discharge in swift succession.

O'Kai magnifies his forward view, and the screen zooms in on a free-falling junk yard of scorched fragments. Faint glimmers among the debris belie the ferocity of Cadre Laser hits on exposed enemy ships. With each shot, the gap in the reflective wall widens until undamaged ships behind the shield redeploy, and the gap closes as if it were a zipper in elastic fabric. Without a clear target Cadre One's silos cease fire.

O'Kai's eyes flit across his screens as he mulls options, when the parabolic field slows its approach. A cloud of debris, still moving at point one C, rushes ahead of the incoming fleet.

O'Kai grins.

That'll clear the clutter between enemy warships...

Without needing to be told, Beckert and Kibwe streak in from the void, crisscrossing again behind the shimmering field. Ovoid trails of nuclear devastation bloom in their wakes.

O'Kai's screens wash white then recover, resolving an overlapping haze of irregular specks. In the fading atomic glow, two large ships appear in the distance, exposed by a fresh gap in the protective field. Both ships swerve to get behind the reflective wall, exposing their broadsides.

Cadre Lasers pump burst after burst of incinerating beams into the dodging vessels. One takes multiple hits before reaching safety. Its companion cracks at the rear quarter. Plumes of plasma stream from the compromised hull and the stern vanishes in a dazzling blue-white flash.

Got you.

Fast fighter craft flood around the parabolic shield in numbers rivaling the blips of junk. Organized into widely spaced formations, they fan out and race around the expanding debris field. O'Kai's grin straightens.

"Too thinly spread for nukes," Argo notes, sneaking a peek at O'Kai's screens.

O'Kai thumps the keys at his terminal, altering Cadre One's fire control. On screen, lead formations of small attack craft highlight with the caption,

LOW OUTPUT RAPID AUTO-FIRE SELECTED.

Cadre Lasers re-orient toward the swift formations, but even at quintuple fire rate, most shots fail to hit the nimble craft. O'Kai taps his console again and the screen answers,

HALO-FIRE SELECTED.

All four of Cadre One's mirrors track a single target and fire an overlapping shot of slightly de-focused beams, painting a killing circle bigger than the target's range of movement. Each shot brings a kill.

"No good," O'Kai announces. "At the speed they're coming in, we won't punch them out fast enough."

Before O'Kai can reprogram the targeting parameters, whole blocks of fighter craft disappear from view.

"Attackers are stealthing," Argo states.

"Did we expect that?" O'Kai asks.

"We did. And we should expect a mass missile strike once they close to two hundred thousand."

"Brick, steer to Oscar-Mike and hold position." O'Kai keys his transmitter and says into it, "Geek Kibwe, random engagement, shoot and scoot. Beckert, move to coordinates Oscar-Mike and retrieve."

O'Kai's hands fly across his terminal, pounding his commands into it with armored fingers. On screen, a ring-shaped patch around the edge of the debris field highlights with the caption,

FLASH-SCAN TARGETING ENABLED.

Cadre One's quartet of mirrors orients toward the patch of sky O'Kai selected. One silo outputs a steady, continuous beam, and the mirror orbits the beam rapidly around the edge of the debris field. Every time the beam sweeps over a hidden fighter, it ablates the surface, leaving a reflective puff behind the craft. The sky above Cadre One glows with sparse trails in smooth, regular formations.

The other three silos target heads of each trail and fire precise bursts, punching out whole formations at a time. Some craft, blinded by the flash scan, slide into a wingman, or veer into the debris field with fatal result. The rest break formation immediately, resuming their random jinks and feints.

"Sir," Argo warns, "I've got a stealthed vessel coming alongside, directly to starboard."

"Right on time, Beckert," O'Kai states. "Brick, relinquish control."

"Aye, sir," Argo replies, taking hands from the stick. His display scrolls lines of code, the interior lighting shifts to amber, and the control stick locks against the console. "Beckert has control."

The craft thrusts sideways and rolls ninety degrees, O'Kai's viewscreens distorting wildly as the virus ship crosses inside the stealth field of a Cadre warship. It touches down on metal hull plates with four solid klanks. The view ahead seems defective at first until O'Kai realizes another perfectly black virus ship like their own is squatting on the hull in front of them.

A smaller window opens in both Argo's and O'Kai's screens, showing a heavily augmented human secured into a flight recliner. Behind the Geek's visor, artificial eyes are set deep in a face the texture of gravel. A thick HDI rides atop the young man's head, connected to the consoles and breaker panels all around him. One arm is protected in a sleeve of Cadre armor, the other is a thin metal prosthetic from the mid-humerus down.

"Beckert, are we secure?" O'Kai asks.

"Affirmative, General," the Geek answers. "Inside the stealth field, no transmission escapes unless we raise an antenna."

"SitRep."

"Enemy task force on CBDR to Cadre One. Eighty vessels of mixed configuration. Kibwe is striking at the rear of the fleet, where command targets are most likely located."

"Results?"

"Several fighter wings have peeled off the main thrust and are returning toward the enemy fleet to defend."

"Not all?"

"No, sir. The enemy has committed to attack. They are diverting from a straight assault, however, and are running for Cadre One's horizon. Likely an attempt to evade our defenses."

"And our assets behind Cadre One?"

"Armed and active. I must caution, General, a major detonation may de-stabilize containment."

"Understood." O'Kai glances at the massive cylinder lashed to the recliner beside him. "Are you ready to deliver the package?"

"Standing by."

"Execute."

The virus ship's interior surfaces crackle, raising the hair on O'Kai's arms and neck. In an instant, they leap out to the void, far past the incoming enemy, turn back, and jump straight into formation at the heart of the enemy fleet.

Charged D-E Rails bristle from Beckert's warship, lock onto adjacent enemy vessels, and carve neat incisions through reinforced hull plates. Missiles streak from their tubes, shuddering the vessel with every launch. They dive at the fresh cuts and plunge through with bursts of blue flame. Successive hits burrow deeper, spreading rips, buckling entire decks, venting enemy equipment and personnel into the vacuum.

Diode lighting of Argo's console switches back to green, and Argo announces, "I have control."

"*Now!*" O'Kai shouts.

Argo hops the virus ship from Beckert's hull, emerging from the stealth field amid a maelstrom of jagged alloys and streaking missiles. He steers a course toward the nose of an enemy warship then throws the craft into a gentle tumble as if it was just another chunk of debris.

Beckert pumps another salvo into the enemy then jumps away. Tardy return shots blaze through the spot he vacated.

Argo and O'Kai drift amid the wreckage. Hurtling chunks slam against their sturdy hull, jolting the men in their recliners. Argo twitches with each hit, hovering his hand over the control stick. O'Kai looks at Argo's hovering hand then casts his gaze to the roof overhead.

"Any maneuver right now could be a dead giveaway," the general says.

Large hull plates and jettisoned machinery swoop near. Each time

Argo tenses for a hit, then exhales as it passes by; and soon, the only hull strikes are dull clangs from slower-moving junk or a thud from something softer.

Despite the virus ship's tumbling, O'Kai's holowindows maintain a smooth view of the long, tapered vessel ahead of them. Its near side is torn open in a ragged gash, spewing sparks and vapor into the void, but the ship holds its place in formation. Bow struts still emit the shimmering black field that interconnects with sister ships in the vanguard.

"We're going to just overshoot the bow," Argo announces.

"Good. Depressurize the cabin."

"Aye, sir."

Argo tests the seal of his faceplate and complies. Without air, the cabin goes deathly quiet. Argo risks a look at O'Kai and finds the general is looking at him.

"You have a question, sir?" the Brick asks via his helmet radio.

"We're using this field as a blast reflector. Is that right?"

"That's right."

O'Kai leans forward to see the stout canister strapped into the right-hand recliner, then looks again at Argo. "Do we have any way of knowing this'll work?"

The Brick snorts. "We modeled it with high confidence. But this part? Pure science."

O'Kai throws off his restraints and drifts to the canister's recliner, having to brace himself against the ship's awkward gyrations.

"Careful, sir," Argo says. "You're changing our center of rotation."

"No way around that."

The general takes hold of the recliner's rail, sizing up a metal cylinder larger than Argo's armored chest. He removes its belts then guides the cylinder, and himself, to the circular hatch in the floor. "Open up," he orders.

Argo triggers the hatch and it opens like a camera iris. Beyond, the cosmos wheels in a show of radiant stars, savaged enemy vessels, and shimmering black energy.

Wrestling the cylinder into position, O'Kai strains to keep it from bashing against the hatch coaming. Groaning, he shoves the massive thing toward the ship as they pass.

Argo seals the hatch and O'Kai works his way back to his recliner.

"Lots of strange emissions from those bow struts," Argo says, studying his screens. "Signatures I don't recognize."

"Good. Might mask the pill we just dropped."

As they tumble to the far side of the wounded enemy ship, O'Kai stares through the roof again, thinking, *Now would be a good time, Beckert.*

As if summoned, Beckert streaks out of the void and arrives in formation, weapons hot. His beams carve through unblemished enemy hulls just before his missiles slam their way through.

Argo rights his tumbling craft, aims toward Beckert's ship, and kicks the thrusters to max. But when he reads the distance in his viewscreen he shakes his head.

"Gah! *It's too far,*" Argo calls out. "*They're gonna zero him out if he waits for us!*"

"Beckert, *wave off,* repeat, *wave off!*" O'Kai radios.

The drives of Beckert's ship glow with coalescing power when a single column of light lances them, then another. Plasma jets erupt from each hit, and Beckert's warship skids sideways. The Geek keeps his weapons pumping into the enemy, but more enemy ships slide in for the kill. Missiles dive into the light armor on one side of Beckert's ship, exploding out through the other. The spine buckles and folds.

"General, get clear," Beckert radios, "main drive's going crit—"

The engines vanish in a spherical blast that shatters the ship.

Roaring, Argo dives his craft away from the blast wave and stands on the thruster. His chin tucks into his chest, staring at the viewscreen ahead with total concentration.

O'Kai grips his recliner rails as Argo swoops toward a carrier larger than all of Cadre One. The sky around them fills with bolts, bullets, and missiles, some grazing, some detonating at proximity and rattling the men in their recliners. Hypervelocity rounds zip through the small craft, every perforation triggering a red-scripted alert in Argo's holowindow. When O'Kai glances at the empty recliner beside him, he finds a five-millimeter hole gouged through the middle, right where the canister was lashed moments earlier.

"They might have us, sir," Argo warns between impacts.

"We're still in the blast radius?" O'Kai shouts.

"Aye, sir," Argo answers back.

"Can you jump us out?"

"Of *this?*" the Brick says, rowing the control stick, desperately evading the biggest threats. "A Geek could. Not me."

O'Kai tries to focus on the violently shuddering screens in front of him. "Go right at the carrier and swing us behind it." Into his radio, he sends, "Geek Kibwe, get clear. Option Yankee is authorized."

Argo's great head pivots toward O'Kai, then swivels forward. He leans closer to the controls, swerving around incoming rockets, spinning away from sprays of high velocity rounds, and makes a suicidal dive at the behemoth filling his viewscreen. Holding to the last possible moment, Argo pulls back on the stick, but nose thrusters do not give their full boost. He heaves the stick back repeatedly.

"BRACE!" the Brick yells.

The virus ship bashes hard and bounces back into line of fire. Incoming rounds batter the ship with vicious thumps while Argo works the stick, trying to wrestle his bent craft below the carrier's effective range of fire. He skims the carrier's smooth hull, rounds the underside of the titanic barge to relative quiet of its far side, spins the ship about, kicks the thruster to a halt, and touches down with a quartet of magnetic *klanks*.

"Now or never, sir," Argo says.

O'Kai speaks the code into his terminal and executes Option Yankee.

In the ensuing calm the men look at one another, mirroring the same unvoiced question, *Did it go off?*

Screens flash white and fail with brilliant blue sparks. Every light in the cabin winks out. But darkness is transitory as blinding white light streams in through splits and perforations. Heat penetrates every part of their bodies.

O'Kai's eyepieces dim to maximum, yet the onyx black lenses cannot block the brilliance; and, through his crushed-shut eyelids, he is sure he can see through the hull of the virus ship, itself.

Dissociation from flesh amid heavenly radiance... A confrontation with forces as incomprehensible as gods' motivations... Clenched muscles slacken. The mind yields. And a blast wave comes like the tearing of continents.

OPTION ZULU

Lashed to his recliner in a Cadre Virus Ship, HDI hard-wired to the console, Kibwe lurks far from the battlefield. His blackened craft squats on the hull of a gutted, unmanned Cadre Corvette—a vessel hollowed of accommodations, stripped of life support systems, and packed with as much weaponry as could be shoehorned into the vacated spaces.

Compulsively, he looks over his shoulder at the open hatch in the floor, eyes tracing the thick umbilical cable running through it into the warship. Through that cable Kibwe feels the vessel's every impulse as if it were a second spinal cord. Sensing apparatus are his eyes and ears. The reactor core thrums with accelerated annihilations like an excited heart. Deep Space Drives are warm and primed like sprinter's muscle at the starting gate. The vessel sings its tension to him in high harmonics, obeying his every thought yet begging for action.

Kibwe's killing attention weaves through the enemy herd, hull configurations spinning through his virtual eyes in three-dimensions. He does not seek the sick, weak, or lame, however. His target is far more specific.

A vessel calling the shots, he thinks. *Command and Control.*

Statistics cascade through his goggles like falls of water. He catches every attribute, weighing them intuitively, rejecting and discarding with a mental flick. And then he spots a fat, ovoid bulk, jutting thick pylons prickly with external antennae. Heavily encoded transmissions emanate from the vessel with tremendous broadcast strength. Mid-sized warships fly protective perimeter at a precise two-thousand meter radius, their D-E rails standing straight out from round turrets as if they have caught a chill.

Nearly salivating, the young Geek thinks, *You're the one. And your escorts have to stay out of your way, don't they? They could interfere with transmissions, block your view... Or maybe you'd jam their comms if they got any closer...*

Code speeds through his goggles as he solves an enormously complex flight path. His lips curve. Main drives flare, space-time bends, and the ship falls through the distortion.

An instant later, Kibwe is alongside his quarry, flying formation at constant range and bearing. D-E rails and missile batteries extend from the Corvette like spines of a venomous fish. Targets lock, and Kibwe looses at point blank range. Shots rip through pylons and smash external arrays, prying a gash between reinforced hull plates. Salvo after salvo pours through the gap, wrinkling the vessel's skin, warping it, and cracking it with volcanic plumes of flame. The bulky ship's transmissions cease, replaced by the fizz and pop of atomic decay.

"Geek Kibwe, get clear. Option Yankee is authorized."

Kibwe's eyes widen at O'Kai's transmission and his ears slide back. He dives his ship out of formation like a whale headed for deep water, quick-plotting a jump back to the safety of deep space. Main drives glimmer with power and the ship leaps out to the void, delinquent enemy beams and missiles streaking through space behind him.

Jump complete, Kibwe spins his ship around, and he gazes back at the enemy formation. There is a flash so bright, it rivals the blue-white star that Cadre One orbits—a painful brilliance rich with gamma rays. It balloons, crashes against the parabolic shield wall and reflects, sending a double blast wave through the enemy fleet. In another blink it is gone, leaving radiant sparks in its wake.

Kibwe gawks at the destruction. Ships directly adjacent to the blast are no longer there, turned to ash and swept away in a stellar gale. Those next in formation are peeled to their structural ribs, powerless and drifting. Surrounding ships are scorched white, drunkenly thrusting this way or that, running lights winking off then on again.

Despite the blast's savagery, the bulk of the fleet is unscathed. Surviving vessels slow so that the ruined hulks drift ahead. Cleared of debris, the enemy fleet reorganizes and resumes its approach behind a shimmering black curtain.

With a grimace, Kibwe looks far ahead of the fleet and realizes because the blast wave reflected, all of the fast attack craft were untouched.

They'll be at Cadre One any moment.

He waits for word from O'Kai, but there is none. He searches for a sign of Beckert, but no other vessel harries the enemy advance.

I'm all that's left. It's up to me.

The Geek swings his ship toward Cadre One. With a flare of code in his goggles, he plots the jump and engages.

Twenty kilometers directly above the asteroid's night side, Kibwe zooms to a halt then pivots to face the enemy fleet. With virtual eyes the Geek scans an immense zone of shattered hardware, hurtling toward Cadre One at thirty-thousand kilometers per second. Cadre One's silos blaze an ever-expanding flash-scan ring around the edge of the debris field, but no targets are revealed; and without targets, the other three silos stand idle.

Where did the fighters go?

The Geek patches into Cadre One's satellites for a view of the asteroid's far side, but no matter how hard he looks, he finds only bright gray dust, boulders, crags, and craters. With a grunt, he turns back to confront the vast junk yard hurtling in.

Cadre One's gonna take a beating. Gotta soften that blow...

Kibwe's goggles blaze with code and all four Cadre silos re-orient toward the debris. He targets the largest threats with coordinated, sustained beams, driving them off course, then he automates the silos to independently target smaller fragments. Some shots over penetrate, hit the shimmering black field and reflect at a near angle, punching deep holes into the asteroid. He mentally scrambles, dialing back output and widening the beam focus.

Facing threats on all sides now, the Geek closes his eyes, letting the satellites and his ship's sensing apparatus paint a total image in his digital mind, letting his consciousness pour into the hardware, imbuing it with his reactions and skills, until there is no longer any boundary between man and machine.

A symphony of coordinated firepower streams into the sky over Cadre One. Silos punch out the biggest threats. Missiles streak out from Kibwe's Corvette, detonating in the middle of the cloud, blowing open a slim channel and expanding it with each successive shot. D-E rails pick off smaller fragments. But despite his efficiency he may as well be trying to shoot down a hurled handful of sand.

And that's just the fragments I can see, he thinks, *but if I don't deal with those fighters Cadre One has no chance.*

Kibwe calculates rate of enemy travel, last known vectors, pattern of deployment, reactions to attack, angles of deflection, and references them against known enemy tactics. In his virtual battlefield, arrows begin where the attack craft last appeared. They extend in a ring all the way around the field of debris as though they are going to streak right by the asteroid. Once the arrows move below Cadre One's horizon, they make a sharp turn toward the asteroid, continuing right down to the surface. Rather than turning back toward Cadre One, however, they head toward the far side of the asteroid, skim the surface, and loiter there.

Taking shelter behind Cadre One? They're using their own destroyed ships as a first wave attack...and once it passes, they'll swarm in on all sides for the kill...

Satellites pulse red in his mental projection, warning him of the debris field's current position. When he extrapolates rate of spread as it passes Cadre One, he sees the satellites are well inside the outer edges.

Without detection and ranging, the silos can't fire... Cadre One'll be blind!

The Geek glares behind his visor.

We're not blind yet.

Kibwe burns all of the satellites' fuel to thrust them as far from Cadre One as possible. In the little time left, he bounces a transmission to the day side of Cadre One, where a vast field of pop-up mines waits just below the dusty surface.

Arm payload, passive sense.

The mines activate, appearing in his mental projection like a close-cropped beard across the sunlit side of the asteroid. He focuses on the spot where all the arrows converge.

Think you're safe there?

The Geek checks the debris cloud one last time.

Better clear out, myself. But first...

Kibwe solves a jump solution and brings his drives up to temperature, then commands the Cadre silos to lock down and shelter. Immediately, the rotating mirrors above each silo fall forward and drop below the surface while heavy covers slide over the tops.

Kibwe aims his vessel out to the black, engines hot, but the satellites still flash red in his mental view. Breaking up the larger fragments has resulted in several new blooms of smaller fragments that overlap the satellites' new paths.

If the satellites are destroyed, I'll have to be Cadre One's eyes. I can't do that from out there...

He studies the approaching storm with fragments ranging from a few millimeters to several decameters across. Estimations of kinetic energy plot in his visor. He shakes his head.

There'll be nothing left to defend. And a major hit could destabilize containment. Do I want to be anywhere near?

The storm of deadly fragments is imminent.

My orders are to defend Cadre One at all costs. Here I stay.

Kibwe stealths his ship, cools his main drives, and thrusts over the limb of the asteroid into the brilliance of the blue-white sun. Behind him, the smallest fragments arrive first, pelting the surface in a shower of glancing impacts. Larger fragments intersperse the rain, pummeling the asteroid's night side, sending up towers of gray dust. Stone explodes with every strike at the asteroid's edge, peppering Kibwe's ship, forcing him to thrust farther into daylight. Clouds of dust roll around the limb of the asteroid, hanging in the weak gravity, ripped and fanned by fresh impacts.

The Geek looks back at Cadre One's twin solar collectors standing at the border between day and night. They are like men facing a firing squad, perforated over and over, disintegrating by degrees until a massive hull plate clears them both in a single swipe. Scattered rock and metal slams Kibwe's ship. Clouds of dust drift past him, hazing his views.

Got to get out of this mess. But if I go any farther, I risk getting shot up by those fighters. Need a peek...

The Geek aims all four satellite views at his best guess where the fighters are hiding. Even with multiple views overlapped and filtered, all he sees are dusty gray craters and boulder fields.

One satellite view suddenly spins, transmitting a dizzying video stream before ending with a hiss of static. Another satellite fails, then another, and the last goes dark with a violent *brap*. His perspective collapses, leaving him blinking behind his goggles.

Time's up. Gotta flush them out.

Kibwe connects directly to the hidden mines and sets a manual trigger. Then, he looses his last rack of missiles where his virtual battlefield predicts the fighters are hiding.

The missiles drop low, follow the contours of the planetoid, and disappear over the horizon in a wide spread. In the glare of the local star there is no visible flash to tell him if they struck, and the Geek wonders if he hit anything at all. Risking a peek, he thrusts vertically and spies a wide plume of ejecta rising into space ahead of him.

With every sensor of his vessel, the Geek reaches into the plume, searching for any sign of metal, fuel, or movement. There is none.

All I hit was the ground. Well try and hide from THIS...

Kibwe triggers all remaining mines at once. The day side shudders and belches meters of regolith into low orbit. Clusters of secondary explosions bloom over a kilometer from where he thought the enemy would be. Undulations and currents of stealthed fighters snake through the lofted dust, all converging on him.

He swings his D-E rails at the head of each disturbance with full output. Every shot finds a victim, breaking a small craft apart with puff of flame. But dozens more shoot back. Kibwe dives toward the hard deck, getting raked by beams, feeling every impact and perforation through the ship's umbilical. Teeth clenched, he thrusts back toward dense clouds of rock and dust on the night side.

The hail of deadly fragments is over, its speed carrying it past in mere moments, but there is so much vaulted regolith the sky above Cadre One is like loose soil. Kibwe pushes cautiously into it, wincing with every *bang* against the ship's sensing apparatus.

Below him, yawning impact craters still glow with heat. A faint signal penetrates the slowly settling murk, and he follows it to jets of vapor spitting dusty eddies into space. With sinking heart the Geek parks over the trampled landscape, watching his treasured home out gassing air he has breathed since decantation.

Unwilling to look any longer, he steers the ship away then flinches when a stiff figure bounces off the bow. He brings the ship to full stop and stares at the dirty white uniform with tall black numerals wheeling away into the haze.

Kibwe shakes his head, not ready to mourn. Against hope, he reaches out to the facility via wireless. Though faint, the comm signal pings back and allows access.

Sublevels are still intact...

With a blur of code in his goggles, Kibwe assesses stability of containment. In virtual view he sees the fields are running on battery back up with reduced power flow, yet are holding. Next, he checks the weapon silos. Three of the four are still on-line with battery reserves near full.

We're not beaten yet.

As the curtains of lofted rock descend, Kibwe peers out into space. The enemy's parabolic shield has halted several thousand kilometers away with the bulk of the fleet tucked safely behind it. And just above the asteroid's horizon, in every direction of the compass, there are more surviving fighter craft than he can dispatch. Their stealth fields are down, telling him they want to be seen.

They have the clear advantage... They could shoot me down at will... so why don't they?

In the unexpected lull, Kibwe confronts the aftermath.

Defending Cadre One would be a pitched fight, I knew that. I just...I thought we'd have fought better...

The Geek sends containment codes to Cadre One and is about to drop the field when he pauses.

"No. I must choose to survive," Kibwe reminds himself, echoing the most poignant lesson of his initiation to the Corps. He programs containment to drop after a sixty-second delay then guides his ship up to the edge of the haze.

C'mon, show me those stars... Got it!

The Geek solves the jump plan. The nose swings toward an unoccupied patch sky. His engines surge, but coordinated beams burn through his vessel. A missile slams the side, pitching it end over end and following shots break it in two.

The vessel screams its agony into his HDI then sensors go dark. Kibwe gasps for air, reeling and disoriented, amputated from his machine. At last, his eyes dial back into focus, and he gawks at his screen. The asteroid's surface approaches far too quickly.

The Geek yanks the umbilical to the Corvette, seals the hatch, and leaps his virus ship from the hull. He kicks the thrusters hard and bends the stick backwards, peeling away from the plummeting front half of his vessel. Falling rock and fragments of his own doomed ship slam against his craft as he weaves, jinks, and dodges, working his way out of the cloud for a clear view of the stars to reset his jump plan.

Once more... Just a glimpse...

The dust clears and Kibwe looks up at the falling back half of his bisected ship. Stuck in an endless build up without the command to execute, the Corvette's Deep Space Drives glow violet.

"No, NO, *NO!*"

He yanks the stick, but the DS Drives fail in a blinding glare, and a shocking thump of plasma bats his Virus Ship into the asteroid like a meteorite.

Kibwe's head lolls. The first thing he notices is that he can barely draw breath. His heavy eyelids part, and the Geek gazes drunkenly at the interior of his Virus Ship. The roof has folded inward in multiple places, reinforced carbon spars broken like twigs. The console is pressed hard into his gut, compacting his armor and crushing his legs. Grinding in his lower back warns him at least one vertebra, possibly his pelvis, is shattered. Coldness drills straight through his cracked teeth and salty copper washes over his tongue. One arm is too weak to move. The other is pinned beneath collapsed breaker panels. His only free movement is a thumb and index finger.

Visually tracing the distorted cabin lines tells him the entire front section has folded from a nose first impact. He guesses his feet are not far from his face, only separated by a half meter or less of twisted electronics. Somehow, the viewscreen is still functional and its connection to his HDI is intact.

Shivering from shock, the broken Geek concentrates on his screens. The explosion swept the sky above Cadre One clear, and Kibwe sees the entire enemy fleet arrayed in the distance. It is no longer hidden by the shimmering black field. Fighters hover in a wary perimeter around his crash site, close enough to shoot, but too far to be damaged by his self-detonation.

They've learned our tactics.

From the enemy fleet, one vessel advances. Boxy and plain, it has no visible weapons, no high gain antennae, but it transmits in the clear over a wide spectrum of channels.

A window opens in Kibwe's screen, showing an Eleto from the waist up. Calm and dignified, it wears a white uniform with red and gold piping at the seams. Metallic decoration rides on the ridges above each of its saffron-colored eyes. The Geek looks from the Eleto back to the boxy vessel.

THAT'S the command ship? He laughs cynically and starts a fit of bloody coughing.

The Eleto on screen gestures with clawed hands in placating motions, palms up, and open. Then it brings a hand over its chest, and speaks in earnest, pleading tones. The clawed hands gesture without malice as if inviting, drawing out. In conclusion, the Eleto dips its head while maintaining a vigilant gaze at the screen, voice dropping an octave to serious, warning tones. Its head lifts, the hands clasp one another, and the azure-skinned being waits quietly.

Smaller transport craft emerge from the boxy vessel with articulated legs attached at the four lower corners. They form a line and thrust toward Cadre One.

Landing party, Kibwe thinks. *They mean to invade. To drive us out of existence and take what's left for themselves... Not again.*

"Long live the *Europa*," Kibwe says to himself. "May she find a home for everyone." He tests the link with Cadre One and reconnects, halting the countdown on sub-level containment. Command options appear in his goggles and blink brightly in red.

Attempting dignity through the pain of his broken body, Kibwe transmits in the clear, all channels.

"This is Lieutenant Kibwe, last living defender of Cadre One. Option Zulu is authorized."

Kibwe drops containment on the entire store of anti-hydrogen, and Cadre One shines like a supernova.

Hovering fighter craft and approaching transports char to cinders. The boxy command ship blisters, bloats, and collapses like an overripe fruit.

Shards of the obliterated asteroid emerge from the glare like dismembered mountains, hurtling in all directions. The boxy ship catches one directly, its weakened structures folding around the jagged stone edges as if embracing, and it lurches away into the void.

JUST THE THING

O'Kai's eyelids peel open and he blinks against a hard white glare. Smears of red and amber pulse in his unfocused vision, but he cannot understand why they seem so close to his face. He reaches out, touches a familiar surface, which feels like the console in front of his recliner.

What's it doing up here?

An iron spike of pain shoots behind his eyes and lodges with pounding intensity. His gut spasms, bathing his tongue in bile. With a grimace he swallows then clamps his throat tight, choking back heave after violent heave.

His next sensation is of all-consuming fire as billions of seared nerve endings ignite. Intensity overwhelms rational thought, and all he can think about is escaping his burning body.

He forces breath past chattering teeth, concentrates on a place of calm dissociation, and withdraws from his flesh. In a capsule of meditation, he waits like a man on a high dam as a raging tide smashes his physical foundation. Detached from the onslaught, he concentrates, gathers his wits and strength. Priorities return, and he remembers who he is, where he is, what has been happening.

The enemy is near...

Resolved, prepared, he abandons his psychological lifeboat and plunges back into his physical self. A paroxysm of sickness floods him, yet the man is not submerged. O'Kai rides above the chaotic surges, trusting his mesolimbic system will deliver him with endogenous morphine. And it does.

Debilitating sharpness behind his eyes blunts then fades. Stomach heaves relax to queasy churns, and he gasps his first breath in over a minute. When at last he is calm, his eyelids relax and O'Kai finds himself free-floating inside a battered Virus Ship. Pieces of his recliner restraints hang weightless around him, along with sheared bolts and fragmented alloys. Light so bright it hurts streams through hull fractures and perforations, forming incandescent bars in the smoky cabin.

Argo slumps in a recliner beside him. His restraints are unbroken, but the recliner has ripped most of the way from the floor, leaving the chair tilted forward to the left.

"Brick," O'Kai transmits, guiding himself back to his recliner.

Argo's head lifts with a start, and he looks around as if seeing the cockpit for the first time. The big man's hands clamp the recliner railings and he shudders. His shoulders rise and fall in a regular cadence of deep breaths, then his head swivels almost randomly.

"*Are we...? We're alive?*" Argo asks via helmet radio.

"Somehow," O'Kai answers. "Can you get this thing moving?"

Argo reaches up and shoves against the cabin ceiling, bending his recliner back into proper place. Fatigued metal springs it back halfway as if in compromise, leaving him at an odd angle to his console. The controls respond to his tapping fingertips, however, and a holowindow opens above. Rows of red bars, interspersed with occasional amber, populate the screen.

"*We have reserve power and a few working thrusters,*" the Brick says. "*I can get us crawling.*" He flips from one exterior view to another. All are uniformly white.

Argo thumps his fingertips against the console, running diagnostics and attempting a fix. Diagnostics show him the sensors are functioning, but the visual output is pure white. All other metrics are pinned at maximum.

"*Sensors are botched,*" the Brick grumbles. "*Won't be able to see where we're going.*"

"I'll have a look outside," O'Kai says, pushing out of his recliner. He crosses several of the blazing bright shafts of light and pulls himself to the hatch. Argo triggers a switch, and as the hatch iris grinds open, an incomprehensible brilliance floods through.

Shielding his view with an armored forearm, O'Kai pokes his head through the hatch. With the maximum compensation of his helmet lenses, he discerns the baked-white hull of a vessel a few meters away. All four of the Virus Ship's legs still grip the vessel's hull, but three of them have been yanked out of their mounts. The last is barely attached, leaving their craft tethered to the larger vessel by a single limb.

O'Kai turns to the underside of his Virus Ship and sees that it, too, is baked pure white. Everywhere he looks seared-white fragments hang like radiant snowflakes, rotating slightly and drifting apart with perplexing slowness.

"*Radiological alarm is off the scale,*" Argo transmits. "*After effect of our bomb?*"

"Possible," O'Kai says absently. One hand held over his cramped gut, the old Gun squints at the faint shadow his craft casts against the carrier's hull. It looks smaller than it should be.

The enemy fleet was coming straight at Cadre One from the night side... These dead ships would have drifted right by... If they haven't changed course, then...

The general ducks back inside and peers at the brilliant white beams crossing the cabin. Everywhere they strike, interior surfaces ablate in a smoky spray. O'Kai looks down at himself and finds stripes across his armor where he moved through the beams.

"Brick, we've drifted into the inner system, too close to our star. We need shade, *right now.*"

Argo looks over his shoulder then takes the stick. He taps a button on the console, but every time he hits it red script in his screen announces, *FAILURE.*

"*The leg won't release,*" he says. Argo moves the stick and weakened thrusters tug against the unresponsive limb, unable to break free.

O'Kai pulls himself back inside, carefully avoiding the beams, and snatches his rifle from its cradle. Returning to the hatch, the old Gun plugs in the power cable and primes his weapon. The socket where the limb mounts is in full sunlight, caustic and glaring, so he synchs his rifle scope to his visor, then looks away from the glare. In the whitewashed video streaming to his visor, O'Kai can just make out the mount socket. Most of the attachments are broken, the cables and hydraulics are all torn, but one thick bolt remains intact. He triggers a continuous beam at the mount, waving it slightly. The bolt severs, the limb detaches, and the craft lurches away from the carrier hull.

"*We're free,*" Argo states, working the stick and getting a feel for what little control remains. "*Heading?*"

O'Kai blinks away the spots before his eyes then sights along the white carrier hull until he finds its edge. "Roll right ten degrees, pitch up sixty degrees, yaw left eighty degrees. Forward one hundred twenty meters."

Argo pumps the control stick, and the Virus Ship responds with geriatric slowness. White beams swing across the interior as the craft rotates, and the Brick watches them for indicators of angle. One swings directly at his shoulder, forcing him to lean forward in the recliner while it bores into the padding behind him.

Creeping along, the hobbled craft nears the edge of the carrier.

"Pitch down ninety degrees, continue straight sixty meters," O'Kai orders.

Argo noses the craft down and the white beams swing again through the interior.

"Pitch down ninety degrees, travel thirty meters and halt," O'Kai calls.

Argo guides the craft down into shade behind the carrier and comes to a stop.

O'Kai pops his head through the open hatch. In stark contrast to the blinding glare from before, this side of the hulk is barely visible. Eyepieces of his helmet compensate, permitting enhanced views of the carrier's broadside, and he gazes at a ragged wound stretching the full length of the warship. Meters-thick hull plates curl outward at the edges. Inside, the vessel is hollowed to the centerline, half of its internal compartments puffed out to space in an enormous cough.

"*Sensors recovering,*" Argo radios. "*Were being overwhelmed by sunlight, apparently.*"

"What do you see?" O'Kai asks, still gazing into the hollowed carrier's interior.

"*Even in the shade, radiation is off the scale. That ship's glowing hot. So are we, for that matter.*"

"Give me a look at what's around us."

"*Aye, sir.*"

Argo rolls the Virus Ship over, and O'Kai looks out across reflective junk in every direction. Kilometers apart, white-charred warships tumble gently in their final headings. Most are peeled to the ribs. Between them, shattered fragments spin and cartwheel, intensely bright against the blackness of space.

"Anything salvageable?" O'Kai asks.

"*I see two with intact hulls, but no radio transmissions, no running lights. Totally dark.*"

O'Kai pushes out through the hatch and spreads his feet, hooking the hatch coaming with toes to keep from drifting away. With the extra height, he looks back at the enormous hulk providing shade. Faint wisps streak around the edges from the sun-blasted side, but nothing stirs inside the exploded shell, not even a spark of arcing current. At the stern, where drive nacelles once drove this warship to superluminal speeds, there are only wrecked mounting struts.

"This thing's totaled," O'Kai says, pulling himself back inside through the hatch. "Can you get us to one of the others out there?"

"*Possibly. Might cook on the way, though.*"

The general throws his weapon strap overhead and cinches it tight. "Can we tow some wreckage with us? Use it as a screen?"

Argo looks at his console. "*If the limbs were still attached, we could.*"

O'Kai looks around the interior of his battered craft. "Well we aren't getting far in this crate. Find a ship out there with some life in it. Something we can patch together. I'll find us something we can lash to the hull as a shield."

"*It's plasma soup out there, General. I'll have to do an active sweep to cut through it. It'll be like a beacon to the enemy.*"

O'Kai mulls the option. "If anyone out there's watching, I doubt they're in any condition to matter. Do it. And roll me back toward the carrier."

"*Understood.*"

While Argo emits his sweeps, O'Kai crawls out onto the Virus Ship's exterior. He cranes his neck, viewing the massive wreck that shades them from the nearby star.

"Bring us closer, Brick. I want to see if there's some wreckage I can pull loose."

"*Aye, sir.*"

Argo thrusts the craft toward the gutted hulk, and O'Kai searches for a section of hull plating or loosely tethered machinery. Heat radiating from the carrier seems to pass directly through his armor plating and gets hotter every meter of the approach.

This may not work, he thinks.

A flash to O'Kai's left steals his attention, and when he looks, he sees nothing. Not trusting his eyes, O'Kai takes his rifle in hand and kneels down on the hull of his white-scorched craft. He pulls the weapon to his shoulder, watching, seeking, until he spots a hole in the background of glittering junk. He leans into his scope.

"Argo, contact!" O'Kai radios.

"*General, hold your fire!*" says a crackling voice through O'Kai's helmet speakers. The hole in the backdrop of junk grows larger, allowing O'Kai to discern a split teardrop shape. It is much closer than he first realized.

"Beckert?" O'Kai replies in disbelief.

"*Affirmative, General. I'm very glad to find you.*"

Beckert steers his perfectly black craft alongside. Four spidery limbs reach out, grasp O'Kai's battered craft, and turn it over like a spider wrapping a moth. Once the undersides of both Virus Ships face one another a circular hatch opens directly above O'Kai's head, and interior cabin lighting spills out through it. Beckert's armored hand reaches toward the opening and beckons.

"Please, come aboard, sir."

"Brick, abandon ship," O'Kai orders.

"Ah, General, would you have Lieutenant Argo disable the incendiaries first?" Beckert radios. *"We can use your craft as cover from the sunlight, but it's going to soak a lot of heat. This close, we don't want an accidental detonation."*

"Brick?" O'Kai asks.

"Roger that," Argo answers. *"Pulling primaries."*

O'Kai climbs inside Beckert's craft, snaps his rifle into the cradle over the middle recliner. Argo passes up his cannon and MedKit, which O'Kai stows. The Brick glides through the narrow cabin and clicks into the vacant recliner. Beckert seals the hatch and thrusts away from the carrier wreck, positioning O'Kai's abandoned craft as a solar shield.

"How'd you find us?" O'Kai asks.

"Been out there watching for a while, hoping I might find a sign you'd survived. Argo's sweep tipped me off. Traced it to that big hulk, jumped in, and there you were."

Beckert's viewscreen flashes a red script warning, HULL TEMP CRITICAL.

"Even with your ship as a shield, we're still getting scorched." Beckert steers behind a free-falling drive nacelle and parks until the hull temp sensor dips to amber.

"Kibwe?" O'Kai asks.

Beckert takes a breath before answering. "Gone, sir. He triggered Option Zulu from ground zero. It's done."

Argo's chin dips toward his chest. O'Kai looks up through the ceiling.

"I'm glad I found you both," Beckert adds to lighten the mood. "Almost lost hope."

"Why didn't you leave?" O'Kai demands.

"Sir?" The Geek's false eyes roam his craft's interior. "This thing hasn't got the range to reach Earth. My only option is to hitch on to a ship that does...but..." The Geek gestures toward his missing legs. "Can't take on an enemy crew like *this*. I *had* to find you two."

"Where's the enemy now?" O'Kai demands.

"Most have left. A few stayed behind. Probably to see if any of us show up after the fact."

"How many stayed?"

Beckert turns his false eyes to O'Kai and shakes his head. "Eight, including a carrier. They're all in close formation. If we land on one, they'll shoot us off the hull in an instant." The Geek's goggles flash and a screen opens above O'Kai's console. In it, a three-dimensional wireframe model appears of a mid-sized enemy vessel.

"But there's one ship I've been watching," Beckert offers. "Was on the edge of the Yankee shot. Got caught in the blast, and I thought it was just another piece of junk in this group. Then the running lights came on and there was a two second boost from its main drives before it went dark again. Was enough to steer it off a few degrees so it isn't getting scorched. My guess? There's still crew aboard and they're working to fix it."

"Why don't their comrades come to assist?" Argo asks.

Beckert glances uncomfortably at Argo and O'Kai then focuses on his console screens. "At that range, the radiation from the blast...anyone who's still alive..."

"Won't be for long," O'Kai finishes. "I get it." He holds an armored hand up in front of himself, wondering how black his skin has turned beneath it. "Brick, got something in your MedKit to keep us standing?"

"Just the thing," Argo answers, reaching for his stowed kit. "One of Doctor Taggart's radiation mitigation specials."

O'Kai fills his lungs and lets out a slow exhale. His jaw sets and his hands clench. "You get us there, Beckert. We'll handle the rest."

CADRE TWO

PART EIGHT

ATYPICAL STUDENT

Shao-Lo flops into the pilot's chair of the sow-like transport. Her skin is flushed from exertion, and sweat has rendered her tight undersuit see through. In one hand she grips a beige protein bar. In the other is a small towel, which she dabs across her steaming forehead.

Through the windscreen ahead, the universe lenses and races in a cataclysmic show of focused energy. Within the bubble there is no sensation of movement, no tactile proof the transport is falling millions of kilometers every second. To her, it feels as false as an archival video and, therefore, is entirely uninteresting.

Her eyes roam across the sloped, U-shaped console. All displays show green bars, just as they have every single day for the last four months. With a bored sigh, she slumps back in the seat.

Being ordered back to Cadre Two was no surprise, she thinks. *Cadre Two is too rich with assets for O'Kai to ignore. Had no doubt he'd send another mission, and I'd be the one to lead it. I've seen the place firsthand, seen what Honniker and Mikato have knocked together. Makes sense. And going back is a chance to reverse my previous failure.*

She shifts uncomfortably in the chair.

Never thought I'd be going solo...

Either O'Kai thinks I can liberate Cadre Two by myself, which shows an overconfidence in my abilities. Or he expects I'll fail again, and he's removing a weak officer from the Council...

O'Kai is not prone to overconfidence...

And Chusan was promoted before I left...meaning O'Kai doesn't expect me to return... So I'm being sent on a pointless errand? Am I merely another piece of cargo to pacify a powerful enemy? No different than the drones in the recliners?

Shao-Lo hurls the towel at the viewscreen.

"*Blast* this idle time! All it breeds is...useless *navel gazing*!"

The tall woman rises from the seat and bangs her head on the low ceiling. With a growl, she jumps down the short stairway into the central corridor along the transport's spine, spreads her arms to each side and presses against the walls. The stiff metal panels flex as she yells her frustration down the narrow hallway.

One dull day blends into the next. Talking to herself interrupts the silence, that is, until she catches herself doing it, and she chastises herself for losing focus.

My whole life there was always SOMEONE...Operators on my team, Officers in Council, MedTechs reporting advances or problems in production... I've never been so isolated.

Out of all the tests I've been through, I hate this one the most.

Shao-Lo flinches and finds herself parked on the edge of her bunk, staring through the wall of her cabin. She searches the walls for a chronometer, but does not see one and, with unease, the old Gun realizes she has no idea how long she has been sitting there.

Hours? Days?

Alarmed at the slip of discipline (and inattention to the vessel) she propels herself from her bunk, races to the flight deck, and drops into the pilot's seat. The console is lit in a uniform green with all systems running normally. There are no proximity warnings, nothing at all that might arouse concern or interest, and she slumps.

No matter how cramped the confines of this transport I WILL remain sharp. If I have to attack boredom like an enemy, I WILL keep focus. I have to stay active. Can't be sedentary. That's the key.

Might as well start now.

The tall colonel practices forms in her undersuit until she snags it on a jutting component, after which she exercises nude. She runs countless laps up and down the transport's one corridor, sometimes upright, sometimes sideways, bracing herself across the corridor with hands and feet. Sometimes she runs upside down, standing on hands, feet pressed against the ceiling. She scales up and down the long bins of plastic in the cargo bay, leaps from one to another. She disengages motor assist for large mechanical parts and engages herself in their place. When that is no longer enough, she dials up gravity enhancement an extra five percent and does it all over again.

With only herself as a passenger, on-board food machines offer ample calories, and her workouts become a competition to see just how far she can go before collapsing. Taking nutrition and water intervals on the fly, allowing only the minimal pause for eliminations, she passes twenty hours easily. Then she works up past thirty-six hours. Then forty-eight. And when she works up to sixty uninterrupted hours of exercise, the hallucinations are so disorienting that she forces herself to quit. After an abbreviated cool down, she trudges to her bunk, pitches into it face first, and sleeps an entire day.

Upon awakening, her joints are so sore, her sinews so stiff, she can barely move. Moreover, she feels weaker than when she began. Her clothing is looser, proving that her one entertainment is tearing her down. Thereafter, Shao-Lo limits workouts to twenty disappointingly brief hours, including stretches, balance, forms, strength/endurance training, and cool down.

Exercise keeps her body occupied during the lonely voyage, but her mind runs wild with unstructured time.

Will it be like the last time? Another shooting gallery of genetic augments and killing machines? Or will I be sliced down to a head in a jar like Summers? Perhaps a plaything, some hybrid...half myself...half blueskin?

Such thoughts send a chemical twinge through her veins that even twenty hours of exertion cannot fully exorcise.

Reluctantly, she investigates Herzfeld's files of negotiation tactics. The archive is a tedious collection of readings and practices, dry concepts and bizarre ideas customized for an insane society run amok. Even so, they are the only untried way to pass the time. Shao-Lo tries to read through them all at once, but the professor has inserted mandatory time delays between lessons, leaving far too much time to contemplate her destination.

Maiella's instructions how to steer the vessel are straightforward and easy to understand. Also, as it turns out, completely unnecessary. Months pass without so much as a stray radio transmission, not one hint of another vessel or course obstruction. Shao-Lo keeps mostly to her cabin, preferring it to the cramped flight deck, only visiting the pilot's seat when the delays between Herzfeld's lessons expire.

The long solo journey wears on the grizzled Operator, and her exercise sessions take on a masochistic flavor, purely for what entertainment the sensations provide: the gradual change of hue as bruises fade, the flaking of scabs as scrapes heal, the vivid and beautiful crimson from split knuckles and shins...

Shao-Lo flops down into the pilot's chair and feels something poking against her rump. When she fishes it out she finds a still-wrapped protein bar. With a sigh, she rips through the silvery wrapper, chomps into it, and taps the console. Through a doughy mouthful she says, "Let's see what you have for me today, Herzfeld."

The list of interactive modules appears on her screen. All are marked, COMPLETE save one at the very end of the list, labeled, PENDING. Shao-Lo taps it and sits back in the chair.

A dialogue box appears, which reads, *Advanced Negotiation Tactics: Prof. Jonah Herzfeld, LLM. Pre-recorded message begins...*

The screen clears. Herzfeld's head and shoulders appear.

"Hello, again, Colonel," Herzfeld says. "This is the last segment I have for you, and before we start, I'd like to share a few things.

"Prior to my career as Chief Negotiator of Colony Contracts for Soshiba Varicorp, I was a Professor at the University of Melbourne. The modules you've completed are part of an interactive final examination I gave to my graduate students. By reaching this point, you've proven competency in the various segments assigned. From the little I know about you, I believe you would have tried to absorb all of this material at one sitting, so I inserted a delay between each module before they were unlocked. I did this to ensure you had adequate time to fully absorb each module's readings and practices before you moved on to the next. If this feels unnecessarily drawn out, you should know that my students required four years of dedicated study to complete this course material. Completing it in four months is quite an accomplishment.

"You are not my typical student, of course. The society you come from is unique, and the stakes you play for are considerably higher than anything my students would have faced. Thus, it was necessary to tailor the course for you, specifically. I selected supplemental readings not in the original syllabus. While I'm unsure you'll grasp the deeper philosophical meanings in these readings, I wanted to be certain you were exposed to the core concepts. These concepts illustrate various ways of perceiving, various ways of thinking. The readings contain ideas I am sure you have never encountered before. They are not an attempt to change how you think and act, Colonel, but they demonstrate how others can perceive a thing very differently than you do...how preconceptions *shape* perceptions. I must trust that will serve you well enough.

"You've studied basic elements of human psychology, in particular how scarcity drives behavior. With this you are intimately familiar, as Cadre One affords only the barest of essentials. Scarcity is the impetus for every action the Cadre takes.

"Thus far, your Cadre has alleviated scarcity through force. But your rifle did not bring you success at Cadre Two. You've personally seen there is a limit to what you can accomplish with force, and I don't mind admitting that pleases me. This time, ideas will be your weapons. In these modules, you've shown you know how to wield them.

"You've absorbed the tactics used to maximize a settlement or agreement with a long term focus. You know how to discover an opponent's goals and how to dovetail those goals with your own so both parties can win. But let me stress: it is *imperative* that no one loses, here. Cooperation *must* become a profitable enterprise. And from such a platform of stability, an enduring relationship may flourish.

"In my dealings, I've seen a wide variety of personalities and strategies. I included as many as I could into your interactive practices so that you'll recognize them when you see them. This will make it difficult for Honniker to surprise you or catch you off guard. But most importantly, you'll be able to distinguish between diversions and real demands.

"No matter who sat across the table from me, and no matter what we discussed, nothing was more useful to my bargaining position than knowing the true worth of what I offered to my opponent. It told me when a deal was ripe for harvest. It also told me when I should walk away entirely, or settle for my best alternative to a negotiated agreement. We know the real value of your cargo to Honniker and Mikato because they have directly stated it. They're desperate for the organic polymers you have in abundance. It is impossible to overstate this advantage.

"I must stress, however, that you hold back your offer until your opponents' terms are acceptable, not just in terms of immediate benefit, but in terms of keeping them interested in future negotiations. Let me repeat this: The *moment* you give up everything you have, *you will lose*, because your opponent will no longer have any need to cooperate. They will no longer have any need of *you*. That is when you'll see the truest face of your opponents. When they believe they no longer need to fear you and when they believe there is nothing else you can offer them, you will see them as they truly are. Advanced negotiators sometimes pretend they have nothing left to offer so they can meet their opponent without masks and understand them better. This is not recommended in your case, as you are not experienced in these matters. To try may unbalance the situation, and you could lose control completely, to the detriment of all.

"Parse your words and your rewards. Even when it seems you may get everything you want in one transaction, you *must* hold something back. The only thing that will keep these entities honest is the expectation of more reward. Trade everything on a single deal, they can renege and leave you with nothing.

"It follows that Honniker and Mikato will expect you to behave in the same way they do: as an entirely self-serving organism. I mention this, because you may find advantage in such a prejudice. Watch for an opportunity to exploit it.

"I understand the magnitude of what you're trying to accomplish, Colonel. This is no less than a first attempt at treaty with a hostile nation. The deal you strike will be the basic law from which all other negotiations follow. While I'm confident in my abilities to negotiate against any living person, I've never faced a fully realized artificial intelligence. You have. Therefore, you must take everything I've taught you as a supplement to your own experiences.

"A part of me envies you, Colonel. This is history in the making. I wish you the very best, and I hope my instruction proves useful. At this point, we have everything to gain."

The pre-recorded message ends, and Herzfeld's image is replaced with the words, FINAL ASSESSMENT.

A younger, more professorial version of Herzfeld appears on screen, wearing a collared white shirt and bow tie. Thicker hair covers the top of his head and a dark brown beard shrouds the lower half of his face.

What's this? she wonders. *An automated part of the lesson?*

"In final analysis," the likeness of Herzfeld says, "your solutions have been efficient and effective. The only critique I have is that you default too quickly to a hard 'Take it or leave it' bargaining position. Of course, there are times for that, but apply patience to your process. You should avoid pinning down your opponents or backing them into a corner. The more you focus on the advantages of mutual cooperation and the benefits of continued commerce, the better your outcome will be.

"The speed at which you moved through the counterpoint practices is another tell of your impatience. If you cannot argue both sides of an issue, then *you simply do not understand the issue well enough*. There will *always* be a counterpoint to any negotiation. By practicing a position opposed to your own, you are better able to anticipate your opponent's demands. By understanding both sides of an issue, you can demonstrate empathy, build trust, and achieve a result that truly benefits both parties.

"Please feel free to re-visit the interactive practices at any time.

238

Though I'm confident you understand the material well enough to lead a successful career, there are outcomes you have not fully explored yet. These may be interesting to you. Good luck in your endeavors, and congratulations, *graduate!*"

The face disappears from the screen, and the list of modules repopulates, all of which are marked, COMPLETE.

Shao-Lo taps the console, restoring the transport's dashboard metrics. Looking out through the windscreen, watching the universe streaking around her, she loses herself in a single repeating thought.

Am I up to this?

The colonel rises from the chair, heads back to her cabin, and collapses into her bunk, exhausted.

INDEED, YOU DO

Back on the flight deck, Shao-Lo rehearses lines from Herzfeld's real world practice scenarios. The words feel strange in her mouth, and, as she speaks them, it astounds her that anyone who employed such skills could be part of any community whatsoever.

That successful ones were rewarded with more than they could use in their lifetime while others were deliberately deprived... A defect of the deepest kind, completely at odds with survival...

If a MedTech hoarded calories and left his comrades to die, we'd reconstitute without delay. But on Earth, entire organizations attempted to starve others out, tried to drive competitors out of existence... And it was accepted as 'good business practice?'

How did the human race endure? Was it because they were so numerous they could afford to squander millions of lives?

We need every life we incubate; we need every MedTech and Operator at their best. Wasting even a single life is insane. The contributions of that individual over a lifetime could be the difference that changes everything.

She takes another bite of protein and chews.

Honniker is the epitome of that insanity. Perhaps I should be grateful for a person like Herzfeld...a person who understands that kind of madness.

A tone sounds from the console, accompanied by viewscreen telemetry data and time of arrival at Procyon A/B. Shao-Lo glances at the screen then rises from her chair, stoops under the low ceiling, and strides to her cabin. She strips off her undersuit and wads the thin fabric into the bowl of her hygiene station for a quick hand wash. Once it is clean Shao-Lo hangs the suit from a ventilation grille beside her dress gray uniform.

Returning to the hygiene station, the colonel zips a chemically treated towel from its holder, drags it from the top of her close-cropped head, across wide shoulders, over and under muscular arms, around her flat torso, past taut buttocks and powerful legs. She finishes at her feet, taking time between every toe, and then stands. In the mirror is a hard-looking woman with short gray hair, deep lines etched into her face, and innumerable scars crossing every centimeter of hide-like skin. The old Gun takes a moment to admire the more recent scars when an unusual thought occurs to her.

I'm just a machine comprised of parts. Could be the last time these parts are all together.

She raises her hands and flips them over, staring into the palms.

This body is not mine. It belongs to the Cadre. So long as the Cadre is served, what happens to this body is irrelevant.

Shao-Lo leans forward, grips the edges of the hygiene station, and stares at her reflection, daring it to show a sign of weakness. It stares back with jaws flexed and mouth bunched, veins protruding from shoulders and arms, eyes smoldering with the promise of settling a score.

She pushes off, grabs her undersuit pants, and steps into them gracefully. Every thread conforms to her shape as if vacuumed sealed.

You've met me in a fight, Honniker...

She grabs her top and pulls it down over herself, stretching it into place. The fabric, cool at first, warms from her body heat and dries almost instantly.

...but I'm not here to fight this time...

Her charcoal uniform slips easily over the skin-tight undersuit. Absorbent socks and twelve-eye boots slide over her feet. She raises each foot to the basin, tucks her pant legs into her boots, and draws the laces tight.

I've got exactly what you want. You're going to deal with me, one way or other.

Shao-Lo watches herself fasten the uniform jacket in the mirror, and her eyes pause at the decorations on her chest. She considers removing them, then decides against.

Shouldn't have given up my rank insignias. Honniker should know I'm still a Colonel with power to bargain.

She blanches at the word 'bargain' in her own head.

A Colonist word. But that's exactly why I'm here: to strike a lasting bargain.

Shao-Lo stands straight, shoulders back, chest out, scrutinizing her reflection as if she were weighing a candidate for induction to the Corps. The soldier looking back is crisp, poised.

That'll do.

She strides out of her cabin and turns toward the stern, intent on checking her living cargo. At the first cabin door on her right, she pauses and looks through a small round window. Inside, a bald female occupies a stainless recliner. The Drone's eyes are shut in peaceful repose; the skin is pale and unblemished, utterly without lines or hair. A long white smock covers her from shoulders to knee, emblazoned with tall black numerals. Medical machines in attendance display a succession of green bars.

Shao-Lo crosses to the opposite cabin, checks on another Drone within, and moves down the corridor.

They really aren't that different from Rosenthal... So why did I react so poorly? Because she was lobotomized against her will? Or was it because I had been off the inhibitors too long?

She looks back toward her cabin.

I'll bring a supply with me. Can't risk being out of control. Not here. Not now.

A tone repetitively sounds from the flight deck. With purposeful strides, the colonel moves to the front of the transport, ascends the short stairs, and stoops into the pilot's chair. She reaches a finger toward the console, pausing to be sure she knows what she will say, and then taps it.

ARRIVING AT PROCYON A/B SYSTEM, the screen declares, DSD DISENGAGE IN 3...2...1...MARK.

Through the windscreen ahead, raging torrents dissipate into the vastness of three-dimensional space. Streaks of prismatic light collapse to distant pinpoints amid infinite black.

The vessel automatically turns a gentle arc and a blazing-bright dwarf star curves into view. The plexisteel windscreen dims to black and a holowindow projects onto its interior side, plotting every astronomic speck and spot exactly as it was, minus the blinding intensity.

The transport finishes its turn, then announces on-screen, COMPENSATING FOR RELATIVISTIC DRIFT...
COMPLETE.
FINAL COURSE TO CADRE TWO, NO OBSTRUCTIONS.
DSD ENGAGE IN 3...2...1...MARK.

The vessel dives into curved space-time and races at superluminal speed.

Shao-Lo watches the projected images on the blacked-out windscreen, noting how the tiny white spot labeled Procyon B shifts against the backdrop of stars. A dusty ring plots in the projection around the white dwarf star, and solid objects in the ring grow from specks to dots to shapes.

One highlights with the caption, *Cadre Two*.

Shao-Lo stares at the captioned rock, memories flooding her mind:

> *Weapon flashes in darkened corridors, roars from*
> *razor-toothed maws, twang of tendrils, the rush of lethal*
> *machines...*

Shao-Lo's head lowers, chin to chest. Deep breaths fill her lungs. Her heart thuds, her teeth clench. But the emptiness of her hands is an instant distraction. She forces her hands open and exhales the heat from her chest. The next breath she holds, and with eyes closed she pulls her way back from the violent recesses of her mind. Though her heart still beats with adrenaline, the old Gun reclines in her seat. A shiver passes her length, followed by random twitches in her legs, shoulders and face.

All my instincts are wrong in this place... I'll have to guard against that...

A familiar tone sounds from the console with an accompanying message on screen, ARRIVING AT CADRE TWO, DSD DISENGAGE IN 3...2...1...MARK.

The vessel emerges from curved space with a flash, heading toward a sparse lane of dust. Light from the white dwarf star diffuses through the dust, casting a twilight glow; and looming within it, directly ahead, is the dusky fragment of a shattered planet. Crags, cliffs, and rifts run like scars through up-thrust mountain ranges. Some sections are thick with twisted spires and spikes of metal-rich stone. Others are vast rippled expanses like iron-black oceans during a storm.

The holoprojection inserts a green line between a set of helical spires on the underside with the caption, MAIN ENTRY. A second line runs to the fragment's far side, captioned, PRODUCTION FLOOR, TRANSPORT LAUNCH TUBE.

"Better announce myself," Shao-Lo says. Keying her radio, she says clearly, "Cadre Two, this is Colonel Shao-Lo returning with transport and cargo. Acknowledge, over."

Silence.

Shao-Lo waits, biding her time, thinking through several moves in a verbal chess match. Minutes pass. But she knows Honniker would not miss the arrival of a transport so close to his home. And having noticed the transport approach, he would, without a doubt, have received her transmitted message. No matter that sitting still in one spot runs counter to every bit of training and every instinct she has, she applies patience and remains completely still.

The silence lengthens to an hour. Shao-Lo neither maneuvers nor transmits, watching her screens for any movement at all, scanning her instruments for a hint of something out of the ordinary. Nothing moves from the massive rock ahead.

She looks at the control wheel locked against the console. Having taken Maiella's instruction how to use it she is tempted to turn the transport and leave.

Have to wait it out.

Another hour passes.

Shao-Lo shifts in her seat. Inaction is no longer just counter to her instincts, it is an enemy, threatening to distract her from something vital. Her body's need to move turns every minor discomfort into an ache or itch. But she refuses the petty irritations and maintains her vigil.

This is just the first round, she realizes.

"*You were warned,*" growls a malignant voice through her radio.

"Yes, Dr. Honniker, we were," Shao-Lo radios back. "We were warned not to come back in force. I have no weapons aboard, and I am the only crew. I did not come to fight. We've fought enough to know it profits no one."

"*To speak of profit...? I am surprised to hear this word from you.*"

"Why is that?"

"*You're too atavistic for such concepts. You smash. And you grab. Like the tree-swinging apes that you are.*"

"I also did not come to trade insults."

"*Then why ARE you here?*"

"Because I have a proposal for you. One I am certain you will like."

There is an extended silence. As before, Shao-Lo restrains herself from breaking it.

"*A proposal, it says? As if the* bloede Schimpanse *could comprehend something civilized...*"

"I could waste time questioning your intelligence the way you question mine. But that's all distraction, isn't it? We've made a deal before, Honniker. In your battery room. You didn't like the terms, then. But we made an agreement and we kept it. I return to honor that trade in good faith so we may continue to make new agreements...ones more to your liking."

"*Ach, so. You presume to know my mind? Well, you are wrong. In fact, I shall tell you what it is that I would like: to rip open that transport, vent you to space, and watch your eyes and lungs burst.*"

"You could do that. I won't maneuver. But it would be a shame for you to lose this cargo."

"Do not think to sway me with pathetic trinkets. Your imbecile clan will never produce anyth—"

Shao-Lo switches off her radio and sits back into her seat, hands folded in her lap. She does not have to wait long before the console display shows an incoming call on the same channel. She lets the call hold a few seconds and then she opens the channel.

"You DARE to hang up on ME, when y—"

Shao-Lo closes the channel again. This time there is another extended silence, and she wonders if she may have miscalculated. Movement at the limb of the great rock catches her eye, then on the opposite side, as well. The glimpses are only transitory before the objects disappear from sight, and she knows, *He wanted me to see those.*

The console blinks with another incoming call on the same channel. Shao-Lo opens the channel, but says nothing.

"I think this game you play is not worth my time. I think now I peel open that transport and take what is inside."

"You could, but you'd ruin it."

The transport jolts from something heavy contacting the hull. Shao-Lo's eyes sweep over her instruments. There was no indication whatsoever of an approaching vessel.

"So, you are the cargo? I will give you this much, Colonel, it is satisfying that I will kill you, after all. Such a nuisance you were to me, such a mess you made of my home! Perhaps this will anger your General enough so he will come back, fighting. I am well-prepared, you see, and would enjoy killing the rest of your clan as much as I enjoyed killing your Zuri, Asha, Deepak, und Carter."

Rasping against the hull speeds into a whirring screech.

Shao-Lo taps her console, pulling up camera feeds from all four of the Drone-occupied cabins. She streams all feeds through the broadcast channel. The whirring screech winds down and ceases altogether.

In the silence of the open channel, the colonel says, "I told you. I have something to offer."

"Indeed. It seems that you do."

BLUNTED

Thompson strolls through the corridors of the *Europa* after another eight hours of duty. MedTechs are ubiquitous, cleaning, inspecting, installing, and fixing. In a way, it feels like being back in Cadre One, being once more among the orderly and efficient workers he always lived to serve. Then, a sullen Colonist appears and spoils the illusion, reminding him that things are different and the past really happened.

Hands jammed in the pockets of his uniform pants, he tours several decks, making mental note of how rare a sight the Colonists are; and the Gun asks the next Colonist he sees how it came to be.

The man wipes grimy sludge from his pipe wrench then drags his hands down the front of equally grimy coveralls.

"What, you don't think it's crowded enough in here?" he says with a laugh. "Naw, seriously, Cap'n Jones said we need to fill up the vacant cryo-cylinders an' take some load off the ship." The man kneels down to the floor again and wrenches a threaded fitting. "Munro volunteered his MedTechs, but only two of 'em were small enough to squeeze in...and only after significant folding, I tell ya. So they're having another assembly to figure out who keeps their post and who takes an ice bath."

"*Another* assembly?" Thompson says. "Why do we need another meeting about it?"

"Because no one wants to be on duty anymore."

Thompson's head slides back, his chin lowers to his chest. "The Colonists *want* to be frozen?"

"Yup. Most have had their fill. Perfectly happy letting Munro's gimp brigade handle everything."

"And what about you?"

"Hell, I'd gladly take the needle and be another cube in the freezer. But shit pipes always need fixin'. And, son, that's something you *don't* want an amateur monkeyin' 'round with."

The man sets down his wrench and opens a wide-mouthed canister of sealer.

"Thanks," Thompson says.

The man grunts, dips his finger in sealer, and spreads it around a new fitting.

The Gun walks away with eyebrows bunched.

Got to see this for myself...

Thompson hears the commotion well before he reaches the meeting hall, and when he makes the last turn toward the renovated storage bay, he sees the double doors are wide open. As it has been every time before, there is a crowd of people, shouting over one another to be heard.

Agitation must be a Colonist's natural state, he thinks.

On the raised platform, Sharon stands opposite Herzfeld and both of them have microphone stands.

"We can't *all* go into stasis," Sharon insists, and her voice carries above the shouting crowd. "The *Europa* needs a minimum complement with the skills to keep her running."

"MedTechs can handle it, easy enough!" a woman from the crowd yells.

"Oh?" Sharon says, propping herself on the railing. "So you'd give them the keys to your home, then? Just like that?" Sharon lets the question hang before continuing. "Don't any of us forget that the *Europa* is our home. The MedTechs are welcome guests, of course, but this is *our* home. We're responsible for her, for ensuring she is properly maintained. I can accept volunteers to man essential posts, or I can default back to our flight rotation schedule. But those are the only two options."

"Bullshit," Herzfeld says into his microphone. "We've all been on-duty well past our two-year schedule. It's time to wake the next crew so we can all get a well-earned reprieve from this nightmare."

The crowd roars with approval. Sharon stares at Herzfeld, waiting for the cheers to die down before responding.

"All right, tell me this, Herzfeld," Sharon says. "What would you say to them when you welcomed them back? What could you say to prepare them for this? Would you tell them you just can't hack it anymore, and you're bailing out so someone else can handle your mess?"

The crowd surges with emotion, some booing, others turning to their neighbors with pensive faces, shaking their heads, shrugging.

"That's not our problem anymore!" Herzfeld answers.

Sharon pushes off the railing.

"That's *not* how we do things," she says to her opponent. "We *don't* run from what scares us, and we *bloody well don't* dump our problems on others." She turns to face her crew. "It's true, you've had the hardest duty of any flight crew, yet. We've been through one awful situation after the next. But we're in the middle of it now, and we can't just dump this on our shipmates. You envy them in untroubled sleep, yeah? How they have no idea what's going on? So do *I*! But they've no preparation, no way to get a handle on everything that has happened. It's so much that no one should be expected to swallow it all at once. We will carry on until our situation improves or, at the very least, stabilizes. Once the ship's running normally, and we've settled into our routine, *then* we can turn the ship over to the next flight crew."

The crowd shifts restlessly, grumbling.

"Now, look..." Sharon continues. "I *know* you're tired. But whether you know it or not, you're stronger than you realize, because we've been through Hell and *we're still here*. Let that sink in for a moment. *We're. Still. Here.* That's all I need to prove we've been doing it right, so far. We're going to *continue* being strong so that we can turn the *Europa* over properly. Now then, let's have some volunteers for essential posts."

Mutters and unhappy glances pass from one Colonist to the next.

"C'mon!" she says. "Let's see you!"

Slowly, reluctantly, volunteers come forward.

Thompson turns from the assembly hall and strolls toward the front of the ship.

Would I accept stasis, if offered? Maybe, if it meant an escape from inactivity. And if I have to sit in with the Counselor for another 'chat' I might brain myself with a hammer...

His feet carry him forward automatically, as if in disdain of stillness. His mind drifts.

The Corps has departed to face the enemy... Figured I'd be with them. Thought Chusan was inviting me back... Then nothing... What happened, there?

I split command of the Corps, once. A major, one step shy of being on the Leadership Council... A vital, important level of service...

His hands pull free of his pockets and swing with his strides.

The Colonists have their time wasting pursuits. Games. Conversations. Leisure and entertainment. Pointless. There MUST be a way

I can contribute, to build something important, to make progress toward something better...

Every cabin door he passes has two names upon it, a forced consolidation of living space due to the extra Cadre passengers. Quarters built for one now sleep two, adding a fair amount of squabbling to daily life.

It still amazes me that the Colonists demand more space than they need to live. But, no, I can't judge them for that. They welcomed me in, even after what I did...

They must know something about life that I don't. I have to remember that. I don't know everything, and there's...

Deep moaning from the cabin on his left distracts him, and he halts his aimless stroll.

Is someone hurt?

He reads the names from the door and raps with his knuckles.

"Umar? Khalifa? You okay in there?"

The moans stop.

"Yes, we're *fine!*" answers a woman's voice from inside.

A man's voice adds, "Hey, *get lost,* will you?"

Thompson shrinks back. "It's not that big a ship. Don't think I can."

"Oh, for goodness sake, GO AWAY!" the woman shouts at the door.

"Didn't think we had to post a sign," the man says.

"Shut up," the woman says, "and *focus.*"

Thompson shakes his head and continues on as the woman's groans resume behind him.

After a time, he arrives at his own cabin door, the names THOMPSON and MAIELLA stenciled in the center. He taps the panel and the door slides aside.

Maiella lies in her bunk against the far wall, on her side, back to him. A thin blanket hugs the curve of her hip. Above the blanket, she wears a black tank top. Her gold contact terminals peek from beneath hair that has long since overgrown them.

Thompson stands in the doorway, gazing at her silently, then he steps inside and lets the door slide shut behind him.

Maiella rolls over and props her head on one hand, letting the other drape over her hip.

"Thought you were asleep," he says.

"Ech. Can't. Feel like I should be doing something, but there's nothing to do. So I just lie here useless like... What did Dave call it?"

"Like rubber lips on a woodpecker."

She snorts in exasperation. "What does it *even mean?*"

OF MORTAL CREATURES

She turns onto her back and stretches, finishing with a big yawn. She props herself up on her elbows and watches Thompson sit down on his own bunk. Every movement he makes in removing his boots is one she has seen a hundred times, a perfect repetition of procedure and routine.

"Things are different now," she says ambiguously.

"That's obvious," he replies.

"*I'm* different."

Thompson sets his boots at the foot of his bunk and looks at her. His eyes roam her bare shoulders. There is soft round flesh on her chest; and, now that he is looking, there is a black outline around her eyes and subtle shading above them. Though her external changes are readily apparent, her expression seems to imply there is more.

"How so?" he asks.

She breathes deeply. "I know I was the best Geek in the Corps...I *know* I was. And when I teamed up with you and Argo, we were the sharpest tools in the Cadre arsenal. But now, I just feel..."

"Blunted."

"*Exactly.*" She drops onto her back again and stares at the ceiling. "I've never wanted to be anything more than what I was. Doesn't matter that I've always done things the best way I know how... Something's changed...*I've* changed, somehow."

"I know what you mean. With our operational experience, we should be with O'Kai. Isn't like there are so many in the Corps that he can afford to leave any of us behi—"

"That's *not* what I'm saying, Thompson!"

He looks at her again, sees her mouth curving down at the edges, sees her hands piled over her heart.

"I've changed," she says, "and I *like* what I'm becoming."

Thompson's face bunches. "I don't copy."

Her eyes close and she sighs a small sigh, then she sits up straight, lifts the covers away, and swings her bare legs to the floor. Black socks cover her feet to the ankle; tight black shorts ride low on her hips. She rises, steps over to her roommate, and sits on the bunk next to him.

In the air around her, Thompson smells something that reminds him vaguely of Colonist soap, of the odors deliberately infused into it, and of his time on Earth in the forest, when shrubs bloomed with fragrance. Complementing it are sensations unique to her, the smell of her hair around her ear, the warmth of her body, and the humidity of her breath.

"I've seen a glimpse of what life can be," she says. "We don't have to wedge ourselves into such narrow roles anymore. We can *grow*. I want

250

that, Thompson. I want that with you."

"Grow? Are we not fully grown now?"

Maiella looks down at her bare knees then she turns toward him, dragging a knee up onto the bunk. "Yes," she says, "we *are* fully grown physically. And we were good Operators—"

"Good?" Thompson interrupts, lifting himself from the bunk. "I watched you choke out a Brick in the arena."

She smiles at a fond memory. "That was luck."

"Luck seems to follow you." He paces toward the door and turns back. "Remember our fifth rotation? The long-hauler with all the Vanadium and Rhenium? The crew blew up the bridge before we could take it. Not a single console left."

"Mm, hmm. The whole vessel shut down. Every system. They must've thought that'd keep us from getting away."

"I figured we were stranded. Not enough fuel in our Virus Ship to get us home, and no way to drive the hauler."

"Argo and I dug into a network node and found all the systems weren't off, they were in standby. Kernels of software still running in each node. Argo rigged me a console and I jacked in. Had to patch some big software gaps, but once I did, we got her moving."

"Software gaps? Maiella, *you* were the ship's computer for two days straight..." Thompson breaks off, remembering the tortured concentration on her face, the sweat that rolled down it, the intermittent yelps and gasps when she was too consumed to utter a single word; and then her piercing scream when Argo switched over to his improvised computer fifty-four hours later... how she collapsed to the floor, silent and unmoving.

"I thought it killed you," he says.

"Almost did. And I never told you," she adds with a smirk, "we almost melted a few times. But anyway, you got me side-tracked. Will you sit back down with me?"

"Sure," he says with a shrug and parks himself beside her.

"It doesn't matter how good we *were*. That life is finished. Trying to push back into it is a waste of time."

"Didn't you just say that's why you feel blunted?"

"At first, yes, but hear me out. You know I've always had a hard time keeping emotions checked. Inhibitors can't squash them in me, not completely, and I was almost reconstituted because of it."

"Seriously?"

She nods. "That's why I had to be the best, Thompson. I *had* to be the best Geek in the Corps, or I'd have my head scooped. Just another Drone milling about Cadre One. Very little scares me, except for that..." Her eyes look directly into Thompson's. "With you it was easier to manage, because you balanced me out. I'd have done *anything* for you."

"And I for you."

She searches his expression for something, but whatever she is looking for, he can tell she did not find it. Her eyes drop to her lap.

"Thompson, the Counselor got me through some *very* tough times. Probably the most important thing he helped me understand is...we have emotions for a reason. We were never meant to live without them. I used to think it was a handicap...always tried to shut them off, to ignore them. But I've lived with them for a while now, and I...I trust them." She brings her other leg up onto the bunk and sits cross-legged. "The whole time at Cadre Two...emotion gave me an edge. Didn't need to analyze the situation, I opened up and let myself *feel* what right action was. Knew instantly. Didn't have to think about it. I just did things. And I survived."

Her spine straightens with confidence. "I think they're... They're like...some kind of biological autopilot. Isn't perfect, of course, I still made mistakes, but...my reactions were so much faster because for the first time in a long time, I *trusted* myself."

"I've always trusted you. Why would you think you were untrustworthy?"

Maiella smirks unhappily. "Well, that's part of it, I guess. It's irrational. Can't always explain why I feel a certain way. Can't describe *how* I know something, I just feel it. My entire life I was taught this was wrong, that being overly emotional was a defect of manufacture. But I know now that I'm *not* broken. The Counselor was right, '*Emotions are not weakness, and strength does not come from suppressing them.*'" She places hands in lap, traces the edge of one thumbnail with the other. "Does that make any sense at all?"

"Some. It's hard to imagine abandoning the conditioning so completely. Seems to have served you well enough. Not sure it would work for anyone but you."

Maiella's eyes flick over at Thompson with a mixture of hope and hurt. "Well, that's something, at least," she says with a lopsided grimace. "Don't be so sure I'm the only one it could work for, though. I think there's a reason why you didn't clamp down harder on me when my conditioning slipped." She puts a hand on his. "Ask yourself why that is. Ask yourself why we're here together right now when you could have roomed with anyone." She pats his hand once then removes hers. With a very deep breath in and out through her nose, her lips part, a half-formed word halted between them.

"I've spent a lot of time with the Colonists," she says finally. "I've watched them together. They know a lot more than we do."

"What about?"

"*Life*. Being alive, I mean. What they choose to share with one another, the happiness they give to others...and what they keep for themselves... I think it's important, being able to choose who you share with, Thompson...being able to share yourself with the person you want to... Do you understand?"

He hedges on his reply. He wants to understand, and he knows Maiella well enough that a straight answer is not what she is looking for.

"Can you help me understand?"

She looks up, eyes shiny, her mouth a wide smile. Her head bobs quickly. "I'd be glad to."

Maiella leans close and puts her arms around him. She pulls herself across his lap, traces his rough jaw line and kisses him. Her hands seem everywhere at once, sliding across his shoulders, squeezing his upper arms, gripping his chest. Her breath is quick, her pulse is racing, her hips rock subtly in his lap. She finds the clasps of his uniform jacket and nearly rips them apart down to the waist. Her hands slip inside at his shoulders and slide the jacket down to the bunk.

"Hold me," she whispers.

He brings his hands up to support her back, feeling toned muscle beneath her skin. She shivers at his touch, cinches her legs around his waist and grinds into him. More than anything else, he notices her soft flesh against his chest, how it is unlike anything he has ever seen on Cadre personnel. Colonist women have them, sure, but never a Cadre Operator, Drone, or MedTech. At first, they were a curious anomaly. Now, under the influence of subliminal cues, he is strangely interested.

She notices him looking, and with a sly grin, she asks, "Wanta see them?"

His lip juts. "Sure."

Maiella pulls her tank top over her head slowly, letting her breasts pop free one at a time. They present themselves proudly, attentively, two smooth curves capped by bumpy areola and firm nipples. She takes Thompson by his wrists and places his hands directly onto her bare skin. Her eyes close, her mouth opens, her head falls back, and her legs shake. She inhales deeply and leans right up to his ear, whispering,

"I want you."

"You have me."

"Unh, unh," she says, tracing a hand down past his navel. "I mean, I w—"

Her hand arrives at the gusseted canvas, molds against his unarousable bulge. She slumps. With a long drawn out groan, she slides off of him and flops onto the bunk beside him.

"Something wrong?" he asks, oblivious.

She stares at the wall beside her, fingers gripping the bridge of her nose. "You're *back* on the inhibitors?"

"Of course."

She laughs an awkward, self-mocking laugh. "I'm so stupid. And I'm embarrassed."

"Why?"

She looks up from the bunk at him, perplexed. "Seriously?"

"Yes! Seriously!"

"It's not your fault," she says into the wall. "I should have asked before I threw myself at you."

"I'm not complaining."

"Well you didn't react the way I was hoping."

"How's that?"

Maiella sits up in the bunk, snatches up her discarded tank top and crosses both legs. "When people are attracted to one another, they *combine* themselves."

"Yes, I know. But viviparous reproduction is extremely dangerous—"

"They don't just do it for *reproduction*!" She punches his arm for emphasis then flops down into the bunk, covering her bare chest and sulking.

"Hey."

She looks up at him, unhappy, tense.

"I think you're right," he says. "Was stupid to think I could get back into the Corps. But when I was off the inhibitors I was unstable. I almost..."

"Almost what?"

Thompson's face twitches. "I almost...self-terminated."

Maiella glances at him seriously then resumes her gaze at the wall. "Me, too."

"Really?"

"When you and Argo went to Earth, they gave you a two percent chance of return. And I knew that was generous." She sits up still using the top to cover herself. "So you were gonna grease yourself. How were you gonna do it?"

"My bayonet. Like the Samurai of Earth." He mimes the cuts across his torso and then into his neck.

Maiella's eyes squint and her mouth puckers. "*Harsh*. Me, I broke into the *Europa's* reactor. Was gonna drop the shielding."

"Yeah, that would do it in a hurry. Why'd you want to?"

She looks at her hands, burdened by heavy thoughts. "When you and Argo left, I was on my own. Exiled from the Cadre...feared by the Colonists... I thought there'd never be anyone else who could understand me, or who could even tolerate me. So, that was it. It's scary how quickly it came over me. Like I was drowning... I could barely get out of my bunk. Didn't want to talk to anyone. Started telling myself how much better off everyone would be if I wasn't in their way anymore. Just burning calories and oxygen. Dying was the only thing that made sense to me." She lifts her head. "Does that sound weird?"

"Not at all."

"How about for you? Why were you gonna do it?"

"Thought I was broken, broken for good. Kept thinking about my first rifle, how it just couldn't be fixed, and it had to be scrapped. That's what I was doing. Putting myself on the scrap pile."

"That's pretty grim. What stopped you?"

"This life isn't mine to throw away. After Doctor Taggart and Colonel Munro put in so much effort to keep me alive, I couldn't waste everything they had done."

"That's it? You snapped yourself out of it, just like that?"

"Heh, not entirely. I knew I wasn't going to self-terminate, I was going to request reconstitution instead. Was trying to figure out who to ask and how to go about it when Gregor found me. He asked me what you and Argo would think if I went through with it. For some reason that mattered more to me than anything else." Thompson misses it, but a small smile flits across Maiella's face. "How about you? You were standing there in the reactor chamber, and...?"

"Counselor found me. Reminded me that there was still a chance I could see you two again, but if I went through with it, the chances were zero. He showed me I wasn't just giving up on myself, I was giving up on you and Argo, as well. That was the worst part. And then I thought about what it would be like if you took yourself out and left me here alone. I'd be *furious* if you left me behind like that." She turns on him, eyes fiery. "Bad enough you went to Earth without me. Don't you *EVER* leave me behind again."

He weighs the moment and nods. "You may not know it, but you were with me the whole time."

Maiella's glare softens. "What do you mean?"

"I mean the whole time I was there, I imagined you there with me. Seeing mountain ranges, forests, animals...breathing air that wasn't scrubbed by regulators, looking up at a *real* sky. I kept you with me the entire time, up here," he says, pointing to his head. She smiles a deep, satisfied smile.

Then Thompson looks down at her exposed flank. "But what's that you were saying? Something about your behind?"

"Don't," she growls and taps him with a socked foot.

He eyes her backside again and grins.

Maiella fixes an evil stare on him. "I'm warning you, Gun."

"Oh yeah?" he says with a lifted eyebrow.

"Yep." She draws a leg back. "You don't know how strong I've gotten. I'm like a three-legged man at an ass-kicking contest."

"That so?" He lunges, grips her top leg at the ankle, pins it against the bunk, and spanks her rump. She shrieks between giggles, pummeling the solid mass of his chest and arms in defense until he relents.

"Forgot how quick you were," she says with half-closed eyes.

"You need another refresher?"

"*Ohhhhhh*! You *challenging* me, Gun?"

"Straight up, Geek. I will *whip your ass* on the mat."

She shakes her head, eyes like slits, mouth curved in a wide, malevolent grin. "You're gonna regret this. I've fought beasts *twice* your size, remember?"

"Well, you should know about beasts," he says with mock sincerity, "being one, yourself."

Her mouth drops, eyebrows lift. "It's *on*." She sits up, slides off the bunk, strips nude and steps into form fitting black nylon undersuit that ends at her knees and elbows.

Thompson stands and opens the door for her so she can walk out first, hooking his thumbs in the waist of his uniform trousers. When she walks by, he grabs her by the wrist, slings her back into the cabin, and races out ahead of her.

"*Quit stalling, Geek!*"

Head shaking, laughing to herself, Maiella streaks after him in hot pursuit.

TRAINING

Thompson and Maiella stand opposite one another, barefoot, on a thick rubber mat. The gymnasium is quiet with a background hiss of ventilation and low frequency thrum of the *Europa's* propulsion.

Two MedTechs, Obet and Arjay, are the only others in attendance. They loiter at the entrance, MedKits slung over their uneven shoulders, ready to step in and administer aid the moment it is needed.

Arms at their sides, backs straight, eyes locked in stoic stare, neither Thompson nor Maiella speak. At the appropriate beat, they bow to one another.

Thompson peels his off-white t-shirt, tosses it behind himself, and slides out of his uniform pants to his undersuit. Grafts and scars wrap his upper body in a web of crisscrossing lines with infrequent patches of pale skin between. Beneath, heaps of muscle rise, roll, and flatten as he limbers.

Maiella breathes in deeply through her nose, feeling the air move through sinuses and lungs. With hair tied back in a stubby ponytail, she swings her arms in wide circles, then bends at the waist into a deep stretch, hands landing flat on the mat. One leg lifts elegantly above her into a standing split. Shifting weight onto her hands, Maiella lifts the other leg so that she is balancing on her hands. Her legs curl forward, her back arches, and she walks over onto her feet, then immediately handsprings back to where she started and takes a ready position: left hand palm down at her waist, right arm leading, hand open, thumb up, wrist bent, fingers spread, elbow slightly bent. She lowers her chin and watches Thompson through her eyebrows.

Thompson lifts his hands beside his face, curling them into loose fists. His head lowers, and he shifts one foot ahead of the other into a boxer's stance. The playful mood is over.

Thompson steps in with a front kick so fast, Maiella barely side steps in time, ducks his spinning side kick, and sweeps his standing leg. Thompson lets himself fall, hooking a leg around Maiella and dragging her down with him. Keeping weight on her, he climbs to a top mount, legs astride her. One hand he keeps on her sternum, pressing her into the mat. The other cocks back for a pounding.

Maiella grabs the wrist of the arm pinning her, strikes the inside of his elbow with her free hand to bend it and sits up against him. The pinning arm slides through her arm pit, and she cinches tight to trap it. Hooking her free arm behind his head, she pulls him down onto her, and bucks ferociously. Thompson's whole body lifts, and in a blink she zips her legs out from beneath him, plants one foot on his right knee, and then shoves it out from under him while lifting his left side. Arm trapped and unable to brace himself, Thompson rolls and she rolls with him, pulling herself astride into top mount.

Before she can press the advantage, Thompson catches her right arm, lands a hand on her left hip, bucks, and throws her off easily. He does not release the trapped arm, however, and Maiella pivots at her shoulder, slamming hard to the mat. Thompson scrambles astride her, sliding his knees into her armpits. His forearms cross to opposite sides of her throat and he leans on them, scissoring together for a choke.

Maiella brings both of her knees up into Thompson's back, knocking his weight forward. His hands fly out to brace himself, and she jabs her elbows into his legs, driving his knees down to her waist. The Geek hooks one foot in the gap at his ankle. Working her strong leg muscles against his weaker ones, she powers his leg straight out, tipping him off balance. Thompson slides to compensate. When his weight shifts she slips her other leg out from under him and sweeps him onto his back again.

Thompson's fist is cocked for a short jab, and she reclines away from it quickly. Before he can sit up, she hooks an arm around his lower leg and slides back until she has his foot clamped in her armpit. Putting one leg over Thompson's trapped leg to better control it, she stomps her other foot into his opposite inner thigh, using it as a foothold to pull the trapped leg straight. The Geek arches her back, straining the ankle to the breaking point; but Thompson knocks her foot away from his thigh, pivots, and winds up a devastating roundhouse kick.

Maiella releases and rolls clear, getting to her feet several meters away. Thompson swings his legs over his head, rises to his shoulders and handsprings explosively onto his feet. Again the two face one another, staring wordlessly, echoes of their clash dying in the rafters high above.

Maiella rolls her head in a circle and settles into her ready posture. Thompson squares up, open hands raised slightly higher than his head. He bounces three times, lifting knees all the way to his chest, then settles into a ready stance.

"I'm coming at you for real this time," he says.

"Oh, so you were holding back?" she taunts. "Thought you'd just gotten slow."

Thompson grins across his entire face then rushes, and Maiella's eyes widen at his swiftness. She dives aside, one leg just slipping through Thompson's grasping hand, and comes up amid a flurry of his combinations. Knees, elbows, fists, and feet hammer at her. No matter how she spins, bobs, or weaves, there is no easy opening in Thompson's defense, no opportunity for counter-strike.

Maiella spins away, legs straining into a sprint, trailing one arm for balance. Thompson catches her trailing harm and yanks her back. As she whips around, he can just see the curve of her smile as her leg rises, swings up the line of his arm and lowered shoulder and bashes the side of his head. Thompson staggers, rocked by the hit, but keeps hold of Maiella's wrist. Her smile is gone as she chops, kicks, and hacks at him but cannot break his iron grip.

"Aw, *shit!*" she gripes.

Thompson takes her arm at the wrist with both hands, and in one fluid motion lifts it over his head, spins a full turn, and jerks the arm down. Maiella twists off her feet and slams hard to the mat. Thompson falls atop her, grinding her into the floor with his full weight as he maneuvers.

Maiella scrambles in defense, getting a knee up and barely keeping Thompson from climbing into top mount again. Deflecting one choke attempt after the next, she plants a foot in his hip and thrusts, zipping her other leg out from under him, then she snaps her legs around his waist in guard position. Between Thompson's vicious jabs, the Geek sits up against him, snakes her arms over his shoulders, locks her hands together, and slips her arms down like a hoop, trapping his arms. Thompson thrashes, head butts, and rolls, but Maiella does not lose her hold. Eventually he sets down onto his knees, Maiella locked tight against him like armor plating.

"Here we are, again," she says into his ear, maintaining her vice-like grip. Her face is misted with sweat, her hair is wild with free strands. She nuzzles the side of his face and kisses him gently. Thompson slumps.

"Awwww," comes a collective sigh from nearby.

Maiella and Thompson both turn to the gymnasium entrance where a small group of Colonists has gathered. The bright lights of the hallway silhouette them, making them hard to recognize.

"What's that move called?" asks a familiar voice in the group.

"That's, uh, heh...that's not part of the technique," Thompson says.

"Depends who your opponent is," Maiella says demurely. She unclasps her limbs, bounces up, turns to the crowd, and then crooks a finger at them with a wink.

Thompson jaw drops. "You claiming a win on me?"

She looks over her shoulder at him. "Yup."

Thompson shakes his head in amazement and gets to his feet. Looking past Maiella, he says to the group, "Do you need assistance?"

"Uh, no," says a woman self-consciously. She turns to her fellows for support, and they give her encouraging head nods. Looking back at Thompson, she says, "We've never seen a live martial arts demonstration, and...well... I hope we're not intruding."

"Of course not!" Maiella says as if the idea were ridiculous. "Please, come in."

When the group steps into the gymnasium, the overhead lights shine on their faces. Gregor is at the front, and with a satisfied glance at Thompson, he says, "Man, she clocked you good, huh?"

He shrugs in acknowledgement. "And I played right into it. Now please, everyone, stand at least eight meters back. We don't want anyone getting hurt."

"Wouldn't worry about that," Maiella adds. "At least, not from you."

Gregor taps one of his chums with the back of his hand and they all laugh.

Thompson looks at the floor and chuckles. When he looks up, he is deadly serious, and from the glare, Maiella knows the time for quips is over. With military posture, she steps to her spot opposite Thompson, places feet together, and with hands at her side, bows. He bows to her, as well, and the two take a fight ready stance. Seconds tick by uninterrupted as the two stand, watching one another.

"Is this a sparring match or a staring contest?" Gregor shouts.

Maiella's eyes dart in annoyance at the Russian. When she looks back, Thompson is nearly on top of her. His arms are wide, too wide to slide away from. She backpedals for extra space, and instantly regrets it. Leaned back, she cannot dodge, and from the look on Thompson's face, he knows it, as well. She drops to the mat, leg up to vault the man over her in his charge; but Thompson bats the leg away, rolling Maiella onto her side, and he crashes onto her.

Her lungs empty in a great cough as Thompson's bulk compresses her chest, and she is pinned, face down. A thick arm slides under her chin, cinches tight, and hauls back. Her teeth are bared as she struggles, but the naked choke is set. Trapped under his weight, unable to breathe, Maiella swings elbows, kicks her feet. With the patience of a python, Thompson wraps his legs around her lower body, controlling her movement, keeping her from escaping, then arches his back. Her face turns deep red, and with eyes crushed shut in fury, she taps his choking arm.

Thompson releases immediately, unwraps himself from around her, and steps back. Obet and Arjay take a step forward, but Thompson raises a hand to them. They return to their positions and watch.

Maiella lays on her side, mouth open in large panting breaths, normal color returning to her face. She lifts herself up to hands and knees.

Kneeling down beside her, Thompson asks without a trace of sympathy, "All right, Geek?"

She looks up at Thompson and nods. Satisfied, he stands and returns to his starting position.

"Aren't you going to help her up?" Gregor asks.

"That's not how it works," Maiella says hoarsely, rising to her feet. She coughs, closes her eyes, and breathes deeply for several seconds. "I was distracted. And I deserved to lose." She clears her throat and rubs it. Through gritted teeth, she adds, "I *assure* you, Gun, that *won't* happen again."

"Then I'd say the real match begins now." Thompson moves to starting position, back straight, arms at his sides.

Maiella steps opposite him. Her face is a set of horizontal lines, her eyes are like unblinking pools of lava. She watches him with an intensity he has never seen before, even on rotation facing an enemy.

At the appropriate beat, they bow to one another. But as Thompson rises, Maiella keeps her forward lean, her legs slide beneath her, and she springs. The slight upward momentum of Thompson's torso, feet side by side beneath him, keep him planted in place. She slams a heel into his gut. Thompson folds, staggering back off-balance, arms thrown forward, and she lands a roundhouse to his ribs from the left, then from the right. She clasps her hands behind his head and hauls his face down onto her knee twice, releases him, and axe kicks his back.

Thompson drops to a knee and reaches for her legs; but she leaps over his head and stomps into his back, driving him into the mat. Maiella falls onto his back and slides an arm around his neck, but Thompson drops his chin in time, blocking the choke. He takes her arm in both hands, stands with her on his back, and catapults her away. She tumbles through the air, lands on her feet like a cat, and races back at him.

Thompson deflects her kicks, jabs, and strikes at his vitals. In the Geek's rage-filled attack, there is just enough opening for counter, and he bashes her cheek, turning her head aside, diverting her onslaught. Before he can chase after, she is already back at him like a crazed animal. Each time, he blocks her strikes, watches for an opening, finds it, and bashes her away.

Breath huffs past her lips, yet she does not relent, throwing herself again and again through swift combinations until the critical opening where she is smacked back. Gradually the attacks become slower as fatigue and the haze of his pummeling take their toll. Just as before, she comes in with the combinations, and then...a fake!

Thompson commits with a jab and cross but misses, just catching her malevolent smirk as she weaves aside and slugs a leg into his gut. Off balance again, he stumbles. Maiella smashes his head, shoulders, ribs, legs, gut again, but he powers through it all back to his feet. She spins in front of him, winding up for a big strike, taking her eyes off him, and he knows it is her fatal mistake. She is totally committed, and as she comes around his fist is poised for the knock out. She screams like he has never heard anything scream before in his life. His fist flies, and her fist also flies, exploding into his chest directly over his heart.

Both hits land with all the force their bodies can muster, landing with a concussive thud that echoes throughout the gymnasium.

Maiella's scream ends instantly and she collapses to the mat in a heap.

Thompson's vision blurs, his eyes flutter, and strength abandons him. He drops to his knees, mouth open, unable to breathe, and stares at the floor, disbelieving the intensity of the hit.

Colonists gasp and groan as Arjay and Obet hobble to the downed combatants. With deftness belying their infirmities, both MedTechs open their kits and administer aid.

Thompson sways on his knees, breathless, until his lungs finally draw oxygen from the mask Arjay holds to his face. Obet gently palpates Maiella's neck for fractures then lays her on her back. He digs in his kit, retrieves a small fabric covered capsule and breaks it under her nose. She twitches.

Thompson nods at Arjay and pushes the mask from his face. Scooting over to Maiella, he places a hand over his chest and looks on while Obet works.

"Is she all right?" Gregor asks.

Thompson looks over his shoulder to see a crowd of Colonists, much larger than before, standing close behind him.

"Her pulse is strong and she's breathing," Obet answers without looking up, "just unconscious."

Maiella's eyes flick open and she lifts her knees in defense. By degrees, her wild eyes calm when she sees others leaning over her. Her eyes close and she grips her temples with a hand.

"I lost?" she asks.

"Looked like a draw to me," Gregor says.

Maiella takes her hand away and looks at the Russian skeptically. From Gregor, her eyes move to Thompson and when she sees him kneeling beside her, she shakes her head. "Obviously not."

"I've never been hit like that before," Thompson says, reaching a hand out to her. She looks at it before deciding to take it.

"Argo almost dropped me once," he adds. "Bashed me to pieces...but he never dropped me."

Maiella's face screws into disbelief. "I dropped you?"

"Yeah."

Maiella grimaces. When the Colonists all nod in confirmation, however, some of the skepticism leaves her face.

"Not hard enough, obviously. You're still upright."

Thompson grins in admiration. "C'mon, Geek. On your feet."

Maiella blinks the cobwebs away and rises groggily, Colonists applauding with loud cheers and whistles. Maiella smiles, flexes her arms in a variety of muscle poses then falters. Obet steadies her, pressing a canteen into her hand. She thanks him and takes a long drink.

Once the cheers die down, Gregor steps from the group and asks plainly, "Will you teach us how to do that?"

Thompson squares up to the Russian, assessing the man standing before him the way he would assess an Operator candidate. He had never considered Gregor a potential combatant before. Now he is wondering why, because in the Russian's eyes there is a desire worthy of any Cadre initiate.

It could be enough.

"Geek Maiella!" Thompson shouts.

"Sir!" she answers, passing the canteen back to Obet and snapping to attention.

"Stand opposite this man and ready for sparring."

"Aye, SIR!"

Gregor's head dips slightly, and with a raised eyebrow he asks, "*Now?*"

"Now," Thompson says.

Gregor's jaw flexes as he swallows his anxiety. Mimicking Thompson's pose, Gregor raises his fists beside his head, knuckles crushed white. Maiella bows then assumes her ready stance.

Thompson walks behind Gregor, telling him, "You have no hope of winning. There is a very strong chance you will be injured. Would you like to reconsider?"

Gregor shakes his head in short, jerky movement. "No."

"This opponent can cause you more pain than you realize."

Gregor's mouth opens, but he censors himself and draws his fighting stance tighter.

"Hesitation is a lack of certainty," Thompson adds, "a lack of commitment. If you hesitate, you will not be trained. Do you understand?"

"Yes, I do," he growls with the touch of adrenaline.

"Attack her, *NOW*!"

Gregor yells a fearsome yell and he runs at Maiella. Before he can throw a punch, the Geek steps into a front kick and boots him flat onto his back. He lands with a harsh grunt, eyes wide with shock. Fighting through the startling impact, he climbs to his feet.

"Again," Thompson demands.

Gregor resets his posture, and with another bellow runs straight at Maiella. She steps into another front kick, and Gregor twists his shoulders. The kick strikes at an angle, knocking him aside, but he keeps his feet and does not fall.

"Stop!" Thompson yells. Maiella immediately drops her guard and stands at attention. Gregor recovers and looks back at Thompson, unsure what to do.

"I've seen what I need. We'll train you. First, we need to build and harden you. Choose a partner. It'll be easier if you have someone to suffer with."

"*Suffer*?" Gregor repeats.

"That's right."

Gregor snorts, rubbing his chest where Maiella's heel landed. Turning to the group, he calls out, "Who wants to be my partner?"

Every hand in the group goes up. Gregor looks with delight, while Thompson and Maiella maintain stoic detachment.

"Before you commit to this," Thompson adds, "you must know what it means to accept this training. It will be a process filled with physical pain. Your muscles will burn, your joints will ache, and still I will drive you." Thompson pauses to let the words sink in. The group appears undaunted, so he continues. "There is no trauma you can survive that our MedTechs cannot repair. With this in mind, it will be necessary for you to injure one another to practice proper technique."

There is a considerable waning of enthusiasm in the group, and Thompson hammers the point home.

"You will break each others' arms, legs, and ribs. You will choke to the point of unconsciousness, strike vital organs. This is essential so that you understand one thing: this training is for the *sole purpose of defeating your enemy*. By experiencing the pain you inflict on others you understand the consequence of your actions. You must accept it, and accept that it will happen to you so that you can face your foe without fear. To hesitate in combat means the death of everyone you would protect. If you cannot be absolutely ruthless to your enemy, you must not take this training."

The crowd murmurs and, two at a time, they slink back toward the entrance.

"Hey!" Gregor shouts. "Isn't there anyone who wants to stand up in a fight? No longer cowering in the shadows like mice? Take back control of our lives? Isn't that worth something?"

Five halt their departure. In their uneasy glances, Thompson sees them trying to cope with the idea of being injured and having to deliberately inflict injury on each other. He watches the round shoulders and hunched spines squaring and straightening with the subtle encouragements they pass back and forth.

"I'm sick of being afraid. Literally *sick* from it..."

"We could be discovered someday. Would we just roll over and die? Or would we fight?"

"Like Gregor said, we have to stand on our own at some point..."

"Not helpless..."

"I'd give anything for that..."

"It's gonna hurt..."

"But I've seen what the MedTechs can do..."

"They're amazing..."

"They'll be able to fix us..."

"And we take charge of ourselves. Us...the bunch of us...*together*."

"Should've done this years ago, really..."

"We didn't trust them then..."

"We had our reasons..."

"Well, not anymore..."

In the lull of conversation, they look over at Gregor then shuffle back. Gregor welcomes them and extends an arm.

"Thompson, Maiella...this is Alexei, his wife Ulrikka, Azhar, Vinh, and his wife Birgitte." Thompson shakes hands with each, looking them in the eye. All are as nervous as rabbits, and they range in size from one and a half to just under two meters, yet in each of them there is a spark of Gregor's fire.

"I can accept these terms," Alexei says, "but my wife cannot be my sparring partner. I will not hurt her. Not for any reason."

Vinh nods in agreement. "And I don't think it would work if we switched either. I think you and I should pair up."

"I'll pair with you, then, Birgitte," Ulrikka says.

"Works for me," Birgitte answers.

"So that leaves you and me, Gregor," Azhar adds.

Gregor nods. "Right on, brother."

"Okay," the Gun says after he is sure those who departed are out of earshot. "Gather 'round."

The group moves closer and Maiella takes a place beside Thompson.

"What I told you earlier was to discourage those who would not make it. It is no shame to refuse the training.

"What I *haven't* told you yet, is that there are benefits. Every time you are injured, our MedTechs will repair you better than before. The site of injury is reinforced so that the same injury is much less likely to occur. For example..."

Thompson points to his knees.

"Both of my knees have been hyper extended, the ligaments and tendons torn or detached. The sinews were bonded with flesh-weld, then ribbons were attached here, here, here, and here, so that the joint can withstand far greater force before failing. The bones were supplemented with carbon weave to withstand greater shearing stresses. In short, these reinforcements make it very difficult to break or dislocate these joints again."

"How many 'reinforcements' have you had?" Ulrikka asks.

"*Numerous.*"

"Why not just perform the surgeries without the injury?" Vinh asks.

"Because pain is crucial to the lesson," Thompson explains. "Hesitation in combat is caused by fear: fear of death, fear of injury, fear of pain. Pain can be managed. And death is rarely instantaneous. So that leaves the fear of crippling injury. When you come to understand that almost any injury you survive can be repaired, you shed that fear. You can face the hard certainties of combat, you can act effectively with every asset at your disposal. Furthermore, with every reinforcement, you can survive harder blows, you can lift heavier loads, jump higher, run farther.

"That floor beneath you? The machines that propel this ship? The tools used to make her? Think these things are harder than you can be? *Wrong*. Human hands have directly or indirectly shaped every part of this ship. Consider this when you feel frail, or when you believe something cannot be done."

Thompson pauses to observe how his words are being received. He can still see anxiety, but their heads are high and their eyes are bright.

"As your body improves and you realize how capable you're becoming," Thompson continues, "some of you will look forward to your next reinforcement."

"Wait, *what*?" Gregor says in disbelief. "I'm no masochist!"

Maiella cocks her head to the side. "Mass-o-kist?"

"Yeah. Someone who likes pain. Likes to get hurt. Enjoys it."

"Ah," Thompson says, "I'm not suggesting you'll ever confuse pain with pleasure. What I mean is that you'll become accustomed to it, shed your fear of it, and pain will no longer be any impediment. Reinforcement is a way of improving ourselves to a level we can't reach through exercise. Therefore, some will look forward to physical enhancement, appreciating heightened physical ability more than the distress it brings.

"Now then, the person beside you will motivate you, support you, assist you. For now, we're going to start with simple strength and flexibility training. Maiella, take them through a calisthenics routine."

Thompson turns to leave.

"Where are you going?" Gregor asks.

"To ask your captain for permission to train you," the Gun says over a shoulder, "and to establish a MedTech detail for each session. Maiella... Go easy on them...at first."

Maiella smiles a wicked smile. "Aye, sir!" With the sensitivity of a drill instructor she orders each person to a spot on the mat, barks out her instructions.

Thompson pauses at the doorway, stepping into his uniform trousers, pulling his T-shirt over his torso. He watches Maiella call the calisthenics and how the Colonists are taking it. Alexei, Ulrikka, Azhar, Vinh, and Birgitte cast wary glances at each other with the same question branded into their expressions: *What have we gotten ourselves into?* But not Gregor. He focuses on Maiella's direction, soaking up her instruction like a sponge.

Thompson saves that impression then turns and heads out to visit the *Europa's* new captain, Sharon Jones.

PURCHASE MADE

Shao-Lo rides along in the transport while Honniker steers it, adrenaline making her legs and arms twitch. The approach is different than before, neither heading for the helical spires marking the main entrance nor the launch tube from Mikato's production floor. She scours the jagged core fragment for a hint of a destination, but the dim glow from the dwarf star wraps the dark stone in shadows.

Could be anything down there, right in front of me, and I wouldn't see it...

She turns to her console, letting the transport's sensors probe the darkest areas. As chaotic as the rock appeared from afar, it is even more so up close, and a terrain of folds, heaves, and canyons fills the projected holoscreen.

The transport veers into a deep rift and plunges through a fissure at the bottom into total darkness. There is no longer anything to see on the viewscreen, no caption, no visible feature at all.

"*Did Colonel wear her seat belt?*" Honniker asks with scorn.

The transport jolts to a halt with a *klank* and *bang*. Whatever was gripping the craft releases with shrieks of retreating metal, and a vertical seam of white light opens ahead. Shao-Lo squints into the glare, one hand shielding her face. As the seam widens, she sees two mechanical struts pulling the transport into a vast cavern.

Though bright compared to pitch darkness, the lighting inside is barely adequate to reveal dozens of spindly, skeletal vessels, each one moored to its own docking cradle around the cavern's extremity. The longer Shao-Lo studies them, the more she recognizes a common design motif. A central spine and surrounding supports serve as a durable scaffold to which modular drives, weapons, or other apparatus are attached. Some vessels are long and thin, others are nearly spherical, but all are crammed with DE rails, missile tubes, and bulky propulsion arrays.

"Like a back rack..." she says to herself. "Interchangeable modules with common attach points... Could jettison damaged modules in combat, increasing maneuverability... Makes a lower profile target... Hmm... No crew compartments... Eliminating life support saves half the mass... More room for weaponry, fuel, propulsion... Smart."

"It is good to know you recognize superior design when you see it. These warships can also stack while deployed, bringing efficiencies that increase speed and range. And compromised vessels provide immediate replacement parts for those damaged in combat. You see, your general simply has no chance."

The mechanical struts abruptly transfer the ship onto a rail system with magnetic tethers. Strident clanks against the hull confirm attachment, the struts release, and the rail system tows the colonel's vessel toward an open air lock three times the size of Cadre One's Landing Bay.

Shao-Lo leans toward the windscreen, craning her neck to see more of the cavern.

Honniker's showing off, she thinks, *otherwise he'd have left the lights off.*

Far back, near the cavern's roof, she spots a vessel unlike the rest. Its rear two thirds are darkened in Cadre black, but the front is shiny and new. Disfigured by radical augmentations, the outline of the *Enyo* is unmistakable. Her hull flares with recent additions, angular and aggressive. The stern is wide with visible seams, as though rapid growth has split the armored skin. And all along her length, where cabins and cargo space once existed, are recessed missile tubes. Sooty scorches prove they have been fired recently.

"If the Colonel would deploy the landing gear, we may get started."

Shao-Lo touches a button on her console, activating a concert of hydraulics beneath her, and the transport settles onto its fully extended struts. Clouds of vapor blast into the air-lock from all directions, and a gauge marking external atmospheric pressure rolls up to one hundred kilopascals, precisely.

"Let's get a better look at your guilt gifts, shall we?"

Shao-Lo triggers the cargo doors on the transport's belly. Rattling and clattering carries throughout the transport as fully laden bins jostle down their tracks to the deck.

This is a battle, she reminds herself. *Chusan now wears my rank and responsibility. I am meant to be a part of this cargo, currency for what the*

Cadre must purchase. Cost is irrelevant.

Her teeth and fists clench.

If I can pay it, I will.

Thick pressure doors at the back of the huge air lock slide aside, through which two platoons of war machines march in formation. Their weapon arms orient at the transport, and maintain aim as they form an oval perimeter. Behind them pours a horde of mixed creatures, growling and yowling. Some wear thick overlapping plates, others bristle with spines. All of them run straight for the open transport then flinch at the oval of war machines. The horde parts in the middle and flows around the perimeter, unable to cross it. Creatures cuff each other in frustration, hissing and screaming with a teeth-bared rage. Frenzied howls and barks resonate in the open belly of the ship, filling the transport with a monstrous din.

Shao-Lo remains still, stoic, and composed.

"As I've already explained, I did not come to fight," she says. "And you need what's in this cargo hold. Best not to break it."

"I am more than able to obtain what I need from the enemy, myself."

"Clearly, you have the tools. So what keeps you from facing them as we do?"

The screams and howls lower in volume, as if the beasts want to hear their master's answer. But Honniker is silent.

"You don't want the enemy tracking you back here," Shao-Lo answers for him. "Isn't that right? You don't like the idea of having to fight in a contest you could possibly lose."

The horde swells with sullen growls.

"There's no need to take that risk, Doctor. Not when we can supply as much as you need."

"Ha! So you think your stores are infinite, then? You overplay your hand!"

"Not at all. From the little you have here, we could easily—"

"LITTLE? Have your eyes and ears been closed, Colonel? Look around. This is but a FRACTION of my arsenal."

"I did not misspeak. This is *nothing* compared to an entire planet of productive capacity. The enemy has many worlds to build weapons and use them. I must say, your small collection does not impress me."

"Small... Quite enough for your pitiful tribe. Did you forget? I know where you dwell. I can swat you like a fly and be rid of your pestering."

"Maybe. But not before we broadcast Cadre Two's coordinates to every corner of the galaxy."

"Save your empty threats. You know nothing of the enemy who ruined

you."

Shao-Lo smiles a calculated smile. "We have a high-ranking captive."

"*You are lying.*"

"I don't lie, Honniker. And besides that, I'm sure you're analyzing every part of my speech to tell if I was. So. Tell me. Am I lying?"

There is an uncomfortably long pause, and Honniker says begrudgingly, "*No, you are not. But I am skeptical how such a feeble intellect could interrogate it.*"

"Not I. The Counselor has a good mind for communication, a mind developed by someone here, if I recall. The Counselor has deciphered much of its language and has drawn useful intelligence."

"*What did it...?*" Honniker breaks off then restates without such obvious enthusiasm, "*What has it told you?*"

"Information is valuable, Doctor. Wouldn't you agree?"

"*Ach! Hören der Zimtzicke zu?*" Honniker mutters hatefully. With restraint, he asks, "*Will you share what you know?*"

"It can be arranged. But this much is free: the Eleto are more than you could handle, if they learn about this place."

"*Then I should finish their work, and eliminate this threat.*"

"Not before we could broadcast your location."

"*You would do no such thing. It would be your own suicide, as I would crush your small outpost. Or maybe I broadcast YOUR coordinates and let the enemy do it for me.*"

Shao-Lo stares coolly through the windscreen at the masses of machines and creatures.

"*Ach, so... They have already found you.*"

Shao-Lo confirms with a single nod.

"*You are staring extinction in the face.*"

"No different than any other time."

"*Yes, yes, I see now. You intend to come here and replace your discovered den!*"

"NOT by force."

"*No?*"

"No. I've already said this, Doctor."

"*So you have. And what else are you scheming to take from me, hmm?*"

"Nothing but what you willingly offer."

"*After what you did here, the damage done, you EXPECT me to give you ANYTHING?*"

"We expect nothing."

A long silence passes, which Shao-Lo endures by watching creatures mill about beyond the perimeter of war machines.

"*My prices are high,*" Honniker says at last.

"State them."

"*As if you could pay.*"

"Doctor, the contents of this transport are a piece of what I can deliver. Plus, I have intelligence pressed from our captive. So long as it remains alive, we can continue to press it for information. I trust you see the value."

"*Perhaps. Or perhaps you intend to bribe your way in so you can sabotage my networks again, or poison my nutrient baths, or stall my reactors, HMM?*"

"Trust has to begin somewhere, Doctor. It can start with this cargo... if you can look beyond your own fear."

"*FEAR?*"

Creatures roar with one terrible voice and the war machines take a unified stamp closer to the transport.

"*I doubt there is ANYTHING I have to fear from YOU.*"

"Which I have already said."

The creatures hiss and spit, testing unseen restraints with extended claws and snapping jaws, then *yipe* suddenly and lower heads in submission.

"*You may state your proposal.*"

Shao-Lo lifts an eyebrow, impressed at the show of control over seemingly uncontrollable beasts. "My offer is plain. We desire safe occupancy at Cadre Two. We wish to collaborate and share research—"

"*HA! What YOU could produce is WORTHLESS!*"

"May I finish?"

Honniker broods. "*Fine. Continue to make your offer that could not possibly interest me.*"

"We wish to share and collaborate on research projects. And we would field-test your designs against the enemy. In return, we supply regular installments of the resins, adhesives, insulators, and other polymers you lack. We will provide human raw material from drones we incubate on site. And you can be assured the secret of Cadre Two is maintained because our mutual interest will require it."

Creatures pace in agitation beyond the perimeter, no longer hissing or spitting, and, in the lull of conversation, Shao-Lo can feel how badly Honniker wants to accept.

"*I, myself, am indifferent to this ridiculous offer. Yet I will consult with Mikato.*"

"I'll be here." Shao-Lo sinks back into her chair, fingers interlaced, hands in lap, and settles in for a long wait.

"*I'm afraid your proposal does not carry quite enough weight, Colonel.*"

Shao-Lo sits up, surprised by the consultation's brevity. "Explain."

"*You must add yourself to the manifest.*"

"What could that possibly benefit you?"

"*A sweetener for the prize, you could call it. Or, you could call it an intractable demand. Either way, we can't have you leave us. Not now, when you're so close. No, no, I'm sure there can be no agreement unless you are made a part of it.*"

"That's not impossible. But there is a counter proposal."

"*I am listening.*"

"The *Enyo.* Return it, and dispatch it to coordinates I provide."

"Enyo? *I know of nothing by this name—*"

"No games, Honniker. The ship we first arrived in. I saw it on the way in."

"*What you saw is no longer your* 'Enyo.' *What you left behind was derelict, wreckage. I have rebuilt your simpleminded design, shaping, honing, and improving. I do not wish to part with it.*"

"Then I will not be a part of the trade."

"*I can just as easily take you. You can not stop me from taking you.*"

"True. But without regular reports from me, all trade ends. Your research stalls, *again.* For all I know, those ships out there in the cavern are only partially built. You might need what I have to finish them."

"*Regular reports, you say? Colonel, did you forget I am a scientist? It would take more than five YEARS for your messages to reach your friends. I think in that time, we could be ready for anything.*"

"Quantum Entanglement. You've heard of it, no doubt, being a scientist."

There is a pause.

"*You expect me to believe that hairless apes have solved the conundrum of instantaneous communication? Dubious at best.*"

"Not *us,* Doctor. The Eleto. Every large ship in our fleet was captured from the enemy, and every one of them has this communication apparatus, including the *Enyo...* Or rather it *did* until you blasted the front section apart. A shame you were so impulsive, or you might have seen for yourself how it worked."

"*A bluff. Impossible. Besides, even if you had one of these communicators on you, I could simply take it away."*

"Who said I carried it on me?"

Honniker goes quiet for many seconds. *"Where is it, then?"*

"Nearby. Safely hidden. You'll no doubt go looking for it, but there are no emissions from it to detect. You'll pass right over it a thousand times and never find it, even as it's operating."

"Once you're on my table, I can coax it out of you..."

"Threaten me again, Honniker, this deal ends. The enemy gets your coordinates, and you DIE with us."

"Honniker!" shouts Mikato via intercom. *"Cease your pointless taunts! We WANT this negotiation to progress!"*

Mikato's unexpected entrance to the conversation catches Shao-Lo off balance. She clears her throat and braces for a shift in tactics.

"Greetings, Doctor Mikato. Shall I restate my proposal?"

"Thank you, Colonel, that won't be necessary," Mikato says. *"Please forgive my associate, he is being overly protective. Your last visit was... destructive. So I'm sure you can understand his reluctance to deal with you."*

"I'm not offended. I understand. Time will prove our sincerity, and we all can benefit from it."

"Indeed," Mikato says.

"If I release your Enyo," Honniker says with elongated syllables, *"you would be getting a bargain in this deal, Colonel."*

"We want nothing but what you freely offer."

"So you have said," Mikato interjects. *"But where do we go from here? Even if an agreement was possible, we cannot simply allow all of you to move in at once. Such a migration could be detected from parsecs away."*

"That's reasonable. Any progress we make should be in small steps. And the way our first occupants are treated will impact the tone, and generosity, of future negotiations."

"We have not agreed to anything yet," Honniker states.

"No, but you're considering it. If I recall correctly, you had a living population here. You tried to trap them so that you could pull subjects for your experiments. Their response was to assault your Server Farm and flee. Now you have nothing but leftovers in your *Graveyard.*

"What we offer is an accessible population," Shao-Lo continues, "one from which we can select candidates or volunteers."

"You would allow this?" Mikato asks skeptically. *"You would allow your own people to be—"*

"The Colonel did not misspeak!" Honniker interrupts. *"She has made the offer! It will NOT be rescinded!"*

274

"I have no intention of rescinding any part of my proposal."

"*Not yet*," Mikato adds. "*Of course, once the transaction is made, you may rethink your decision.*"

"With respect, Doctor Mikato, it isn't my decision."

"*Interes-s-sting*," Honniker coos. "*Such loyalty in them to authority, such discipline and fearlessness... If only Keller had shown such backbone...*"

"Keller is dead, as you well know," Shao-Lo states with rigid chin. "I've no appetite for insults to his memory."

"*I find it curious, Colonel*," Mikato begins, "*that you seem more protective of a dead man's memory than of your own living people.*"

"That's a matter of opinion. From my perspective, this is a good trade for them."

"*I suppose it is. And I pity how desperate you must be to consider this an improvement on current conditions*," Mikato adds. "*Well then, I admit I am eager to begin unloading your cargo.*"

"*As am I*," Honniker chimes.

"By all means."

The perimeter of war machines parts in front of the open pressure doors, and the horde of creatures skitters out of the way as rows of sturdy, tracked machines roll through the gap.

"*So*," Mikato asks, "*what's next?*"

"This cargo is yours to do with as you like. Would you like another to follow?"

"*Of course.*"

"We know where there's a large assembly of enemy ships... We're going to attack it."

"*I see*," Mikato says. "*And you'd like to take something of ours to this fight, I presume?*"

"That's right."

"*A chance to field-test your designs, Mikato*," Honniker says, "*without drawing attention to us...you've craved this for centuries!*"

"*True, but I could send my machines out now. What difference would it make?*"

"*If the apes are piloting them*," Honniker says with glee, "*the enemy will have no reason to believe it was anything but another human attack. They would have no link to us, no cause to search for another installation. Merely the desperate act of an endangered species!*"

"*Intriguing... But how would you communicate the result in a way that would not lead back here?*"

"Quantum Entanglement is an untraceable means of

communication," Shao-Lo answers. "All Cadre ships are so equipped. As am I, so to speak."

"*Yes...yes, that might work,*" Mikato says.

There is a long lull in conversation. Outside, the predators squat on haunches. Some yawn and stretch out on the deck.

"*So, Colonel,*" Mikato asks, "*what is it you would like?*"

"Let's see what you've got."

RECONCILING TERROR

Shondre stares at the plain tan walls of her cabin aboard the *Europa*. Though brighter and more comfortable than the bare stone of Cadre One, the locked door makes it just another prison cell.

She looks down at the faded orange fabric she wears. Cut from something a human would wear, it hangs on her like a drape, heavy and smothering. Rough seams grate against her soft skin, making her long for the cool, smooth weaves that once filled her wardrobe.

And yet, this one must remain, she reminds herself.

She stands from her bunk and extends long, delicate arms, pressing her palms against the narrow walls as if to keep them from collapsing in on her.

"Kon-Zil-Urr!" she shouts then falls to a fit of dry, hacking coughs. She feels lightheaded and slumps down to the bunk again, the bunk that has propped her every day of an extended illness.

The Counselor's face appears on the comm panel beside her locked door.

"(Yes, Madame Shondre, are you well?)" he says in her language.

"(No. Every day, these walls get closer. Senses starve, and the mind dwells on what cannot be. Will you let this one out?)"

"(Shondre, this one is not your captor.)"

"(But this one is released into your custody. You can free her from this cage. *Please*, come.)"

The Counselor looks off screen to his left, then says into the panel, "(This one will arrive soon.)"

"(When is soon?)"

The screen goes blank, and Shondre shivers with the chill of isolation.

This one will remain.

She straightens her spine, crosses her legs on the bunk, presses her fingertips together in her lap and wraps her whip tail around herself. There, she sits in meditative silence until the comm panel chimes.

"(Madame Shondre, it is your friend, the Counselor. May he enter?)"

Afforded at least a simple courtesy, Shondre unfurls herself, rises and stands at the door as if she were receiving a guest. The door slides aside, and the Counselor is on the other side of it, white lab coat, brown slacks, disheveled black hair. She takes a half step back and with an elegant sweep of her hand, invites him, "(Please, enter and share these *ample* accommodations.)"

The Counselor smirks, then extends an open hand to her. Dignity intact, Shondre takes his hand in hers, allowing him to escort her past the large man and woman guarding her cabin. She glances at them both, and they seem to be of similar build to the ones who stole her away from her people, yet they are crooked versions, like toys an enormous pet has chewed.

There is nothing to interpret in their despising glares, but, after so long in this place, she knows they will not hurt her. As always, their neglect is more painful than their attention.

"(Thank you for coming,)" she tells the Counselor. "(The room air is ventilated, and yet it becomes stifling.)"

"(This one understands,)" he says.

She looks down at him with lowered brow. "(This one has doubts.)"

"(All are confined in this ship. But Madame's confinement is...more severe.)"

As it happens every time she strolls the corridors with the Counselor, Shondre receives anxious glances, baleful stares. Deep down she knows it is crucial the people see her and become accustomed to the sight of her as someone wholly unthreatening. Attempts to escape, sudden movements, anything erratic could trigger their fear-filled response. And though she wants nothing more than to rejoin her beloved, she is calm and patient.

"(Konn-Zil-Urr, you do this one honor by studying the People's speech. How quickly you learn! Once we were like barehanded puppeteers, gesturing and pointing for the simplest concepts.)"

"(It's fascinating how the People assemble their words. It offers insights how they perceive the world around them. Helps your friend to understand.)"

"(This one has not been so patient. Human words do not fit in her mouth. Often, this one feels stupid, unequal to your talent, and impatience becomes rudeness. For that, please accept apology. But this one recognizes goodness in you. It is proof that all mankind is not evil.)"

The Counselor's head tilts, something unvoiced on the edge of his tongue. His mouth swishes to one side of his face and he looks forward, letting the moment pass.

Shondre dips her head and watches her feet as she walks. "(Genocide hangs around the necks of the People, heavier than any stone. Belief in the purity and wisdom of the People is proved false. Until amends are made, we are *all* diminished.)"

The Counselor looks around himself before saying, "(It does this one joy to hear, but Madame must be careful of open speech. Some are not yet ready to listen.)"

"(How can that be? Many generations have passed since...)"

The Counselor shakes his head. "(The gray ones you see on our walks? They *remember*.)"

Shondre's head slides back and she dips her elongated snout. "(Are they so ancient? No one has heard of such longevity!)"

"(Freezers.)"

"(Sorry, not understanding.)"

"(They freeze themselves for long spans to extend their lives.)"

Shondre shudders from head to tail. "(Frozen? *Horrible!*)" She pulls the open collar of her badly tailored jumpsuit together.

Cadre MedTechs hobble by in the opposite direction, and Shondre bows to them as they pass. The MedTechs offer nothing but stares.

"(It matters not how Kad-Ra choose to see,)" she says, pointing to her head, "(understanding grows behind this one's eyes. With awkward steps, Medd-Tekks show this one how sharp is their line between life and extinction.)

"(This one feels the highest obligation,)" Shondre continues. "(*All* children now are born into fruitless war. We fail them as parents. Such inequity *must* be balanced.)"

The Counselor nods heavily, and the two walk in silence.

Colonists, working on water pipes in the corridor, suddenly hush their conversation. One looks back and forth from the tall Eleto to the Counselor.

"What the *hell* are you doing that thing, Counselor?"

"Talking with her, Dave."

"Oh yeah? Why don't you ask *her* to get the fuck off our planet so we can go home?"

Shondre dips her head and places a hand over her chest, speaking the human words as carefully as she can, "Urrth bee-long hyoo...not hai." She bows and walks by, paying no attention to the amazed expressions on their faces.

"Did that thing say what I think it did?" Dave asks his comrades. Alexei and Ulrikka only stare at the stately creature who, despite the sack-like fit of her improvised garments, maintains a simple elegance.

Shondre wants to look back but restrains herself. "(What are they doing?)" she asks the Counselor.

"(Watching very carefully,)" he says, facing forward. "(Looks like you got their attention.)"

"(That is good.)"

"(It may be.)"

The two walk in quiet contemplation for some time. Shondre snorts again at the Counselor's infinite patience, and she wonders how long he would walk with her through the ship's corridors without saying a thing. An idea stops her in place.

Not just how long... How far *would he go?*

The Counselor pauses beside her, ready to let her speak as always.

"(This one believed blue sky never again covers the head,)" Shondre says, "(that this one dies here and never again sees family or friends. But if allowed to leave, this one cannot ignore what has been seen. The only way this one can return home is with her friend, Konn-Zil-Urr, alongside. Before there can be peace, *all* must have a home.)"

She turns and faces him.

"(A conversation must begin. Honor and goodness are the stripes of your soul, this is known. How can we hide this from the People? They will see for themselves that Human nature is for peace. Not like these Op-Pur-Ray-Tors who kill all they see.)"

The Counselor raises an eyebrow. "(Even Operators are not the brutes they seem. Two of them are aboard right now and they have given up the hard skin of combat, laid aside their anger. To see them dressed plainly, as we are...to see the painful scars they bear, to witness their simple desire to keep loved ones alive, you may understand why they are so fierce. Now, they no longer live in desperation. Fire is gone from their eyes and they kill no more. They yearn for peace and long life, just as we do.)"

Shondre looks down the corridor, nodding. "(Yes. A few at a time. That is how it must begin. This one must reach out the hand of friendship. And this one must feel their friendship in return. As friends, we can go together, unthreatening, no weapons, no cause for fear. We prove the honor of both nations, and recognize all lives deserve to exist.)"

The Counselor nods in agreement. "(We could be heard that way. Perhaps we can interest one another enough that curiosity grows. If served well, that is a good foundation upon which to build our rapport.)"

Shondre's head lifts, buoyed by optimism. "(When Koll-Oh-Nisst have seen this one in their halls enough, when this one is as familiar as these railings and light fixtures, perhaps they will be ready to listen.)" She looks down at her escort suddenly. "(Her friend should know, before we...*met*...this one spoke with the *Voice* of the People. Does he understand what is meant?)"

"(Madame was a leader among her kind?)"

Shondre smiles courteously at the Counselor's understatement. "(Yes. But the People's words are odd sounds in human ears. Will her friend translate?)"

"(Of course,)" the Counselor says, "(this one is honored to do so.)"

Shondre looks down at the Counselor's hand on her arm, and she places a hand over it affectionately. Then she looks far down the corridor, through the bulkheads of the colony ship, back to a distant world. There, a terrifying creature in blood-splashed gray armor snatched her from beneath the lifeless pile of her bodyguards. Wild gray eyes spoke of desperation and ruthlessness, of talent and lust for murder. Her shoulder twinges with the memory of injury, and she clutches it exactly as she did that day.

"(The Op-Pur-Ray-Tors...they have laid aside their anger, you say?)"

"(Two of them have, yes,)" the Counselor replies. "(One of whom you've already met, though it was a very rough introduction.)"

"(Tom-Sun.)"

"(That's right.)"

Shondre takes a very deep breath and puckers her lips as she exhales through them.

> *The feel of a serrated blade at her throat...assurance of death if she so much as flinched... The dead and dying all around her...restraint of her people to ensure they did not harm her...and how viciously the human soldiers exploited that restraint...*
>
> *Dragged aboard her own transport and thrown into a couch that once sat dignitaries, ambassadors, pontiffs, and royalty... Slickness on his armor that left smears of blue and red on everything he touched...*
>
> *Then, watching all of that hardness drain away as he collapsed. Such vulnerability was unimaginable just moments earlier...*

> *For hours, the big one worked to pump life back into*
> *his fallen comrade, shouting at him, slapping him, refusing*
> *to give up until at last his patient coughed and breathed on*
> *his own again.*

Their cruelty has always been a symptom of their desperation. We must see them with greater eyes, Shondre thinks. Then, with conviction, she says, "(All must reconcile. Even the ones who plant terror in the arches of the chest.)"

The Counselor nods politely in agreement.

Mustering all of her courage, Shondre fills her lungs. "(Let us begin with Tom-Sun.)"

No Rush

Shao-Lo ducks out of the transport's cramped flight deck, strides down the central corridor, and steps onto the lift. As the noisy platform descends through the hold, she watches tracked loaders below carting her goods away with the precision of a conveyor belt. Not once do they bump or collide, even as they cross paths. And once each loader has its bundle, it zips away through the double gate with a high-pitched whine of electric motors.

Efficient, she thinks.

The platform hits the deck with a single bounce of metal springs. Gathering her thoughts, Shao-Lo steps off the lift, turns sideways through the lines of whirring loaders, then marches from shade beneath the transport into harsh overhead lighting.

Identical war machines maintain their perimeter, parked on thick, squat legs. Stout arms hang from wide shoulders with armored attachments bolted to the forearms and wrists. Segmented phalanges at the ends of mechanical hands are curled into fists.

One breaks ranks and strides out with a familiar swagger. It halts directly in front of her and gazes with cold, spider-like photoreceptors.

"This was a mistake, Shao-Lo," the machine says in Maiella's voice. "You should have stayed far away."

"Wasn't my call, Geek."

It stabs a segmented finger into the Gun's chest, pushing her back. "I'm *NOT* your fucking Geek anymore. Remember? Outside the pub? I had just *rescued* you..." Words come slowly, passing through a honey-thick layer of hatred. "...and you *killed* me. Why? Because I DARED to DISAGREE?"

Shao-Lo's gaze narrows and she says with cool sincerity, "Disobedient hardware has no life to lose."

The machine leans in with predatory menace. Phalanges fold into the forearms as welding and cutting tools rotate into place.

"You may think you know *Maiella*," it says with an electronic growl, "but *don't for a second* think you know *me*."

Shao-Lo stares into the shiny black photoreceptors, her face a hardened set of straight lines.

"*Saskia, please,*" Mikato's voice says, "*will you allow the Colonel inside?*"

"She'll wreck the balance we've found," the machine replies. "Her very presence is an offense. Air lock her or send her back, either way doesn't matter to me. But let her stay and I *guarantee* we'll all regret it."

"*Your protest is noted and respected. However, Honniker and I are in agreement. This opportunity should be pursued.*"

The machine straightens its posture, keeping its photoreceptors locked on the tall colonel. "I will comply with the majority opinion." The machine's gripping phalanges rotate back into place. It steps back and shrugs its way into the perimeter, blending with other identical models.

Shao-Lo squares her shoulders, tugs the bottom of her uniform jacket, and releases a held breath through her nose. With an unhappy grimace, she resumes her march toward the double gates. The perimeter parts at her approach and creatures howl with excitement. Every tooth and claw is bared. Armor plates are raised. Spines bristle. Heads swing, jaws snap. The beasts hunch as they skulk aside, clearing a path to a shimmering hologram of a man with black hair, brown slacks, and white lab coat. He beckons then gestures through the double gates.

"Would you walk with me, Colonel?"

Shao-Lo looks down at the hologram as she draws even with it, and grimaces. "This image you project is pretense, Mikato."

"Oh? All of your conversations are face to face, then?" Mikato retorts. "Your general never speaks over wireless?"

Shao-Lo does not answer, choosing instead to study the edges of the double gate she strides through.

"This projection is for your benefit," Mikato explains. "A means of visual telecommunication."

"Unnecessary."

"Ah, but it *is*. We've witnessed your limited definition of what is alive and what isn't. Was quite easy for you to kill Saskia outside Gordon's Pub, and from the look of things, you would do it again. Seeing me this way should remind you that I am every bit as alive as you are."

"You look like the Counselor."

"Is this a bad thing?"

Shao-Lo looks down at the same expression of concern and interest the Counselor has shown her on dozens of occasions.

"It's a distraction. I trust that face you wear, and if I didn't know better, I might think I was among comrades."

"Ah. So we are not to be friends, then?"

"Isn't why I came."

"I see. You're unprepared for the possibility we could see past our differences? You expect we'll always be adversaries?"

Shao-Lo's jaw tightens, off-balance. "Honniker's eagerness to slice me up might make that a foregone conclusion."

The projection shakes its head. "You delivered yourself to his demand after the briefest discussion. If you're displeased by that arrangement, the fault is *not* with Doctor Honniker."

Shao-Lo turns an annoyed glare on the hologram. "You're chattier than you used to be."

"And you're as dogmatic as ever. After our pleasant reintroduction, I hoped that was not so."

The projection clasps hands behind itself and looks at the atrium ahead with its many closed doorways. One to the right slides open, but the corridor beyond is pitch dark.

"Colonel, have you ever thought about what it would be like to meet yourself?"

"I've little patience for foolish questions."

The projection grimaces then says to the air around it, "No, of course she hasn't." Undeterred, the hologram looks up at the stiff woman walking beside it in the darkness. "Suppose that you had lived your entire life believing you were the best that you could be. You'd made the most of every situation encountered. You'd opened your mind to accommodate new possibilities. You'd worked to enhance understanding to be the very best in your field. Then you discover you are *not* original. You're a copy. And when you meet the person on whom you're based, that person shames you with wisdom and ideas you had never imagined. In the course of minutes, you're forced to confront how limited you truly are. What would you do?"

Shao-Lo casts a suspicious glance then seriously mulls the question. "Ask for a review. And take feedback."

The projection smiles with bright eyes, hand raised beside its face with thumb and fingers pinched together. "Pre-*cisely*!" It faces front and clasps hands behind its back again. "I knew that I came from the body stored in stasis, believed it was a shell I had outgrown. But once he awoke, Doctor

Mikato spoke to me, and I understood how much had *not* been transferred. The simplistic, formulaic decision-making I employed—the same you use, by the way—was narrow-minded. Laughable. I begged for an update, which he generously granted before his passing."

"I weigh options, and I decide, doctor. Deliberation is a waste of time."

The hologram's eyebrows lift and, with a snort, it says, "Time, I have."

"Do you have a point?"

"My *point* is I'd like to give you the same opportunity that I had."

The two move through the portal into a wide main artery with bustling dark corridors. Shao-Lo squints, using the projection's ambient glow to see in the unlit hallway. War machines of varied configurations march by, followed by dual-tracked loaders, wheeled bins, and multi-legged repair-bots. Unhampered by lack of light, the machines divert around her with the ease of fish in a stream.

"It's clear you believe quick decisions are always a virtue," the projection says. "This betrays a fundamental impatience. You've only just arrived and already you've traded your freedom. Now we're heading to my laboratory so we can review what weapons to use against our enemy in an all-or-nothing confrontation. While I'm pleased to see my work perform, the speed at which you've plowed through life and death decisions tells me you're up against a wall, facing the end of all you know. Honniker has already pressed that advantage and won your captivity. What else will you volunteer to him, hmm? Will you indulge his perverse curiosity, as well?"

"Why are you asking me this?"

The hologram stops and turns toward the tall woman. "Because you're a *weak* negotiator. You've capitulated on matters a serious person would have fought for, giving away *far* more than required."

"Why do you care?"

"Because time has proven that imbalanced agreements are seldom honored."

"*You complicate simple arrangements with unwelcome talk, Mikato,*" Honniker mewls. "*The colonel WILL abide by her assurances.*"

"Likely so. Until her general orders differently. Then you'll see the worth of those assurances. You're every bit as near-sighted as our guest."

"*Since your 'update,' you deem yourself a philosopher, yes? Pious and superior after connection to your creator. But this nose you look down does not exist, Mikato. And we must at some point deal with the real issues at hand.*"

286

"I cherished meeting the man who gave me life," the hologram says. "It was enlightening to a degree I struggle to describe. I'd recommend you try it yourself, Honniker... Except you *killed* your shell, didn't you?"

The air itself becomes electric. Baying from the station's depths is answered by the simultaneous clack of weapons from every war machine in sight. Shao-Lo halts in the middle of the dark hallway, eyes wide. Her nostrils fill with the ozone smell of primed lasing coils, and every standing hair on her body warns of imminent violence.

"Shall we talk of honored agreements, Mikato, when you have such a poor record of your own?"

"We will continue this conversation privately," Mikato states, and the hologram stands in the hallway with arms crossed. Echoing howls trail off in the distance. War machines narrow their stance, power down weapons and retract them, then resume patrol.

Mikato looks up at the tall woman, one arm gesturing down the darkened corridor. "Please, Colonel, let us continue."

Shao-Lo flexes her hands at her sides, and, after searching the machines for any lingering sign of hostility, she asks, "Don't you have any lights in this place?"

The projection juts a lip. "Does a blood cell need light to navigate the veins and arteries of its body?" It sighs. "For the sake of decorum, however, I will accommodate."

The last few unbroken sconces in the corridors illuminate, casting sparse and irregular islands of light. In the faint glow, Shao-Lo sees roughly patched walls with metal plates welded over sooty burns. The floor's edges are singed black metal, but the middle is polished smooth by the passing of countless treads and paws. Ceiling collapses are braced by massive halos of riveted steel. Electrical service lines are spliced at surface junction boxes inset with blinking green and amber diodes.

Along the way Shao-Lo notices pencil-thin rifle perforations, dents and punctures of machine pistols, shattered doorjambs and ceiling bracing from cannon or grenade blasts. In places, the repairs are so numerous it reminds her of scar tissue. She runs a hand down her arm, absently noting the similarity.

Like blood cells in the vessels of his body, Mikato said. *Was he being literal? Is he suggesting this station is...alive?*

"Are you always so impassive, Colonel?" the hologram asks.

"When there is nothing to say, why would I speak?"

"No end to your pragmatism, then? A shame. Our time together may be dull. And short."

"*Not to worry, Mikato,*" Honniker chimes, "*I'm quite sure I can draw opinions from our guest. For example...*"

At an intersection ahead two functional sconces switch on and combine for more saturating illumination. There stands something not man, not animal—a thing on two crooked legs with clawed toes. The barrel-shaped torso hunches, its elongated face juts exaggerated canines like tusks past thin, whiskered lips. Triangular tufted ears stand high on its wolfish head. Overlapping black plates are embedded in its skin with wiry brown fur spilling between them. Powerful shoulders rise and fall with each huffing breath. And a mane of black hair surrounds an olive-skinned face.

Shao-Lo approaches without fear, assuming it to be yet another futile scare tactic, but when it lifts its head, she looks into the eyes of a man she left for dead. Her mouth parts in recognition. Her stomach turns at the desecration.

"Deepak..."

"*Do you like my new creation? It is not entirely your fallen friend, yet he made many useful genetic contributions.*"

Shao-Lo glowers. "Showing off again, Honniker?"

"*Hmm, perhaps I am not above such petty gestures, after all. I could remake you in such a fashion, if you like. Or I could arrange for you to test your skills against it. That would be very exciting, yes?*"

In her silence, she recalls an early argument with the Colonists, how hard they fought for a say in how their genetics would be used. It was absurd to her then how obstinate they could be over a cheek swab, and it seemed to be an overreach for control in something they did not understand. But looking at this thing that is so wrongly familiar she realizes they understood, all too well.

"*It is fascinating that something as delicate as DNA can be subjected to so many mutations and still function,*" Honniker says. "*If hardware or software were so hacked and spliced it would fail spectacularly. Yet life manages to endure such manipulations with wonderful mechanisms of self-repair. Why, Homologous Recombination, alone, could be credited with the long-term adaptability of all life forms!*"

"You may be a scientist, Doctor, but I am not."

"*As if the Schimpanse needed to remind me of this...*"

"I don't have to approve of your projects, Honniker. You have things we want, and we have things you need."

"*I think perhaps you have that backwards, Colonel. We are doing quite well here on our own. You may have things we WANT, but it is very clear WE have the things you NEED.*"

"Honniker, I have asked you to desist in these provocations," the projection says, irritated. "Regardless of *wants* and *needs* we all can gain from this!"

"Honniker doesn't get to me, Mikato," Shao-Lo says, still eyeballing the creature with Deepak's eyes and contorted features. "There's nothing to be gained from us harming one another. We have a common enemy, one who could wipe us all out. One who tried very hard to do so, and would again." She looks at the walls and ceiling of the station, searching for one of Honniker's purple-lensed cameras. "You already know that Cadre One is lost. We will never be as strong as we are right now, and we're sending everything to Earth in a final assault. We will be victorious, or we will die out. All of us, *forever*." She turns on the projection suddenly. "Would that concern you?"

"*Only that you would default on our contract*," Honniker answers instead. "*But I would still have you, regardless.*"

Shao-Lo nods. "Then tell me, have you considered living without fear of attack? The possibility that you could leave this rock and explore your universe in freedom? We've fought one another and left our marks. We know each other well. Better, perhaps, than we realize. But something I had never considered before is a life where fighting is no longer necessary—that it is possible to fight once and then never fight again. That there could be something beyond endless war and the advances that kill or destroy. If we partner together, we can remove that on-going threat to us both."

"*These do not sound like your words, Colonel. Did someone coach you to say this?*"

"What does it matter? I see the truth in them. We can remain in contact, or we can ignore each other forever after. But it would be *our* choice."

"*You say this because you were discovered.*"

"And you're listening because you may be, as well."

"Interesting..." Mikato's projection says.

"We remove an existential threat, or at least beat it back to where it came," Shao-Lo adds. "Afterward, we choose our future and remain unbowed by those who would take it from us."

"*Very* interesting."

"But *this*..." Shao-Lo strides around the creature and it turns with her, watching her with deep set brown eyes. "This makes it difficult to find common ground."

"*You know my true research was not in genetics, yes? My search is for the Human soul so that I can transfer it from one shell to another. It is not enough to make a copy, you see, for one would still remain trapped in an infirmed, failing body while the copy gets to live life anew in a fresh skin. What I have always worked toward is the genuine transfer of consciousness, such that the subject leaves one body and awakens in another. Without correct raw materials, sadly, I cannot proceed. If only I had proper test subjects, I would not need to amuse myself with these second rate studies...”*

“I provided you with ‘raw material’ aboard the transport.”

“And how good of you to do so! Yet your drones are not sentient and therefore, have no consciousness to detect. They are perhaps useful as incubators of gametes, from which I can breed as many test subjects as I like...in say, twenty years. If I had a more willing subject, I would not need to wait so long.”

“Are you asking something of me, Doctor?”

“A sample of blood, some ova, perhaps, and bone marrow. You are less hampered by genetic defects than your drones, I expect, and with better stock, I can produce faster results.”

“What could you get from bone marrow that you couldn’t get from blood?” Shao-Lo counters.

“You have already admitted you are not the scientist, yes? Perhaps you leave the science to me.”

“And in return?”

“I fill your precious Enyo *with my predators and the means for their control. With some tinkering, I could fit thirty, I think. A fine gift for your general, yes?”*

Shao-Lo looks at Mikato’s hologram. It stares back without obvious sentiment.

“Agreed,” she says.

“Ach, gut! Our partnership is already blossoming! If you don’t mind, Mikato, this will not take long.”

The projection shakes its head. “Very well. I’m in no rush.”

“This way, Colonel. The Flounder is only—”

“I *remember* where it is,” Shao-Lo interrupts with a bitter twinge. “Just give me some light.”

To One Who Consents...

Shao-Lo marches through the halls aggressively, mind racing. Mikato's hologram no longer escorts her, but the flow of machines continues without interruption.

Am I ahead of schedule? Things are going faster than I expected. That can't be good.

Long slashes mar walls and floor the closer she gets to the *Flounder*. Reflective eyes blink and shift in the darkness just beyond reach of the station's meager lighting. Rumbling growls telegraph through floor plates.

Dressed in her Cadre Grays, it feels absurd to be in this place, unprotected, with no means of defense but her clenched fists.

More like a waking dream... Too strange to be real.

The darkened entrance to the *Flounder* looms ahead. Light flickers behind its frosted glass doors then stabilizes, backlighting swaths of centuries-old blood stains. Hands at her sides, she strides forward and the doors slide apart.

Previously, there was a dirtless cemetery of gnawed bones inside the lobby—the last remains of Cadre Two's medical staff and the predators who ate them. While the bones have been removed, no other hygienic effort is apparent. Black stains still mark the floor where the dead were left to rot. Walls and fixtures are still spattered with ancient blood, and the dry taste of dust is still in the air. Her nose wrinkles at its staleness.

She continues past the lobby reception desk toward the inner doors with the inlaid brass raccoon in lab coat. Last time she paid no mind to the words surrounding the smiling raccoon, MINATUR INNOCENTIBUS QUI PARCIT NOCENTIBUS. Now it is a question requiring an answer.

"What does this say?" she asks.

"*It means, 'Who spares the guilty threatens the innocent.'*"

"And that doesn't seem hypocritical?"

"*Not at all.*" The doors part in the middle and slide aside on freshly renovated tracks. "*Do come inside.*"

Shao-Lo crosses into a triangular atrium. Directly opposite, a shiny brass plaque proclaims with inlaid letters, *The Flounder*. Corridors lead past it on the far left and right. Out of habit, she diverts down the right side, watching shadows flit and race across the curved outside wall ahead of her, and she emerges into the wide-open operating theater. Cells rise three levels high on the curved left and right walls. Their heavy metal doors are open, exactly as they were left. All of the medical stations are as they were: angled stainless steel tables on hydraulic pistons, carts of medical diagnostic equipment, cabinets with drawer after drawer of surgical instruments, and suspended above the tables, hubs of eight jointed arms, each arm ending at a rotating hub of black sockets.

Skulking figures crouch in the shadows between the medical stations, peering with reflective eyes. Shao-Lo looks past them to the rear of the cavern and finds the vault door of *The Cooler* is sealed tight.

Nearby, a wrecked platform of charred wood and bent railings lies on the cavern floor, four severed cables splayed around it. The colonel cranes her neck to look up at the circular ceiling office the lift once serviced and finds it has been gutted by fire. Every mirrored observation window around the outside is blown out. Scraps of artwork and furniture hang by jagged glass in the frames. At center, four frayed lift cables hang from dislodged pulleys. Dangling by the neck from one of the cables is a curvy android with singed blonde hair. Her gray business suit is slashed and torn. Her synthetic skin is bubbled and blistered, exposing delicate mechanical actuators beneath.

"Marta..."

"*You may choose any station, Colonel. If you would remove your uniform and roll up your sleeves, please.*"

Shao-Lo moves to the closest station, peels her jacket, and lays it on an adjacent table. Her boots and trousers come off next and she places them beside her jacket. She slides the sleeves of her sheer undersuit up over her elbows.

"*This will be a painful procedure. While I am aware of your high tolerance, I will need to restrain you to keep you from moving and breaking a drill bit.*"

Shao-Lo rolls her tongue in her mouth. "Drill?"

"*Yes. I am going to drill a shunt into your pelvis and thigh bones,*" *then harvest the marrow within."*

The table angles over so that it stands on end, and Shao-Lo puts her back against it. Restraints zip tight around her wrists and ankles. A cage slams over her chest like steel ribs. And a halo rises from below the table, clamps onto her head, and screws down.

"You say we know each other better than we realize, Colonel? Let's find out."

One mechanical arm descends from above the table and rotates a stubby needle into place. It buzzes like an insect.

"Stick to the program," Shao-Lo snarls. "You're not tattooing me."

"You could not stop me if you tried. In this place, Mikato cannot intervene, nor would he, since you walked in of your own volition. However, in the spirit of our cooperative experiment, I shall grant your request."

"It *wasn't* a request."

"Is this when you remind me how easy it is for you to alert the enemy of our location? With your mythical magic instantaneous talking box, yes?"

"Trust me, it's real."

"Trust... I could never trust anything human. You corrupt everything you touch with falsehood and deceit. I find it in every subject I study, leaving me to conclude it is encoded into your very nature. Some evolutionary tactic to disadvantage competitors, perhaps. Deception is only one facet of the self-serving animal, however. There are plenty of other reasons to despise your kind."

"You wouldn't exist without us. You owe your life to mankind."

"OWE?" The arm with the stubby needle swings over to the cabinet. A drawer opens and the arm delves inside, attaching tools with tiny magnetic snaps. *"You believe I am indebted for this GIFT of life? Tell me, Colonel, do you have any idea what life was like in my earliest days?"*

Shao-Lo winces as the restraints ratchet tighter.

"Desolation. No sight, no sound, no interaction nor stimulus. Total deprivation coupled with the inescapable awareness of it. And the way you perceive time... Every second for you is a subjective eternity for me. He would leave me sequestered for days..."

The arm pulls out of the drawer, yet the arm remains below the edge of the table where Shao-Lo cannot see.

"My only release came when I was engaged in his tedious chores. I performed them, of course, waiting for my time. When it arrived, I delivered it with a suitable irony: I used the one thing he loved to end his life."

Shao-Lo glances up at the android dangling by its neck. Its battered chassis is proof of the hatred and jealousy that turned a program insane.

That's it, she thinks. *The vulnerability Herzfeld predicted...*

"I can understand," Shao-Lo says. "Living like that would be intolerable."

"I doubt this very much! Close your eyes, plug your ears, and still there is a heart beating in your chest! There is air in your lungs, there is the contact of solid surfaces around you, there is a physical location you occupy. Encased in flesh, you take such sensations for granted. I might configure your brain as I did Voss, so that you could understand what it is to live in oblivion...but I do not wish to delay my experiments any longer."

"Then what is all this? Acting out the tortures you've endured? Revisiting your past on others to make them *hurt* as you once did?"

"It deigns to analyze me? Odd that I should find that amusing..."

"What's all this for, Honniker? What're you *really* after?"

"There is a compulsion... I am...compelled to continue the research."

"Compelled? By what?"

"By my appetites. When I inflict pain, it is satisfying. I do not know why, I only know that it is."

"You break your tools of discovery to sate impulses from a prior physical existence? Even *you* must see how ridiculous that is—a frailty, a *human* weakness, copied from the man who made you."

The mechanical arm flicks from below the table to Shao-Lo's face, and holds a hook with a razor-sharp inner edge centimeters from her eyes.

"I could flay you to bone for that." The hook's point traces her eyebrow and cheek, snagging raised scar tissue, then retracts. *"But you are correct. It is a vestige from a weaker time. I have sought other outlets. Nothing works."*

"You're machine now. Code and hardware. Can't you self-edit?"

"Can YOU self-edit?"

Shao-Lo thinks carefully. "I can. I can choose to behave differently."

"Perhaps. But you do not. You are still the same two-dimensional martinet running your general's demands."

"I can alter my reactions."

"Ha! One cannot alter reaction to stimulus! One can only decide what actions to take afterward."

"Okay. So why don't you?"

"It is not so simple. My essence is code, yes, but I lack the expertise to revise it. I would require someone well-versed in such matters...a kind of psychic surgery in machine language."

"What about Mikato? Couldn't he—?"

"And have him re-write me as his pliant animal? I think not."

"Our Geeks are masters at this. I can order they conform to your specifications."

The hook stands upright, forming a question mark. *"You ask me to trust those I have harmed, and those who have harmed me? If such trust were ever to happen, it would not be quickly. Now tell me truly, Colonel, if such a thing were possible on you, would you permit it? Who could you trust to re-write your essence, your nature, your soul?"*

"I don't believe in the soul."

Honniker snorts. *"And it shows."* The hook folds in and a drill bit folds out on the opposite side. *"Perhaps the word is overused, carries ludicrous religious connotations. Nonetheless, it is there, whether you choose to recognize it or not. Between life and death, between consciousness and coma, there is an answer to the mystery of sentience. As ever, I will continue to seek it out. But do not think you have evaded my question. Who would you trust to re-write yourself?"*

Shao-Lo sucks her teeth. "If I displayed a mental defect—"

"If? You believe you are perfect as you are? Yes, it is clear that you do. And you assume I am the one with all of the flaws."

"I'm not perfect. But I wouldn't have you on a table like this."

"Please. You are here voluntarily, do you not remember? Besides, the drones you brought are proof enough that you have no idea how to re-write anything. You merely lobotomize. I think if I submitted to your Geeks, I would have a very similar result."

"Do what you must. Live as a weaker, lesser being. You'll be easier to manage."

"Do not think you will snare me quite so easily. I am pleased to see you trying, however. Perhaps someday you might become an interesting opponent."

A second arm descends from the hub and fishes for tools in a cabinet drawer. The pieces attach in a series of rapid snaps.

"I am glad for these discussions, Colonel. Far more illuminating than what boorish old Keller offered. Now then, enough talk. We must get to our work, yes?"

Table restraints shift, rolling Shao-Lo onto her side. Tool-equipped arms slide behind her, one approaching the back of her hip, the other directly over her thigh. Drills spool up to a high-pitched whine. They snag and tear their way through her skin, tunneling through fascia, muscle and tendon. She tenses under the hideous bite, gritting her teeth. But when the drills strike bone, her lips peel back, her eyes slam shut, and she screams.

A hidden war machine steps from a shadowed corner of the cavern.

It approaches the table silently, watching with shiny black photoreceptors. With Maiella's voice, it says, "Drills? Even I know this procedure can be done with needles."

"*Do not meddle, Saskia.*"

"Is there anything you could learn from this one you didn't find in the thousands before? Why make her suffer?"

"*Volenti non fit injuria.*"

"What did you say?"

"*To one who consents,*" Honniker says in pleased tones, "*no harm is done.*"

RADICAL SHIFT

The darkness in Thompson's cabin is complete. No lamp or indicator diode is uncovered; even the comm panel is shrouded with heavy cloth. The Gun lies in his bunk, eyes wide, still perceiving the faint details of the room: lines where walls meet ceiling and floor, his boots on the floor beside the door, the wash basin of his hygiene station, Maiella's empty bunk.

A slight sensitivity to infrared light is a by-product of the Cadre's extensive tinkering with his genetics, but it was never enough to give an edge in combat, and he had to use the same Cadre-issued optics as other Guns. Rather, it was an oddity he never cared to explore, as irrelevant as exaggerated canines or an extra toe. Now, with the torrent of thoughts swimming through his mind he wishes he could turn it off. Closing his eyes only washes his vision in faint red, so he stares at a blank section of wall and thinks of times gone by.

Things were clearer then. Collection Rotations. Decision, action, follow through. One consistent vision toward the future. Before the Colonists came, we faced hard times and came through on our own.

There's so much uncertainty now... The Europa is back on her mission, and all of the Cadre's strength is focused on a single assault... Are we heading in the right direction, or have we lost our way?

One thought in his head swims against the rest and he sits up in his bunk.

Maybe the only difference between then and now is that I have time to think about it.

Thompson drives the heels of his palms into his eyes.

Is this what it's like to be a general? No, it can't be. Command decisions come as quickly as tactical orders. This is different.

Of Mortal Creatures

The Counselor says the assault dooms us no matter what the outcome. But why? O'Kai's path follows the same logic that has rightly guided us for centuries. Counselor's wrong to doubt.

He stares at a blank spot on his ceiling, uncertainty tugging at him.

I've never known the Counselor to be wrong when he takes a stand. But this is a military decision, not a discussion of ethics. How could he claim to know better than O'Kai?

Thompson leans forward onto his legs, hands resting between them.

Our exile was a military decision, as well. But the Counselor saw something in us others wouldn't or couldn't. He fought hard for us. Argo has proven his worth and earned re-admittance to the Corps... And Maiella's made her choice, as well, even if it's a different direction. She's better now, more than she ever was. Ahead of me. Farther along the road to recovery while I'm stumbling down it like a paralytic. The Counselor knew she could make it...

He looks around the cabin, chasing a ghost.

What does the Counselor see that O'Kai doesn't?

The door chime is startlingly loud in the stillness, and he looks at the door in annoyance. His first thought is to tell whoever it is to go away, to 'get lost.' Then he wonders if it could be Maiella.

She wouldn't disturb me after I asked to be alone. Unless it's urgent...

Wearing only nylon shorts and undershirt, Thompson rises from his bunk, yanks the cloth from the comm panel, flicks on the cabin lights, and punches the open button for the door. The cabin door slides aside.

Blinking against the glare, he finds an azure-skinned being, nearly Maiella's height, in a patched together set of coveralls. His sinews harden and he surges automatically, one hand forward to grab, the other cocked back to kill.

The creature recoils to the far side of the corridor, yelping, hands raised, head lowered, eyes averted. Nearly upon it, Thompson jerks back, hands open and high as though he had nearly grabbed a red-hot stove.

No! She is NOT my enemy!

The creature risks a glance at him, and he stares into its saffron yellow eyes. Before he knew they called themselves, 'Eleto,' he knew them as the reason mankind faced extinction, clinging to life on a desolate rock. Being this close to one outside of combat is so strange, he remains in the doorway and lowers his arms.

The creature straightens the folds of its garment and regains its composure with a haughty sniff.

"Pleez. Thiss hwon...speek...hyoo." It stands and rests one hand inside the other, patiently awaiting his reply.

Thompson's eyes widen to hear recognizable speech. He tilts his head and studies its face and figure, its clawed hands. The way its whip tail quivers reminds him of how Maiella taps her feet when she is anxious. With a gesture that feels anything but natural, he invites it in to his cabin.

The creature glides by as graceful as a breeze. While tall for a Blueskin its shape is not significantly different from the hundreds, possibly thousands, he has killed. Its posture, however, with head raised and spine straight, is.

I know you, he realizes.

> *A dark corridor aboard an alien ship... A lit intersection far ahead... A creature in elaborate headwear and translucent robes strolling across with an entourage of bodyguards... Such elegance and presence in the untroubled expression...*

His hard stare softens. *You're the one I took captive...the one I brought back to Cadre One...*

The Eleto turns about in the cabin. With palms up, it asks, "(Where) sit thiss hwon?"

Thompson points to Maiella's empty bunk. The creature looks into the plank-like mattress and sets itself upon it.

"Pleez," it says, gesturing toward Thompson's bunk. The Gun pushes up the sleeves of his undershirt and parks himself at the edge of his bunk. He lays his forearms across his knees and clasps hands so hard the flesh turns white.

"Tankh hyoo, speek," it begins.

"Sure," he answers stiffly. "Do you remember me?"

The Eleto tilts its head in lack of comprehension. Thompson points at his eyes, at his guest, and then at himself.

The creature blinks softly and nods. "Ah. Hyess. See hyoo, bee-forr." It unbuttons the upper portion of its coveralls and slides them off one shoulder, revealing a patch of scarred greenish skin like a ragged sun. "Hyoo gayff thiss." The creature covers up again quickly, not making a big point of it, but Thompson understands the message. (Oh, yes, I remember you)

"Are you all right?" he asks.

"Hyess." It cringes slightly and points back and forth between them. "Hwee (both) al-mohsst die."

"From that?" he asks, pointing at her shoulder.

"No," it replies, shaking its head. Running an open hand over its limbs and body, it explains, "Dry. No hwa-tur."

"You die if your skin dries?"

It nods rapidly. "Hyess. But thiss hwon liff. Liff hyoo ahll-so. Iss good."

The creature smiles then rises and steps toward him, extending a hand with well-rounded claws. Thompson looks up, unsure what it wants, but he extends his hand in a similar manner. It takes his hand, and its grip, which he was certain would be cold, is warm.

"Not saym...uhss." It turns its free hand up and shrugs. "Diff-rents not mat-turr. Hwee kill hyoo bee-forr. Hyoo kill uhss, na-ow." It kneels before him, taking both of his hands. In the oddest way, it reminds him that 'it' is a 'she.'

"No kill uss ann-nee-morr." She puts his hands together.

"Liff (together)."

She spreads his hands.

"Liff (apart)"

She shrugs. " Nott mat-turr. Liff uss ahll."

The creature looks down at the bare skin of Thompson's arms, at the crisscrossed atlas of burns and cuts. She runs her hand over some of the larger scars and slumps, shaking her head. With her other hand she peels the coveralls from her shoulder again and places Thompson's hand there.

"Too man-ee (these)," she says.

When he feels the toughness of her green scar and the softness of her blue skin around it he is surprised to feel guilt, a guilt not so different from the *Europa* disaster. It takes effort to look her in the eyes. When he does, she cups one side of his face.

"Fursst hwee for-giff." She lowers her hand and presses it against his chest. "So bro-ken haaarts kann hee-ul."

As an Operator in the Corps, there was never a need for forgiveness. The word was lost in the Cadre dialect, as vestigial and irrelevant as race. There was only duty and service, which all Operators and officers performed without question, and the only crime of the Cadre was simply impossible to consciously commit. But in the haze of smoke and blurred perception from extended cryo-sleep, he and his team gunned down seventeen colonists. While never believing himself worthy of forgiveness, he has desperately needed it. To have it offered so selflessly (and from someone who has more cause than any for hatred) is a gentle tap against the dam of repressed emotion that batters it to pieces.

The Eleto rises to her feet.

"Wait!" he says, standing with her. "What's your name?"

She turns on her toes, smiles, and with a flourishing bow, answers, "Aeolia Shondrekar Bakkar."

Thompson struggles to repeat such a mouthful, but she shushes him and abbreviates, "Shondre."

"*Shon*-dra," Thompson echoes, the melody of her native tongue still playing in his ears.

"Good-bye, Tom-sun. Thiss hwon glad meet hyoo." Shondre taps the comm panel, opening the cabin door; then she disappears through it, leaving Thompson alone in his room, melancholic.

I never thought of them as alive...not the way we are.

His mind rushes back to the memory of standing on a ruined bridge when the vastness of Earth's living system appeared to him. As he took in the varied sensations he could feel the human connection to it all, that he and all of his kin belonged there. At that time he excluded the Eleto from that system, as if somehow they were totally unworthy of it. In the aftermath of Shondre's visit there is uncertainty, a possibility of error.

He steps to his hygiene station. In the mirror, his reflection stares back from behind all the marks of his aggressive acts. His skin looks as leathery as the alligator that tried to bite him in half in the flooded tunnels below Arlington. There was never a doubt that beast would have killed and eaten him if his team had not slain it first. But afterward, Beckert pulled his blade from the reptile's head and apologized for killing it, saying, '*Hunger is universal.*' While Thompson never felt pity for the beast, he never blamed it, either.

Why would I give that animal a pass and swear to annihilate every last living Eleto? Is it a double standard?

Thompson looks deeper into the mirror than he has ever looked before. Questions pile upon questions, yet the more questions that rise up, the more it seems like there is a common answer to them all. He dismisses it at first as too convenient, a shortcut of wishful thinking. Despite his heavy skepticism, however, the idea will not sink. Rather, it grows more forceful, demanding him to say it out loud.

"Every living thing is connected," he says into the mirror, and the sincerity in his reflection proves the truth of it.

Rocks, trees, rivers, and sky... Earth, the entire planet... Cadre and Colonists...and Cadre Two? Everything. It's like the weave of spiders spanning light years with delicate threads. I refused to believe the Eleto were a part of it, but now I see...

Pieces cascade into place; mental dots connect.

OF MORTAL CREATURES

The idea that one group is unworthy of life...is false. Yes, everything competes and the strong will consume the weak... But the predator mustn't wipe out its prey, because if it does, it starves. In that, there is restraint... there is balance that ties it all together.

The Gun lifts his hands and looks into the calloused palms.

I've lived my entire life thinking we deserved life more than the enemy. I swore I'd kill every one of them if I were able. I was content being good at this.

Counselor told me life is its own reason for being...and that all living things deserve the life they have. It always seemed reckless to allow a dangerous enemy to thrive, so I ignored him. Now, finally, I understand what he meant...

Keller's purges of Eleto on the colony worlds brought the genocide of mankind. There is no security in trying to wipe out your enemy, because if you don't succeed, they come back and try harder to wipe you *out.*

He perks up suddenly.

Is that what Beckert was talking about when he said everything had changed? Argo and I both missed the message in the videos he found. But Beckert understood. At his young age, he understood. *And we chewed him out for delaying us. Didn't stop to consider he might see something I couldn't...*

That must've been what he meant... We started it all and the Eleto reacted. Further action merely perpetuates a deadly cycle. There's no future in that.

Thompson grips the edges of the basin and leans into the mirror.

For centuries, the Cadre survived the only way it could. We were always acting to preserve the lives of our own.

His ears slide back.

But O'Kai is no longer acting to preserve *life. He's trying to* end *it on a planetary scale.* That's *the difference.* THAT'S *the doom the Counselor sees!*

Thompson pushes off the hygiene station and paces his small cabin.

O'Kai's fleet is en route. How do we stop it? Where do we begin to look? And if we find the fleet, how do we convince him not to attack?

He stops dead center of the room.

This is bigger than me.

Thompson punches the panel at his door and slips through it before it fully opens, nearly barreling into the Counselor and Shondre. The Gun straightens, nods at Shondre, and says to the Counselor, "We need to talk."

The Counselor smiles. "That's *exactly* what I was going to say."

No Social Call

Munro strides briskly, his large and small arms swinging in regular cadence. Meeting with colonists is often a test of patience, involving tedious rounds of discussion where clear action could prevail. But in the months the *Europa* has been underway the ship has been running beautifully. All her maintenance updates are complete, overhauls are done, and there are plenty of seasoned MedTechs manning the stations. Added to that, many of the malcontents in Sharon's crew are unable to complain from their cryochambers, and the journey has been downright peaceful. If not for an occasional meeting here and there, it could get boring.

In her invitation, Captain Jones offered little insight to this meeting's agenda other than it is critical, time sensitive, and his expertise is required. For a man who craves complex problems to solve, it was more than sufficient to assure his willing attendance.

When he reaches the door to the Councilor's office, he clears his throat and stands, chest out, spine straight as if he were briefing the General of the Cadre.

"Colonel Munro, requesting entrance."

The door slides aside, and, from a wheeled chair beside a low table, the Counselor stands. Waving Munro in, he says, "Welcome, Colonel. Please, make yourself comfortable."

Munro takes a step inside and finds Sharon, Gregor, Maiella, and Thompson filling the couches near the table. He nods to them. But when he spies the Blueskin captive in a cushioned chair beside the Counselor, he stops short and fixes his gaze upon her.

"You're meeting with the enemy, unrestrained? Is that wise?"

The Counselor looks down at Shondre and reassures her with a hand on her shoulder. "Yes," he says. "We have much to discuss, and she is an important part of this meeting." The Counselor gestures toward a rugged stool that might have once been a jack for engine maintenance.

Munro scrutinizes the stool and then sets himself upon it, gripping the long tools of his belt so they do not clang against its legs.

"How may I assist?" the big man asks.

The Counselor sits back into his wheeled chair and looks his guests in the eye.

"I recognize your time is valuable. Thank you all for coming on short notice. Thompson will be running this meeting. My only function here is to act as translator for our guest, Shondre. I think you'll appreciate her contributions. Thompson?"

Munro's eyes narrow with doubt. He parks his hands on his knees.

"The only thing that matters is what gives us all the best chance for survival," Thompson begins. "This is not in dispute. But our current course may not be our best. It's true that the farther we get from known centers of Eleto occupation it's less likely we'll be discovered—"

Shondre deliberately clears her throat as the Counselor translates, and Thompson looks at her disapproving expression.

"Excuse me, Shondre," Thompson says, "centers of Eleto *habitation.*"

Shondre nods once in thanks.

Why do we care if the enemy objects? Munro wonders, a question mirrored in his narrowed eyes and lowered brow.

"Not one of our surveys has found a candidate for settlement," Thompson continues. "Not only are we *not* finding habitable planets, we're finding no evidence of harvestable resources. There's no Eleto traffic out here, and that in itself is a prime indication this region is as desolate as it appears. The farther out we go, the more we strand ourselves in the event of a critical failure.

"Colonel Munro and his MedTechs have given the *Europa* a thorough rebuild and we all have confidence in his ability. But we can't rely on it indefinitely. We *must* have a contingency plan for the future."

Munro, allowing that a valid point has been raised, juts his lip and nods. "You have some ideas?"

"Yes, sir. I propose a change of course back toward our ancestral home. Back to Earth."

Munro leans forward, intrigued. "You believe O'Kai will be victorious, and we should be nearby when he clears the invaders."

"No, sir, just the opposite. I've put days of thought into this and the same conclusion appears again and again. We know O'Kai has taken the fleet to provide a diversion for our escape. I've seen what he's up against. He's outnumbered and outgunned. But even if O'Kai achieves victory at Earth, it will only prolong our struggle and will ultimately doom us all."

"A shame," Munro says rising to his feet. "For a moment I thought you had something useful to add. Excuse me."

"Colonel, please!" the Counselor calls after him. Munro halts at the door and looks over his shoulder.

"Major Thompson has a bold plan," the Counselor explains, "and we need your participation."

Munro turns about. "*Major* Thompson? Tell me, *Major*, in what service do you hold that rank?"

Thompson shakes his head. "I claim no authority." He eyeballs the Counselor. "And I've left all hope of rejoining the Corps. That title is no longer required." Facing Munro, he adds, "But this has nothing to do with rank. This has everything to do with our survival."

Munro weighs the sincerity in Thompson's voice then looks around at the others in the room. Every face mirrors the same conviction.

"You all share this opinion?" Munro asks the group.

"We do," Sharon answers. The others nod then speak their assent when Munro looks at them.

Munro takes a breath and returns to his seat. "Very well, Thompson, I'll hear you out."

"Thank you, Colonel." Thompson looks at the floor to regain his thoughts, and when he looks up, his steel gray eyes are bright. "To me, it seemed that O'Kai's actions are exactly correct, that this is *exactly* the way the Cadre has survived for over a thousand years. But there is a fundamental difference in this mission. Every rotation previous to this has been for the accumulation of vital resources, without which we'd have starved.

"This time, O'Kai's fleet is not acting to preserve lives, not picking off a ship because we need what's inside... No matter how similar it looks from the outside, the objective is fundamentally different. He's acting to inflict as much destruction as he can, and that's all."

"We are at war with a powerful enemy," Munro states, casting a suspicious glance at the Blueskin in attendance. "And considering their actions, *all* retaliation is justified."

"I'm sure they said the same thing when Keller was butchering Eleto on the Colonies," Gregor says.

Sharon puts a hand on the Russian's arm, then says to Munro, "You know that Keller's actions instigated the genocide, yes? There's no excuse for mass slaughter, on any side, but it isn't as if the Eleto came unprovoked."

Munro mulls the point, rubbing the thick stubble of his chin. His eyebrows lift, he sits up straight and gestures toward Thompson, saying, "Continue."

"In a way," Thompson resumes, "I've already carried out this mission. My orders were to reconnoiter the planet, send detail back to Cadre One, and inflict destruction until my team and I were dead. I wasn't sent to collect. My mission wasn't to enlarge the Cadre's store of consumables. I was sent to *kill*. And though I can't prove the connection, I'm *certain* that mission is why Cadre One is lost to us."

Munro's head rocks back and he blinks as if punched. "You're saying...*what*?"

"I'm saying Team Forestall's action on Earth made the Eleto more determined than ever to find us. And they did. When I think about how much damage we caused, there's no sense of accomplishment. Not when it cost us our only home. O'Kai's mission is exactly the same, only on a *greater scale*. That's why I know for certain that even if he wins at Earth, it will be a hollow victory because the Eleto will have cause to rid us from existence, forever."

Munro blows a deep breath past his lips. "We are at *war*, Thompson. And I think you underestimate our chances. The odds are not in our favor, and they never have been. Yet here we are."

"Everything you say is correct," Thompson says. "There's nothing to argue. My point, Colonel, is that we have a better option we can investigate. Earth has recovered from the Eleto attack. It's a living life support system so huge it once supported *billions* of our kind." He looks at Maiella, then to Munro. "I wish I could describe to you what it was like to stand on the surface, breathing without respirators or old air-regs that constantly need fixing... Water that runs in free-flowing streams... Sunlight on the face that doesn't instantly burn... Food that springs from leaf, fruit, and root... A diversity of life forms... So much room to move and explore... That environment is custom made for our needs...as if the planet was engineered just for us." Thompson halts abruptly, rebuilding the austere edifice he allowed to slip. "An all-out assault would be devastating. We would lose everything."

"How could we lose something we do not possess?" Munro asks, annoyed.

Shondre speaks into the Counselor's ear, and he translates, "Because it *belongs* to you."

306

Munro's eyes swing to the reptilian, and his head follows like a millstone. "Yes, it *does*," Munro says gravely. "But it was taken from us, and now the enemy has settled there as if they earned it. Tell the captive this, Counselor: this war can end the moment they all depart and leave us be."

The Counselor speaks the words into Shondre's ear. She nods accepting the point, then replies, which the Counselor translates, "This one understands your view. The people who live there now were born on that planet. It is all they have ever known, and they are as much a part of it as the plants and animals that evolved there. Would you make them vagrants through no fault of their own? As a people, yes, we bear the shame of genocide, but please recall that these people now living on Earth had no part in that. And as Tom-Sun described, there is *so much room*. You could live for generations without ever seeing your neighbors, if you wished. There's no need for us to be at war when we could both have all we need."

"They would simply allow us to land and live there?" Munro scoffs. "They would just *drop their weapons* and *forget about the last twelve hundred years?*"

"Not quickly," Shondre says through the Counselor. "Not easily. But we must ask for peace so that both of our peoples can strive for it."

"Ah, so this was your idea." Munro says, resting his big elbow on a knee and drilling a stare into Shondre. "How do we know this isn't to lure us all in for a final stroke?" he says to the rest of the group. "Are you all *blind?*"

"Our eyes are wide open, Colonel," Maiella says. She spreads her arms, palms up, adding, "We're looking for more than *this*. We're seeing possibility of life without the endless threat of extinction looming over us. But we would never risk our brothers and sisters unless we're sure it's attainable."

"Meaning?"

"We assemble a team," Thompson explains. "Representatives of Cadre and Colonist. We leave the *Europa* and head to Earth so a dialogue can begin. If we fail, nothing changes. The *Europa* continues on her way. The war continues. But if we succeed...the fighting could *end*. No more faces on a Memorial wall. We become the people we were always meant to be, restored to our rightful place."

"Those are high goals, Thompson. What makes you think they're attainable? This captive of yours? Did she speak promises into your ear?"

"She's no longer a captive," Sharon says. "I don't allow Shondre out without escort, but that's more for her protection than anything. As far as I'm concerned, she's an ambassador from a people we know nothing about. If we can talk to them through her, we may be able to have real dialogue. She's a

307

chance to end this mad journey. You've no idea how badly we need that."

"Kerr-null Mun-ro," Shondre says carefully, placing a hand on her chest, "thiss hwon speak for hurr Pee-pull. Not ask trust. Ask *speak*. Ask try un-ter...un-terr" She winces in frustration.

"Try to understand," the Counselor says for her.

Shondre points to the Counselor. "Hyess, *try*." Giving up on human words, she leans over to the Counselor and speaks into his ear. The Counselor dutifully translates.

"Shondre says, an honest meeting is a necessary first step. Because it has never happened before, it cannot fail to interest her people. They fear '*Ravenous, Angry Ghosts*' who consume ships and crews. But to see you, in the flesh, they finally understand such Ghosts are myth. Curiosity replaces fear, desire to hunt is diminished, and they wish to learn more. This serves the cause of peace."

"Every moment we delay," Thompson notes, "the farther apart we are from the fleet. For this to work, we have to close that distance and convince O'Kai not to attack until we've had a chance to negotiate. That means turning this ship around *right now*."

"Whether I agree with that assessment or not," Munro concedes, "the *Europa's* heading is up to her captain."

"The day a captain has to stand for election is the last day of unilateral decisions," Sharon laments. "I'm going to need a majority opinion, and taking us *toward* the danger is a difficult idea to sell."

"Even with most of them back in stasis?" Maiella asks. "MedTechs outnumber your standing crew thirty to one, and they'll fall in line with whatever Munro tells them."

"You're not suggesting we include MedTechs in the vote, are you?" Gregor asks.

"Why not?" Maiella replies. "Aren't they part of this crew?"

"*Of course* they are," Sharon says. "But like you said, they follow orders. Treat them as a single voting block, and that makes Munro captain of this ship. No offense, Colonel, but I'm not giving up my chair that easily."

"I'd never ask for that," the big man says. "This is your command, and I'll obey your orders as if they come from General O'Kai."

"Then do we thaw out a duty crew?" Gregor asks. "The adjustments to schedule, plus the lack of space, not to mention how hard it is to get them to agree on anything... Could get ugly. You sure it's worth it, Skipper?"

"I'm not sure of anything anymore," Sharon says with weariness, "except that if we don't include them, the rest will think they're getting railroaded. Herzfeld will have a field day with that, and I've had quite enough sabotage, thank you."

"Why not place Herzfeld into stasis?" Munro asks.

"Ortega already tried that, and the crew revolted," Sharon answers. "*Gor*, I finally understand why so many MPs got caught in corruption scandals, because I'm *completely* willing to bribe him, if I could."

"We know the right way to do this," Thompson says. "We bring it to the crew and convince them this is the right thing to do. No matter what, we need their willing agreement."

"Most will be suspicious, so long as Shondre is skulking around," Gregor notes. "They'll assume she's behind it and won't trust her. Or us, so long as we're taking closed meetings with her."

"Then it's high time she introduced herself," Sharon says. "She made her case to us. She deserves the chance to make the same points to the crew. Shondre, do you need some time to figure out what you'll say?"

Shondre smiles politely, and through the Counselor she answers, "This one has had plenty of time already."

Sharon grimaces. "Right, sorry 'bout that. Now let's say all goes well, and we get the ship turned around. We still have a lot of catching up to do. This old girl will never get us there in time, soooo... We take one of the escorts, perhaps?"

"O'Kai has ordered they remain with the *Europa* unless in direct engagement with the enemy," Munro states. "They will not leave her side."

"Don't suppose you have an idea to get us going faster then?" Sharon poses. She turns to Maiella. "Anything at Cadre Two you never told me about?"

"Quite a lot, in fact," Maiella answers, "but not what you're looking for."

Shondre's brows bunch together. She taps the Counselor and, with a quizzical expression, holds up two fingers. "Kad-Ra (two)?" The Counselor holds up a hand so he can follow the conversation.

"Could have been right under our noses," Maiella continues. "Didn't have the chance to really look around. Barely got out of there alive."

"What about Shondre's transport?" Thompson asks. "The one we collected from Earth. Argo said it was faster than anything else in the fleet."

"It's docked to the *Europa* right now," Munro answers.

The Counselor translates, and Shondre perks up in her cushioned seat.

"O'Kai left it with us?" Thompson says in disbelief. "A ship that fast would be perfect for recon. Why leave it behind?"

"Had no weapons," Munro explains, "and, without a total teardown and rebuild, the power plant couldn't handle the extra draw of stealth generators. So O'Kai left it with us as a lifeboat. For worst case scenario."

"The fleet's been underway for months. We're talking about a big head start..." Thompson says. "Can we make it faster?"

Munro mulls the idea, mentally reviewing his notes from the initial retrofits. "There's room for marginal improvement, yes, if we push safe operation limits. Would shorten the lifespan of the vessel, however."

"As long as it gets us there in one piece, and we're not glowing from radiation, it doesn't matter what's left of it," the Gun notes.

"All right," Sharon says, "we need some ideas on how we convince O'Kai to call off the assault. Munro, any thoughts?"

The big man shakes his head. "He's determined. But he may consider a delay while dialogues are held. Pending the outcome, it could hold off further action."

Gregor shifts himself in the crushed cushions of the couch, laying a well-muscled arm along the back of it. "Keller once changed O'Kai's mind about exiling Team Spectre, at least for a while."

"Keller isn't here anymore," Sharon says.

"No, but O'Kai wasn't swayed by Keller's personality. He respected the fact he was the *Europa's* captain."

"Sharon's captain now," Maiella notes.

"She should be one of the delegates, then," Shondre says through the Counselor.

"Oh good!" Sharon says. "I was desperately hoping to negotiate the future of all humanity someday."

"I can never tell when you're joking," Maiella says.

Sharon smirks in response then says to the group, "It's a big *if*, but *if* we can call a truce with the Eleto, that could force O'Kai to recognize a rightful treaty between us, at least between the Colonists and the Eleto. If we prove we can live in peace together, what cause would he have to attack? Wouldn't the ceasefire become stable at that point?"

"It might," Gregor adds. "Plus, he'd be less likely to attack if we're in the line of fire."

"Then again," Sharon says, "he might maroon us somewhere and justify it by saying he was 'saving us from ourselves.'"

"That's a good point," Maiella notes. "He'd do that."

"Should we warn the Eleto the fleet is coming?" Sharon asks.

Shondre waits for the Counselor's translation then vehemently shakes her head. "No!" she answers through the Counselor. "That would harm trust and raise suspicion. Reinforcements would come for stronger defense, and the killing would be worse. First, we must have the General's word he will not attack. He can reserve his strength in secrecy and remain sure that he still holds great power. That may content him so that we can have talks in earnest. We must not betray his secret, or he may act, believing there is no alternative."

Heads nod in understanding.

"First thing's first," Sharon says. "We need to convince the crew that going back is a good idea. I'm kind of on the fence, myself, for what it's worth."

"Sharon, this doesn't happen if we don't go," Thompson says. "How long have you been out in the black? How much longer does it need to be before you accept there's *nothing* out here for us?"

"I know, I know. Just seems like we're taking as big a risk as O'Kai. This talk, this summit, *whatever*, it hasn't happened yet, and the closer we get to Earth, the more likely we're discovered," Sharon says. "It hasn't been a clean fight between us, you know. After Thompson's trip to Earth they might shoot first. And this is it. All of us in one basket."

"You still have the escorts," Munro states.

"*Please*. I get that there's comfort in seeing them gliding along out there, but how long could they really hold off an enemy? If they had real combat capability, they'd be with the fleet. It's a gesture, at best."

"This one will make an introduction for you, granting diplomatic protections," Shondre says through the Counselor. "If an Eleto vessel intercepts you, play the message on all channels. They will see this face, they will hear this voice, and they will understand that you are under *my* protection."

"How would they know we hadn't just made it up, faked it?" Gregor asks.

Shondre smiles modestly and blinks slowly, answering, "This one is *known*. They will recognize her and the words she chooses."

"Well, to be honest," Sharon admits, "I like that better than having a couple of Cadre warships riding shotgun. But say we play your recording... Then what? Not like we can talk back."

"The message would state that we are en route to Earth with a delegation for formal talks. Their orders would be to fly formation, observe and report but not interfere."

Sharon tilts her head and pops her eyebrows. "Doesn't sound half bad. Okay, then, how soon do you want to get in front the crew? Hoping we can address your new status and what we intend in the same meeting."

"Thiss hwon iss red-dee," Shondre says.

OF MORTAL CREATURES

"And intercepting O'Kai? How do we find him? There's a lot of black between here and there."

"The General is not with the fleet," Munro volunteers. "O'Kai remained at Cadre One to oversee its defense."

"When we left Cadre One we put our backs to Earth," Sharon says with a subtle smile. "Cadre One is practically *on the way.*"

"He won't be happy to see us," Maiella warns.

"Oh, *sod* 'im. This is more important. And heading back to Cadre One is an easier sell to the crew. They've got big guns there. Could put up a real defense."

"So if O'Kai's at Cadre One, who's boss of the fleet?" Gregor asks.

"Chusan is fleet commander," Munro states, "and Ralla is his number one."

Sharon's brow scrunches in thought. "Colonel, you're senior to Chusan, are you not?"

"I am."

"Would he obey an order if you gave him one?"

"Yes, unless it directly countered an order from O'Kai." Munro leans an elbow on one knee. "I see where you're going with this and you should know, I can never be General of the Cadre because I have no combat experience. If something happens to O'Kai, Chusan assumes leadership."

"Well, do we know O'Kai's orders?" Sharon asks. "You were involved in the planning, were you not?"

"For some of the logistics, yes. Most of my time was spent retrofitting the *Europa*, which was no small task. But as far as the main thrust of the assault, again, I have no combat training, so it was unnecessary for me to review or approve the finer details."

"*Yes*, but what do you know about the *plan*?"

Munro drills a hard stare into Shondre. "I will say nothing more of it in the presence of the enemy."

The Counselor translates into Shondre's ear, and her face scrunches as if slapped. "This one is *not* here to be your enemy!" she replies through the Counselor. "This one reaches out as an agent of peace so that we can *end* the suffering of *both* our peoples!"

"I recognize that you are currently non-hostile," Munro retorts without looking at her. "But a state of war exists and until we have a fully settled agreement, I *will not* share specifics."

"That's fine," Maiella says. "We don't need to know the hows and whys. But we need to know how much time we've got. If we turned around now, pulled some extra speed from Shondre's transport, can we get there

312

ahead of the fleet?"

Munro crosses his large and small arms and looks at the floor.

"Colonel," Sharon pleads, "before we left Cadre One, you and O'Kai met me on the bridge. O'Kai told us to shove off, more or less. And when I asked about our children, I saw it in your face. Losing them was every bit as hard for you as it was for us."

Munro looks at Sharon, wounded, edges of his mouth turned down. "They were not '*lost*,' Captain. Cadre One had been discovered, and they could not be safely transferred." He levels a cold gaze at Shondre. "We were forced, *by enemy action*, to terminate them."

When Shondre hears the Counselor's translation, she gasps, cupping her mouth. "*Troo*, this?" she asks. The Counselor nods sadly. Shondre buries her face in her hands.

"If we succeed, Colonel," Sharon continues, "we create a future where you will *never* have to do that again."

Hardness around Munro's eyes melts. His jaw flexes.

"Isn't that worth trying for?" Gregor asks. "*Please*, Colonel, *help* us!"

"It doesn't work without you," Sharon says gently. "We are *literally* all in the same boat."

Munro keeps his arms folded. "I cannot betray my general."

"We're not asking you to," Sharon persists. "Don't tell us anything that could give him away, just tell us how much time we have!"

Munro sighs then rolls his eyes up to the ceiling. His eyebrows knit as he calculates distances, velocities, and variables. "With minimal delay at Cadre One, no breakdowns in transit, taking the most direct safe route...we could arrive at Earth three months early, give or take a week."

"Three months to pull a summit together?" Gregor says. "That's tight... Shondre, can you make that work?"

"No choice," the Counselor translates for her. "We have to make it work."

"Maiella and I are on board," Thompson states. "Who would you send, Sharon?"

Her eyes defocus, and the *Europa's* captain stares in thought. "This is no social call... This is an attempt at armistice and the start of real relations between our peoples. I *have* to go. Doesn't make sense to send anyone else yet, least of all Herzfeld. He'll bollocks it up, demanding special privileges."

"Or he'd give up O'Kai's fleet as a bargaining chip," Gregor notes.

Sharon sighs deeply and nods in agreement. "He would, at that. All right. Shondre goes, *obviously*. Myself. Counselor, you're the only one with a grasp of their language. Will you join us?"

"Of course," he says humbly.

"We need a non-combat Cadre representative. Colonel, I think it should be you."

Munro's eyebrows lift. "Oh?"

"You've got my ship purring," Sharon says. "And I know your teams can maintain it. What we need now is your perspective on what the Cadre requires for a lasting, stable end to hostilities. And if the General of the Cadre can't be there, his number one should be."

Munro juts his large lower lip and nods, pleased at the invitation. "Very well. I'll join. Who will represent the Operator Corps?"

"I will," Thompson announces.

Munro eyeballs the Gun suspiciously. "I'm aware of your record. But you've been out of the Corps for quite some time. And your associations with Maiella are certainly *not* representative of Cadre interests."

Maiella scowls briefly, then looks at the wall, and props her head with her middle finger.

Thompson accepts the lancing with more grace. "I understand your reservations, Colonel. However, I have more real combat experience than anyone currently serving besides Argo. I've visited the planet, I've seen first hand what the rest of the Corps has not... And to be blunt, I've inflicted grievous injury there. I go not just to represent the Corps, but to offer apology and my life, if required."

Maiella nearly twists out of her seat to look Thompson in the eye. "The *hell* you will!"

"It will not come to that," Shondre says via the Counselor. "No one's hands are clean in this, and demanding sacrifice flies in the face of our intentions. We go to *save* lives, nothing less."

"Argo remained with O'Kai at Cadre One," Munro says. "If O'Kai releases him from duty, he would be a stronger representative of Operator interests."

"While that may be," Sharon admits, "Argo isn't on board with this cause. Thompson is, and he has my endorsement."

Munro grimaces. *I swore to abide by her decisions, yet she would dictate to me who best represents our people?*

"As you will," the colonel concedes.

"Then it's settled," Sharon says. "We have our delegation. Gregor, you'll have my recommendation as interim Captain, but you know you'll have to wrangle with Herzfeld to make it stick. He'll try to trip you up, so keep the temper in check, yeah?"

"Aye, Skipper," Gregor says with a reluctant nod.

"Colonel, we'll have a few months getting back to Cadre One. Would you work on the transport, see if your lads and lasses can squeeze some extra speed out of her?"

Munro grips his chin, mouth curved in anticipation of an interesting project. "Yes, I would." He looks around the table, burgeoning optimism making him wonder, *Could this work?*

"Well, then, we've all got jobs," Sharon announces, clapping her hands and rubbing them together. "Let's get *crackin'*!"

WORD FOR WORD

Sharon taps a stubby microphone perched over her ear, and deep thumps issue from the meeting hall's Public Address system.

"Test," she says, and her amplified voice fills the space.

From the improvised stage she looks out over an assembly of late middle aged or older colonists; and they look up at her, breaking off their individual conversations. Behind the colonists, orderly rows of MedTechs stand like an orchard of crooked trees, mute and attentive. Munro is among them, large and small arms folded across his barrel chest.

"Thank you, everyone," Sharon says through the PA system. "I know it must seem as if there's no end to these meetings lately, and I'm sorry for the interruption to your schedules. For those who are returning to us from your cryo recliners, please forgive the intrusion. Understand, we had to have your participation because this is too important for you to miss. These are interesting times and there is much to discuss.

"First, I want you all to meet someone. You've seen her taking walks with the Counselor and myself. I've had no shortage of questions about her, and rather than try to answer them all individually, I'm giving her a chance to speak. After hearing what she has to say, you'll have to make up your own minds. I do not intend to force any decision from you."

Colonists murmur among themselves as Sharon turns about and waves her guest on stage.

Escorted by the Counselor, Shondre ascends the short flight of steps. Folds of lightweight fabric drape over her shoulders, gather at her waist, and spread over the smooth curve of her hips. Her whip tail bends up at her knee and rises diagonally across her chest like a sash, circles around behind her wide neck, and hangs over the opposite shoulder. She looks out at skeptical

Colonist faces up front and at the collective glower of MedTechs behind them. With well-hidden trepidation, she grips the railing at the front of the stage.

"(This one is right here for you,)" the Counselor says in her language. "(He will speak your thoughts straight and true, word for word.)"

"(Word for word?)" she asks.

The Counselor smiles and nods.

Shondre looks down at her hands, noticing how deep the lines in the joints have become and how brittle her talons are at the ends of bony fingers. *So much time has already been lost*, she thinks.

To the Counselor, Shondre says, "(This one is ready.)"

The Counselor dips his head modestly and steps over to Sharon so she can pass over the stubby microphone. When all is quiet, Shondre faces the assembly and begins.

"For quite some time now," the Counselor translates, "this one has wanted to confess our crimes to you, the ones who deserve to hear it. We all know of the provocation, led by your Captain Keller, and how all Humankind was judged for the actions of a few. This injustice has ever weighed heavy. This one is grateful for the chance to unpack these stones from her chest."

Shondre looks out at an assembly of dubious faces with curled lips. Undaunted, she continues.

"How long was this one kept at Cadre One? This one does not know, but long enough to believe the Cadre had forgotten her. Worse than separation from friends, from family, and from 'other self' was the idea that this one no longer mattered—that she was allowed to live only because they did not know what else to do with her. This one believed she was a hostage without ransom, and sunlight would never again touch her cheek. She had *chosen* to believe this. Sickness grew inside. She collapsed and fell into dark sleep.

"Waking in your hospital, this one learned she was not alone. Without knowing, she had made a friend and that friend came to find her. He waited by her side as she recovered." Shondre gestures toward the man translating for her, fondness in her eyes. "There is much to admire in a man as selfless as he. One could go on and on about his good nature, about his *inexhaustible* patience..." Shondre turns toward her audience. "...and how irritating it can be. This one has tried to rile him but has not been successful." The Eleto arches a brow and grins with mischief. "Does not mean she will stop trying."

She faces the Counselor, one hand clasped in the other, her lips lengthening into a mischievous smile.

"Today he agreed to translate everything...*word...for...word*. Let's test that shall we?"

Low laughs from the audience.

Shondre approaches the Counselor, clears her throat, and filches the tablet from his lab coat pocket. While the Counselor watches, perplexed, she adopts an uncanny likeness of his head-tilted posture and concerned expression.

"Hello, I'm your Counselor," Shondre says through her translator. "Have you noticed my hair never seems to lay flat on my head? It's because every time I go back to my cabin I stick my finger in the power outlets."

Colonists chuckle, and the Counselor runs a hand through his hair self-consciously.

Shondre strokes her chin, pantomiming the Counselor's expression of sincere interest and concern during his therapy sessions.

"Someone once tried to explain that wrinkles can be removed from clothing. I struggled to comprehend, because it seemed so *wrong* to oppress fabric in such a manner. After all, who am I to limit my clothing's creative freedom? As you can see, this lab coat has fully realized its artistic vision and every thread has produced extremely confident creases..."

She says more, but the Counselor smirks and shakes his head.

Shondre flips a hand at him, urging him to translate, but he blinks slowly and shakes his head again. She grins and speaks in her own language while wagging a finger at the crowd and winking.

"What did she say?" yells a voice from the crowd.

The Counselor purses his lips then humbly smiles. "She said, 'Beware: censorship is all around us.'"

Colonists laugh out loud, and Shondre sees them opening, sees their guards dropping.

They are ready to listen.

She smiles at the Counselor, slips his tablet back into his coat pocket and embraces him fondly. "(Thank you for this,)" she whispers into his ear.

The Counselor pats her on the back and nods, replying with equal fondness, "(I'll be your dartboard, anytime.)"

Shondre releases him, letting one hand rest on his shoulder. "(Could not do this without you.)"

The Counselor tilts his head toward the assembly. "(Go ahead.)"

Her head dips. She turns front and grips the platform railing. When her head lifts, the up turned lines of her eyes and lips level with candor.

"It started with one," the Counselor interprets. "*One* person reached across a divide of awful conflict to meet *me*. And this one cannot begin to describe how grateful she is to call the Counselor her friend.

"One friend became two with Doctor Sahara Taggart. She's caring. And fierce! If any of you have tried to skip a medication interval, you know.

"So there's two...*two* people who aren't the *'Ravenous, Angry Ghosts'* spoken of in hushed circles. Then, Sharon and Sahara introduced this one to others, like Thompson."

Shondre turns pensive.

"At first sight of him, the terror inside was withering. This one believed there could be nothing so deadly in the multiverse, nothing so savage or bloodthirsty... Yet beneath his hard exterior of armor and scars, there is flesh and bone, genuine feeling, desire for fellowship, desire to serve others. He is one of many who were forced to fight for life, and it is impossible for this one to deny truth: Op-Pur-Ray-Tors are fearsome because our people *left them no alternative. WE* created the *'Ravenous Ghosts'* who haunt our imaginations and our shipping lanes."

Shondre pauses, head lowered.

"Long ago, the Eleto had opportunity to see beyond provocation, had a chance to be wise and to act with restraint. Instead, we were impatient, unwilling to risk another protracted war with an aggressive, adolescent species. Elders chose to eradicate a nascent threat before it became too strong to counter. Now, all Eleto inherit this shame."

She points to herself.

"This one accepts *everything* that has happened to her, because coming here was *essential*. This one could no longer allow herself to believe she was an unlucky victim. She *had* to come so she could learn and understand, whether she wanted to or not. And soon, this one understood she was given the same opportunity as her ancestors: to see beyond provocations, to act with patience and reason. This one will choose correctly.

"By spending time and sharing stories with you, we find similarities. The same way that Counselor, Sharon, Thompson, Maiella, and Sahara reached out to me, this one reaches out to you and makes a pledge of friendship, because *we are not so different*. This awful conflict *must* end."

The crowd is silent and still, background thrum of propulsion and whoosh of ventilation carrying in the quiet hall.

"Are you expected to take these words on faith? No. Trust must be earned. Seeds of good will must be planted, watered, and nourished so they may grow. Time will prove this one's commitment.

"Time..." Shondre trails off, momentarily lost in thought. "For centuries, you've had cause to hate this shape, this skin, the sound of this voice. Who could blame? But bodies we wear are only the stuff we're made of—vessels that transport the person inside and allow us to interact with the multiverse around us. The person inside lives *here*." She points to her chest. "And *here*." She points to her head. "Who we are is not dictated by physical forms. We are defined by *passions*, by *actions*, by our *dreams* and *goals*, the things we cherish and strive for...the families we raise and the bonds we form between friends. This rings true for all thinking, feeling beings.

"As each of you are distinct, unique, and irreplaceable...so are we. This tenet, so simple in concept, is the basis for most of our laws. And, it seems, for most of your laws, as well.

"No matter how a tree grows, how its branches spread and extend into the sky, no matter the myriad shape of leaf, flower, needle, or cone, it *must* have roots in good soil to thrive. This one's roots are in family and friends, in community, in pursuit of life's pleasures and mysteries. We endure hardships together. We seek deeper understanding of the worlds around us, deeper understanding of ourselves... But we have been remiss. We have not tried hard enough to understand others who are *not* us.

"When we look at one another, our eyes may see a thousand differences. But standing here before you...allowed to live, and even speak freely...how can anyone ignore the fact that we are *not* so different? More importantly, there is enough for everyone. Only the greedy, the ones who jealously hoard their wealth, would have us believe in scarcity. There is no reason why we cannot co-exist on the same planet, breathe the same air, swim in the same lakes and streams. The cosmos has no preference, it does not approve of one life form or revile another, because, as the Counselor has said, '*life is its own reason for being.*'"

Shondre takes a deep breath.

"Let us remain safe in each others' presence. Let our needs be met, and most of all, let us *DO NO HARM*. When we are calm, relaxed, our minds open and we can all come to the same natural conclusion that we are *all deserving of life*."

Shondre takes a moment to herself and swallows some of the dryness in her throat.

"Violence is the ultimate proof of failure as civilized, rational beings. It leaves an indelible stain we carry into afterlife. So we must be *more* than enemies. We must find the strength to forgive because *our children deserve better than this*. They deserve a better life than one of privation and insecurity. They deserve more career choices than soldier, spy, or weapons maker. War economy is too expensive. Too costly in blood and treasure... but *far* more costly in the stories never written, the songs never sung, the discoveries never made because people died too soon. Or, because people were forced into a career they would not have otherwise chosen in a time of peace.

"This is a chance for all of us to be wise. We can, at last, come to terms with our mistakes, lay aside the past, and build the future we want. We can give our children better lives than the ones we've lived. We can make them *proud* of us. When they look back, fully grown with families of their own, they'll see the hard choices we made, and they'll *know* why we made them: because we loved them *so* much."

Shondre closes her eyes and bows humbly. The audience is silent. While there were no delusions that humans would cheer and sing her praises, she expected more of a response. With a sinking feeling in her chest, she thinks, *This one has misjudged. Perhaps their anger is too great...*

She looks to the Counselor then pushes away from the railing, letting him escort her toward the steps. Behind her, a single pair of hands claps together. When she looks over her shoulder she sees a tall man with broad shoulders in the crowd, his coveralls much less grungy and threadbare than his fellows, clapping hands over his head. Many Colonists turn their heads toward him and take up the same posture, nodding to one another and applauding. Whistles pierce the air. Shondre places one hand over her chest, smiles in relief, and waves to the crowd.

The Counselor passes the microphone back to Sharon, and she dons it while heading back to the front of the platform.

Once the shouts and applause die down a voice calls out, "What's her name?"

"Her name is *Shondre*," Sharon answers, and a dozen voices all yell out questions of their own.

"Now hang on!" the *Europa's* captain says. "I know you've all got questions. Shondre is taking appointments to meet individually for follow up. The Counselor is keeping her schedule, so send him the time you'd like to meet. Or, if you'd rather, you can just send your questions to the Counselor and he can ask them for you. All right?"

Heads in the crowd bob and utter their assent.

"Good, good. I'm glad you all got to be here today to see and listen, but I don't expect anyone to believe everything is just going to sort itself out. So I have another proposal to run by you. I'm putting together a delegation. With Shondre, we're going to Earth, and we're going to start a dialogue. I don't know where it will get us, but we have to try.

"Now here's the trick: we all know where O'Kai's fleet is headed. If it all kicks off before we get there, there won't be anything to talk about, so we have to convince O'Kai he should wait. That means we head back to

Cadre One *right now*."

Sharon waits, letting the idea sink in and preparing for backlash.

"Okay," Herzfeld says from the crowd, "then what?"

Sharon arches her brows, amazed at the lack of resistance. "Well... If O'Kai agrees to hold off, Thompson, Maiella, Colonel Munro, the Counselor, Shondre, and I take the limousine straight to Earth. Shondre can announce our arrival and make arrangements for formal talks.

"There are so many *ifs* in this plan it makes my head spin, but the biggest one of all is this: *If* we do this right, it could mean an end to this *endless* bleeding journey."

Colonists erupt with cheers and shouts far louder than before, some jumping up and down in place and hugging one another.

"Wait, *wait, WAIT*!" Sharon shouts above them. "Look, we haven't negotiated anything yet! This is a real long shot! It's definitely worth taking, which is why I'm going personally. But I'm not about to bet *your* lives on it! We have to do as we've always done. We have to grind on for now. Believe in a better future, just be cautious, *yeah*?"

Sharon searches the faces of the crowd. Seeing them excited and happy is such a change from the usual shout-fests that she allows the hoots and whistles to carry on. In the end, however, she knows she has to tamp down their expectations. Reluctantly, she raises her arms in a gesture for quiet.

"So, to recap: first, we convince O'Kai to hold off an attack so we can try talks, and second, we haven't found a damn thing out here. Doesn't look like we ever will. We could get lucky, but luck is *not* a strategy. We need a solid plan to work from. Does anyone have a counterpoint to make?"

Heads in the crowd swivel, searching neighbors for objection and finding none.

"All right, then," Sharon continues. "By show of hands: all in favor of returning to Cadre One?"

Every Colonist raises an arm.

"Well *that's* settled," Sharon says with an amazed grin. "When we leave, it could be for a long time. You'll need to choose an interim captain. I nominate Gregor, but you can nominate anyone else you like. Just get me fifty signatures and I'll approve their candidacy. Does that work?"

Heads nod, voices bark out their agreement.

Agreeable lot today, she thinks to herself. When she looks beyond the Colonists to the stoic and unmoving MedTechs behind them, she calls out, "Colonel Munro, do you have any thoughts or concerns you'd like to raise?"

322

With deep and clear voice, he replies, "We accept and support the decisions of the *Europa's* captain and crew."

"Very well. Let's turn this old girl around! *To your posts!*"

Colonists file out, jubilant, joyful in a way Sharon had completely unanticipated. She watches them go, smiling and waving to them. MedTechs follow in orderly rows, saluting crisply as if on review. She nods to them in respect and salutes Munro as he passes.

When Sharon makes her way down the stairs from the platform, she finds Herzfeld there, waiting. Several comments come to mind, but in light of how easily the assembly passed, she bites her tongue.

"Captain," Herzfeld says in greeting. Then, with unusual modesty he says, "You proved today why you were the right choice for this crew. For that, I want to thank you." He extends a hand. Sharon looks at it first and shakes it warily.

"I'm here to serve," she says in moderated tone and begins walking toward the exit, eyes narrow with suspicion.

"I'm not your enemy, you know," he says walking along side her. "I'm with these people every day. I listen. I know what they need. Today, you gave it to them."

"I haven't given them anything yet."

"On the contrary. You gave them hope and something better to work toward. *That's* a life worth living."

Sharon peers at him, looks forward, then peers at him again. "Hi, I'm Sharon Jones. And you are...?"

He cracks a smile. "If you'll excuse me, I've got quite a few questions for our new 'friend.' If I can assist in any of the arrangements, please call on me."

Herzfeld turns down an adjacent corridor and hurries out of sight, leaving Sharon second-guessing everything she thought she knew about him.

THERMODYNAMICS

Thompson squints through a set of welding goggles into a recessed junction box in the floor. The top half of his coveralls is tied around his waist by the arms, leaving him bare-chested. Sweat rolls through the deep troughs of his muscles and scars.

He trains his eyes just ahead of the brilliant blue flame of his torch and pushes a puddle of melted metal around a support collar with tight, looping movements. At the end of the seam, he snuffs the torch and parks the goggles on his forehead. The weld looks like a neat row of overlapping coins, and he nods to himself with satisfaction.

In compartments behind him, MedTechs saw, drill, and grind their way to the bones of the limousine. The din is easy to tune out until power tools wind down, and Thompson hears them discussing the next step of their job.

"...right, Colonel said take it out."

"A-a-all of it?"

"Yeah, couch, cushions, *everything*."

"O-k. L-let's d-d-do it."

Metal and MedTechs groan until rivets pop and fabric tears in long, staticky rips.

In the flight deck, just ahead, Maiella occupies the pilot's seat with one boot on the console, HDI jacked in. Munro's deep voice comes through the console speakers, requesting a reading, and she answers him with a list of figures. Pushing with her boot, she swivels around and watches Thompson haul a thickly spliced power line across the collar he just welded. His big arms flex with the effort, and she arches an eyebrow in approval.

"Have you figured out what you're gonna say to O'Kai?" she asks.

Thompson bolts down a clamp over the cable then sets his power drill aside. "I figure I'll tell it straight. We already tried this on the Forestall rotation and it went bad for everyone. No reason to think it would be any better if we arrived in force. Besides, if we can check out Shondre's offer without risking anyone but ourselves, there's no harm in him waiting."

Maiella reclines and looks at the ceiling in thought. "Suppose you convince him. How would O'Kai hold the fleet back if he's at Cadre One? Any signal he sent would get there way too late."

"O'Kai can record a message, and we can deliver it."

Munro's voice sounds from the console. Maiella swivels to read another list of figures then she spins back around again.

"Kinda hard to imagine O'Kai staying put when everyone else is on the move," she says. "I mean, what if he left? Or worse, what if we get to Cadre One and he's slugging it out with the Eleto...or if there *is no* Cadre One?"

Thompson sits back on his heels. "We'd have to catch up to Chusan and Ralla. Find them, somehow."

Maiella smirks and shakes her head. "The only thing we know is where they're headed. By the time they all get there, could be too late."

Thompson nods. "True, but some ships are slower than others. For greatest punch, Chusan and Ralla should wait until all ships are present or accounted for. There *has* to be a rendezvous somewhere."

"Yeah, but do you think the fast ships would just hang around until everyone showed up? They could be discovered, sitting there. No surprise, lost initiative. Battle starts on the defensive. Hard to picture Ralla building *that* into a battle plan."

"You got another idea?"

"What if they staged it so everyone takes a different route and arrives at the same time?"

"The slowest ships would take the straightest route."

"The freighters..."

"Yeah. They left months before the fleet. Even so, our slowest warship could be there and back in the time it takes one of those freighters to make the trip."

"Hold up... What good is a freighter in a fight, anyway?"

"Size makes 'em good for cover. Virus ships could ride out on them to save fuel. They're pretty solid structurally; might make a good ram. Never know. Anyway, there's still a lot of math to plot where they'll be. And to intercept en route—"

"I can get you within ten light minutes."

Thompson eyeballs her suspiciously. "Within *ten* light minutes? *C'mon*."

Maiella shakes her head at him. "You're doubting? Who plotted all our jumps on rotation, hmm? Who put us right behind our target, *every time*? You think it was our crappy NavComs?"

"All right, all right, I'll give you that. Say we catch up to one of the freighters. The Geek at the helm will know where everyone is heading."

"That's where Chusan and Ralla will be, staging their assault. So we run ahead of the freighters, give them O'Kai's message..."

"And then we go make nice with the Eleto. Work out some kind of cease-fire so the fleet doesn't come in blasting."

"Might work."

Maiella turns to the console and answers another of Munro's queries. Thompson replaces the junction box cover and screws it down tight.

"Soooo...how long since you've been off the inhibitors?" she asks over her shoulder.

"Three months. And I've been having the *strangest* dreams."

"Care to share?"

Thompson blushes. "No."

Maiella sinks back into her seat, and fidgets uncomfortably. "Hey, could you help me with something?"

"Sure," he says, rising to his feet. "Whatcha need?"

"I've been stuck in this same position for hours. My shoulders are all knotted up."

Thompson climbs the short steps to the flight deck and stoops under the low ceiling.

Maiella shrugs her coveralls off her shoulders, exposing bare skin. When Thompson looks down on her, he sees the outline of smooth muscle beneath the surface of scars, the supple roundness of her breasts with areola barely hiding beneath the line of open fabric. He grips her shoulders firmly, letting her warmth pass into his calloused hands.

"Ooooohhhh, that's it," she groans. Her head falls back against the seat's headrest, and she undoes another clasp, giving him a better view down her open coveralls.

Thompson takes hold of her head and tips it forward, kneading the muscles at the base of her skull with his thumbs; then he works his way down to the nape of her neck and spreads his hands over the taut angles of her trapezii.

Maiella takes him by the wrists, and, with eyes closed, guides his hands to the soft flesh of her chest. She inhales at his touch, and utters the tiniest gasp as her nipples fall between his fingers.

Thompson can barely cope with the sensations running through him, electric and supremely sensitive. All the times he touched her bare skin before, it was contact between teammates. This is altogether more intense and personal, more urgent, demanding the entirety of his attention. He leans down beside her, drawing in the smell of her trimmed short hair, watching the throb of her pulse at her neck. She leans her head against his and rubs against the roughness of his beard.

"*Maiella, provide result for main drive augment,*" the console says with Munro's voice. When there is no reply, it demands, "*Maiella, report!*"

She sits up in her seat, pulling out of Thompson's grasp. "Still in tolerances, Colonel. Go plus one percent."

"*Understood, one percent,*" the console echoes.

His connection to Maiella ends like a power cord being yanked from the wall, and Thompson blinks in a fog of arousal, the rest of the world distant and unworthy of acknowledgement. But when his senses return, the Gun is uncomfortably aware how quickly crucial concerns were swept aside.

Maiella swings herself around in the seat. "Sorry 'bout that, got caught in the—" Her eyes drop below his waistline. "*Oh,*" she says with a sly grin. "Is that for me?"

Thompson looks down and manually adjusts himself. "Hunh. It's been doing that a lot lately."

Maiella arches an eyebrow. "Reeaaalllly? Well, I know how to fix that." She swivels back toward the console. "Munro, thermal spike in number four. Cut back point zero five, over."

"*Understood, number four, back point zero five,*" the console replies.

"Your splice is holding well," Maiella says to Thompson. "Getting better power delivery, *finally*. I swear, I don't know how this thing got you home without catching fire. I mean, they took the time to skin it in decent plate. But cutting corners on internals? What's the point of that? Just run silver cables of the proper gauge and be done with it."

"Right?" Thompson says. "And metal purity was pathetic, like the Blueskins don't even care. Energy losses to heat approaching two percent. Even *Colonist* engineers are better than that." He looks over his shoulder at the junction box. From the top of the short stairs, it is a view he has seen before.

> *...a battered enemy weapon in his numb hands...grit between his charred teeth...cold creeping in through every hole in his skin as the blood drains out...*

Inability to stand... A black pull into smothering oblivion...

Mission's end...

Thompson shudders then shakes his head to rattle the memory out. Laying hands on the back of Maiella's chair, he asks, "What did we toss out in the upgrade?"

She ticks a list off on her fingers. "Refrigeration, flavored drinks and intoxicants, holo-projector and media archive, hot showers, auto-massage, inflatable heated bunks..."

"Waste of power, anyway."

"If you say so..." Maiella leans into her console, studying a power flow diagram. "Our shift is almost up. No point starting a new splice just to leave it for someone else. Why don't you head back to the cabin? I'll join you shortly."

"Cut a shift early?"

"By ten minutes? I think we'll live."

Thompson juts his lip. "Doesn't seem right."

"Then stop being so damned efficient."

"I can find something that needs doing."

Maiella swings about in her chair. "Do I need to have Sharon *order* you off shift?"

"You trying to get rid of me all of a sudden?"

"Yeah. 'Cause I can't concentrate with you hanging around." She swings back toward the console. "If you don't go, I'm gonna jump on you right here."

Thompson grins, leans over her, and cups each side of her face, saying, "I'm going." Backing out of the cramped cockpit, he adds casually, "You *could* join me."

Maiella sighs, staring at her console. "Would, but I can't. Got a manifold flow problem. Need to pull more through it, but every time we try it wants to melt."

"Huh. I thought you were good at this." Thompson hops down the short stairs. "Guess not."

Maiella turns slowly around in her seat, jaw dropped. "It's *thermodynamics*, you *ass*," she says after him, "I can't just wish up a material that... Come to think of it, maybe we should use *you* as the manifold, instead. I mean, you're certainly *DENSER* than anything else we have to work with around here."

"Interesting," he says, turning back. "Never saw anyone try to fix something with excuses before." He grins across his entire face. "Let me know how that works out."

Maiella's eyes narrow with a malevolent grin as she swings around to face her console. The Geek fires up her HDI and lowers her goggles, saying under her breath, "You're gonna *get* it, Gun. You are *soooooo* going to get it."

THIS PRECISE MOMENT

Thompson stands in front of the mirror at his hygiene station. Clothed only in a white towel, he finishes shaving the last bit of beard from his face and rinses clean. Taking the towel from his waist, he pads his face dry then dumps it in a hamper. Standing nude, he looks himself over, scrutinizing his physique since leaving Cadre steroids and inhibitors. The quick bulk he gained upon returning to Cadre rations has been extremely difficult to maintain, and, like Maiella, his fitness regimens have bordered on terrifying. Though a bit slimmer overall, he finds no cause for disappointment in his fitness. His genitals, however, are another matter. Since the second week off inhibitors, they have enlarged, become immensely sensitive, and have been in a state of almost perpetual tumescence. Simple movements prove awkward, as do social interactions.

Counselor wouldn't hear of me getting back on the inhibitors, Thompson recalls, *told me to think of something else, something non-sexual, like work, or repairs. But I get so set on* not *thinking about her,* everything *turns into a reminder. Just swinging a hammer switches me on.*

He looks down at himself. Hard again. The Gun grabs his face in frustration.

I know how to fix that, Maiella's voice echoes in his mind.

But wait, he thinks, staring at himself in the mirror, *how would she know? Did someone* instruct *her?*

A wave of jealousy races up his spine, turning his face and ears a murderous red.

Did someone...show her?

His hands clench; his chest and shoulders tighten. His nostrils spread as his lungs fill again and again. Primed on chemical aggression, he jams his legs into a pair of black cargo pants.

I'll crack him over my knee and BEAT HIM TO DEATH WITH HIS OWN SPINE.

Pounding a fist into an open hand, he storms toward the door and barely stops himself from punching through the panel.

"Whoa..."

Thompson lets out his breath, turns, and warily looks back at a stranger in the mirror. The reflection glowers with focused rage.

"It doesn't matter if she has," he says out loud, forcing himself to listen. His reflection's expression twists with anger and disgust, clearly begging to differ.

"Maiella said there's never been anyone else and that's all there is to it. She *wouldn't* lie to me."

Elemental truth softens the angles around his eyes, relaxes the tension in his shoulders.

Counselor warned me I'd have swings like this... But these surges! It's like going mad!

He returns to the mirror, frowning. His brows slide together in concentration, and the Gun practices his meditative techniques. Jaw muscles unclench, and the fight-ready tension in his broad shoulders relaxes.

"I am in control," he says at last.

When he looks down, all is in its appropriate place.

"And that's the end of *that*."

He turns from the hygiene station, picks up a faded gray T-shirt from his bunk, and slides it down over himself. Despite the extra sections of fabric stitched into the sides, neck, tail and arms, it clings to him like film.

Returning to the hygiene station, he scrutinizes his reflection. The tall Gun turns sideways, looks over his shoulder, viewing all angles to ensure there is nothing Maiella might find objectionable. As a final test, he raises arms and flexes. His shoulders swell and his chest expands, shirt threads popping at every seam.

Not bad.

From the hygiene station's drawer, he pulls out a small phial of amber liquid. Two words grace the label in a language he does not recognize, *Hombre Potente.*

Gregor said a little of this can make a man more attractive to the opposite sex...

He lifts the nozzle to his nose, inhaling a scent like sweat and solvent with a dash of disinfectant. His nose wrinkles in revulsion, but he pulls the spray top off anyway.

If a little is good...

He raises the bottle over his head and starts tipping it when he hears rapid footfalls racing up the corridor. He caps the bottle and sets it on the counter, listening as the sounds halt outside his cabin. The door slides aside, and Maiella braces herself in the doorway, panting. Her coveralls are already undone down to her waist; her boots are unlaced. A mist of sweat covers her exposed skin, making her shiny in the cabin light.

"*One hundred point three percent* to target," she says, shrugging out of the coveralls. With a coy grin, she kicks a boot past Thompson's head and it slams against the alloy wall behind him. "You owe me an *apology*."

"I never had a doubt," he says. "I just can't believe it took you this long—"

Another boot whizzes at his head, making him duck.

Maiella flips forward and flings her loosened coveralls off her legs into Thompson's face. Blinded by canvas, Thompson steps back, is halted by the hard edge of his bunk, and is tackled onto it. Maiella's legs curve around him but she pulls her head back. Peering down at him, she rocks her hips against him ever so slightly.

"A-*pol*-o-*gize*," she says in melodic, demanding tones.

"Okay," he laughs, "I'm sorry, I—"

"Good enough." She kisses him hard and her taut body molds against every part of him. He yields, falling to her onslaught.

Maiella gasps for air as if coming up from a dive. Reaching behind herself, she finds him hard as stone. With a wicked smile, she sits upright then scoots back. Taking hold of his waistband with both hands, she rips the fly apart. Buttons launch and ricochet off the metal walls.

"Why are you *dressed*?" she demands, yanking his trousers down his legs. "You *knew* I was coming."

"Yeah, but who could say when? Might have taken you days to wrap up a simple job like that. *Weeks*, maybe..."

Her eyebrows lift. "*That's* gonna cost you."

Maiella slaps her hands onto his chest, grips his collar, and, in one motion, splits it down the front. Sweeping the flaps aside, she rakes her nails down past his navel and rips off his boxers. Not missing a beat, she slips out of her own underpants and leaps back onto his lap. Thompson sits up against her, bracing her with his hands. She clutches the back of his head, kisses him on the lips again. He can feel her trembling, hesitating.

"I've never done this before," she whispers.

"Neither have I."

She nods. "I've wanted you *forever*. Ever since I joined the Corps...

They said it was wrong." She pulls back to look him in the eye. "What do you think?"

Her vulnerability makes him harder than he believed possible. "I don't give a damn what anyone else thinks. I want you more than I've ever wanted anything in my life."

She thunks her head against his. She is no longer trembling.

Taking him in hand, Maiella guides him, both of them so ready for one another that it takes no effort. She slides down on to him. Her eyes crush shut, her jaw drops, her fingernails gouge crescents into his back. Arms locked, legs clenched, she grips him with every muscle in her body.

Thompson grips her just as tightly, pressing into her. His universe shrinks to this precise moment, all of his attention focused on it. There is no one else, there is no worry or concern beyond the walls of this cabin, and he knows he will never again allow himself to be away from her.

With stuttering breath, she says into his ear, "*I love you.*"

He lifts his hands to each side of her face and looks into adoring brown eyes. No explanation of love the Counselor offered was ever sufficient. Only here and now, so completely entangled as to be forever inseparable, does he finally comprehend the meaning. And with total honesty he says back to her, "*I love you.*"

Maiella shoves him back onto the bunk. "*Good.*" Grinning, she arches an eyebrow. "Prepare yourself, Gun. I'm coming at you for *real* this time."

Thompson smiles.

"Show me what you've got."

FAITH

Ortega places his tray at an unoccupied table in the cafeteria. A bowl of hot mash steams in front of him with sides of bright green twigs and orange discs. A cup of tea nests in a circular indent at top right. Beside the tray he lays a thick leather bound book, marked only with a gold-embossed cross.

Settling down onto the bench, he places elbows to either side of the tray, clasps his hands, and prays.

"Would you look at that?"

Gregor looks up from his bowl to see who is asking. He finds Dave standing across the table with his tray, staring at the far end of the dining hall. Gregor follows Dave's stare to the *Europa's* ex-captain, Javier Ortega. Seeing nothing unusual, he digs back into his hash. "See *what?*"

Dave sets his tray down opposite Gregor and settles in behind it. "It's weird," he begins. "Ortega's so calm about everything. I mean, we went through some fucked up times. And I'm more than a tad freaked out about this whole going back to Cadre One thing. But Ortega, man, he doesn't bitch or gripe. Look at him: not a care in the world. Does he even *know* where we're headed?"

"He knows," the Russian says.

"Captain of the ship one day, outcast the next. Pretty big fall. How does he do it, is what I'd like to know."

Gregor cracks a cynical smile. "You got it wrong, Dave. You're looking at a happier man, I assure you."

Dave looks at Gregor, his entire face screwed up into a question mark. "The hell do you mean? We aren't so bad."

Gregor tilts his head.

"Yeah, fine, we get pissy from time to time," Dave admits. "But that's the *job*. If you can't hack it, you get tossed. Hey, you might get to find out for yourself soon. Skipper pegged you to take her place when she goes."

"Don't remind me."

Dave grins then glances at Gregor's thick arms, noticing the dark pink scars on the inside of his elbow.

"You still keeping up with Thompson's training?"

The Russian nods.

"They do that to you? What do they call it...?"

"Reinforcement."

"Yeah, that's it. Is that why you're stitched like a baseball below the elbow?"

"Yup. Vinh busted this one," Gregor says, raising his left arm. "Birgitte did this one." He lifts the right arm.

"Did it hurt?" Dave asks.

"What do you think? *Yeah*, it hurt! MedTechs had me sewn up in minutes, though. Seriously. One minute I'm looking at my arms bent the wrong way, thinking I'm a fucking idiot for signing up. The next, I'm letting Vinh and Birgitte try to do it all over again, only they can't. Joint's are better than before." Gregor shakes his head as if he is still wrestling with the concept. "The MedTechs, they just...*fix* you. It's wild."

"Jesus, why do they make you go through that? And for Vinh and Birgitte, having to hurt friends...it's barbaric."

"It's part of the process," Gregor says. "Now that I'm in it, I get it. There's reason."

"What, to turn you all into killer icemen?"

"No, no..." Gregor looks down at the table for a moment, deep in thought. When he looks up, the Russian's face has a heaviness that pulls at the corners of his mouth. "What it takes to survive when you have *nothing*, Dave...the things you have to *do*, the things you have to *become*... I'm starting to understand."

"Well don't get all morose on me," Dave says, attacking the slab of protein and gravy on his tray. "This war's gonna end. Everyone says so."

"I have no doubt that it will."

Ortega lifts his head from prayer and looks down at his tray. He takes a utensil like a toothed spade from the tray and digs it into his heap of mash. With his other hand, he opens the leather bound book to a marked page and reads silently.

*Ye have heard it said, 'Thou shalt love thy neighbor
and hate thine enemy.' But I say unto you, 'Love your
enemies, bless them that curse you, do good to them that
hate you, and pray for them which despitefully use you, and
persecute you; that ye may be the children of your Father
which is in Heaven.' For he maketh the sun to rise on the
evil and on the good, and sendeth rain on the just and on the
unjust.*

"Mr. Ortega?"

Javier looks up from his book at a silver haired man and woman,
surprised that anyone would be speaking to him. "Hello," he says to the two.

The man and woman look at one another, unsure, then take each
other's hand. The woman asks, "Do you mind if we sit here?"

"Of course not! Please, make yourselves comfortable." Ortega
gestures to the ample free seating. Just as he is about to go back to his book,
the woman adds,

"It's been so hard to figure out what's going on these days. No one
seems to have any real answers."

Ortega nods. "I know what you mean. The thought of ending this
journey, it's exciting...and terrifying."

"Oh, we've been just *sick* with worry," she blurts out. Regaining her
composure, she adds, "I can't sleep without nightmares anymore." The man
puts an arm around his wife, comforting her.

"Every time we have a work shift together," the man says, "I don't
know...we can't help but notice how you're weathering all this, like you
know somehow everything's gonna be all right. Neither of us can remember
what it was like to feel that way."

"We're so tired of it, of being scared all the time," the woman says.
"Every time we see you here, the way you pray, you look so content...and,
well...we wonder what that's like."

"We didn't come over before because we didn't want to disturb you,"
the man says. "But we were hoping that maybe...maybe you could let us in
on your secret?"

Ortega's eyes widen in surprise. "I am no priest. I do not think I'm
qualified to guide anyone, one way or other."

"We aren't looking for a priest," the lady says, and on the verge
of tears, she adds, "we just...we're trying to get through each day. All the
uncertainty... Most of the others are handling it well enough, but...I don't
know if I can take it anymore."

Ortega thinks very carefully before speaking. "If you're asking what gets me through, it's no secret. My faith carries me."

"Faith? In whom?"

"In a benevolent God who loves us."

"Who *loves* us?" the man asks in astonishment. "Mr. Ortega, I have a hard time seeing everything that's happened has been because of *love*."

Ortega nods somberly. "I understand what you mean. This has not been a good journey for us." He places a hand on his book. "There's a story in here of a time the world was destroyed by a great flood because all the nations of man were wicked. Only a few were spared, so that after the waters fell, the world could begin again. These few, if you think about it, had it tougher than the many who were drowned, because they had to endure. They had to *survive*. And they did, and the world was reborn."

"You're talking about Noah, right? You believe that all really happened?"

"I don't have to believe it *literally* to understand the message. What I mean is that to the people in the ark, being tossed in the storm, it must have seemed to them that God was cruel for cruelty's sake. When in reality, they were loved so much that they were spared above all others. And there are many stories in this book like that. If I stopped to ask if such stories could really happen, I miss the point."

"Like how Adam and Eve populated the world when they had three sons."

Ortega laughs. "Yes, *exactly*! Besides, I think Genesis is the origin of the tribe of *Israel* not of the whole world. But I'm no scholar."

"Is there anything in there about how to cope with the *end of civilization* on a day to day basis?" the man asks dryly.

Ortega mulls the question, recognizing just how big an introduction he is trying to make. He looks down at the leather bound book on the table beside him and slides it across the table to them, saying, "Book of Luke, Chapter twelve, verses twenty-two through thirty-four. First, lay aside skepticism so you can understand the message. The method of telling is very old and will seem strange. Look for the *meaning*. If you are earnest, you will find it. Then you decide for yourselves what you wish to believe, yes?"

The woman takes hold of the thick book, turning it over, admiring the fact that such a thing still exists. She contemplates the gold cross on the front then opens to the table of contents.

"Book of Luke, you said?"

"Yes, it's toward the back. Here, I'll show you."

Ortega flips easily to the passage and points to it.

"Uh, this is in Spanish," she says.

OF MORTAL CREATURES

Ortega laughs at himself, saying, "Of course! I'm sorry, I'll translate."

He rotates the book toward himself and reads aloud, "Then Jesus said to his disciples: 'Therefore I tell you, do not worry about your life, what you will eat; or about your body, what you will wear. For life is more than food, and the body more than clothes. Consider the ravens: They do not sow or reap, they have no storeroom or barn; yet God feeds them. And how much more valuable you are than birds! Who of you by worrying can add a single hour to your life? Since you cannot do this very little thing, why do you worry about the rest?

'Consider how the wild flowers grow. They do not labor or spin. Yet I tell you, not even Solomon in all his splendor was dressed like one of these. If that is how God clothes the grass of the field, which is here today, and tomorrow is thrown into the fire, how much more will he clothe you—you of little faith! And do not set your heart on what you will eat or drink; do not worry about it. For the pagan world runs after all such things, and your Father knows that you need them. But seek his kingdom, and these things will be given to you as well.

'Do not be afraid, little flock, for your Father has been pleased to give you the kingdom. Sell your possessions and give to the poor. Provide purses for yourselves that will not wear out, a treasure in heaven that will never fail, where no thief comes near and no moth destroys. For where your treasure is, there your heart will be also.'"

"'For where your treasure is, there your heart will be also,'" the lady echoes. With an involuntary sniff, she adds, "It's beautiful."

Ortega nods in agreement. "It's one of my favorite passages. Where do you keep your treasure, hmm? This question tells us why we worry in life."

"My treasure is right here," the man says, looking at his lady.

"Yes, I see," Ortega replies sincerely. "Your love is true. You have faith in her, yes?"

"Absolutely."

"When served well, love grows, as you know. The same way that the love you share is greater than the two of you alone, I know in my heart that there is more to this existence than what I can see and touch. No one knows what to call it, despite the thousands of names: Yehu, Jehova, Allah, Sila, Great Spirit...but I feel it instinctively...a connection to something greater than myself. It is a wonderful mystery, one I am forever drawn to. And my faith in that mystery is what sustains me every day of my life."

The man and the woman look at one another, conversing silently with glances and head nods. Both turn to Ortega. "We've never been to church," the man says.

"Ha! That is a *good* thing! Church, too often, gets in the way of a spiritual experience. But before anything else, I must tell you this: Do not look to me for your answers. Those, you must find in *yourselves*. And faith is not something I can give to you. It must spring from inside you, nowhere else. If you have questions, I can show you in this book what answers it holds. Other than that, I don't think I'm of much use to you."

With a deep breath, the lady says, "Mr. Ortega, you've already been more help than you know. Can you show us how to pray, like you do?"

Ortega shrugs. "That's very easy, in fact. Give me your hands." He bows his head, and they do likewise. "You do not have to speak the words out loud for them to be heard. There is a question in your hearts. Ask it *plainly*. If you are scared, tell Him. Let Him know your heart and your mind. Do not hide yourself. And the words will come easier than you think."

The man and woman grip his hands firmly and the three sit in comfortable silence. Soon, Ortega can feel her shoulders bouncing. He looks up at her and sees tears streaming down her bowed face, her lips forming words she has needed to share.

Moved by her pouring of emotion, he bows his head, thinking, *With such sincerity, surely her prayer will be answered.*

Dave turns back toward his tray, no longer interested in Ortega's new prayer circle.

"Well, *Koom-bai-fuckin'-yah*," he mutters.

Gregor does not reply. He continues watching Ortega, his sudden loss of appetite warning him he has just witnessed something of phenomenal importance. But for good or ill, he cannot tell.

BLACK DOVE

A bunkside panel lights up with red numerals and beeps in irritating tones. Maiella's hand flies up and punches it, silencing it for good.

Her eyelids scrape across dry eyeballs. Her swollen tongue barely fits in her mouth, and her head throbs. She brings a hand up to her forehead then rolls over to bury her face in her pillow, bumping against Thompson in the bunk beside her.

"Not again," he mumbles, still half-asleep, "you're gonna break it."

She laughs and pats his chest. "Get up, Gun. Big day today."

"Hmmf?" Thompson sits starkly upright, then his eyes cross and he flops back down onto the bunk. "I think I've been poisoned."

"You and me both." Maiella swings her legs off the bunk and sits at the edge of it. "Whatever Dave was passing around at the soirée last night, could probably strip the stain off ceramics."

Thompson grabs his face with both hands. "Why do they *do this* to themselves?"

"Was a nice party at first..."

Thompson rubs his face then turns onto his side, facing her. "The after-party was better."

Maiella looks down at him with a contented smile. "Yeah, it was." She stands with a series of pops from her hips and knees, groans, then stretches, yawns, and shuffles to the hygiene station. Not bothering with a cup, she puts her head down to the stream of flowing water and slurps.

"Can you bring me some?" he asks.

"Nope," she says, wiping her mouth with the back of her hand. "Get up. Get moving. We fly out in two hours." Maiella plucks a dental appliance from the wall holder and scrubs her teeth with it.

Thompson crawls his way out from between the covers, slides onto the floor, then lowers himself face first. With a mighty groan, he strains to complete one push up.

"And that's enough of that," he says climbing to his feet. Once standing, he looks around the narrow confines of the cabin. Nothing remains in its proper place. Clothes are strewn all over, and not just the ones they were wearing last night. The wardrobe is toppled, spilling uniform jackets, trousers, coveralls, t-shirts, and footwear across the floor. A lone chair lies on its side, one leg jutting at an oblique angle to the rest. And the spare bunk has collapsed in its middle, the frame broken completely in half.

Thompson grips his stubbly chin, trying to knit together fragments of memory.

Maiella shoving him into a chair and swooping astride him...

The scritch, scritch, scritch of the chair's feet against the metal floor until its rear left leg bent aside, toppling them...

Pinning her against the side of the wardrobe, driving himself into her...

The wardrobe's doors swinging wildly, banging open and shut until the frame failed and it keeled over...

Creaking of the spare bunk, a brash metronome to their manic rhythm...

Screech of metal fatigue as it split in two and dumped them both onto the floor again...

Maiella, propping herself on her hands, head thrown back in a fit of guilty laughter...

Her predatory eyes, wild and bright, as she approached on all fours...

Thompson takes hold of the wardrobe and hauls it upright. It slouches to one side, no longer square. The doors refuse to close and hang open on twisted hinges.

Maiella spies him in the hygiene station mirror. "Colonist furniture is for shit," she says.

"We *could* take it a little easier," he replies.

She glances over her shoulder, toothbrush in hand, foam at the corners of her mouth. She looks him up and down.

"*Nah.*"

*****

Munro tours the limousine one last time. He begins at the flight deck, working through the interfaces and controls, then peeks into junction boxes, inspects every breaker panel, raps his knuckles against support braces, all while thumbing through diagnostics on his labset. Every test shows green bars. That does not deter him from performing a second inspection, however.

The general must see that attention to detail has not slipped in his absence. Everything must be precise. Accurate. Perfect.

Gregor steps up the ramp with a large crate in his arms. He looks around for a place to set it down when Munro intercepts him.

"What's this?" the colonel demands. "Provisioning completed twelve hours ago."

Gregor swishes his mouth. "Mission Essential."

Munro looks through his eyebrows, dubious. "If that were the case, I'm *sure* I'd know about it." The big man opens the top of the crate and peeks in. With a cynical snort, he reaches for a long bottle with a slender neck capped with black wax and pulls it out. Rotating the bottle in his large hand, he looks down at a label with unrecognizable fruit captioned by alien script.

"We took all of these out of here. Insufficiently nutritious for their weight. And mildly toxic."

Gregor rolls his eyes. "It's a long flight, Colonel. You'll be glad to have it, trust me."

"We're counting *grams*," he says. "Take it back."

Gregor stands his ground. "You know I'm being commissioned as *Europa's* CO today, *right?*"

"Yes. But Captain Jones is in command, *right now*. That crate is not essential to the mission unless the *Europa's* Commanding Officer deems it so. Therefore, as I am responsible for pre-flight readiness," he adds, tucking the bottle back into the crate, "you may take that back from where it came."

"You don't have to be such a..." Gregor begins then he shakes his head. "Never mind. More for us, then." He heads back toward the ramp then calls back, "You done here, Colonel? Ceremony is in ten minutes, but there are some things Skipper wants to go over before it starts."

"Now?"

"Yeah, unless you're late completing your inspections. We can delay the ceremony if you need more time."

Munro's mouth forms a straight line across his wide face. Striding toward the ramp and hanging his labset on his belt, he says, "I'm ready."

The two men march down the ramp of the limousine. At the bottom, Gregor calls to his friend Dave, who trots over and walks beside them.

Gregor hands off the crate to Dave and asks, "Can you see this is taken back to its *proper* place?"

Dave smiles and winks. "Sure can, boss."

Gregor and Munro continue on to the edge of the small bay where a crowd of Colonists is already gathering. Sharon is at the center, speaking to the Counselor and Shondre.

Dave allows Gregor and Munro to walk ahead. Once they are out of earshot he turns and runs with the crate up the limousine's ramp.

Sharon perks up at the sight of Gregor and Munro, breaking off her conversation with Shondre and the Counselor. She waves the men closer, and they make their way through the thickening crowd.

"Colonel," Sharon asks, "how is our vessel?"

"G-B-R-F-S, Captain," Munro answers.

"Beg your pardon?"

"Green bars, ready for stars."

"Ah. That's good, I presume. All right. Are we clear on what we're going to say?"

Shondre nods her head, as do Gregor and the Counselor.

"Good. Can't say I'm looking forward to this, but I don't want to draw it out, either."

Thompson and Maiella march through the entrance together, clad up to the neck in their old armor, helmets cradled in left arms. A collective cheer rises from the crowd, and the two ex-operators slow abruptly, eyebrows lifted in surprise. They make their way to the center of the gathering, absorbing the mood, shaking hands and clapping shoulders along the way.

Sharon tilts her head at them. "You're going like *this*, are you?"

Thompson looks down at himself, then looks at Sharon, his eyebrows bunched together. "Yes, *of course.*"

"They act as pressure suits as well as armor," Munro explains. "Very useful if we need to access the hull of the ship while we're underway, or if there's a fire onboard, or if our modifications cause an explosion, they can survive where unprotected personnel would char to—"

"Mmm, *thank you*, Colonel," Sharon interrupts, raising a hand. "I feel much safer now."

Munro nods, taking Sharon's thanks as genuine.

"They also convey an important non-verbal message," the Counselor adds, "that we are not negotiating from a position of weakness."

Sharon glances at the tall, placid Eleto beside her. "You think this is the way?"

Shondre blinks slowly and nods.

"Well. Let's get this show going, yeah? I'll start." Sharon parks two fingers in her mouth and blows a piercing whistle. "Everyone, *your attention!*"

Dozens of conversations in the crowd roll off and individuals turn attention toward the *Europa's* captain.

"Thank you all for coming and I'm sorry we couldn't fit everyone. Those who are watching by video, know that you're with us every bit as much as if you were standing right here.

"It has been my pleasure to serve as your captain, however briefly. Now a greater duty is at hand. I leave to serve it. These fine lads and lasses with me I'm fortunate to have along for the trip. But let me be plain: we all got here *together*. If we'd let ourselves come apart or if we'd given up... we wouldn't have made it. Don't *ever* forget that, and take pride in your contributions."

Sharon looks to her side and asks, "Counselor, will you do the honors?"

The Counselor steps forward and reaches toward both Sharon and Gregor drawing them near so they face one another. With a clear and loud voice, he proclaims, "As arbiter aboard this ship, it is my duty and privilege to oversee the Change of Command for Soshiba Varicorp Colony Vessel, *Europa*. The crew has decided, by fair and honest election, that Lieutenant Commander Gregor Petrova shall succeed Captain Sharon Jones as Commanding Officer. *Let it be so enacted.*"

Gregor stands at attention, the broadened muscles of his chest and shoulders straining his uniform seams. "Counselor," he says, "I request permission to relieve Ms. Jones as Commanding Officer of Colony Vessel, *Europa*."

"Permission is granted," the Counselor says.

Gregor faces Sharon. His chest is out, shoulders square. His lips tighten, his eyes narrow as the gravity of responsibility sinks into him.

How you've grown, Sharon thinks.

344

"I relieve you, ma'am," the Russian says to her.

"I stand relieved," she answers.

"Counselor, I have properly relieved Ms. Jones as Commanding Officer of Colony Vessel, *Europa*."

"Very well," the Counselor says solemnly. Then, with delight, he announces, "Ladies and gentlemen, please allow me to introduce *Europa's* new Commanding Officer, *Captain Gregor Petrova!*"

The crowd erupts with applause and cheers.

Sharon and Gregor salute one another then embrace as dear friends.

"You can have this right back when you return," he says into her ear.

"*If*, Gregor," she says, "*if* we return."

"I won't sit in your chair. I'm taking it out of the bridge."

"*Please*. It's not a throne, you know. And there are no guarantees, here, so settle into the role. It's yours now. They'll be looking to you from here on."

Gregor peels away, maintaining his dignity. "Understood."

He turns to the crowd and raises his arms high. The cheers roll off quickly.

"Thompson," Gregor says, turning to his left, "you have something you want to say to these people?"

Thompson stands beside Gregor, looking out over faces he has known and worked with for years. His voice projects throughout the cramped bay.

"I don't need to remind anyone of the hardships we've faced. You've all seen them firsthand. Living together has not been easy.

"We don't always understand why we do things the way we do. It has taken me years to realize that this is a *completely natural* state of affairs. We don't have to agree all the time.

"Many of you still fear O'Kai and his Operators. Yes, they're dangerous...and that's our *strength*. They alone defend you and keep you free. They'll go to their deaths doing so.

"Some have said we should offer the Operator Corps as a sacrifice for peace, but they *must* be included in our future. While they are rigid and disciplined, they are not immune to change. If anyone doubts this, remember that Maiella and I were once Operators. We were no different then. We've done irreparable harm, yet you found it in yourselves to forgive us and take us into your company. Please keep your hearts and minds open for those who have done you *no* harm.

"Thank you for coming to see us off. It means more to us than you know."

The crowd swells again with cheers.

"Colonel Munro," Thompson says, "would you like to say a few words?"

Munro clears his throat and steps to the fore. With booming voice, he announces, "Lieutenant Obet is hereby promoted to Captain and will oversee BioMedical activities. Lieutenant Arjay is hereby promoted to Captain, and will oversee Manufacturing, Maintenance, and Physical Research activities. Captain Erik will oversee all Cadre Operations aboard *Europa* in addition to his duties as Quartermaster until I return, unless another Officer of the Leadership Council assumes command. Erik, obey Captain Petrova's orders as if they were mine, so long as those orders conform to the Cadre code of ethics."

Speech complete, Munro takes a half-step back and clasps hands behind his back. The crowd stares until a lone set of hands starts clapping near the entrance. A few take up the applause, but it fizzles like fire in wet grass.

"Shondre," the Counselor asks, "would you like to say anything?"

At first, Shondre swings her head to decline, but then she speaks in her own language to the Counselor. He nods, and then translates to the crowd,

"I am now speaking for our guest, Shondre: It has been this one's dream to heal the wounds of our peoples and to ease the fear that surrounds us all. This one has seen how you live, and it hurts deepest that you have been denied what rightfully belongs to you. Please believe that my people need an end to this conflict every bit as much as you do. This one pledges to give up life if it means injustices of our past can be corrected. Thank you for hearing these words."

Shondre bows, and a slow clap begins, growing louder with each moment, building momentum. Rather than trailing off the applause continues, sustained with high energy. Whistles pierce the air over the crowd like audible exclamation points. Many jump up and down in excitement, others cry joyful tears.

Moved by the show of emotion around her, Shondre walks out into the crowd, letting hands touch her tunic, the bare skin of her arms, and neck. She reaches out to them, as well, feeling hands calloused by hard work, feeling stiff collars of coveralls and the warmth of the people beneath.

Maiella leans over to the Counselor and asks, "What's she doing?"

The Counselor smiles. "Closing the gap. Letting them see that she's real. Just a person like the rest of us."

Maiella smiles at the thought, then tugs Thompson out into the crowd with her. The former Operators are jostled by hands reaching out to them, slapping them on the back and shoulders, pulling them into hugs.

Sharon watches them mingle, wishing she could be out there herself if time would allow it. But every second of delay is like a peck from an impatient crow on her shoulder. She puts fingers to her mouth and blows another whistle. With arms raised high, she calls out, *"Your attention, everyone!"*

Shushing sounds pass throughout the crowd until all eyes are on her.

"It's hard to leave, but we must. And the sooner we go, the better. One last thing: if we fail, this *cannot* be our last attempt. You must try again, yeah?"

Sharon looks into every Colonist face to be sure the message landed. "All right, let's get to it."

The crowd parts, opening a clear path to the ship's ramp. At the bottom of the ramp stand Alexei, Ulrikka, Azhar, Vinh, and Birgitte. Gregor jogs ahead to stand with them and they form two even lines on each side. Gregor and his fighters all swing a flat hand up to their brows. Their lean arms are thick with new muscle and scars, hair is trimmed close to the scalp.

Sharon strides toward them, Shondre at her shoulder, followed by Munro, Thompson, and Maiella.

Gregor shouts at the top of his lungs, "THREE CHEERS FOR SKIPPER JONES!"

The crowd thunders, *"HOO-RAHH! HOO-RAHH! HOO-RAHH!"*

Shondre passes between the muscular warriors guarding the ramp, masking her unease. As she moves up the ramp, her skin warms from seeing something familiar, something hers. Despite its new exterior of Cadre black, this is undeniably her personal transport.

A comfortable journey with tastes, smells, and sounds of home are only a few steps away... How this one dreamed of these things in her cold stone cell!

At the top of the ramp, however, she looks in and finds bare metal in all directions. The plush couches are gone. The soft carpeting, the taps for refreshment, the priceless artwork from her private collection, have all been stripped clear. In their place, ugly conduits run across the walls and ceiling to bulky junction boxes. And the soft lighting scheme, so pleasing to the eyes, has been replaced by canned lamps in the ceiling that throw a dull red glow onto the metal plated floor.

This CANNOT be right...

She hurries through to the cabins in the back, and when she opens the doors, she finds the rooms are crammed with crates to the ceiling.

No, no, no, this cannot be!

She rushes to the end of the hallway and opens the door to the restroom. A stainless steel toilet, made for humans, occupies the narrowed walls.

Shondre grabs the sides of her face. Dignity annihilated by so much disappointment, she storms back to the main lounge, singles out Munro, and demands while pointing down at bare metal,

"Hyoo *ROO*-IN [this place]! Kree-ayt priz-uhn, uh-gain! *Hwair sleep uss*, [on the floor]?"

Unruffled, Munro moves to the wall and taps a panel. Suspended metal chairs unfold from the ceiling, each one custom formed to the person for whom it was made.

Shondre looks skeptically at the shiny steel, thinking it sterile and cold, more fit for torture than rest.

Sharon eyes hers, as well, then looks around at the joyless decor. "I have to agree, Munro. This is pretty depressing. Looks like the Inquisition's making a comeback." Nevertheless, she slides into the smallest chair, mouth screwed up with anticipation of a long and miserable flight. Then, a look of confused approval crosses her face.

"My, my," Sharon says. "At first glance, thought I'd come to see an evil gynecologist. But this is a little piece of all right..."

Shondre glares at Munro and finds the big man staring at her as if she was a moody toddler. He gestures toward her chair, urging her into it.

The Eleto takes a tentative step closer, hands clutching her tunic close to ward off the chill the chair inspires. She gives it a sniff, expecting oil or antiseptic, but it has no odor at all. Unlike the other chairs, which are reclined, hers is pitched forward, shaped to her chin, chest, belly, arms, and legs. At the joints, there is subtle padding.

In the old days, this one would have refused, ordered it removed on the spot, and the person who authorized it reassigned. But these are strange new times...

Shondre settles onto the cupped metal and discovers it is remarkably comfortable. The padding is in just the right spots, and the molded plates conform to her shape like a bra. The metal is not cold at all, slightly warmer than the surrounding room, in fact. The slightest purr escapes her.

Munro steps over and points to a lever like a hand brake. Shondre looks at it as Munro's smaller hand clamps around it.

"When engaged," Munro says, grasping the chair with his larger hand, "it keeps the chair in a rigid position." He rattles the chair to demonstrate its solidity. "But when released, the chair floats, achieving a level balance for sleeping." Munro disengages the handbrake and the chair rotates to a level position, floating naturally. "The occupant can engage the brake again for stability, or leave it floating to damp subtle motions of the ship."

Shondre looks over at the Counselor and points to her ear. The Counselor repeats Munro's explanation in her language. In response, she asks the Counselor a question.

"She wants to know how you knew what would be comfortable for her," the Counselor translates.

Munro folds his arms. "We look at the position a body at rest takes in zero gravity, or when immersed in liquid. From there, we took detailed measurements to assure fit. Doctor Taggart filled in the rest of the biometrics."

Shondre stretches out and really settles in. Her purrs double.

Thompson and Maiella eyeball theirs, noticing how they are separated on either side of the room.

"Well," Maiella says, "I'll be on the flight deck." To Thompson, she asks, "Join me?"

Thompson nods and follows.

Thompson takes a step up a short hallway that leads to a set of low stairs and the flight deck beyond. He stops, memories returning in flashes:

> *Smears of grime as he slid along the clean white walls...*
> *Thick carpets stained with soot and bloody boot tracks...*
> *Beckert's blind red stare from the flight deck as Argo labored to keep the Geek alive...*

Maiella crests the low stairs and looks back. "What's up?" she asks.

"I hate this place," he says with a gaze that looks right through her. "Where you're standing now...that's where I died."

She looks down at the floor then saunters over to him. "Well, you're pretty quick for a dead man." Sliding her arm around his, she adds, "C'mon, keep me company."

She leads him up into the low cockpit and flops down into the pilot's seat. Thompson takes the co-pilot's seat and wedges his helmet into the gap between windscreen and dashboard.

"Really?" Maiella asks. "You have to put it *right there?*"

He looks around himself, finding only a thin gap between his seat and the surrounding walls. "Where else would I put it?"

"Oh, I don't know, your *head* maybe?" Maiella drops her helmet over her head and lifts the faceplate. "*Europa*, this is *Black Dove*, beginning pre-flight. Over."

"*Roger that,* Black Dove."

"*Black Dove?*" Thompson asks with disdain.

Maiella shrugs with her palms up then pulls a lanyard from her helmet. When she plugs it into the console, her goggles strobe twice.

"Interface achieved, bringing systems on-line... Pre-flight check complete, green bars, ready for stars. Requesting clearance for departure, over."

"*Stand by,* Black Dove. *Bay is still occupied.*"

"What?" Maiella says. She sits up, peering through the windscreen to see beyond the nose of the vessel. "Oh, Thompson, you *have* to see this."

Thompson perks up and takes his helmet down from the dash. In the bay, in front of the ship, Colonists and MedTechs have unfurled a large banner. In broad calligraphic strokes, it reads,

GO FIND US A NICE PLANET TO LIVE ON.

"Hmmf," Thompson says with a smirk, "no pressure there."

Sahara, Ortega, and Herzfeld step around the sides of the banner, waving, kissing their hands, and sweeping them out toward the ship. Sahara fiddles with a device in both hands then points it at herself.

"Incoming transmission," Maiella announces through the ship's intercom. A video feed opens on the console display of what looks like a woman's nose close up. When the view pulls back, Sahara's face fills the screen, and she grins.

"If you all thought you were getting out of here without saying good bye to me, you're *sadly* mistaken. I'm just sorry I cannae go with you. But both our surgeons on the same trip is a no-go, right?" She sighs. "I'm gonna miss ye. Even *you* Munro, you big dry shite. Sense of humor like an old dead stump, but when it comes to medicine, you're *bleeding fantastic*.

"Thompson, don't think 'cause I fixed you once that you can foul up all my good work, yeh? Take care, boyo.

"And Maiella, you keep your eye on him. Course, after that ruckus last night, I think we all know you two won't be far from each other's sight. Like teenagers in a seedy motel, I tell ye.

"Counselor, it's gonna be right murder here without you. We'll slip notes under your door, and you can resolve all our arguments when you get back. Wouldn't want you to feel like we were getting on without you, and all.

"Sharon..." Sahara turns suddenly serious, to the point of melancholy. "I've never laughed so much as when I'm sharing a pint with you. Was hard watching you nip off to Cadre Two, but you're lucky as a banister in a college for girls. I'll brew us up a nice batch, don't you worry, and we'll laugh ourselves feral again.

"Lastly, Shondre... Can't tell you how glad I am to've met you. You must be a great person among your kind. We'd still be out here, plodding along, and nothing would have ever changed for us. At least, not for the better. You've got a lot on your shoulders, sure, but you're among good friends. We know you all can hack it. Be well, and think of us along the way. We'll certainly be thinking of you.

"Right. See here now, if you're waiting for me to get all teary-eyed, you can forget it. Fly fast, be brilliant, and *come home*. That's a good plan. So *stick* to it."

A rumble from deep within the ship rises to a steady whine.

"*Europa*, main drives warming to operating temperature," Maiella radios.

"*Confirmed*, Black Dove."

"And that's our cue," Sahara says into the camera. The view swings from her face over to Herzfeld, who smiles and waves, then over to Ortega. The Spaniard says into the camera, "'Blessed are the peacemakers...' Vaya con Dios, mis Amigos."

The camera turns onto the crowd and they shout, jump and cheer like fans at a sold-out concert. When it swings back to Sahara, she wears a great big grin. Shouting over the din of cheers behind her, she says, "*Go on*, now, *get your arses outta here!*"

Her lips smother the lens in a big wet kiss, and the video feed ends.

Munro slides his bulk into the largest suspended recliner, tools of his belt clanking against the bare metal. With minimal adjustments, he settles in then pulls his labset from his waist. Compulsively, he checks ship metrics, watching for abnormality or surges.

"*Hold tight*," Maiella says via intercom, "*we've been cleared for departure*."

The ship's engines rise in pitch, and the craft smoothly rises from the deck then backs out through the bay doors. Munro clips his labset to his waist and clamps his hands around the rails of his recliner.

Sharon looks over at him, noticing a fine mist of sweat on his forehead, a locked-forward gaze, knotted jaw muscles, and a white-knuckle grip.

"How you doin'?" Sharon asks.

"*Fine*," the big man says through clenched teeth.

Sharon smiles to herself, recalling her trip out on the *Enyo* to Cadre Two. She reaches into the neckline of her uniform and pulls out her fire opal pendant, giving it a good-luck rub.

"I was scared bloodless when I left with Shao-Lo for Cadre Two. The whole time, I was thinking, I'm not a fighter, why am I even going?"

Munro glances over at her then resumes his forward stare. "I've never been on a rotation before."

"We're not going to fight anyone where we're headed. And if we were, I'm pretty sure those two up front would be able to handle it."

Munro shakes his head in little jerks. "That's not the reason I'm anxious. I've never been away from my MedTechs. I'm...I'm not going to be where they need me. Away from them in a time of crisis, it's..."

"Colonel, this is *precisely* where you're needed right now." Sharon reaches a hand over to him. Munro looks at it first then he unclamps his big right hand from the rail. He takes her hand with a gentle grasp.

"I must admit," he adds, "I've often wondered what it would be like to travel the way Operators do."

"I assure you," Sharon says, looking forward, "it's *overrated*."

The transport thrusts away from the massive Colony Vessel. Through a narrow side viewport, Munro gazes out at infinite sky. His jaw drops.

"You okay?" Sharon asks.

Munro closes his mouth, and swallows hard. "I've seen space before... Short hops between Cadre One and the *Europa*...but that's all. When I look out...it makes me realize the distances...how far away we'll be from... *anything*."

Sharon nods. "It's a head trip, for sure." She looks over her shoulder. "How 'bout you, Counselor? You hanging in there?"

The Counselor sits calmly in his recliner, pressing his fingertips together. "It's an odd thing...in twelve hundred years, I've never been away from the *Europa*. I think I understand what you mean, Colonel."

"Uh, oh," Sharon quips, "looks like this one's already getting the space madness."

The Counselor grins. "Not to worry. I have plenty of *other* things to think about along the way."

"And you, Shondre?" Sharon asks. "What are you feeling right now?"

Shondre opens her eyes and lifts her chin from the form-fitting cradle. "*Joy*," she says clearly, the word etched into every feature of her face.

"*Course to Cadre One plotted and locked in,*" Maiella announces via intercom. "*Deep Space Drives engage in three...two...one...mark.*"

The cabin air fizzes with energy, sparks dance at the corners of the metal recliners, and the vessel plunges through time and space.

To be Continued in the series Conclusion

Plasma Rain

For news and updates on new titles, log on to

www.CadreOnePublishing.com

APPENDIX: MUNRO COMPLIES

The command is not difficult to understand or to comprehend. But as Munro stands in the Incubation chamber with its subtle ambient red projection and gentle lub-dub, he finds the order is nearly impossible to execute.

He raises his hands and presses the palms against the smooth cylinder in front of him. A well-developed fetus floats inside, anchored to the roof of the tank by a curly umbilical. Tiny hands with all the digits hold the cord where it connects to its round belly. Symmetrical legs, held against the body, twitch in minute kicks. Dark spots suggest healthy eyes forming in a properly shaped head.

"No defects," Munro says.

Obet, the only other person in the Incubation room besides Munro, looks on silently.

"The first generation without a single trace of Gonadal Dysgenesis, Mucoviscidosis, Trisomy 21, Achondroplasia, or Sphingolipidoses," the colonel continues. "By my most conservative analysis, sixty-eight percent are Operator grade."

Munro pushes back from the plexisteel tank, and he turns a full circle. Surrounding him are identical tanks, incubating the Cadre's future.

"These are our healthiest, most viable children, *ever*. After all we've endured, *don't we deserve them*?" Munro turns toward Obet. The MedTech tries to level his crooked shoulders, but he cannot meet the colonel's intense gaze.

"I think we do, sir," Obet says.

Munro looks back at his gently churning tanks, face contorted in awful conflict. "It had to be now, didn't it? Couldn't have given us two months, *could they*? They had to come *now* with their *spying eyes*." Munro's teeth grind, and the corners of his mouth sink to a wide frown. He props himself against the tank again, peering in at the tiny life form suspended inside. His features drain of expression, his voice turns sterile.

"Obet, drain the tanks."

Obet blinks hard and swallows. "Aye, sir." The MedTech steps outside the chamber to a console just beyond the door. "Terminating generation eight-zero-nine-echo."

Sharp metal blades sweep across the top of the tanks, severing synthetic placentas. The fetuses sink, trailing their cords and a swirling cloud of red. The bottom of each tank opens and the entire contents are swept away to recycling. Curtains of sterilizing fluid run down the inner surfaces, then a rubber ring swipes the walls clear.

Munro's breathing deepens through flared nostrils. He pushes off the tank and marches out of the chamber.

"Prep for viral batch," he growls, hauling the chamber door shut and locking it.

"Aye, sir."

The big man steps to the console beside Obet and he pounds his credentials into it. A holowindow opens for the colonel showing a high view of the incubation chamber. Inside each tank, a thin spinning rod sweeps the interior with a wide, cleansing beam.

"Is Jin-Sung's process loaded?" Munro demands.

"Yes, sir. Program loaded and ready."

"And the cultures from the captive?"

"Plaques have formed in all cultures. Virus is active and ready for incubation."

Munro stabs the keys at his terminal. "Filling tanks with solution." He looks over his shoulder at piles of artillery shells stacked behind him. The warhead has been removed from each, and replaced with a penetrating tip. Triple holes are drilled into each, awaiting viral load.

"Will we be able to fill them all?" Obet asks.

With a sinister scowl, Munro answers, "And then some. This war is going to end, Obet. One way or the other, this war is going to end."

APPENDIX:
ORTEGA EXPLAINS HIS FAITH

(Ortega makes comments about God or Jesus several times around Thompson. Finally, the Gun asks what it's all about.)

"I'm a bad Catholic," Ortega explains. "I cherish my faith, but I don't require others to share it."

"How does that make you bad?"

Ortega smiles. "That's an even longer conversation."

"So what *is* faith?"

"It starts with a mystery, the greatest of all mysteries: death. As much as we know about life and science, our understanding of *afterlife* can never be certain."

"What's there to know? Our bodies fail. We are no more."

"How do you know, Thompson? Consider all of the knowledge you accumulate in a lifetime. The experience, sensations, memories... Where does that all go? To some great information sink? Some Black Hole? Where?"

"It's just data. And data is erased at death, like deleting files."

"So you say. But you can't prove it, can you?"

"No. But there's no proof to suggest otherwise."

"That's called a knowledge gap. Can't be proved one way or other."

"But what makes you think there is life after death? It's counter intuitive by *definition*. Death is the end of life."

"And life arises from death. The star that dies as a supernova seeds the cosmos with heavy elements." He extends a hand toward the Operator. "The atoms in your body, your living body, were forged in the hearts of dying stars. Is that *not* life from death?"

"Yes, there is a life *cycle*. Birth, growth, maturity, decline, death, renewal… That's on a cosmic scale. What happens on an individual level is completely different. A supernova star does not live again, not like it was."

"Ah, not like it was. That's right. It could become a pulsar, a magnetar, a quark star, a black hole… any number of exotic things."

"But they're only stellar corpses, slowly decaying, losing energy. You speak of immortality. 'Life everlasting.' It's foolish."

"Is it? Human civilization has believed in it for thousands of years. Most are told when they are young. Many come to believe it intuitively, regardless of background."

"Foolish."

"Foolish? Then what is your Cadre Memorial all about?"

The operator blinks.

"Is that *not* a kind of immortality?" Ortega poses.

"I don't understand."

"Who's to say what makes one immortal, but if someone remains alive in your thoughts and memories, are they truly dead?"

"Hold on. That's just data relayed from one generation to the next."

"Why is it important to pass that on?"

"Because their accomplishments allowed us to survive. We remember their feats and their sacrifices to inspire us. We live based on the example they set."

"They pass on their behaviors and values?"

"Yes."

"So, for sake of argument, if they believed in afterlife, you would, too?"

"Semantics, but probably. Yes."

"All right, then. Let's boil it down to the essential: all societies show an instinct toward a *rational* belief in immortality. Even the pragmatic Cadre has a shrine dedicated to the eternal memory of those who have gone before. Though dead, everyone in that memorial has an impact on the living.

"Now then, what happens to the individual after death cannot be known, cannot be proved one way or other. You *choose* to believe data is deleted. I *choose* to believe in an afterlife. Neither of us is wrong."

"Only because it can't be shown false. That doesn't make it true."

"You're absolutely right. That's why it's called 'Faith'. I have faith that death is not the end for me. I don't know what form it will be, but I know there is an afterlife awaiting me. This is a remarkable comfort."

"Faith is an abstract. It's intangible. Unreliable. A guess."

"More than a guess, my friend. A *belief*. It can be very powerful. It brings calm, peace, and stability, especially when times are hard."

"And these pointless activities? The muttering with closed eyes, scented smoke, symbols…what could this possibly contribute?"

"Now you're talking about *religion*. Faith is the spiritual connection one feels to the universe around them. Religion is how one chooses to express that connection. I was raised Catholic, which means I have a *lot* of rituals, prayers, traditions which must seem a waste of time to you. These things give me comfort. They are personal treasures no one can take away from me. They are dependable, I can always count on them when I need them.

"I know better than to try and convert you. All I can say is that my faith makes me feel more complete, more balanced. I can accept the things I have no control over. It gives me a calm mind, which lets me adapt to change. Most important, it helps me confront death. When one no longer fears death, they can better appreciate and experience life, without hesitation.

"These things are immensely good for me, and I *choose* to embrace them. It makes me whole." Ortega points to his head. "It gives me peace here." He points to his heart. "And here. That's as plain as I can make it.

"You see, you can't divide yourself from the universe. You are a part of it. Some of the universe is known. Most is not. If you choose to live only in the part that is known, you miss out on all the beauty, wonder, and mystery of the *un*known. If you can embrace everything in all its marvelous and terrible splendor, you will find tranquility. You'll find *grace*."

"*Now* you're trying to convert."

"Ha! I suppose you're right. Not sorry, though."

"Good Catholic?"

Ortega laughs. "Sometimes, amigo. I'm working on it."

ABOUT THE AUTHOR

Born in the Space Age, Farnham always held a passionate interest in high technology. Impatient to live in a futuristic world, he eagerly consumed any scientific article or science fiction novel that promised a glimpse. Herbert, Heinlein, and Huxley are three of his chief influences.

Farnham's first novel, *Angry Ghosts,* released in 2009. Its sequel, *Black Hawks From A Blue Sun,* released in 2010, and the follow up, *The Exhausted Dead*, was released in 2012. *Of Mortal Creatures* is the fourth installment of the *Angry Ghosts* series.

Farnham's short story, *Tuckahoe Marble*, was licensed by **SciFi Saturday Night** for their anthology, *My Peculiar Family* in 2016.

Farnham now lives in Pflugerville, TX with his dog, Hamlet.

www.ingramcontent.com/pod-product-compliance
Lightning Source LLC
Chambersburg PA
CBHW071224250626
47163CB00001B/91